ONE RED ROSE FOREVER

One Red Rose Forever

BY

MILDRED JORDAN

1941

NEW YORK · ALFRED · A · KNOPF

Copyright 1941 by Mildred Jordan

Manufactured in the United States of America

FIRST EDITION

Published simultaneously in Canada by The Ryerson Press

*T*O THOSE

WHO HAVE BELIEVED

IN ME

MATTHEW 7:26

And everyone that heareth these sayings of mine, and doeth them not, shall be likened unto a foolish man, which built his house upon the sand:

27: *And the rain descended, and the floods came, and the winds blew, and beat upon that house; and it fell: and great was the fall of it.*

ONE RED ROSE FOREVER

Prologue

O N THE FIRST Sunday of June, 1892, Mr. and Mrs. Stiegel of Virginia alighted from their train at the station of Manheim, Pennsylvania, and a cannon boomed their welcome.

Four black chargers and a landau waited to draw them through the streets. Riders on horseback preceded them, and a band played music of the colonial days. Horses and buggies lined the pavement, filled with laughing young girls and curious young men. Manheim seemed to bloom in a profusion of flowers, gay summer dresses, music and laughter.

Mrs. Stiegel smiled self-consciously beside her husband in the landau, and whispered, "Do you suppose your famous ancestor had as much fuss as this, John? I think it must have been rather fun. . . . Imagine the coach, cream and scarlet. And the postillions and barking dogs, and band!"

In the afternoon, at the Lutheran Church, payment of a red rose was made to John Stiegel, for when Henry William Stiegel deeded property to the Zion Evangelical Lutheran Church of Manheim in 1772, he stipulated the rental of "One Red Rose in the Month of June forever, if the same shall be lawfully demanded by the heirs, executors, or assigns."

For one hundred and twenty years after Stiegel's gift to the church, the clause of the payment was forgotten. In the meantime, the church grew slowly. In 1820 the walls of the crude little cabin were plastered, a wood floor was put in, and the small tower bragged a new five-hundred-pound bell, and a spear instead of a cock to predict the weather. The second church was built in 1857, a one-story building of Grecian structure, and then an eight-hundred-pound bell was cast from the metal of the old one. The legend of Henry William Stiegel still slept, not quite old enough for romantic interest, perhaps.

Some years later, a young physician, Dr. Sieling, began to browse through the church records, and came across the original deed given to the congregation by the famous German glass manufacturer, and his wife, Elizabeth. Manheim lay under the enchantment of the old story. It was rumored that the very red roses so luxuriant in the church-yard had been brought by "Baron" Stiegel from England on one of his business trips; that the "Baron" had demanded a bud each time he passed.

"One Red Rose Forever." . . . There was a long-standing debt to be paid to Stiegel, thought Dr. Sieling. The story of the "Baron" was revived, heralded, and exaggerated in news stories.

A letter of inquiry as to the meaning of all this came to the minister from a John C. Stiegel of Harrisonburg, Virginia. On proving he was a descendant, he was invited to come to Manheim to receive the Rose. Since then, the ceremony has been repeated each year on the second Sunday of June. The altar of the church is a fragrant dedication to the love which Stiegel had for God and his fellow-men; the very fountain outside is a living flower. Dr. Knittle, the present pastor, and distinguished visiting preachers give

memorial sermons. Stiegel is spoken of reverently, and his
sins of prodigality are extolled. The least of his enterprises,
a small gift to the church, has brought him enduring fame.

There is still material evidence of his extravagant mode
of living. His house near Brickerville is standing and in good
repair, but not as much of a mansion today as yesterday.
Elizabeth Furnace has been owned by the Coleman family
since Revolutionary days, and many of the original furnishings are in the rooms. But the caretaker's wife with the
flannel about her throat will admit no visitor, so you can
only peer over her shoulder while you question her, and see
as much of the old kitchen as possible.

Although a modest department store has replaced the
Stiegel house in Manheim, the mansion George Ege built
at Charming Forge is still beautiful, and the boxwood at the
stone steps has grown to man's estate. The old tenant houses
remain too, and the tiny office across from the home. Stiegel's desk stands in the very bedroom where he died, and
the closet shelves are stuffed with his old ledgers and account books of the owners of the Forge before he bought
it. Thin, fascinating writing in spectral ink!

And yet, in spite of Stiegel's fame, no one seems to know
where the "Baron" lies buried. Some say his grave is at the
Corner Church in Heidelberg Township, north of Robe-
sonia; others say he was laid to rest at Schaefferstown, or in
an unmarked grave beside his first little Elizabeth, in the
cemetery at Brickerville. The winter he died, the snows
were severe, and I like to think he is buried under a tree of
Diane's orchard, behind George Ege's mansion—near the
river which still runs humming out to sea.

But what does it matter?

When Stiegel glass on a shelf comes alive with sunlight,
and when Manheim dedicates to him each June her loveliest
red rose—these are better memorials to young Heinrich Wilhelm Stiegel from Cologne than a name upon a headstone.

1

THE "NANCY" lay exhausted in the Philadelphia harbor. For a month she had been buffeted westward by a temperamental ocean, tossing her fifty passengers like so many ninepins. Now, on this last day of August, 1750, she emptied them onto the Market Street wharf and turned her mind to Cowes, out of which she had come.

Heinrich Wilhelm Stiegel, being twenty-one, had left Germany with flaring confidence.

"But I don't want you to go," Minnie had whispered to him that last spring day in the woods. "Why must you go, Heinrich?"

"Because in America I shall be both rich and famous!"

"But the young men who wish to be famous musicians come to Germany to study! . . . In America there are only Indians, Heinrich."

He laughed, oddly touched and irritated by the wilted wild flowers in her hand. He would always think of Minnie with the mingled warmth of spring and summer, with the earthy richness of molding leaves and early tender blooms.

"I want everything, Liebling," he said. "And there is everything waiting for me in America. Great forests. Great

rivers. Land that men have never even seen. Men and
women who have courage. And who long for beautiful
music. . . ."

"But some day you would be famous in Germany, too,"
Minnie persisted stubbornly.

Heinrich shrugged. Minnie knew no more about America than she did about genius. He could not explain to her
that he did not need these masters any longer. And that
Germany was filled with poor musicians who played in
beer gardens.

"I cannot wait so long as some day," he said with impatience.

"In America you will be famous right away?"

Her stupidity vexed him, and he nodded.

"And rich?"

"Ach, Minnie, I have told you, nicht? that my uncle has
wrote to Herr Huber, who will very like take me into the
iron business?"

He crushed her next foolish question with his lips. And
he thought, as she closed her eyes to hide the tears, "In
America, too, there are women who can love without tears.
Men and women who can see deep into my soul because
they have learned to live full in a dangerous new land. My
music is for them—not for the old country. I will share with
them what I feel, and they will understand because we are
so young together, so strong. We are not like Germany,
where life is half-finished . . . where the stones crumble.
We are new, these men and women and I. We are the best
of life. . . ."

And now Minnie and her soft abandon were a blur in the
excitement of landing. And here he was, dumped out in
anti-climactic fashion on the shore of this new country, a
country that continued to roll barrels and disregard him
entirely. In Cologne he had never felt so insignificant as in
this feverish America, Stiegel thought.

Beside the "Nancy" on one side was a West Indies ship, being disembowelled of sweating, skulking Negroes, naked and half-mad with fright, and waiting patiently to lap up colonial products—corn, lumber, fur, and inferior rum. On the other side was a vista of the chaste and respectable water front, with its somber Quaker warehouses. It meandered for a mile or more, fretting with little shore boats, reeking conscientiously of tar and hemp, and vaguely of oysters. All along were boats that had braved the sea, and in their shadows were other boats in construction. Ships lading on one side of the wharf, ships sprouting on the other; teeming with men, all of them.

No sooner had a ship come in than The Sign of the Three Mariners at the river's edge was raucous with pig-tailed sailors and steaming punch; The Penny Pot Inn, close by, took the overflow of seamen, and for the bruised passenger there was the more sedate Coach and Horses or the London Coffee House.

It was to this last tavern that Stiegel took his mother, a pudgy, lugubrious woman in widow's weeds, and his brother Anthony, bursting with eleven years of unquenchable curiosity.

They drove over to the tavern in a lumbering old wagon, their sea chests and carpet bags shifting at their feet. Anthony was pale, and rested his head on the all-sufficient arm of his mother. The fascinating new scene which he had painted with such braggart optimism to envious playmates in Cologne, passed him by in swimming confusion.

But to Frau Stiegel there was nothing fascinating about the scene. The newness only served to make her wary and suspicious and she longed for the beloved familiarity of her Cologne—the little home she had left there, the neighbors who were of her own kind; the mounds of her four little dead children and her husband in the cemetery.

"Ach, Gott," she wailed, knowing in her heart that she

would never again see her beloved Vaterland.

"If only things would stand on their feet," sighed Heinrich, "and not be all angles!"

The London Coffee House was astir with activity. Little groups of men clung together jokingly at its door; guests hurried in and out. A friendly clamor issued from its barroom; laughter, the clank of stacked dishes and mugs, the tinkle of toddy-sticks. The innkeeper in a leather apron rubbed his hands in gratification at their arrival, and made a great ado over his distinguished guests. And what news had they of the other side of the water?

Suddenly, the newcomers were surrounded by Americans hungry for news from "the other side." They had come aboard the "Nancy"? Where was her captain? When would he bring the mail? What cargo had they carried? What sort of voyage had there been? Had the King been behaving himself well? How many victims of the smallpox had been tossed overboard? And (this from a little feminine voice in the background) was Madame de Pompadour still wearing lavender kid gloves?

The air stirred lazily with smoke and the odors of punch, and Stiegel gripped the stair rail with sudden premonition. He felt that the "Nancy" was still part of him, body and soul. He suppressed his love of imparting information and followed his host up to the two small whitewashed rooms.

Frau Stiegel took off her traveling cape, donned a fresh sacque, and sat at the window, stolidly, challengingly. In Germany people did not give up. She watched the gay procession of afternoon strollers, and her fingers knitted assiduously. Stiegel fell across the bed, and rode the billows once more. Anthony, persistently curious, leaned from his window and gave a kaleidoscopic report of Philadelphia.

"Such a black one I saw, Heinrich—his face and everything. . . . Oh look, look. . . . Why does that man sit on

the bar with his hands and feet through the wooden holes?
. . . People are throwing things at him. Look, Heinrich,
the dog is trying to reach the well water."

Frau Stiegel followed Anthony's finger. Everything he
pointed out only emphasized her opinion that America was
a crazy place. It was nothing like Cologne. She closed her
lips in tight derision and began to knit faster. A German
woman lived as her husband wanted her to live, and did
not rebel. Well, she must not forget that since Herr Stiegel
was dead, Heinrich was head of the house. She had come
to America for him, and here she must live if he wished it.
Only he must never know that it had broken her heart
to come to this uncivilized country. Well, there was nothing to prevent her living in Cologne in her mind. She need
not even look at these ridiculous things Anthony pointed
out.

"Heinrich, look!" continued Anthony. "What are the
buckets hanging out in front of the houses for? . . . There
is the clock striking twelve. Do you like America, Mutter?
I think I like America now. Do you think they have sauerbraten here, Mutter?"

"Ach, Gott, Anthony, be quiet!" The thought of sauerbraten stabbed her afresh—she would never taste sauerbraten again.

It was almost three when the Stiegels had gathered sufficient courage and control to appear in the taproom for
dinner. Heinrich wondered if some of these jaunty Americans might take him for a Baron. Well, wasn't his uncle a
Baron? And wasn't there nobility in his own even features,
his large pale blue eyes, his high forehead and thick blond
hair? He was well-built and moderately tall, like his uncle,
with the same fresh complexion of the old man. Perhaps
that was why his uncle had always helped him—had, in fact,
given him the money to come to America.

They were seated at a round table with two men, pre-

sumably from the town itself, who had come in out of the
midday sun for a cooling flip.

The taproom was still broiling with life. Several flushed
girls were scurrying about with bobbing skirts and savory
dishes. The proprietor, aglow with enthusiasm, deftly
manipulated glasses in his little barred cage; now he poured
into the beer a dash of rum, now grated a few flecks of
nutmeg into a spicy wine, now thrust a red-hot loggerhead
into his concoction till it frothed over.

The landlord's daughter placed before them the usual
midday meal of leg of mutton, cabbage, ham, roast beef,
and a fat fowl, and laid glasses for the Madeira and ale
which was set out before them.

"Ich will Sauerbraten," announced Anthony, as the odors
lifted energetically in a cloud of steam.

"Nein," answered Stiegel paternally, "du wirst essen was
es gibt, Anthony."

The two men gazed at him curiously. He flushed, annoyed, and glanced at his mother who suffered in silence.
She was dabbling bravely with her food, determined to eat
what she was paying for. The sanded floor of the taproom
rose with slow perseverance, and swam about with gentle
undulations, settling sometimes with a jolt, and leaving a
gay whirlpool in Stiegel's head.

"They are Germans," remarked the Quaker, who had
food on his ruffled jabot.

"I think the 'Nancy' has conveyed them hither," answered his friend with the handsome lace cuffs. He had
evidently just come from the barber, for there was a splotch
of wig-powder on his one eyebrow, making him look very
sinister. "She flew twelve knots. Uncommon wonderful
what can be done this day."

"And yet a rough sea by the captain's logbook." The
Quaker bent a little closer to his companion. "I do not
think they come here new. They scarce would act so

seasoned. I think they travel here from the Moravian colony, for they are German, of a certainty."

"I shall wager you they are indentures who have just arrived," bullied the lace. "Look at the young man's hair. Naked, without wig or even bob. And the mother too, unpowdered like a servant. Do ye note the contouche she wears to her knee? 'Tis not the *ton,* and *that* is German; I wager a sovereign they have come today aboard the 'Nancy'."

The Quaker colored. He did not have a sovereign, but he wished very much to have one, even if the means were unethical. And he could not lose what he did not have. " 'Tis done," he said in an undertone.

The lace fluttered ever so gently. "He sees we have spoke of him. . . . Odd's life, I can hear the clatter of my sovereigns now. And yet, is it possible they do not wear wigs in Germany? Can it be that young men go about the streets there with a pigtail like a seaman? Why, not e'en you Quakers dress so solemn. A fortnight in America would put a solitaire about his hair, or a jewel in his stock. . . . But I'll prove you I'm right. Now, let me think on how ye say it. (It takes me a bit to set to on my German) . . . Aye —mein Freund, du bist von Germany, nicht?"

Stiegel turned to the men thunderously. At the University he had been considered a criterion of fashion, for he was one of a radical group there who dared to imitate the army's hairdress, and who emulated the simpler mode of clothing coming into fashion across the English Channel. It chagrined him, too, that his mother should be mistaken for a servant. Didn't these men know what it meant to be tossed endlessly in a dingy boat, where there were no coiffeurs? . . . He would see that she was powdered, however, before they left for Lancaster. Was it just possible that her going unpowdered was a defiance toward the new country?

For a moment he felt bursting with indignant explanation. But he decided it would be more gratifying to let the
man's curiosity dangle.

"Perhaps you had best ask it from the landlord," he retorted in his most select English, enjoying the humiliation
on the two ruddy faces.

"Come," he besought his mother in German, for she
understood no English, "we shall not sit here to be insulted, especially when none of us can eat today." And
with a continental dignity inborn for generations Stiegel
led his family from the taproom through the hallway and
into the inn parlor.

He wondered how he might rid himself of his charges
for a while. His blood was boiling with the insults of his
table companions, and he felt that his first task here in
America was to thrust their criticisms in their teeth. The
fact that he would never see them again made no difference.
He looked about him through the inn with anguish. It was
true. Every man's head was covered. Stiegel felt suddenly
naked. People would stare at him; they would laugh after
he had passed. No matter how his legs tottered, he must
get his head covered.

He led his mother and Anthony strategically into the
inn parlor, where there was an exhibit of goods to be sold
at a "vendue," the following day. The walls were filled with
alluring pictures and posters announcing the sale, and there
were puppets on strings, statues of great men, and clocks
which were elaborate mountains of rococo gilt. Anthony
pulled his mother from one thing to another, brushing past
little groups of men who were smoking and playing cards.
Frau Stiegel stopped at a table full of India cotton stuffs,
and her eyes rested hungrily on a background of black with
hilarious pink roses. But she turned her back on this too,
for she had bought a best dress for the trip, and she now
wore a sacque which had served her nine years since her

husband's funeral. She felt it was only respectful to wait the full ten years before wearing gaudy roses again.

But the India cotton had served its purpose. She had been so drawn to it that she did not notice the final disappearance of Heinrich, who mumbled that he was going out to get a little air.

She would not have missed Heinrich for some time if Anthony had not gotten himself into trouble. Eager to see what funny American words looked like, although, unlike Heinrich, he knew no English, he had pounced upon a newspaper as soon as the man in the green velvet laid it down. One of the card-players glanced up immediately, and spoke so sharply that Anthony flushed and stammered, "Nein, ich kann nicht. . . ."

The gentleman pointed to a sign above the fireplace: "Gentlemen learning to spell are requested to use last week's newsletter." Anthony looked about wildly for Heinrich. As the man rose, Anthony dropped the paper hastily and slithered over to his mother, who was fingering a shawl. He whispered to her what had happened.

"We are paying our bill here at the inn," she bristled, in her high German, but the man only rose, bowed stiffly from the waist and sat down again, going on with his cards. She would have Heinrich tell this American fool that Anthony would not contaminate his newspaper! She looked about haughtily for her handsome, wigless German son. But he was nowhere to be seen.

2

As HE SEARCHED the square-paned shop windows for evidence of a tailor, Stiegel was certain that the eyes of all passers-by were upon him. He was being taken for some indentured servant, even though his pockets were filled with his uncle's good German gold.

The afternoon parade of pedestrians sauntered along the flat brick footwalks, which were separated from the street by a line of stalwart hitching-posts. Stiegel felt that he had never seen such an array of pretty girls before. In Cologne his eyes would have lingered on the faces bright under their sheltering bonnets. Now it agonized him that these lovely young women were snickering at his naked head. He kept his eyes averted. One pair after the other of red kid heels passed him by. He knew only by their feet what people went along the street. A Quaker's pewter buckles: a Negro boy's bare feet; the stump of a sailor; the silk hose and marcasite buckles of a gentleman. Well, they would not laugh at him long. He must have his wig now, for to-morrow he and his mother and Anthony would ride with the mail to Lancaster; there Frau Stiegel and Anthony were to live with a distant cousin, and Stiegel would leave them

for Brickerville. Supposing he had gone to the Hubers'—
his uncle's friends at Brickerville, without a wig! It was
said there was a daughter. . . .

He reviewed his clothes, dark green, with gray small-
clothes and no furbelows, the ruffles of his jabot and sleeves
a plain, Teutonic cloth. Suddenly he felt as if all life in
Cologne had been dark green and a little stuffy. He knew
now that it had been merely a preparation, a prelude to an
adventure which would flower here in America.

"I have eaten my solid dinner in Cologne," he told himself as he hurried along the brick walks, scarcely aware of
the warm, summer hum of the streets, "and now I have my
dessert before me."

His pulse quickened at the sight of red velvet in a window, and he turned in at the tailor shop, more abashed
than he cared to admit. The proprietor, a Quaker, para-
doxically enough, surveyed him professionally.

"Ah," he exclaimed with sympathy, "thou hast had a mishap to thy wig, friend. But there is nought in fashion thou
wilt not find here. We. . . ."

"In Germany," Stiegel interrupted defensively, "the
young man. . . ."

"Ah, mein Herr, America is not akin to Germany. Thou'rt
handsome, friend, as thou must be well aware. I can see
thee now with a fresh-powdered wig—a Corded Wolf's
Paw or a Spinach-seed would become thee vastly; and
methinks. . . ." He rested his chin on his fist and meditated.
"A crimson velvet coat, and a robin's-egg vest. . . . The
winter is hard by and plush is in the kick of fashion. Ah,
mein Herr, thou hast no silk stockings. E'en yester. . . ."

" 'Tis only a wig I wish," retorted Stiegel curtly, his color
mounting and his desire as well, so that he hastened to
check it. But what would Herr Huber's young daughter
think of him in his dull green? Supposing she knew nothing of fashions at the University? She might be beautiful.

She might be vital and gay, with full red lips like Minnie's.

" 'Tis thy own doing, friend." The shopkeeper shrugged his gray Quaker shoulders. "Thou art redemptioner, mayhap, and cannot pay the sum of 'broidered hose. I beg thy humble pardon, friend. Thy manner is deceiving. Now. . . ."

"Hold your tongue," blazed Stiegel, for the shopkeeper had found the one means to ignite his temper. "I'll show you I can lay out money as I wish. Think you I'd sell myself to some mealy-mouthed or pig-headed Englishman?"

"I prithee forgive me," bowed the Quaker. "But as 'tis a gentleman, mayhap e'en a lord I address, I shall not err in showing him the cloth so late come over on the 'Queen Anne'."

The German gold had soon purchased an impressive wig of the finest human hair, with a scalp of red and blue intertwined ribbons. And the German pride, relenting in this vast display of elegance, had bought two coats of carmine and bright green, which had been ordered by a French dancing-master, now deceased. Now that he had left the University behind him, thought Stiegel, he would set the fashion in a different manner here in America; and he bought smallclothes of shell and fawn silk, jabots of French lace, onyx buttons, shoe buckles of pinchbeck set with marcasite, long flowing handkerchiefs for his braided pockets. Things equally as fine as any of the clothes of his uncle.

Secretly elated, he longed for the moment when he might appear in all his finery, but as he counted over his silver change, the image of the thrifty Frau Stiegel rose formidably before him, and he asked quickly, "What time of morning do you open shop?"

"At the fifth watch, friend."

"Then send a boy with the clothes to the London Coffee House on the morrow, for we ride with the Post to Lancaster. And pack them so small as it is able."

He stood for a moment at the door, struggling with the vision of his mother. He wondered if the walk back to the inn with a wig was not worth all the scorn she might vent on him!

"Wait," he added. "I will wear the Spinach-seed!"

He took it with nervous hands from the Quaker, and looked at himself in the mirror. Yes, he was handsome! Why, he was entirely different. He was somebody else.

As he strode from the shop he was confronted by visions of himself in the future: Herr Stiegel bowing over his pinch-beck buckles to Frau Huber: the Spinach-seed bending over the plump, clinging fingers of her daughter; mein Herr's coat-tails flipping backward as he took seat; the delicate perfume of the pomatum escaping from his wig.

Now he wandered up and down the broad, regular streets of the new city, filled with an exhilaration such as he had never felt in his native Cologne. New worlds to conquer with his violin! When he should once get to Brickerville he would play the German colony into Paradise with his music. His hand searched about in his big pocket to feel reassuringly his letter to Herr Huber. Now he looked people in the eye as he passed them by. They all noticed him, and he held his head high. In his mind he could see the fresh white glistening hair of his wig. He smiled boldly at a pretty servant girl who was going to the well to fill a jug with water. Her strong, regular teeth reminded him of Minnie. It was strange how many pretty young women today had reminded him of Minnie. He was seeing her eyes in one, her ankles in another, and the thought came to him that it was because he was hungry for Minnie, who belonged to a familiar world.

His senses were alive now, and he felt the noise and the color and the motion of the street. Everything stimulated him—the cry of strange voices, the whinnying of horses, the grinding of wagon wheels in a rut. Even the sedate, well-sashed houses, with three and four stories of windows peeping out from heavy shutters. They seemed patriotically alike and secretive, with their trim spotless stairs, fire insurance marks and foot scrapers. But they were exciting. They symbolized the future.

He found himself on Water Street, and thought he had better return to the inn. He waited for a wagon-load of slippery looking, naked Negroes to pass. They were herded together in chains, being taken to an auction block. His eyes furtively followed the young woman with an infant suckling at her breast. Her limpid beast-like eyes fixed on him till she was out of sight, and disturbed him.

Suddenly there seemed to be a stir of excitement, and Stiegel saw people running to the posts, and heard the high-low tap of horses' feet. A gorgeous equipage approached, swirling clouds of dust before and after it with royal nonchalance. He watched it eagerly, avidly, for it seemed the embodiment of the new country. It was a dull red, gilded. As the four alert horses turned the corner close to him, he saw that the coach was lined in palest blue, delicately carved, and embellished with the arms of the owner on the door panels. A gentleman was just barely visible, muffled in protection against his own dust. The footman and coachman withstood it like waxen images, gazing arrogantly beyond the harness so bright with its silver and brass fittings, its bells and plumes.

Heinrich leaned on a post to meditate, listening to the sound of the hoofs which grew faint and left him dreaming.

"This is not real," he said to himself. "I am not just Heinrich Stiegel. I *am* somebody new. Somebody gay. I am going to have a coach like that. I am going to be famous. It is only the spring which makes me feel like this in Cologne. And here. . . ."

He stopped at a shop whose windows were filled with

luxurious importations: capers, nutmeats, English walnuts, anchovies, peppers, mace and cloves. He felt suddenly very generous toward Anthony, toward mankind in general, and purchased a packet of dried currants and olives for the dull moments of the coming trip. For his mother he bought some sweetmeats. He had a small-boy desire to stuff his wig in some out-of-the-way corner. His mother would not say anything about the wig. That was the trouble. But she would make him feel young and inconsequential and foolish. The last hour on the Philadelphia streets had been magic. He did not want it spoiled. But there was nothing to do but face her. At least she wouldn't know about the clothes he had bought.

The porch of the inn was almost deserted. A little group of Negro boys and half-breeds pitched pennies and played at dice along the walk at the side, but the bustle of the business street had subsided, and the petticoats had withdrawn.

Stiegel paused for a moment at the door of the bedroom. It was years since he had had his head covered, and he felt as ridiculous with his wig in the face of his family as he had without it in the face of Philadelphia.

"I am a man," he told himself severely. "I have a right to change my mind. . . . Everything is new. I am new. . . ." And he opened the door.

Anthony had been half hanging out of the window, and he pulled in when he heard the door, bursting into laughter. Stiegel turned scarlet.

His mother was pinching at the ruffles of a fresh cap. She stared at him for a moment, and then, for the first time in a month, she smiled.

Stiegel had been prepared for anything but this. If she had scolded him he would only have felt more important and delightfully abused. But he looked funny to them! Humiliation flooded over him again.

"Now I look like a gentleman," he cried childishly, pulling off the wig, which itched abominably. "Not like some German redemptioner!"

But Frau Stiegel only continued to smile. "Ja!" she said.

Stiegel threw his peace-offering of olives and currants on the counterpane with the gesture of a redemptioner who was now a gentleman, and stalked out to the barroom of the inn.

When he returned he found Anthony lying snug in his night-rail and cap, never moving a hair's breadth, and the tremulous snore of Frau Stiegel came comfortingly from the adjoining room.

Stiegel stood close to the window and looked out upon the darkness of the street, lighted occasionally by the lamp of some house or shop, and the swinging lantern of a pedestrian. Now with his family asleep there seemed to be no obstacle between him and the new world, between him and his ambition. He would meet it fearlessly. He would meet it wholly. Tonight he was filled with a longing for life so painful and so sweet that he had never known anything like it before.

It was at times similar to this that he had always picked up his violin and let his imagination wander from one tune to another, sometimes only playing a few bars of a loved waltz, and then flying off to the leit-motif of the opera he was composing. Now he took up his beloved instrument and started to play.

His bow hung on the opening chords of a Bach Prelude when there was a firm tap on the door. His heart pounded. He had quite forgotten there was anyone else in the world. He opened the door to a chambermaid whose apron was filled with candles. She smiled at him openly, came in, and laying an armful of kindling wood on the floor, sat on it.

He returned the smile, watching the quick rise and fall of her plump bosom after her run up the stairs.

"I was listenin' at the keyhole for a minute, and I says

to meself, 'ye will hear a sight better if ye can *see* him play.' And your candles is all stubs in here anyway. But pray won't you play before I changes the stubs?"

She reminded him of Minnie, but this time, he could not say why, and he was annoyed. He particularly liked to play for anyone who had not yet heard him, and tonight he seemed to want all the praise of which the girl was capable. He began the Prelude again, and forgot her. She sat entranced on her woodpile, and Anthony slept on.

When he had finished the Prelude he put on the mute and tripped through a pot-pourri of German waltzes. They were soft and coaxing, and meant only for her.

"Well?" he asked, stooping down beside her.

"Like the heavenly choir!" she sighed, and gazed at him wide-eyed.

An awkward silence ensued. Then Stiegel said, "You love music, good music?"

"Oh yes. . . . And ye are so grand. . . . Methinks ye are a nobleman to play like that!"

Stiegel laughed. "I have played the violin so long as I can remember. First I learned it in my Vaterland. I played a little to the ladies, too, in the army. And then I have been to the University. And everywhere I go I play. And always I have the best masters."

"Ye are a rich man," she remarked, utterly unfrightened. "And why do ye come to America? Why do ye leave all your castles and come here?"

"I am going to pleasure all America with my violin," announced Stiegel evasively. "I am going to write operas and be on every tongue!"

This was what he had wanted tonight. He had wanted someone to appreciate him. He had wanted to talk to someone who felt that he was different from all the rest of mankind, that greatness was hidden in him.

He opened his heart so freely to the little chambermaid

that it embarrassed him later to recall all he had told her. His whispering was suddenly interrupted by a loud, husky voice, droning in the street, "Hear, brethren, hear, the hour of nine is come; keep pure each heart and chasten every home!"

The girl was startled, and jumped up, scattering the candles which the two of them hastened to gather again.

" 'Tis late. Luddy! I'll have a flogging for this."

His fingers touched hers, and gripped them.

"They wouldn't dare lay a hand on you," he said.

"They've whipped me many a time."

"Then stay here," he whispered ardently. "They can't touch you if you're with me, can they?"

"And then get a floggin' for *that!*" she retaliated.

He pulled her to him, and kissed her pouting lips. But his fingers rebounded from something round and prickly at her waist beneath her apron.

She laughed, like a delighted child. " 'Tis my scent. An apple pricked with cloves is well enough for a barmaid, an't it?"

In a moment he was facing the slammed door. He kicked the pile of wood aside and the clatter wakened Anthony, who jerked up into a sitting position.

Blinking, he recognized Heinrich, and giggled again.

"Donner und Blitzen!" swore Stiegel, infuriated, and he picked up a piece of kindling and tossed it at the wall above Anthony's head. The boy ducked under the covers.

But though Stiegel aimed the wood at Anthony, he knew that he had really thrown it at the chambermaid. Even after he had washed for the night, he could smell the faint pungence of cloves on his fingertips.

3

THE FIRST MORNING of September broke damply in
a sheet of fog. One of the early fires of the season glowed in
the barroom as the Stiegels breakfasted. They did not talk,
but ate their rump steak and fish and eggs almost sullenly.
Frau Stiegel dipped her cake into her coffee briskly. She
had prepared for this ride with resignation, girded with a
weather-skirt, and her face was enshrined in a red handkerchief, so that her cheeks escaped like a thriving case
of mumps. This headdress was to repel flies and fleas and
mosquitoes.

The horses were laden with the baggage, and the postman blew his horn. Frau Stiegel rode apillion behind
Anthony, clinging to a strap about his waist. The postman
smiled to himself. He wondered which of them would be
anchor in case of accident.

Frau Stiegel rested her eyes on the additional package
from the tailor shop.

"Ah, you have been buying again," she remarked in her
thick German.

Stiegel flushed. "Just a . . . a surprise for Herr Huber,"
he compromised.

They rode on silently. Soon, at the edge of town, they saw the ruts of the country road stretching on before them into virgin woods. They left the outlying scattered houses with trepidation, though occasionally they could still hear the voice of the town-crier putting the night to bed:

The clock is six, and from the watch I'm free,
And everyone may his own watchman be.

There were three days of riding before the Stiegels reached Lancaster, and the sun beat relentlessly down on them. It was beautiful rolling country, the Blue Ridge Mountains stretching off misty purple to their right. Very seldom they saw a lone log cabin, and at night when they found an inn it was always among a little cluster of houses.

Now and then they met a horseback-rider and stopped to exchange news with him, or a farmer ploughing his fields, or driving his cows to shed. Otherwise the hours were endless. The horses picked their path over great clots of mire and stones. It was no wonder the postman amused himself by knitting, and that Anthony was continually on the lookout for Indians lurking in the trees.

"Look, is that an Indian?" he would whisper melo-dramatically, as some deer rustled through the under-brush.

"Ach, Gott!" Frau Stiegel whimpered, and Stiegel him-self felt a rush of excitement, half frantic and half pleasur-able.

On the third day the Stiegels were safe with their rela-tives in Lancaster. It was a thriving little village, with square-paned shops like those in Philadelphia. They were all so thankful to have arrived without trouble that the modest houses and their gardens looked like Paradise.

Stiegel himself had not been content to remain in Lan-caster for the night. With Brickerville and the Hubers only fourteen miles away, he must get to his destination, even if

it was after dark. He would be back to see them all in a
week, or in two weeks perhaps.

So he God-blessed his mother and received from her a
volley of moral injunctions. He finally separated himself
from Anthony's hug, and cautioned him to enter at once
into manhood's estate and take good care of their mother.
And then, after a chorus of "Auf Wiedersehens" he sneaked
to Postlethwaite's Tavern.

It was there that the new life began. He unwrapped the
"surprise" for Herr Huber and arrayed himself in its
grandeur. He felt that he had grown taller, broader, hand-
somer. He had left behind his apron-strings, and now he
was a colonial gentleman.

As he rode on, the vales became lower and lovelier, but
the heat of the road clung to him even as he passed through
their shade. He had not had quite the courage to shave his
head, and as he traveled alone he removed the wig, which
had become a mountain of heat he could not endure. Indeed, now that Stiegel had prepared for winter with velvets and plushes, summer tarried relentlessly on.

But he gave little thought to the heat. He drew mental
pictures of Elizabeth Furnace, of the men working there,
of the Hubers and Elizabeth. She would be little and dark,
with sparkling laughter. She would fall in love with him.
He would be quite mad about her. Perhaps he would have
a struggle to win her. Of course she would marry him at
last, unable to resist his ardent love. He would become rich,
like the Baron, his uncle. There would be children . . . a
dozen children at least. Many sons to carry on the name of
the famous musician. . . . How dark it had grown.

This was Brickerville he was coming to, this tiny cluster
of lights on the hill. Now Herr Huber's iron plantation
would only be a mile or more away. Brickerville—a disap-
pointing little settlement of four corners. No more signifi-
cant than a fluttering of fire-flies!

As he left the sleepy village, a rush of fear possessed him. " 'Tis a great venture, all the way from Germany," he thought. "Perhaps he's dead, Herr Huber. And the daughter —one so beautiful would be married. . . . What an ass I am! Well, if I've gam'd too much there's nought to do but return to the cousins in Lancaster. . . . The devil if I would!"

Now as he rode through the woods of God's-Acre itself and came into the opening, the whole night was a contrast of glowing red and black silhouettes. The tall, gaunt chimney of the furnace along the stream sent up sparks into the sky; the spectral water wheel was majestic and still. The whole scene was breath-takingly beautiful, and his imagination quickly etched in the buildings on the outskirts of darkness: the charcoal house, the stable, the mansion, and the blacksmith shop with weird pieces of wagon lying about. There was no sound but the restful plashing of the water in the creek, and the song of the crickets, strangely like the far-off tinkle of sleigh-bells, Stiegel thought. It seemed eerie that a place could be so warmly alive at night.

An ugly middle-aged Negro let him into the house. The hall which seemed yellow in its candlelight after the glare of the furnace shone softly with brass and the rich red of mahogany.

There were voices in the parlor. Stiegel listened intently for the sparkling laughter. He tried to stand straight, and not nervously to twist his hat. This strange, beautiful place, would it ever look familiar to his eyes?

A dapper little man hurried out of the parlor, a Meerschaum pipe hanging from his lips. Stiegel stood a good head above him. His chubby face with its tremendous red nose was surmounted by a green silk cap.

"Ich bin Heinrich Stiegel von Köln," murmured Stiegel, instinctively lapsing into German.

"Ach, my boy," greeted Herr Huber in German too. And

as he patted him joyfully on the shoulder he led him into the parlor. "And how goes it with my old friend, your uncle? Good, I hope? Magdalena, John Frederick Stiegel's boy from Köln."

Stiegel glanced beyond Frau Huber and met the eyes of the daughter. He noted her calm, blonde beauty with a little feeling of resentment. It flashed through his mind that he had wanted her to be someone joyfully awakened, and yet whom he would awaken.

He clicked his heels and bowed low to Frau Huber.

"Is't not great fortune to have as guest a youth from the Rhine, Magdalena?" her husband asked.

Elizabeth lowered her eyes as she met him. She was overcome with confusion. She had never seen anyone quite so splendid and handsome as the visitor.

Stiegel thought of Elizabeth first as a delicate, pink flower. Her hair was puffed and rolled and lay in white curls on her fair skin. A little band of gold beads encircled her throat. The pink and white brocade fell stiffly over its farthingale, and even the slippers which peeped from under the skirt were of pink silk. A long lace apron hung from her stomacher, and in the breast knot of fresh ribbon was a rose.

In frantic embarrassment she curtsied, and her sampler slipped from her hand to the floor.

Stiegel rescued it with agility and smiled to himself. To drop a scented handkerchief was delicate and designing; to drop a sampler with balls of scattering threads was unsophisticated and gauche.

He entrusted the sampler to her trembling hands, snug in their pink, fingerless mittens, and thought, "She is all pink and white and fragile. What devilish luck! I'll wager e'en her eyes are pink, like a rabbit's."

But as her eyes finally met his, in despair, he found them frightened, and too large and blue for her delicate face.

Herr Huber hurried off to instruct Cyrus, the Negro servant, to stable Heinrich's horse, and Frau Huber took
Stiegel to a guest room. She had as many chins as his Tante
Gussie, he thought, but she flew around with her great
weight as if it were only a bundle under her arm.

The following morning Herr Huber took Stiegel on a
tour about the grounds. The romantic, lurid glare of the
furnace by night yielded up by day an amazing little village. The mansion itself was nestled among the trees in a
dip of land, and spreading before it were luxuriant gardens,
the smokehouse, the buttery, servants' quarters, and a
scattering of colliers' cottages and huts. Near the creek in
the offing were sawmill and gristmill, a blacksmith shop,
and a general store where politics were forged at night. The
stables were filled with horses and mules, and there was a
grinding of heavy carts hauling iron and charcoal to the
furnace, like assiduous ants.

"But this is . . . is wunderschön!" exclaimed Stiegel,
amazed, looking about him. "You have everything, nicht?
Cornfields and mountains—and woodland!"

Herr Huber chuckled. "You have not seen the best yet.
Come, I will show you my stoves."

Beside the stream rose the furnace, a truncated pyramid
of stone forty feet in height, its fat base and tapering chimney reminding Stiegel of a Dutch windmill. A translucent
flame with glowing sparks rose and fell from the open
tunnel head, pulsating with the draft from the bellows
below. The water wheel which operated it groaned loudly.

Beyond the stream was a hill, and a roofed runway con-
nected it with the furnace. From the bank, "fillers" were
carrying baskets of charcoal and limestone to the chimney
head, feeding the fire below. For a moment Stiegel and Herr
Huber watched the founder at the hearth, drawing out
shovels full of thick, pasty cinders, and tossing them onto
a heap of slag.

Stiegel felt his pulse racing with the thrill of this new America, with the giant industry before him. Great open spaces, woodland rising thickly in solid walls of oak and pine and chestnut, blackened men sweating in the sun, flocks of sheep, and fields of rye and barley and oats to feed the hungry mouths of these dozens of workers!

He followed Herr Huber through the casting-house, where the iron ran molten over molds of scorched and blackened sand. The "guttermen" grinned at his open admiration.

"I have my own Formschneider for carving my molds," bragged Herr Huber. "He carves so beautiful! The Huber stove is no 'Cain and Abel' pattern from the mold of somebody who goes from one furnace to the other, yet. Magdalena and I, we pick out the Bible stories for our Formschneider. Our patterns are new: 'David and Goliath'; 'Daniel and the Lion.'"

Stiegel was tongue-tied with questions. If Herr Huber had been minting gold he could not have been more dazzled.

"Twenty tons of iron a week—bars, kettles, fire-backs, stoves. Come, I will show you my stoves," Herr Huber persisted, sucking on his pipe, and Stiegel followed him into the storehouse bulging with ware. "My six-plate stove, see? The best in America—like the German stove, nicht?"

"Ah, wie schön!" exclaimed Stiegel again, trailing Herr Huber through the labyrinth of stock and out once more to the open. "And you have built this up alone!"

"Nein. I have partners. Charles and Alexander Stedman in Philadelphia. They own thousands of acres of land here, where we get the wood for our charcoal. But Magdalena and I, we have the ideas. . . . Ach, Himmel, this doesn't go so gut. My legs are not so young any more yet."

Stiegel laughed as Herr Huber rested on a barrel, and rubbed his knee.

He thought again of the pink little creature, Elizabeth. What a pity she could not have been a man, a strong-muscled son to carry on this iron business in the family tradition.

Stiegel wondered if Herr Huber had noticed that his legs were young!

Guests were a rarity and luxury in the community, and Stiegel was the centre of attention for weeks. Neighbors drove over from Brickerville and Germans came from nearby villages when they heard a fellow countryman had recently arrived.

Herr Huber spent hours questioning the young man about conditions in Germany, about old friends and relatives, and changes in customs and business. Stiegel felt, uncomfortably, that he was being studied. He had not mentioned to Herr Huber that his heart was absorbed in music. He was tactful enough to keep his passion to himself. Herr Huber was a practical old iron-master, and to him Heinrich showed only his worldliness. Though he often played for the Hubers in the evening, he kept his score hidden, and worked on it fitfully in his room after the others slept.

He began to spend time at the furnace, asking questions, learning the work.

"Did you know, Elizabeth, that tough oak is worth more than pine? That the finer the wood, the better charcoal it yields?" he would expound, impressed with his new knowledge.

"Of course, Herr Stiegel. I learned that with my nursery rhymes," she teased him.

"But you're a woman. What do you know of business?" he challenged. "How much ore does it take to make a ton of metal?"

"Two or three tons, is't not? And one hundred and eighty bushels of charcoal."

He was astounded and embarrassed, and she laughed at him kindly.

"When I was a little girl, Herr Stiegel, I played every day with the colliers' children. And Frau Habicht used to take me to the furnace."

He no longer boasted of what he knew, but his interest in the business grew. Often he watched the ore being washed before it was used, the big water wheel revolving it in a trough. He chatted with the master miner, the chief collier, the manager. Best of all he liked to watch old Hans, the Formschneider, carving the wooden molds, and mending a broken finger or letter with clay or wax.

Every day which he spent at the Furnace brought sharper realization that here was his great opportunity. Herr Huber was no longer young, and his present manager was a former collier. The Furnace needed someone like Stiegel, keen, vigorous, with social prestige. He was the very man for Herr Huber, and the business was a highway to wealth. A few years with Herr Huber and he would be rich beyond his dreams, and when he was rich he could write music to the end of his days. One evening Stiegel determined that he would bring the matter to a head. Several times he had tried feebly to suggest a change of quarters to the inn, but Herr Huber insisted that he accept their hospitality. And Stiegel knew that Herr Huber had not yet decided what to do. It irritated Stiegel that the old man was so slow in his judgment. Stiegel had been restless for weeks. He could not work openly and satisfactorily on his music, nor could he become an integral part of the life at the Furnace. He felt frustrated, stifled.

The October air had become sharp and penetrating, and the family sat in a group about the parlor fire. Frau Huber, who had been bustling about the house since five o'clock, allowed her head to anchor in its bed of fat little chins, while she dozed, upright as a wall. Stiegel knew she was asleep because her eyes were closed, and her dimpled hands rested on her knitting.

Elizabeth stitched on a linen shirt for her father, occasionally making some little remark to Stiegel about mutual friends.

Herr Huber, humming a tune Elizabeth had just played on the harpsichord, found his eyes blinking from the reflection of the flames on the fire-dogs.

Stiegel began bluntly. " 'Tis high time, Herr Huber, that I return to Lancaster!"

Herr Huber removed his pipe from his mouth. "Pooh, bide till the winter snows are past. Now let there be an end on't."

"But 'tis unfair to you, Herr Huber, and to myself."

Elizabeth's fingers stopped their work.

"I have come to America to make my fortune, sir," Stiegel went on. "Every day which passes is a day lost."

"Don't you . . . don't you like stoves?" stammered Elizabeth.

Stiegel flushed at her ingenuousness, and Herr Huber, slowly chewing on the pipe from which he seldom parted, said, "Ja. Don't you like stoves? Why do you not stay with me here, and make your fortune as an ironmaster?"

Stiegel jumped from his chair and went over to shake the hand of the old man.

"Ach, Herr Huber, you are like a father to me!" he said. "My heart is too full for words!"

The young man went into the business with vigor and imagination, and he wondered if his mother were not reconciled to America now that he was sending her such generous sums of money. Before long, Herr Huber began to turn more and more responsibility over to Stiegel.

The furnace was out of blast for three months while the seventy workmen went to work about the grounds and in the forests. Instead of the splash of the water wheel and the wheezing of the bellows, there was the cold, steely ring of the ax. The mule-carts which had been used for ore now trailed back and forth on the roads, bringing in loads of lumber. Mounds of corded wood were set to burning in pits, for charcoal. Sometimes the wood burned for over a week, and the air was fragrant with smoke.

"We must get some charcoal burners on the next boat from the Old World," said Stiegel to Elizabeth. "They are better than Kemp and Schmidt."

"Otto Schmidt has been with papa for fifteen years."

"But the charcoal isn't so black and glistening like it should be!" Stiegel still did not dare to make business suggestions to Herr Huber.

He helped the founder hew a new hearth for the furnace from sandstone that winter. It was good to feel again the blood rushing through him; to feel the sweat trickling in grooves down his back. It was a long time since he had been to the turnverein, and he had been company for too long, dining on pudding and venison.

Stiegel was buoyant. His future was in his hands! Stoves would bring him gold, and music would bring him happiness. He took out his score casually one night, as if it were a hobby he had forgotten about in the excitement of his new life. He began to work at it in the evenings, and where before he had often accompanied Elizabeth on the harpsichord with his violin, now he withdrew to the desk, and was in a world of his own. Each night of work seemed to absorb him more, and each night he felt more drawn into the magic of this task which he loved so passionately. He dreamed of notes over the fire of the forge, and he hummed to himself as he walked over the crisp path of snow from the house to the furnace. He felt tense, as if he were running downhill and were trying to keep his balance.

The weeks had passed quickly, and he and Elizabeth

seldom seen one another alone. They had gone to meetings together in the draughty little meeting-house, and had
made calls, and drunk tea. Several times when the Hubers
had dozed before the fire, he had put his arm about Elizabeth's waist, and kissed her timid pink lips. But somehow
he found he did not want lips that were afraid. He was so
alive himself, so frighteningly alive.

Just before Christmas a party of young people from
Brickerville went out on a sleigh-ride. They huddled together laughingly in the two sleighs which started from
the meeting-house. The night was crisp and bright, the air
stinging. He drew Elizabeth close to him under the bear
robes. The horses jingled along pleasantly in a fresh-fallen
snow, their lusty odor mingling with the perfume of pine
and chimney smoke.

As they clipped out into the country, the fiddlers on horseback started to play. Stiegel drew Elizabeth closer. She
laughed up at him, her eyes blue-black now with the night
in them. How lovely she was, he thought, like some bit of
pink sky beyond one's reach. She wanted to love him, he
thought suddenly, and didn't quite know how. The idea
amused and taunted him. He might teach her love. He
might open her wide blue eyes still wider with the shock
and the awfulness of passion. As they rode along she rested
her head on his shoulder, and he could see young Klingerman, the minister's son, squirming about often to look at
them. So that was it. When young Klingerman looked about
again Stiegel bent his face down to hers, and held her lips
in a long kiss.

"No, Heinrich—you mustn't!" she pleaded.

"Why not?" he whispered jauntily, his question half lost
among the sleigh bells.

"Not if you do not mean it. . . ."

"What man ever kisses a woman that he does not mean

it?" he returned, pleased with his high-sounding philosophy.

After the ride, the group stopped in at Amanda Powell's for burnt wine. Stiegel and Elizabeth, having to go the added mile to the Furnace, left shortly afterwards with Cyrus, who drove them home. They shivered as they came out of the warm house, the hot wine tingling through their blood.

How the kiss had spoiled her chastity, thought Stiegel. How he wanted suddenly to possess her, to teach her the glory of a winter night throbbing through one's veins and singing in one's heart. That was it, he wanted her to *feel* with him; one went on and on feeling ecstasy alone and then suddenly there must be someone to share it! Cyrus was so muffled in his blankets behind the horses that he looked like some immutable rock, growing out of the seat. It would be so easy to make her forgetful with kisses. . . .

"Elizabeth!" he whispered. "Let's keep on riding through the night!"

"Oh Heinrich, how foolish you are. I'm nigh froze. And Papa ——"

Papa! Stiegel wanted to shake the girl into living.

Well, she had brought him to his senses anyway. What sort of thoughts were these to hold about the daughter of his host? A girl who had never attracted him except in the reflected fullness of his own joy! He dropped her hands and stretched his arms into the open air.

"All I meant to say was, 'How beautiful it is tonight!' "

For several days Stiegel could not rid himself of a sense of strain. The desire he'd had for Elizabeth vexed and repelled him. Then he thought happily of making a trip to Lancaster to see his mother. Herr Huber wondered that he had not made the request before, he said. Elizabeth pouted a little because he was going.

He arrived at the house of his mother's cousins shortly before dinner, and sat down with them all, eager to tell them of the wonderful future which was in store for him at Elizabeth Furnace.

"Herr Huber rich? You should see the gardens, and the fine ——"

Stiegel was struck silent by the entrance of a maid. She was the very image of his Minnie in Cologne! The girl blushed, and set her plate of meat on a trivet by the fire.

"Ja?" reminded Frau Stiegel, dishing out noodle soup from a tureen. "Fine . . . ?"

"Fine . . . furniture," Stiegel finished lamely.

After the old ladies had gone to bed, Stiegel took a lantern and went down to the German club, which met that night at Postlethwaite's Tavern.

The snow cracked beneath his step as he returned home late, and he felt that no amount of ale he had drunk and no amount of quilts would keep him warm in the third floor attic room beneath the eaves.

He began to undress, shivering and laughing to himself over some of the tavern jokes, humming the songs they had sung in their cups. Why wasn't there a fireplace in this attic room? It was damnably cold. He shuddered at the anticipation of the icy damp sheets, and wondered if his mother had thought to put a warming-pan in his bed. No, she hadn't.

He supposed the little German girl would be sleeping across the hall. She might get a warming-pan for him. He tiptoed over to her room, listening at the door, and knocked softly. There was no response, and he knocked again. He fancied he could hear her heavy breathing, and the thought of her began to excite him. He opened the door, and went over to her bed, holding the candle close to her face. She lay huddled in a ball of quilts, and he shook her shoulder gently. As her eyes flickered open, Stiegel saw that she was

about to cry out, and he placed his hand over her warm
lips.

"Shh! Do not be frightened, Gretchen. . . . I have just
come home from the inn, and I am freezing. Would you be
so kind as to get me a warming-pan? The house is strange, or
I would not bother you."

He lighted her candle from his own, and went back to his
room, his hand tingling from the warmth of her lips. They
were full and red. Why did she take so long, he wondered,
waiting for the sound of her footsteps again, and pacing up
and down the room, unable to pause for the cold.

At last her knock came shyly at the door.

"Come," he said, wondering if he had wakened his mother
when he came in. The little German girl stood behind her
candle, and in her hand she held a warming-pan.

He knew that he had wanted her from the minute he saw
her. His heart began to beat hard. Her hair hung in two
thick, blonde braids which came to her waist. She wore a
soft flannel night-gown over her night-shift.

"Come, put it here at the feet. So," he told her in low
German. He closed the door, and sat down on the bed.
"Now, tell me about yourself, Fraulein. You are indentured, I suppose. Sit here, and we will talk."

The girl looked embarrassed, but put her Betty lamp on
the table and sat on the bed beside him. Stiegel saw that
her hands were chapped and red.

"You have no family?" Stiegel asked her in a whisper.

"My mother and father and two sisters. We have all together come over. They are in Lancaster too."

"You like it here?" He saw that she was uneasy, and he
wondered what he might do to reassure her.

"I am homesick," she said, and her lips trembled.

"Sometimes I am homesick too," he admitted. "But it is
for Minnie."

And he began to tell her about Minnie and the things

they had done together. How they had gone into the country on Sundays with a crowd of young folks and danced and sung. How Minnie's father had worked in a glass factory in Cologne, and had made a little bottle the shape of a violin for Stiegel.

"I have a boy in Germany, too."

"Then tell me about him, Gretchen."

He listened absent-mindedly to the girl's words, for his thoughts were really on her lips, and how soon he might have them.

"You must not miss him too much, Gretchen. There are other boys in America."

"They are not like my Karl," she whispered softly, and the tears began to fill her eyes.

Stiegel touched her fingers, her two hands, held her close to him and kissed the lips he had been watching. "Perhaps we are not homesick, Gretchen," he whispered passionately. "Perhaps we only need one another. Do you know what it means to need someone else like this?"

Frightened, trembling under his touch, she shook her head.

"Gretchen—you like me, don't you?"

"Ja," softly.

"You will not mind if I make you forget Karl?"

He watched the tears roll down the side of her face and into the sheet; and he put out the two candles on the table.

From then on, Stiegel went to Lancaster frequently to see his mother. And so the winter slipped by, and then another winter, and the fall had come again. He treated Elizabeth like a little sister, and no longer disturbed her with kisses.

At last his opera was finished, and he sent it off to Germany for the criticism of his old master. But he felt depressed. He had lived for months in the highest emotional pitch, and now his work was finished and he was quite barren.

He applied himself with double effort to his work at the Furnace.

"I have an idea for the improvement of the Benjamin Franklin hearth," he told Herr Huber one day. "With a different back-plate, it might admit of cooking. As it is, 'tis a rich man's stove."

Herr Huber listened to his scheme with interest, and ended as he usually did, by saying, "Go ahead, my boy; go ahead."

Stiegel knew that Herr Huber was pleased with him, by the twinkle in his rheumy eyes. But he was sparing of praise. Stiegel wanted praise. It would be months, perhaps a year before he could ever hear of his opera. The time seemed long and unbearable. Now with the furnace out of blast for the winter, he could not even experiment on the Franklin hearth.

One night Stiegel sat with his back to the family; he had just finished off a letter to his mother. Last week when he was in Lancaster, she had said in her cryptic fashion, "It is time for you to marry!"

He often wondered whether Frau Stiegel knew that Gretchen had forgotten her Karl. Well, no one would ever know what his mother was thinking, anyway.

He began to trim a goose quill which had split, and was so engrossed with his thoughts that he did not hear Frau Huber say, " 'Tis nine o'clock, child, and you must go to bed. How pale you are! I'll brew you a benefit. Do you wherrit yourself with something?"

"Oh, no, mama," exclaimed Elizabeth quickly, "I pray you think nothing of it." And the pink which had faded from her cheeks since the summer rushed into them again.

" 'Tis not your conscience, Elizabeth? You have not opened one of those books on the top shelf? You read your

Bible each day, and say your prayers?"

"Oh yes, mama. 'Tis nothing, indeed, mama."

Herr Huber took his Meerschaum from his lips, and motioned the girl to come to him.

" 'Tisn't a beau vexing you? That young fan-mounter, pox him, has been hanging about you like a leech. And Reverend Klingerman's son, too. You are most seventeen, Liebling. Perhaps you pine for a husband?"

Elizabeth covered her eyes with her hands, and started to run from the room. Her mother rose abruptly.

"Black shame, Elizabeth Huber, to make scenes before your papa. Now bid us good-night like a gentlewoman, miss."

"G-g-good-night, mama and papa."

"Good-night."

"G-g-good-night, Heinrich."

There was no answer but the steady scraping of the pen.

"Heinrich," cried the iron-master so abruptly that the young man leaped up, knocking over the sandbox from the escritoire.

"Elizabeth speaks to you!"

"Oh . . . oh, I beg pardon, mein Herr. . . . What has she said?"

"She has said good-night!"

The girl looked over at Stiegel pitifully, and he thought he would like to shake her into action.

"Good-night, Elizabeth. Schlaf wohl."

Stiegel returned absent-mindedly to his work, but again came Herr Huber's voice with the precision of one who has something on his mind and will speak it out.

"You go to Lancaster often, these days, Heinrich."

"Aye, sir. My mother and cousins are continually urging my visit."

Stiegel felt uncomfortable. It was impossible that Herr Huber knew anything of himself and Gretchen; and yet

Herr Huber knew many Germans in Lancaster, and perhaps Stiegel had not been too discreet in his drinking at the inn.

"I thought perhaps a young man of your age had marriage in his head." Herr Huber puffed slowly and evenly. He would give Stiegel every chance to speak for himself.

"My music has filled my entire thought, as you know, sir."

Stiegel was annoyed. The devil! Would everyone marry him off of a sudden?

"I can scarce believe Elizabeth is grown a woman! 'Tis a pity she is so pale and languid. Some days she is so ill she must keep chamber."

"Aye," assented Stiegel, chewing at the feather of his pen. "She grows very thin."

"Think you she might have fallen in love?"

" 'Tis very like. . . ."

There was a moment's silence, and Stiegel could hear the "pup-pup" of Herr Huber's lips. It was an annoying sound to one who did not make it, and Stiegel thought that he would continue his work in his room, in spite of the cold there. He began to gather up his manuscript sheets.

"The young men who court her, they dare not to speak?" murmured Herr Huber thoughtfully. Let the boy squirm, he smiled to himself. He would soon be on the line. If Elizabeth were a little thin to suit him, marriage would fatten her up to the plumpness of any happy hausfrau.

"I suppose they feel it's taking vantage to ask for the hand of one so lovely, and so rich endowed with worldly goods." Stiegel rose. He'd had enough of this hinting around.

"I thought as much. You're *all* too modest, my boy. And you, Heinrich, are the most modest of the lot!"

Stiegel stared at him in unbelief. For two years he had worked feverishly at the furnace and at his music, and Elizabeth had been a happy interim of pinkness and relaxation. That he should have kissed the girl once in a moment of fancy meant nothing. Or maybe the old man was simply working around to a continental way of arranging a marriage. Well, marriage was the thing farthest from Stiegel's mind right now. Some day he would become a partner in the business, or buy the whole thing out. And some day when he met some fiery little person who would know what it meant to live—then he would marry. At present Gretchen was everything that he could want. He got up from the desk, stretched, and began to whistle as if Herr Huber's remark hadn't required an answer.

But Herr Huber had no intention of letting Stiegel get away from him. He had suddenly realized fully what Elizabeth wanted—and that was what she would get.

"Sit down, sit down," he grunted, and Stiegel reluctantly slipped into Frau Huber's usual chair at the fireside.

"Ja, they're all too modest and carefree. I know how young men are," he mused. "They like to play about a bit before they raise a family. They like to pinch a cheek or two and—I was young, once. I was young!"

Stiegel's mind flashed back to Lancaster. He would have to pretend Gretchen was someone he wanted to marry.

"To be truthful, sir, I *have* met a girl . . . but. . . ."

"I thought as much," the old man murmured. "And why have you not made a proposal of marriage to her?"

Stiegel smiled to himself. It had taken a little lie to wiggle out of the predicament, but it was a white little lie.

"I have just made my start, sir, as you know. I am too poor to take a wife."

"I shall make it easy for you, then. Elizabeth's hand is yours."

"Ach, mein Herr!" expostulated Stiegel, overwhelmed, and groping for a way out. "But 'tis too much!"

"Damn me if 'tis too much. In business you set the Thames on fire . . . and why shouldn't an old man make his daughter happy, nicht?"

"But . . . but it would be years before I could . . . could. . . ."

Herr Huber took his pipe from his lips, pursed his mouth, and nodded as much as to say that he knew everything which was going on in Stiegel's head. "The property goes with her."

Stiegel's head was swirling. Now, at once, he might have what he had thought it would take him years to earn. He would be rich, rich without the years of labor he had anticipated. And the sooner he was rich, the sooner he might give all of his time to music. Once a partner in the business, he would have Time, and with Time he could compose great music. Supposing he did not love her, could never love her with all the passion and soul that was in him? He would always have his music. And she was a little child. She would never know what she had missed.

If he should refuse this match, his career at Elizabeth Furnace would be ended, of course. The years he had already spent here would be lost. There would never be such an opportunity again. He thought with shame of marrying the girl because of what she would bring him. This was not what he had dreamed of back in Cologne. Well, had he stayed there, like as not he would have married for convenience, too.

"The property goes with her. . . ." Herr Huber was repeating, swinging one slippered foot with tantalizing regularity.

"Ach, mein Herr. . . ." cried Stiegel at last, wringing the hand of his new father with a confusion of sentiments.

Herr Huber rose to go to bed, and knocked the tobacco from his pipe. "I give you my permission, Heinrich, my permission!"

4

$\mathcal{G}$OD'S-ACRE, the country adjacent to Brickerville, was in a flurry of excitement. There was more than one femi nine heart that concealed its disappointment that Heinrich Stiegel was to marry. He had indeed been popular, flirting recklessly without prejudice; and consequently many a belle had dropped a finished doily or bit of cloth into her great hope chest with its polished bone, and thought only of the very gay and tantalizing young German and his stolen kisses.

The crescendo of life in the household became more evi dent as the seventh of November approached. Every hidden bit of pewter had been polished to radiance. An old lady from Brickerville was hired at twenty cents a week and her keep to finish the quilt which Frau Huber had worked on intermittently for years, and which was composed of patches of her own and her mother's wedding dress.

The candle-dipping had been finished early. Frau Huber resented the modern invasion of the candlemaker, who rode from house to house each autumn to make candles with his own molds. She always sweated conscientiously over the ripe, boiling bayberries herself, and boxed away hundreds of milky candles in a dark closet to prevent their turning yellow.

A messenger was dispatched to Philadelphia to obtain wedding garments, for there was not time to send to Europe. Great supplies of food were ordered too, delicacies which had been imported from the Indies. Frau Huber rested by cutting into lumps a great cone of sugar, using the blue paper from it to dye her wedding day petticoat. Cyrus made numerous trips to Lancaster and Brickerville, now for a supply of tea from the apothecary, and now for Mistress Elizabeth's bonnets from the mantua-maker. He even invested in a "bob" for himself for the festivities, and greased his new wig with so much pomatum that Frau Huber declared he was odious as a skunk cabbage, and would not allow him in the house for several days.

Elizabeth had her hair washed, and freshly powdered and frizzed. She fluttered about the house like a cloud come to earth, thought Stiegel as he caught her sometimes in his arms, and he wondered again if she would ever be able to feel the sweet earthiness of love. She was half afraid of her elegant lover though she had known him so long; sometimes her timidity vexed him, and then again it provoked him to a fierce desire to shock her.

When Stiegel returned from a hunting-trip with a quantity of partridge, pheasant and plover for the wedding-banquet, he found his wedding-clothes awaiting him. He tried them on before his pier-glass, highly pleased with the new flesh-colored small-clothes, raspberry velvet coat, and the first gold buckles he had ever owned.

He felt somehow as if this marriage were a part of a play in which he was acting. He had made his last trip to Lancaster to see Gretchen. He had meant to tell her, of course, that he was going to be married. It was ridiculous to think that he might miss Gretchen. But she had seemed to adapt

herself so well to his every mood. With all her ignorance, she
had given him a certain understanding, a kind of strength
that he could never have explained in so many words. . . .
Well, he hadn't told Gretchen about his marriage after all;
he had not wanted the memory of her dissolved in tears. He
hated himself for his weakness. But perhaps when she
heard the news from his mother she would become bitter,
and that would be easier for her in the end.

Elizabeth was no longer pale.

"Shall we . . . do you . . . a . . . which chair shall
we use at our bedside?" she asked Stiegel shyly, for they
were planning to use Elizabeth's room for their bridal
chamber, and some of Stiegel's belongings were already
moved into her possession. "And . . . do you like that picture of Martin Luther so *very* much, Heinrich? . . . I think
I shan't like his staring at me in my night-rail. This child at
play with the birds is so beautiful. And mama's sampler
she made when she was a little girl, over there. . . ."

The day of the wedding bloomed in November like a
flower in a patch of weeds. Frau Stiegel and Anthony arrived from Lancaster, and were given Heinrich's bedchamber, for tonight Heinrich would look out of his window at
the eastern stars, and the moon would shine in upon him
and his bride.

As noon approached, the guests drifted in from Brickerville and from the farms. The house glowed with open
hearths, and fiery pewter and spotless linens. The savori-
ness of stuffed fowl filtered through the rooms, and punch
in great bowls, steamed fragrantly.

Stiegel, conventionally, was nervous. Everything seemed
to irritate him. Cyrus had sneaked in to him early in the
morning with a piece of southernwood for his shoe.

"I done give Miz Elizabeth one, too. Yo'll see great 'speri-
ence today with that in yo shoe, Baron." The grandeur of
Stiegel in even his more relaxed moments had evoked this

title from the old servant, and had even spread among Stiegel's friends.

Reverend Klingerman came early with his son, who pouted and desponded in corners, looking off into space, taking out a pinch of snuff and then absent-mindedly playing with it.

Nowhere was Stiegel heeded or wanted. In the panic of preparation he seemed to be merely a figurehead; if he spoke to his mother she gave a choking little cough and dropped stitches in her knitting. Elizabeth was not to be seen, and Frau Huber looked through him with abstraction. Even Herr Huber had hidden his pipe on the mantel and was buried in the coolness of his cellar, selecting, discarding, combining. Anthony, to whom Stiegel turned in despair, had been a little prematurely at the punch and was in a state of quiet recuperation.

Stiegel retired to the little room which had been assigned him to dress in, hoping he would find comfort in working on his new score. The notes, however, refused to come. And now his clock said eleven, and he at last could dress for the ceremony. He ordered some hot water from Cyrus, and put his hone and razor to use. He could hear muffled voices in the next room, where Elizabeth was dressing too. They never ceased, and seemed as important a part of dressing as the lacing of her cherry stays.

The buzz grew more audacious as noon approached. Then the expectant lull came as a clock hastily pounded out the hour. All Brickerville and the élite of Lancaster were motionless with anticipation. And never had there seemed a more properly pale young bride. She rustled slowly in to the minister in her white silk and gauze, crowned with white roses, and exquisite with pearls on her hair, neck and arms. As she approached, borne on relentlessly by a coterie of white muslin bridesmaids, Stiegel felt as though he were watching some strange charade. She halted before him, a

little faint, and the white muslin bridesmaids revived her
with a twinkle of the painted ivory fans she had given them.
He tugged helplessly at his stock. There was utter breathlessness, a few droning words; then he was being kissed by
the beautiful young ladies who had so expectantly dropped
doilies into their hope chests, and Elizabeth's tiny little
hand clenched his arm for support, and people were buzzing about him like a fly after honey, and the odor of punch
which had hung breathless too, poured into the air again
its wedding greeting.

The remainder of the day was a continuous banquet o
roasted fowls and meats, pickled fennel, nasturtium buds,
mushrooms, cakes, always tempered with beer, and rum
from Jamaica, and wine from Lisbon. The men shouted a
ball and bat and at quoits in the lenient November sun
shine, and the women amused themselves exchanging whisperings and new stiches and "pantins." These were the
new French pasteboard figures moved by strings which
put everyone into torrents of laughter with their silly
antics.

As the sun went down, there was a serenade too by an impromptu band from Brickerville. The music shrieked forth
in spirited cacophony from horns of squash vines, cornstalk
fiddles, combs, and aeolian harps made of wooden boxes
with horsehair strings. Following them were real fiddler
from Lancaster who knew the latest dances; in heated succession there followed the Allemandes Valley's, De La
Cours, minuets from Devonshire, and jigs from America
while the voice of the "caller-out" was drowned in excite
ment and hilarity.

The wedding seemed never to end. The house had no
quieted down until the poor little bride was drooping with
exhaustion.

Stiegel tampered with the candles, embarrassed, a
Elizabeth knelt in prayer beside their bed. Seventeen sh

was, and yet slim and tiny and undeveloped as a child. His wife. . . .

He snuffed the candles and crept into bed beside her. She lay still, terrified, exhausted. Stiegel touched her cheek and he felt the tears of humiliation which ran fast from her eyes.

"Liebling . . . why do you cry?" he whispered.

She buried her face in the pillow, and answered him with sobs.

"Is it that you do not love me?" he asked, kissing her arm softly.

"No—no."

"Come then . . . let me hold you in my arms. . . . What a soft little thing you are, Elizabeth." He felt again an overwhelming desire to stir her, to shock her into a breathing, panting life. He held her close to him, and he felt her trembling under his touch.

"Elizabeth, you must not be afraid. . . ."

"No, no . . . Heinrich, . . . do not touch me . . . I am so sh-shamed . . ." she sobbed.

"But you are my wife, little one. . . . Think of it, we belong like this. . . ."

He was suddenly angry with her for her innocence. "You are only lying safe in my arms, Elizabeth. When I kiss you on the lips, so, does it not make you forget your shame a little? . . . Do you not feel something growing inside of you, Liebling?"

"I am so t-tired. . . ." she sobbed, turning away from him, and struggling from his embrace.

Stiegel fought with the desire to crush her into submission. Then he pulled himself out of bed and slipped into his banyan. He would watch the fire of the furnace until she had fallen asleep.

The wedding party stayed on for several days to help with strenuous receptions which followed, for people came drifting in at all hours and always stayed for a dish of tea.

For three or four Sundays after the wedding Elizabeth "came out bride" in church, being given the most prominent pew with her new husband. Each Sunday she was a spectacle of more grandeur than before with a bright colored new gown, her black mode hood lined in white silk, and a large cape extending over her shoulders.

It was only as the Christmas season wore on that life seemed to become normal again. Frau Huber returned to her knitting; Herr Huber rested at night again before the fire-dogs; Elizabeth played hymns on her harpsichord; and Stiegel worked at the escritoire, absorbed by his music. The only difference now was that sometimes Elizabeth stole up to him, leaning over his shoulder, jealously watching the winged notes take form. She was no longer afraid of her husband. She loved him with all the fervor in her fragile little soul.

And for Stiegel, life had become complacent and satisfactory. Elizabeth anticipated his every comfort, and if she was unable to feel with his heart, and think with his mind, it was not because she did not try.

The business had become a passion with him now, for he felt that the furnace was the fire of his own blood, and he avidly watched the sales grow. Sometimes as he worked on his music he found himself distracted by designs of new stoves he had been working on, and he would lay aside his pen, and give himself over to the more practical work.

In February Stiegel went off for a few days with friends from Brickerville to hunt, for the stock of meat of the mansion was greatly depleted, and the little spell of warm weather had been irresistible. He said that he would be home Monday. Elizabeth, who had not been separated from her husband since the wedding, had fretted and pined for three days, and now that he was returning she prepared to dress in her most lavish pink outfit, and even tucked fresh herbs into the little pocket of her English corset.

"Mama," she asked, "would you come lace me? 'Tis harder each day; methinks I have eaten too hearty."

Frau Huber pulled on the laces ruthlessly. She had always been proud of Elizabeth's anaemic waist, but now, indeed, it was unsubmissive.

"Don't, mama. Luddy, 'tis painful," and tears appeared in her great blue eyes.

"Shame, Elizabeth. Have I not taught you a Christian does not snivel at so small a test!"

Elizabeth fell back weakly onto her bed.

"Elizabeth, are you with child?" cried her mother hoarsely.

The girl lifted trembling hands to her face. "Oh no, it can't be that. I have never prayed to God for a baby, mama. Oh no, I should be afraid, terribly afraid!"

Frau Huber left the room quickly. It hurt her that her little girl should have to learn these things as she and all other women had had to learn them, with experience, and shock, and humiliation.

Elizabeth burst wildly into tears. She had quite forgotten that this thing came magically with marriage, and suddenly she hated Heinrich with fervor.

The sun went down, and Cyrus shuffled about, piling fresh wood on the fires and lighting the bayberry candles. The dinner hour came and went, and there was no sound of horse's hoofs.

Elizabeth sat in the dark of her room. What would happen to her if she should be with child! The child would grow larger and larger within her, and there would be nothing she could do, nothing! The child would be too big to be borne from her! Women screamed out for hours with torture, and there was nothing to do to help them. The perspiration broke out on her face. If this thing had happened to her she would not be able to run away from it. . . . Oh, she would never speak to Heinrich again, never let him touch her, no matter how she might ache to lie close to him. . . . But why didn't he come?

"Elizabeth!" called her mother, impatiently. "Why don't you come when I call? The food is all dry."

"Come, Liebchen," called Herr Huber, from the bottom of the stairs. "They won't come today at all, I think."

"But they . . . they promised," replied Elizabeth, complying against her will. The thought of food sickened her lately.

Herr Huber "broke" the goose with good appetite, but Elizabeth sat by with tear-stained face, passing the vegetable basins and refusing to touch a morsel.

"Maybe I will just let him kiss me," she whispered to her conscience.

But by ten o'clock Elizabeth had quite forgotten the fear for herself in her anxiety over Stiegel's safety. She could tell that her parents were pretending to be casual for her sake, and she raised the shutters and stood at the draughty window, shivering. She was being punished for her bitterness toward her own husband; God was punishing her. He might let something frightful happen to Heinrich. . . .

"Now you must go to bed!" commanded her father, at eleven.

"But I . . . I can't sleep," wailed Elizabeth, dragging herself upstairs.

"Ach, they have stopped at an inn, and forgot themselves."

Elizabeth did not believe him. She undressed and knelt at the window where she could see the stars. She thought of Heinrich lying dead in the snow, scalped. She had said she would never speak to him again, would never let him touch her. . . . Oh, if only she could know that he was safe somewhere out there in the woods.

"Dear God," she prayed, "I didn't mean what I said . . .

I was selfish . . . I love him. . . . And . . . if only you
send him back to me . . . he can do whatever he wants!"

At midnight, even Herr Huber became uneasy. Stiegel
had promised to return that morning. He brought out his
Bible and took it in doses between warm sack, glancing
often at Magdalena who sat upright, sound asleep, her knitting in her hands. He had been dozing a little himself when
he looked up and found Elizabeth sitting at his feet, pulling
about her a scarlet night-gown.

"Papa, do you think . . . could the Conestogas be
night-walking?"

"Nonsense, my dear," he whispered, so as not to waken
his wife.

"Some indentured criminal might be prowling at large
through the forests."

"That is a fancy of jingle brains, child."

Elizabeth watched again from the window, though she
could only see a blur of pine as the snow drove down between her and the glow of the furnace. It was long after midnight when she heard Cyrus cry that Stiegel had returned.
The house suddenly wakened, and Elizabeth flew to open
the door. Stiegel half fell in. His coat covered a figure in his
arms which he laid carefully before the fire. He shook a wet
covering of snow from his hat, and fell back, panting, into
a chair.

"Odd's life!" exclaimed Herr Huber. " 'Tis a child. . . .
'Tis a *dead* child!"

Elizabeth shrank from the prostrate figure with a little
cry.

"Not dead; nigh frozen," gasped Stiegel.

"How did you come upon this foundling?" asked Herr
Huber excitedly.

"We'd gone astray. We had to rest . . . and tarried in a
thicket with our game. I lay against the warm shanks of my
horse. . . ." He paused a moment to get his breath. "Then

I saw a fire. It was far off in the woods. I stole close to it, my gun cocked. I could see nothing for the glare. . . . Then I tripped on the girl. She lay near the fire, cold to the death. Indian, I thought, but I can't let her die. . . . Lizzie, can you brew some grog?"

Elizabeth grabbed a Betty lamp and flew to obey him, glad to be rid of the still figure until warmth came into it again. Frau Huber ran upstairs for some quilts; Herr Huber hurried out to help Elizabeth, forgetting his rheumatism; and Stiegel, with effort, knelt and rubbed the slim, stiff hands.

"Come, little one, open your eyes," he coaxed.

As the warmth slowly penetrated her muscles, the girl's eyes fluttered open, and rested on the eager face close to her own. Stiegel was startled at their sudden beauty. They were large and black, and the fire threw miniature flames into them, and onto the smoothness of her black straight hair.

She lay for a moment staring at him, and he whispered anxiously, "Are you all right?"

"Oui," she said softly, and began to smile.

He was suddenly abashed, and dropped her hand as Frau Huber came down the hall.

Stiegel carried the girl to the spare bed, and they forced her to take a little grog. Elizabeth, still frightened, placed a warming-pan at her feet, and timorously touched the girl's garment of mink and the bright beads on her neck. They swaddled her with covers, and when she slept left her hesitantly for the rest of the night.

Elizabeth, uneasy at the thought of those bright beads, lay close to the protective warmth of Stiegel's body. She had looked forward so much to his home-coming, and now there had been all this strange commotion. She had wanted him to think she looked pretty when he returned, and in the excitement he had scarcely noticed her. For a long time she did not sleep, listening to the deep breathing of his fatigue.

5

STIEGEL, who had begun to breakfast with his father-in-law, finished his ale and was about to rise when Elizabeth stood in the doorway with a young woman beside her.

Astounded, he watched them enter, his eyes never moving from the black eyes of the stranger.

"Gott, I thought she was but a child," he said under his breath. "She must be all of thirteen."

The girl was dressed in Elizabeth's clothes, and they hung on her badly, for she was very small. The delicate pink of the cotton print only emphasized the darkness of her skin, and the red morocco slippers shifted about on her tiny bare feet. Her hair was caught back carelessly with a green ribbon and hung unbraided and straight down her back. Stiegel wondered when she had last worn a dress.

She attempted a curtsey, awkwardly, and the eyes which had traveled swiftly about the room rested on him.

"Je suis Diane!" she announced and smiled.

"'Tis ne'er the same . . ." ejaculated Herr Huber, his cheek bulging with unswallowed cake.

"Mais oui. Today I should be very froze and dead but for the kind heart of M'sieu," the girl answered quickly, every word savoring of French.

" 'Tis my husband," informed Elizabeth hurriedly, wondering why her words sounded a bit foolish.

"You—you have slept well?" inquired Herr Huber, still feeling that somehow he had been cheated.

"Non, non, non. You have no sooner left my room than I wake. How can I sleep in milkweed? I gather my blankets about me and lie on the floor."

"You . . . you are Indian then?" asked Elizabeth, aghast.

"Maybe," returned Diane, laughing. "Long ago, maybe two, maybe three years, my mother die in Acadia, because she cannot see France again. She is beautiful, a great lady. . . . She cannot stand the cold. When the Indians come to Acadia my father escape with me. We live in the forest. We try to find New York. My uncle would give us a home. First we find Bostong, after we leave the St. Lawrence. Then we go into the wilderness again. . . ." She looked about at their intent faces, and noted the horror in Elizabeth's eyes. "In the summer we like the wilderness. We eat berries . . . big like the cherry you have. . . . We stab fish in the brook with a big stick, like the Indian. We sleep on the pine needle. At night the wilderness screams. . . . We are afraid. . . . We scream like the animal."

She paused, and the paleness of Elizabeth's face gratified her.

"But the Indians . . ." stammered Elizabeth.

"Oui, we hide from the Indians. Every day we thank God we have not been eat. . . . In New York the Indians are so fierce. . . . They pull out the eye, like this, with the hunting knife." She illustrated with a knife which she seized from the table, so that Elizabeth shrank away from her. "They pull out the tongue, so! But my father, he is not afraid. . . . When the Indians find us, he laugh and shoot at them. They yell. They dance and sing and shout. They tie my father to the stake. Ah, mon Dieu," she cried, with a sudden sob, "before my eye they put him in flame. . . . They . . . they cut off his arm. They give me the blood to drink! . . . They . . . they feed him his flesh!" she cried, the anguish in her voice just tinged with bravado.

Elizabeth screamed and fell fainting against the table, and in the confusion that followed, Diane was for the moment forgotten.

That evening Elizabeth lost the child she had conceived. For days she trembled with emotion at mention of the girl's name. Because the family was so concerned over Elizabeth's condition, Diane was disregarded, and no one suggested what to do with her.

As time went on, Diane helped Frau Huber with the household tasks, learning quickly. When her other work was done, she labored incessantly at the spinning wheel. She seemed to sense the fact that as long as she kept busy none of these people would be cruel enough to turn her out homeless into the cold. Gradually she insinuated herself into Elizabeth's affection, entertaining her as easily with pretty tales of little French children and quaint Acadian customs, as she had at first horrified her. Elizabeth was kept quietly at her sampler or her paper flowers. Diane ran errands for her tirelessly.

As spring came on she planted a very special garden which she called her Garden of Eden. She had planned it carefully so that it would be in shades of yellow, ranging from calendulas to pale yellow pansies.

Sometimes she enveloped herself with a big apron and helped Frau Huber and Frau Habicht, the indentured cook, to make soap. She preserved and pickled, and attempted to read sermons to Herr Huber in her quaint French accent. Stiegel, who had been teaching her English, listened proudly to her progress.

One morning he came from the furnace to the kitchen

yard, and at the sight of Diane picking geese, he leaned against the iron fence and roared. Diane, her head swathed in a kerchief, and an old gown of Frau Habicht's tumbling in loose folds about her, held a goose firmly in one of her brown hands, and jabbered Indian at him. He was squawking angrily, for his head had been done up in a bag to prevent his biting, and he resented this stripping as any modest goose might. A flurry of feathers surrounded them in a gay storm and Diane paused to sneeze, but not before she had plucked the largest quill of all from the insulted bird, and held it out to Stiegel.

"A large pen, Herr Stiegel, to write the large note of music." When Diane was excited, she still forgot the plurals which Heinrich was inflicting upon her so severely.

He put the quill in his hat, and she threw the goose from her. They watched it dipping about the yard in its bonnet, and Stiegel laughed, " 'Tis plain to see he's been dramming."

"Sometimes of a night I lie and hate the geese. They clank so loud. I wonder oft-times which clanks the more, the geese or the stillness in the dark."

"You . . . you still can't sleep in feathers?"

" 'Tis like every bone was broke or crumpled, though 'tis better now. But . . . you will not like me to say this!"

"To say what, Diane?"

"At night when I think of my father's death—and how you snatch me from my own grave ——"

"Hey day, you must think pleasanter."

"Ah, but I do, then. The little—what you say, *Vorspiel*, runs into my head like a brook. And it runs and runs. I see M'sieu sway . . . so . . . with the music under his chin. Then of a sudden, I am tipsy with sleep."

Stiegel, in spite of himself, was flattered. "You're a quaint child," he pondered aloud.

"I am a woman," she corrected.

" 'Tis all of a piece. A child because you choose not to be called one."

She puckered her mouth.

"Well, then, how old are you?"

"I think I must be seventeen."

Stiegel laughed.

Diane shrugged her shoulders. "How many years one is born, M'sieu, does it matter?"

"Frau Huber told me you were fifteen."

"How should I know?" retorted Diane crossly.

As they entered the kitchen, Frau Huber was humming an old German lullaby, and covering crocks with paper for the spring house.

Stiegel helped his mother-in-law carry them to the porch, where they stood chatting for a moment about the pigs.

Diane stripped her comic robe from her with agility, and sang a little French tune in husky, deep tones: "C'est l'amour qui tourne le monde ronde!"

Frau Habicht adjusted the dripping pan under a roasting chicken, giving a little grunt as she straightened up. She was a German indentured servant whom Frau Huber had taken many years before because she had come so well recommended from her cousin in Germany. Her coarse gray hair wound around and around in a coil on her head until it ended in a little pinnacle. She squinted as if she were looking into the bright sun, and her face was covered with thousands of fine little wrinkles which ran down into her neck and arms. Her age had always been a matter of jovial contention in the family.

"She always groans when she stoops," laughed Stiegel at one of these conferences. "She must be a ripe old age."

"Fooh! Wait till you are a ripe old age, my boy," taunted Herr Huber.

Elizabeth had always defended Frau Habicht. "She calls me Püppchen."

"But that does not stop her bones from creaking with age," her mother contended. "She's sixty, I'll tie to that."

"Sixty—she's seventy!" When Herr Huber put his pipe in his mouth that meant the end of an argument.

But there was no doubt that Frau Habicht was along in years. She had hated Diane from the first glimpse of her, and now when she saw Diane fling her dress inside out over a chair, several months of patience gave out.

"Ach, 'twas the like of a dovecote in the yard, ye cooin' to him; him cooin' to ye."

Diane turned like a deer. " 'Twas no more than manners!"

"Sugar-coated manners then, miss!"

"You old pig!" cried Diane, her whole body aflame with fear and wrath.

The woman balanced her German bulk close to the girl, and spat German at her fiercely and volubly.

Diane quivered with rage. Her face became stark white, and a scar which had never been evident before leaped into prominence on her forehead. The angry brown hands seized a pewter tasting-spoon from the wall and flung it at the receding cook.

"What clack is this?" cried Frau Huber petulantly, as she came in with Stiegel.

"She . . . she aims to kill me," sputtered Frau Habicht, rubbing her wound, which began to show crimson.

"Diane, what's this ado?" demanded Frau Huber.

"She . . . she . . ." Diane's eyes shone from beneath their heavy brows like live coals.

"Answer me, miss. Did you trounce Frau Habicht?"

"She . . . she . . ."

"Did you, I say?"

"Oui."

"Then off to your room, miss. 'Tis the most unseemly conduct I have ever seen. Not a bite of food till you bespeak apology."

Diane bristled away.

"The girl goes off like touchwood," blazed Frau Huber. Stiegel felt strangely aquiver.

"She is nought but a child," he maintained.

"Heh! Child! She is sixteen years!" sassed the old cook. "An age to know better, that I'll warrant."

"Ach now, Frau Habicht, she is a poor child that has had no mother since she's born. Nor father of her own. The Indians have had her for years. . . ." Frau Huber did not like dissension in the household, and was truly miserable trying to administer justice. "We must allow for her!"

"Gott!" thought Stiegel, "Diane is a magnificent little liar! But life is not near so dull!"

"Heh! She is like to kill one of us!" thundered Frau Habicht.

"How did this trouble come about?"

"I' faith, I don't know. I beg her to be neat with my gown, and because 'tis old she trundles it about!" The cook waddled off to examine a pot full of potatoes, still nursing her bruises with grunts.

And the incident was seemingly closed, though for the sake of discipline, Diane was locked in her room.

The evening was spent by the family as usual in the parlor before the fire. Elizabeth was sewing again on infant's clothes, stitching infinitesimal tucks into the linen, and hemming it with the most delicate of lace. Her mother had bundled her into a big wing chair, and Herr Huber had supported her back with pillows. Stiegel had propped her feet onto a footstool.

At last she put aside her sewing. "I think I shall raise a tune on the harpsichord. 'Tis very dull without Diane."

"Oh no, my dear," cried her mother. " 'Twould never do for you to pedal."

"Mama, mayn't I take just a chicken wing to Diane? You don't want to bestarve her!"

"Diane is in disgrace, Elizabeth. Were she my own child a fine trouncing she would have for such a temper. As 'tis, I think we must send her back to Acadia."

"Mama," cried Elizabeth, aghast, "I should never be happy again if Diane left me." Two large tears hovered on her eyelashes. "I have never had a sister. . . ."

"Shush, Elizabeth, child. I'll think better on't." Frau Huber forced the girl gently back into her nest.

"Don't you think we are a bit too harsh, shutting up Diane like a child?" asked Herr Huber, clicking his pipe on his teeth.

"You're too lazy to fill your own pipe, since she's here," chided his wife.

"Mama, how you talk! What would any of us do without Diane?"

Stiegel, perturbed, played with the lid on his snuff box. It was true, Diane had changed the household. The first months of his marriage seemed colorless now when he thought of them, and yet they had seemed absorbing enough at the time. Of course, he told himself, Elizabeth had not been well right along. It was only natural that the coming of this gay little animal should make Elizabeth seem more of an invalid.

Then, rather impetuously, he sat on her stool, holding her small white satin feet on his knee.

"If you want Diane to stay, you shall have her!" he declared.

Elizabeth's soft fingers swept over the silky wire of his wig, and caressed his cheek. "My darling," she whispered a little shyly, "it frights me to think what life would be without you!"

At seven, Reverend Klingerman's son arrived noisily from Brickerville in a borrowed gig. He was now the devoted swain of Diane. He had so far recovered from Elizabeth's rejection that he watched with utter equanimity as she smuggled away the infant's clothes. Stiegel took the opportunity of his arrival to steal away from the parlor. A moment later he hurried up the stairs to Diane's room, unlocked the door from without, and knocking quickly, waited a reply.

"Diane," he whispered loudly, "again I rescue you. 'Tis some chicken and cold pie I've pilfered. And the evidence you may fling into the garden!"

The door opened, and in a shadow of candlelight Diane stood before him, proudly pale.

"Have you repented?" he teased, holding the tempting food a little away from her.

"Non!" she cried fiercely.

"Then here is your reward. Howbeit, do not say again you are not a child, Diane!"

She took the napkin from him.

"Thank you, Herr Stiegel!" she said more softly.

As Stiegel locked the door again and turned away, he bumped into his father-in-law, with a plate in his hand.

"Er . . . a . . ." Herr Huber coughed. "When a young man comes sparkin' all the way from Brickerville in a borrowed gig, I can't see the harm of a girl talking to him in the garden! Can you?"

"I have just brought her some food myself," laughed Stiegel, "so she'll be strong enough to speak up to him!"

Herr Huber noisily unlocked the door again, and the two went back a little foolishly to their women in the parlor.

6

Stiegel and Diane were alone in the parlor. The Boston Evening Post had just arrived with the last mail. It was several months old, for it had lain over in some little village or other with each new snowstorm. Stiegel read it avidly, and Diane hung over his shoulder spelling words aloud, and saying them over and over to herself.

"The Congress which con—con ——" she stammered.

Stiegel read on hurriedly for news of the Indian outrages.

"The Con —— What is this, Heinrich?"

"Congress which convened (that means met) at Albany. . . . About the Indians, you know."

"Oh. And why have they met?"

He read on, seeming not to hear her.

"Heinrich, *tell* me!" she demanded.

He turned to her impatiently. Her great black eyes rested on his lips.

"That is what I am trying to read!"

"But the Indians, they do not need a Congress!" she laughed gaily.

"You do not understand, Diane! The Indians have been plundering again. And now the Congress in Albany has

[*66*

given more land to the colonies, land west of the Susque-hanna. The Indians are furious, and they have turned to the French to protect them. And so . . . because the Indians are furious, the Congress gives them gifts . . . to make them happy!"

"Gifts . . . but they do not have their own land?"

"The colonists need it! They must have land too; they must live and grow!"

"The Indians, they are fools!" declared Diane.

"Fools! Fooh! They take gifts for their land, and then they fight for it anyway! They plunder and scalp and creep up on us. . . . There's not a soul of us safe any more on the road."

Diane's eyes shone. She was very excited at the thought of war. Perhaps some day the entire country would become French.

"Do you understand?" Stiegel asked.

"Mais oui. I am the Indian. . . . Elizabeth is the colony. . . . You are the land. You belong to Elizabeth and Congress pays me not to look at you. . . . Herr Huber and Frau Huber are the Congress. . . . They give me everything to make me happy! I take everything they give to make me happy, but I try to get just a little smile from Heinrich Stiegel too! Why do you not laugh and joke with me, Heinrich, like Robert Klingerman and the fools from Brickerville? You are so . . . so *old!*"

"Because I am not like the fools from Brickerville!"

"You do not like me then!" she pouted.

"Of course I like you!" he thundered. "Do you think I would teach you to read if I did not like you? Come now, read this to me. And do not gargle your words."

Diane jauntily read the paragraph he pointed out, but he was so shaken by her metaphor that he let the mistakes go uncorrected. She was nothing but a damned little flirt who wanted no less than the countryside. And she was giving him fair warning of her plan to attack. However childish and confused her analogy had been, it was plain enough.

She had become rather flagrantly beautiful; a wild color lingered on her cheeks, stung by the winds of winter. Her large, luminous black eyes seemed to possess whatever they saw, and her quick, natural laughter reminded him of the woods. Well, if he hadn't been married, he'd have shown her a thing or two. There was no fun quite like breaking the heart of a hardened coquette, he thought.

"You English read with so great a labor," she criticized with French outlook, as she finished her lesson. "And you waste so much time. You fill your mouth e'en with one syllable, while we have spoke a thought with a grunt, n'est-ce pas?"

Early in the spring the family portraits were painted. It was one night shortly after the melting of the last snow that an artist came to the house, his wagon filled with canvases. The Hubers surrounded him, delighted, for of course he bore news of the countryside and details of the war. He scarcely looked artistic in his heavy surtout and bearskin cap. He puffed and panted with the rawness of April, and peeled off some old stockings, soaked in neat's-foot oil, which had covered his boots and legs like tights.

Herr Huber pelted him with questions, but Mr. Baldersnap gave out his news only in frugal spurts.

"England, she sent over an army of 'lobsters,' that's how frightened she was, and told General Braddock to make short work of the job."

With this tidbit he yanked off one stocking.

"Lobsters!" shrieked Diane with mirth. "But they are to eat! N'est-ce pas?"

"Soldiers . . . who wear red coats with long tails," explained Stiegel, laughing.

The family waited tensely while Mr. Baldersnap tried to

get a good grip on the second stocking.

"But he needs wagons and horses!" he jerked out, as the stocking came off.

There was a hubbub of discussion while the artist struggled with his coat, and an anticipatory lull as his arms slipped out of the sleeves.

"Asked Benjamin Franklin what to do!" he conceded.

Herr Huber was greatly upset by the close range of the fighting. Like most of the German colonists, he was a pacifist at heart. He did not want war any more than his comfortable little Frau wanted contention among the servants. He asked nothing more from life than to work peacefully with his iron, and to smoke at night at his wife's side.

Elizabeth leaned on Stiegel's arm, for they had been standing around their guest, and the excitement tired her.

"Mr. Franklin," she whispered to him. "What does he know of fighting? He makes electricity, doesn't he?"

"What are we ever coming to?" wailed Frau Huber, and she handed Mr. Baldersnap the hot grog which she had just brewed.

"Advertised, that's what Mr. Franklin did!" finished up Mr. Baldersnap, as a last admission before the grog. "Advertised (sip) . . . Lancaster, York, and Cumberland Counties (sip). . . . One hundred and fifty wagons with four horses each (sip) . . . and fifteen hundred saddle horses (sip). . . . Advertised—this very week." And Mr. Baldersnap went into a lethargy which lasted until the following day.

"We do not want war! Why does he advertise among us Germans!" cried Herr Huber.

"But we've got the finest horses in the colonies. Where will you find stronger?" returned Stiegel. "Or horses tended so well through the winter and snows? We must help General Braddock, nicht?"

"I do not like war . . ." meditated Herr Huber, puffing on his pipe quickly. "But the Indians are close. . . ."

The following day, Cyrus was sent off to Will's Creek with a wagon and two saddle horses trailing him, the offering of Herr Huber to General Braddock. The entire family watched until he was out of sight.

Mr. Baldersnap, exhilarated by a good night's lodging, laid out his display of canvases to the admiring household. In the winter, snowbound, he had painted a devastating array of headless aristocrats, all garbed in the latest French fashions. There now remained but to choose a favorite costume and paint in a familiar face.

" 'Tis the very portrait for you, with its yellow pelerine and black ribbons," cried Stiegel to Diane, "and there, mein Herr, is a gentleman with pipe in hand, and a banyan of the handsomest green brocade. 'Tis alarming like you."

"Ach, in a few years the pictures would only lie in some attic!" growled the old man.

But Diane thought the torso of yellow pelerine and black ribbons very elegant, and, throwing her arms about Herr Huber's neck, she coaxed, "Oh, please, Herr Huber! 'Twould be such fun to hang on the wall!"

He chuckled, as he always did when Diane hugged him, and smoothed her black hair.

"Yes, well. . . ." he weakened, and the artist was invited to paint the family and became a thirsty and not too diligent guest for some time.

One evening Elizabeth said hesitantly, "I . . . I would like to be painted too, papa."

"Black shame, Elizabeth," chided her mother, "wanting to be painted in your delicate straits."

The tears tumbled down on Elizabeth's flushed cheeks.

"I' faith, I shall ne'er be ought but in a delicate state," whispered Elizabeth, as she fingered a dry elm leaf in her Bible.

"You are a ninny," jibed Diane, and a polar silence filled the room. She turned to Stiegel and found his face scarlet with anger.

"Fluff your waist with a shawl or ruffle your polonaise," suggested Diane hastily, to cover her embarrassment, "and spread before you the large fan with London Bridge painted on't."

"Diane, you are incorrigible," reproved Frau Huber. "Sixteen and noddle-headed. 'Tis small wonder you are an old maid."

"Robert Klingerman swears he will be suicide without me," she retaliated, glancing quickly at Elizabeth.

"The fopling would never have the courage to lie interred at the crossroads with a stake drove through his middle, as custom allows," guaranteed Stiegel.

The talk of Diane's marrying made him uncomfortable. She was so indispensable with her gayety and chatter, he told himself, that life would be a dull thing without her. And more than that, he quickly dismissed from his mind.

As the spring went on she seemed utterly independent of him. He realized bitterly that she coquetted with everyone, himself included. With some she had one stratagem; with others, another. When she ignored him he became angry and restless; and when she flirted with him, he became angry and restless. Elizabeth was unable to do more than dress and sit about pasting leaves in an herbarium. Diane tore into the woods, and came back gloriously radiant, her arms filled with jacks-in-the-pulpit, or her hands overflowing with fragrant arbutus she had unearthed from beneath wet leaves. She brought Elizabeth bits of every plant or flower as it first came up, and watched her a little enviously as she pasted them in her book, writing their names below them in her formal German script.

"Teach me to write," Diane begged of Stiegel one night, as he worked on his long-neglected score.

She pulled her chair to the desk, satisfied that Elizabeth's blue eyes were upon her. "I want so much to melt a vermilion wafer on a billet, and to mix my ink powder till the lumps are gone!"

"*I* shall teach you to write," offered Elizabeth, trying to fight the prick of jealousy which she had so often harbored lately. "Heinrich has little time to spare."

"But you do not write so beautiful as Heinrich!" declared Diane bluntly.

Stiegel found his pupil apt. Sometimes, correcting her impatiently, he colored to find that her eyes had not been on the paper, but had clung to his lips. And he was painfully conscious of the hot, young blood running through her veins. As they worked together, the lace engageants of her sleeve tumbled over his hand, caressing it softly, and driving concentration away.

Diane smiled to herself, for she knew she disturbed him. He was more interesting to capture than the rest of her swains, because he was more vain and stubborn. She did not want to hurt Elizabeth, of course. And yet a wife who couldn't amuse her husband deserved to lose him. Well, if only she could get Stiegel to admit his infatuation for her, she would be quite satisfied. She would toss him back to his little weakling and let them flounder together!

He was much annoyed during the summer by Diane's popularity. In spite of her arrival at the age of spinsterhood, there was an invasion of males young and old, and Diane flirted with them all outrageously. She drove with them to the inn to see dwarfs and cockfights; she rode to Lancaster with them to the race paths, and spent the night with Frau Stiegel, entertaining her with the most ingenious fabrications about the Indians. She pored over almanacs with them and laughed over the jokes. She read to them from "Pilgrim's Progress," slurring the two-syllable words, and inserting witticisms which Bunyan would have expurgated with a blush. She discoursed with them volubly on such favorite debates of the day as Constancy vs. Stability, or on Decorum vs. Impropriety. She dramatized Ophelia and Juliet, to the amusement and languishment of her swains. She read and wrote falteringly, and this appealed like the first steps of a baby. She sang little French songs with a tremor in her voice, and when her suitors paled with emotion, she translated the verse into rollicking words of humor, to the chagrin of the lovesick.

When Cyrus returned and told them that General Braddock's army had been defeated, the family was shocked.

"That Gen'l Braddock, he dead as snuff," gloated Cyrus, who had never felt more important in his life. "De Injuns, dey snuck right into Philadelphia—most in, anyways. . . . Dey thick like mole holes all about, de Injun holes."

"Whatever will become of us!" wailed Frau Huber once more. "Think of those boys lying dead. They all have mothers!"

"We will become French!" cried Diane, triumphantly. She seemed exhilarated and jabbered Indian at the sensitive females who hugged their children to them and dreamed at night of Indian assaults. It was the hour openly to declare her politics, and the Hubers were aghast at her boldness.

But with the same breath that she flaunted her ideas, she ran upstairs for a handkerchief for Frau Huber's tears, or a jar of tobacco for Herr Huber's pipe; and while she was gone, Herr Huber mused, " 'Tis only for the sport of it, she talks so brazen."

Herr Huber secretly chuckled, and thought that if he were a young blade, Diane would not long be single. Who else could so have amused him this summer when his foot was bound up in cabbage leaves and flannel?

With the damp, cool weather of the fall, his rheumatism became worse, and he was incapacitated for active work. He felt perfect confidence, however, in his zealous young son-in-law, and he sat back with his Bible and sermons and withdrew from the fray.

As Stiegel's work increased at the Furnace, he took over most of the correspondence with the Stedmans, Herr Huber's partners in Philadelphia. Charles' interest in the Furnace was largely financial, for he had a thriving law practice, but Alexander Stedman wrote often of customers he had waited upon, and new accounts he was striving to get. It piqued Stiegel that he did not know the Stedmans personally, and if he had been independent he would have made a trip to Philadelphia to meet them. There were many things he would do if he did not have Herr Huber over him at the Furnace, thought Stiegel. It was not easy working for an old man with fixed ideas.

Stiegel sweated and labored long hours. He was discontented, and the thirsty furnace requited him. He had never been truly happy when he was not working on music, and now he told himself hypocritically that this was the reason for his unrest. When Herr Huber was feeling better, Stiegel would have more time for his own ambition. And then life would not seem to be standing still!

Toward the time of Elizabeth's confinement, Diane gave her energy unstintingly to Elizabeth, treating her like a little child who must be coddled and amused. Elizabeth's misgivings disappeared. She had been silly to be jealous of Diane.

But Heinrich seemed ever to become more of a stranger to her, and she battled with the fear that he did not love her. One day, when Diane was not there to watch her, she went down to the kitchen, and in spite of Frau Habicht's protests, slaved in the heat to make Heinrich a cherry pudding. But the closeness of the kitchen proved too much, and she fainted in Frau Habicht's arms.

Stiegel carried her up to her bed.

"You must take care," he scolded, as she opened her eyes.

"But I—I wanted to please you." Her voice trembled.

"If you go on so, we will never have any sons!" he warned her.

And his eyes met Diane's, as she waved the smelling salts before Elizabeth's nose.

He was ashamed. It had sounded somehow as if he cared only for the sons Elizabeth might give him. And she had been a good wife. . . .

Stiegel had planned to go to Lancaster on business the following morning, and suggested that Diane might go along to hear a lecture about Benjamin Franklin's discoveries.

"As a reward for being so faithful to my poor little wife," he qualified.

In the morning Elizabeth was not feeling well.

"Would you like Diane to stay with you today?" Frau Huber asked Elizabeth.

"Oh, no, mama, let her go. She will amuse me with fresh news when she comes home."

Her eyes looked longingly after Diane in her new riding habit, and when Heinrich came to say good-bye, her courage faltered.

"Oh Heinrich, what if I am brought to bed and something should happen to you!" she cried.

"I thought you weren't to deliver the child until Christmas, Liebling," he said, trying to hide the disappointment he felt.

"But I feel so strange. . . ."

" 'Twas folly for you to make the cherry pudding!"

"But you . . . you liked it, Heinrich?"

"The most toothsome cherry pudding I ever ate!"

"Heinrich, I wish I could go to Lancaster with you today."

"It will not be very long before the baby is born, and then we shall have an outing together."

"But then . . . then I shall nurse him; and then, there will always be another baby. . . ."

"Elizabeth, you do not like to bear my children?"

"Oh yes, Heinrich. 'Twill be wonderful to be a mother. Only—sometime do you think we shall be gay together? . . . Like you and Diane?"

She stroked his cheek softly with her fingers, and he felt guilty, though there was nothing for him to feel guilty about.

"We shall be very gay!" he smiled. "And today I shall buy you a ring in Lancaster, and p'r'aps even a pink floor covering!"

When they had gone, Frau Huber came in to give Elizabeth an eggnog.

"Mama," asked Elizabeth hesitantly, "Does papa . . . does papa ever say he loves you?"

"Well, child, since when does one married woman pry into the secrets of another?"

"Don't cozen me, mama. . . . Does he?"

"Ach, my child, what has come into your mind, as you lie abed? For twenty-five years your father and I have been happy. Because he does not fondle me before the servants does not mean he does not say sometimes, 'Magdalena, ich liebe dich.'"

Elizabeth buried her face in the pillow so that her mother wouldn't see the tears.

It was a fine morning, and Stiegel and Diane were jubilant at the outing. Diane was jaunty in a new Brunswick riding habit and a cocked hat with a trailing orange feather.

"You are radiant, Diane, like a sunflower come alive," laughed Stiegel, as they started down the road.

"Was ever such a day!"

"And yet you an old maid!" he teased.

"Think you the Hubers would really be quit of me?"

Diane questioned worriedly. She wondered if Frau Huber had noticed her flirtation with Stiegel. "It is so very pleasant, Heinrich, as it is."

They looked confusedly into one another's eyes, and fell silent.

"Let her keep on," thought Stiegel, "with her wiles. I'll show her soon enough which of us plays with fire!"

After his business appointment he met Diane at his mother's house for lunch, and they went to the lecture together. The inn was crowded with curious folk from all about the countryside. Mr. Kinnersley, an ingenious neighbor of Benjamin Franklin, was going about to the larger towns, giving two talks on electricity. Mr. Franklin himself said he couldn't be bothered capitalizing on his own discoveries. The eager and mystified farmers examined his elegant apparatus, which they were afraid to touch for fear of being "fire-bitten."

It was evening when Stiegel and Diane neared home. The furnace glowed brilliant through the trees from the roadside.

"Like a glimpse of hell!" said Stiegel.

Diane corrected him quickly, "Yet how strange like heaven!"

As they approached Cyrus' little log cabin, Diane suggested that they stop in and give him the earring they had purchased for him. They pushed the door of the cabin open, blustering in. The room, though colorless and plain, bespoke comfort. A bed hung from the wall at one corner. A small table held earthenware, wooden plates and a pewter pitcher, which was not so resplendent as those in the mansion. The floor had been sanded through a sieve, and Cyrus had evidently but finished the artistic operation, for the four corners of the cabin resembled a pinwheel in action, and in the center was outlined a very grotesque and distorted horse, with a tail like a peacock's. A kettle of

watcr bubbled aimlessly on the pot-hook, intended perhaps for a nightcap, and over the mantel hung a fowling-
piece. Diane playfully dropped down on a hard wooden
settle before the fire. Stiegel sat beside her and took out
his snuff box.

"I am joyed that Cyrus is not at home," murmured Diane,
warming her outstretched hands. "I like it here."

"You are a monstrous coquette," affirmed Stiegel, if only
to see the anger blaze up in her eyes.

"Ah no, Heinrich. You slander me. 'Tis being alone with
you . . . I cannot say how to liken it. 'Tis the feeling of
the woods at dusk."

"Now you *are* coquetting!" He rose and leaned against
the mantel, where his face was shadowed. He felt strangely
emotional. He felt something new creeping upon him, the
same hunger he felt when Diane's lace frills had trembled
on his arm. Flirtation had always amused him, satisfying
his sense of vanity. But he had always been arrogantly
principled. No woman had ever come before himself. And
now he was gazing madly at her lips, impassioned, while
the glib, heated words escaped them.

"Heinrich," she was whispering, her scarlet cape falling
to the ground. "Why is it you do not like me, Heinrich?
Why is it you stare at my lips so—and do not kiss them? Am
I so ugly? The others say I am beautiful. They cannot live
without me. . . . And you do not even want a little kiss!"

She came close to him, and his hands slipped magically
to her waist. He covered the shame in his heart by clinging
to her lips.

A piece of burning log slipped from the firedog and
frightened them. There was an awkward silence, and Diane
felt limp in his arms. He had expected her to be cocky,
triumphant, but now that she drooped a little he felt
vaguely annoyed with her. Her very magnetism had been
her inimitable pride and exhilaration.

It was not in his scheme of things to fall in love with Diane. And he did have a vague, unformed scheme of things. He laughed quietly at his folly, and calmly picked up her cape, shook the sand from it, and placed it about her shoulders. Well, it had been quite inevitable. And what harm was there in a kiss, after all?

As they entered the house, silently, Diane pulled her plumed hat from her head, and tossed it upon a chair. She heard a faint cry, and, startled, began to run up the stairs.

Heinrich followed her, taking two steps at a time in his haste.

They were greeted by a flustered and beaming Frau Huber in the hall. Stiegel rushed into his room, dazed and ecstatic at the sound of the infant's cry.

Herr Huber, squinting, was leaning over the big family Bible, holding a dip in one hand and a quill in the other, his beflanneled foot unconsciously holding its weight as of yore, and Diane, with a strange new emptiness, watched him write:

"Barbara Stiegel, born seven minutes to five, November 6, 1756."

Barbara was the very epitome of pinkness, and Elizabeth, whose happiness knew no limit, lay weakly with the small bundle in her arms, hour after hour.

"A daughter!" exclaimed Stiegel, and now that he had time to recover he found that he was highly pleased. He thought of himself in years to come surrounded by beautiful daughters, in a home luxurious and elegant.

Money had been pouring into the business, and Stiegel lavished it on his home and family. He brought home from Lancaster the finest ruby ring he could find for Elizabeth, and for himself a heavy carnelian seal, embellished with a coat of arms. "For the Baron papa!" he joked.

In his excitement and elation at being a father, he had scarcely thought again of the jaunt to Lancaster. Why, the child looked like him. It was amazing! And if she was tiny, and weak, and premature, nevertheless she would be a handsome child, everyone predicted.

"Heinrich," Diane said, when he gave her a pomander on the day of the christening, "you are very proud and happy n'est-ce pas?"

[8o

"Now life is complete!" he said, "but tell the mid-wife to hurry with the child. Frau Huber is waiting in the sleigh, and Reverend Klingerman is waiting in the church!"

He thought, "If she's given one kiss too many, 'tis her own ado, not mine."

Diane helped to hustle the baby into her baptism robe, which was an orgy of tucks and embroidery; and after she had put on Barbara's linen mittens with their trimming of imported lace, she went back to Elizabeth's bedside. She handed her the caudle cup of ale with spice and sugar, and reassured her that the infant would be perfectly safe in the light snowfall.

"Diane, Heinrich has not thought to kiss the baby. Does he like her, do you think?"

"Like! Such a weak little word, Lizzie. Men do not kiss babies, you silly thing."

"He kneeled at my bed, Diane. He said I was pure . . . like snow."

"Are you?" asked Diane, curiously.

"I try to be . . . I want to be just what he wants me to be, Diane."

"How can you say what a man wants you to be!" retorted Diane, so sharply that Elizabeth was startled to tears. "He does not know himself. He wants what you make him want, bête."

"Diane, you're . . . you're not the same . . . something has gone wrong. Robert Klingerman has not come of late."

"I told him I should scalp him if he vexed me more."

Elizabeth sighed, and felt it was very sad that all the world could not be as happy as herself. Her thoughts never left her baby for more than a minute.

"Diane, show me again the baby's pincushions. How many has she now? I like best the one where the pins spell:

'Little life of heaven sent,
May thy years be glorious spent.'

"Diane, you should marry, if e'en for the delights of motherhood."

"I think I shall never marry. Who would really want me to wife? I am not pure . . . like snow."

"Diane!" cried Elizabeth, and her face and neck suffused with a deep scarlet.

"Oh, I have not mated in the straw like an animal," Diane exclaimed, "but for the first time I should like to do this."

"Diane!" cried Elizabeth again, aghast and pulling herself up in bed as if she would rush from such perversion. "Diane, you must not talk so . . ." trembling, "my parents will . . . will throw you out."

Diane tapped the window pane with her brown fingers. She had never felt hurt and aching like this before in her life, and she did not care at all what she said, or who heard it. She knew very well what had happened to her, and she knew still better that she deserved it. But justice made the bafflement no easier to bear.

"Diane, I pray you will never talk so again," pleaded Elizabeth. "But I forgive you. . . . You have had some lover's quarrel. You do not mean these things. . . ."

"I meant . . ." replied Diane sarcastically, "e'en for the delights of motherhood!"

She stirred up the Duffy's Elixir impatiently, and said, as if she were talking to a child, "Come, swallow your medicine like a brave."

That night, Diane lay looking at the moon from her bed. It was an experience for her to lie still and reason things out. She had always acted on impulse, and she had always been sufficiently happy.

She knew now, of course, that she had been stupid beyond words. Stiegel was principled, and prudent and proud. She had been blatant about her flirtation. This was the first time in her life she had been serious, and now she had frightened him into avoiding her! She closed her eyes for a moment and relived the scene in Cyrus' cabin. She dropped her cape on the floor again, lifted her face to his . . . felt his lips. . . . It had been so different, so very different, from what she'd expected. She had known that sometime he would kiss her. . . . What was this thing which had swallowed her? And Stiegel too, the kiss had done something to the two of them together. She dreamed the kiss over and over again, clinching her hands into two tight little fists.

Then she rolled over onto her elbows, and thought, "He wanted me; I wanted him. I must make him want me again. I must not fright him. Non, non, non . . . I must be snow . . . I must be pure."

So, as the months went on, Diane was sedulously pure. She spent much of her time nursing Barbara, who was not strong, being afflicted with ricket fever. She dosed her constantly with syrup of black cherries, thrust her naked in a bucket of cold water in the morning, and if her feet were cold, let a little blood out of them. She washed and primped and played with the child.

Barbara was not pretty, but she was fragile and dainty. The gleam of fire in the furnace fascinated her. Sometimes Stiegel took her to see the workmen, their faces bathed in sweat. She was frightened when they smiled. Their teeth showed bright and terrifying from besmudged countenances. She clung desperately to his neck, and called for "Nan," as she called Diane.

Diane watched Stiegel furtively as she mothered the little girl, and wondered if the child would not bring them together. He must eventually see that she was more of a mother to Barbara than Elizabeth herself, that it was always

Diane the baby cried for. In the fall when she learned to walk, Barbara followed Diane around the house, for Elizabeth was in bed much of the time, pregnant again. Inwardly Diane was annoyed at the fumbling steps of the baby, and the innumerable objects which had to be replaced because she had dragged them off of tables. But she kept thinking to herself, "I must reach him through Barbara. The stronger I am, the weaker is Elizabeth."

As the weeks went on, Diane became more conscious of her failure. For Stiegel worked hard. He rose at five in the morning, breakfasted before the women, and was about the furnace to see the winter dawn ushered in. She saw little of him during the day. His business was more profitable each year, and it seemed to absorb most of his waking hours. Stiegel was not so interested in stoves, at heart; but he was deeply interested in wealth. He had craved it since the first day in America when he had bought the crimson velvet suit.

Diane watched him as he sat at night, quiet, at his desk. These were the hours she looked forward to the whole day as she fed Barbara or dyed the wool. She sat always where she might watch his profile as he worked, a little behind Elizabeth, who could not see how often Diane's eyes rested on his lips, and the broad shoulders, and the strong hands with their little silken red hairs. Oh, she must do something to make him notice her, to make him feel this awful ache she hid in her heart. It was his work, not Barbara, that interested him. That was it, she must reach him through his work. She began to rack her brains, wondering what she could suggest to help him.

One night he sat at his desk, poring over patterns for stoves. The side and end plates of the new stoves had raised designs. Stiegel, knowing his Bible as well as he did, illustrated stories from the Scripture, and added German inscriptions.

"How do you like this?" he asked, looking over a verse which he had composed himself.

> *Baron Stiegel ist der Mann*
> *Der die Ofen giessen kann.*

Diane looked up puzzled, and Elizabeth smiled. She spent most of her time now sewing for Barbara, exquisite little gowns the replica of her own.

"Did I tell you," she said, "Barbara took her anodyne necklace from about her neck her very own self, Heinrich, and swathed her dolly in it?"

"Hm . . ." he answered, absent-mindedly, returning to his sketch.

Elizabeth glanced over at her husband, irritated because he did not answer.

"Heinrich . . . you . . . you do not care one whit!" She dropped her sewing and ran sobbing from the room.

"Ach, Gott!" Stiegel muttered to himself, and he flung aside his pen and got up to follow her.

"Heinrich," Diane spoke up quickly. "I have thought of something to make your stoves sell even faster."

"What does a woman know of business!" he laughed, sitting down again, and chewing at the feather of his pen.

"A woman may not know business, but what does she know better than stoves?" she responded, dropping her sewing and pulling her chair close to his at the desk.

"Verses and pictures from the Bible are all very well, M'sieu," she went on, "but a woman loves beauty, n'est-ce pas? She wearies of seeing Joseph and Paul as she keeps warm of an evening. She would like flowers—tulips, and—tulips!"

Stiegel smiled at her enthusiasm. "I am bad enough as an artist, but tulips!"

"They are so easy!" she cried. "Look, Heinrich, I can

draw for you . . . if you will let me help you of an evening!"

He hesitated.

"Do you not remember my drawings of Frau Habicht and Robert Klingerman?" She put her hand coaxingly on his arm, and he stirred uneasily.

Diane puzzled Stiegel, and he thought of her often as he worked at the furnace. All throughout the summer she had been playing with hearts again. But as for him, she hadn't bothered. She had finished him off with a kiss, he concluded bitterly, and gone in search of new conquests. Whenever he thought of her the idea rankled. It was one thing to dismiss a girl, and another to be dismissed. . . . Well, this was what he had wanted, of course. She understood that he was not a philanderer and excluded him now from her banter.

It was only as the fall and winter came on and he worked with her steadily at night, that he became painfully conscious of her again. Her skill at designing far exceeded his expectations; she was original, and her flowers seemed to have a live, exuberant quality which he failed to get in his own work. Old Herr Huber approved the patterns with a pinch of her cheek, proud of her innovations. The evenings went by so fast that they seemed always just to have begun.

They worked side by side at the desk, and sometimes Diane's fingers handed Stiegel a sketch and lingered on his hand. He began to understand, to know that she was no longer flirting. He began to sense the deepness of her longing, and to know that beneath his unrest there was longing equal to her own. As he worked during the day, the thought of the evening made him impatient. And as he worked beside her at night, he puttered with the sheets before him, and thought over and over, "She's beautiful . . . and her lips are red as holly. . . ."

It was at this point that Herr Huber, who sat every night

smoking while Magdalena helped Elizabeth to bed, told Stiegel that he would like him to go to Philadelphia on business.

"Don't go," Diane's eyes cried, "don't go just when we know what it means to be together!"

While Stiegel was gone, Diane determined that she must learn to accompany him on the harpsichord, and she begged Elizabeth to teach her. Elizabeth thought it would be amusing. She lounged beside the harpsichord, her feet on a stool and port wine on her little table, and pointed out notes and chords. In the six weeks that Stiegel was gone, Diane learned voraciously, rising an hour earlier in the morning to conquer sharps and flats. Whenever she found ten minutes to spare, she practiced. Searching out the music which he played most frequently on his violin, she picked out the tune on the harpsichord, and tried different chords for the left hand, exulting when she had found one that was harmonious, and playing it over and over until it was impressed indelibly on her mind. What a wonderful surprise it would be for Heinrich, and how he must realize soon that she was a part of all the things he cared for most in life!

When he returned from Philadelphia just after Christmas, he tried to ignore her, and she was infuriated that the trip should have brought this breach between them. He was very gay and happy, she thought; his wit had been sharpened by new contacts, and now he seemed to have found a whole new life outside of her world.

The first Sunday morning after his arrival, Stiegel took out his violin when he returned from church, and began to tune up with zest. Diane's heart pounded. Now was the time for her surprise. Her hands were stiff from the January cold, and she rubbed them together, jubilant, and sat down on the chair before the harpsichord, spreading her cherry-colored skirts nervously.

"Shall we play—this one?" she asked, picking from the

pile of music the short waltz she had labored on night and day.

Stiegel thought of course that she was being facetious, and cried, "Ja!" slipping into the melody.

Diane played a few measures stubbornly, trailing a bar behind him.

Stiegel stopped, amazed.

"You have learned to play?" he asked.

She nodded proudly.

"Wunderschön! . . . Well, now, we will begin again."

They started off once more, and Diane felt Stiegel watching her curiously as she struggled to recall the chords. Suddenly the notes dwindled out of her memory completely, and she felt her cheeks going hot, as the playing sounded like something Barbara might have done. She stopped short, and Stiegel's bow slipped from the violin. He laughed heartily, and she banged on the keys with an enraged fist.

"Why do you laugh!" she thundered, and she thought her heart would break.

"If you could see how you look! . . . And if you could hear how we sound! Like an Indian war dance. . . ."

He was laughing at her. She would have killed him gladly. Killed him for the misery he brought her, and the horrible pain of having him close again, laughing.

In the next few weeks she found his eyes lingering on her more than once, and she loved and loathed him furiously, bitterly hurt by his cold constraint. And she kept thinking, feverishly, "There *must* be a way!" And yet it seemed to her, as she lay in bed, watching the clouds smothering the winter moon, that she had tried everything, every way in her power to make him love her.

One night, long after the house was dark, Diane could not sleep. The moonless night seemed stifling, and the members of the household filed through her mind in dull succession. She thought fearfully of Stiegel, and how he seemed to be slipping farther away from her since his journey. "Good morning, Diane," without a glance; "Goodnight, Diane," without a glance, as his fingers continued to balance figures. She admitted over and over again a physical ache to be close to him, to touch him, to be part of him. She did not cry, but lay silent, tortured.

At first she imagined she heard a bar of music. It was so soft she strained to hear it again. The night was soundless. She sat up in bed, listening. Then it came once more from the parlor beneath her, suffocated by shutters and closed doors. She rose hastily and slipped on a nightgown.

Temptation with Diane meant action. She had no means of lighting her candle, and faltered through the hall and down the stairs, her hand resting on the knob of the parlor door for a brief second before she soundlessly entered. A chime clock announced midnight, and she took advantage of the clamor and closed the door, quickly curling up into a ball on the sofa.

He had not heard her. Stiegel, in his brilliant cap and banyan, was a subdued splash of color in the shadows of the room, like the reflection of a tropical sunset in the water. He improvised furiously, softly, without hesitation for ten minutes. He wafted into a waltz of his own composition, his violin swinging like a happy pendulum. He stopped on a trill. He was playing it badly. Irked, he laid the instrument on the table and fingered his bow musingly.

"You are in dire need of practice," murmured Diane.

Stiegel dropped the bow with a clatter, backing into the harpsichord with dumb astonishment.

She smiled at him mischievously, delighted that she had upset his equilibrium at last.

"Diane," he gasped, "get to bed."

"Why should I go to bed?" she retaliated. "Play the thing about the nymphs."

She was coming over to him, handing him the bow from the floor. "Come, Heinrich, do not be afraid of me! I am not going to *eat* you."

He took the bow and began to play, but the notes hung together heavily. Stiegel stopped, in a sharp saccade.

"I . . . can't play to you, Diane."

"I know . . ." she whispered. "You cannot play . . . you cannot sleep either. . . . Like one in love, Heinrich. . . ."

She leaned close to him over the harpsichord, thrusting her hand impulsively into his. "Heinrich, you are afraid to unfold. . . . You are hard, you are cruel to me, but you do not hate me, Heinrich?"

He clenched her arm, pulling her into his embrace roughly. It had been agony enough thinking of her lips for months. Now he must have them again!

His hands caressed her hair, trembled on her cheeks, her breasts.

"Diane," he whispered, "you only do this to torture me. . . ."

"Heinrich, you fool. . . . Look! . . . See what I do to be near you! Think you I am content to nurse Elizabeth? To shush her baby in the cradle? I have come to hate them all, the puling lot!"

"We can't keep on like this, Diane. . . ."

"Why shouldn't we have what belongs to us?" tensely. "Heinrich, there's nothing else in the world but this, but you and me—but this thing which we do to one another. . . ."

He turned away from her abruptly, pretending to hunt his snuff box on the table. He was overcome with emotion, and he was determined not to let her see how much she unbalanced him.

"You are a coward!" she condemned him, her voice quivering huskily.

"I still have a sense of honor!" he retorted.

"Honor! 'Tis only an excuse because you are a coward. You are afraid of Herr Huber! You are afraid of Elizabeth! You are afraid of *me*, Heinrich!"

His face turned crimson.

"You know it!" she went on scathingly. "You are afraid to love!"

"I have my life to live."

"Money, that's what you call your life! You want to be rich—and you are afraid to lose what you have!"

Stiegel felt with a rush of fury that he would like to slap her face. Her impertinence was true, every word of it.

"You will go on having puling babies! You will go on holding Elizabeth dead in your arms! You will go on getting rich, and some day, Heinrich Stiegel," she finished savagely, "you will be hungry for love!"

For a moment there was silence as her words stung into him, and then his voice rose queerly, triumphantly over the quietness like a thing apart from him.

"Take the dip, and get you to bed!"

He stalked over to the window. He was left in total darkness. He felt limp, ill, as if lightning had struck him. He watched the furnace smoldering, like a dragon breathing fire. He could see nothing but the eyes of Diane, aflame.

And he wanted her. He was so sick with desire for her that his thoughts seemed to be at a standstill. He kept watching the fire, and after a long time thought came back again.

"Animal . . . that's all it is, animal. . . . Elizabeth ill so long, her hands and feet swollen. Her face drawn and yellow . . . dutiful . . . and dead. . . . God, why must I feel so alive, so strong and—and animal! Would it be so wrong? She's swift, like my blood. . . . She's wild. . . . We breathe the same breath. . . . But that isn't . . . love!"

He struggled again and again with his sense of duty and

honor. Tonight he was convinced that Diane was not merely trifling with him. For months he had been obsessed with the idea that all she wanted was victory, but her lips had been hot against his own, and her body lithe and impelling in his arms.

He sank down on a chair, his head in his hands, and tried to reason clearly. He had come to America to make his fortune. Herr Huber had offered him that fortune. Without it, he would never be able to give himself to his music. With the fortune went Elizabeth. She was willing to rear his sons. She loved him, and he wanted to hurt her. . . . But it was true, the only reason he wouldn't betray her was because she meant the success of his future. . . . He must see that Diane married. He would not let her block his plans. . . . Let her call him a coward if she liked. She must marry, and then life would settle into contentment . . . at least. She must marry someone like herself, hungry, eager, volatile. Never Robert Klingerman. . . . He could never bear to see her throw herself away to some weakling. Not Diane, so beautiful, so live . . . lips hot, moist, scarlet. . . .

The next few days Diane was gay, and flip and mercurial. She imitated shopkeepers and townspeople to the great delight of Herr Huber; she sang new songs to Elizabeth, in French; and jabbered incessantly, stumbling over big words as of old, and swallowing them indifferently with French skill. At every opportunity she flaunted her beauty before Stiegel, tormenting him with a word or a glance. Later, when she entered her cold room, her candle spurting unsteadily in the draught, she flung herself hysterically on the bed. Her act was over, and she had performed well!

One morning Diane did not come down for breakfast. Frau Huber, who supposed she had stopped first to give Elizabeth her tooth powder, or to freshen up the baby, thought nothing of the delay. As the men were finishing their breakfast, and Herr Huber was about to read from Job, Barbara came pattering into the dining room in her bare feet and night-rail, her nightcap coyly down over one eye.

"Nan?" she queried. "Nan?"

A curious look was passed from one to another, and Frau Huber placed Barbara on her father's knee before the fire and hastily bounced away.

Diane had vanished. Her bed had been slept in, but clothes and gimcracks lay strewn about the room. Bits of ribbons and fans overflowed from a chair, and yet nothing seemed to be missing.

They searched the house, the outbuildings, the grounds. Frau Huber bounced from one place to another like a rubber ball.

"But surely you must have seen her early this morning," Frau Huber accused Frau Habicht.

The old cook paused. "Heh! Many's the time I told her the woods is no place for a woman alone."

"I'se been warnin' her, too," put in Cyrus. "But she only laughs when I tells her the Indians likes their squaws beautif ——"

"The Indians!" cried Frau Huber, her strength giving out suddenly.

The household was in a clamor. "The Indians" was on every tongue. Cyrus was sent out at once into the neighborhood to get help to search for Diane.

Stiegel tried to remain aloof from the family, for he felt that his eyes would betray him. He listened to their assumptions and said nothing. He felt an emptiness greater than he had ever known, and yet a flood of relief and thanksgiving; a frustration because he and Diane had never realized the passion they felt for one another, and along with it a prayer of gratitude that he had been strong. Diane too, was strong—and he knew what had happened.

The men formed a scouting party at once, and the neighbors at Brickerville joined in the search. There had been a mild spell of weather for days, in which the snow had been entirely absorbed; along the bank of the stream Robert Klingerman found Diane's pattens, which she had evidently discarded, regardless of mud.

Stiegel watched the boy as he wiped off a patten with his handkerchief, and sickened at his sentimentality.

Further footsteps had sprung softly level with the earth, and the men went blindly into the woods, knowing that their quest was hopeless. After a week, the search was abandoned.

During that time, Elizabeth grieved hysterically, and nothing could be done to assuage her. At last she weakly gave birth to her child, another daughter, Jerusha. Stiegel tried to hide his disappointment that the child was not a son.

Elizabeth, instead of becoming stronger and being out of bed in a fortnight after her baby's birth, had taken cold and developed a "broken" or abscessed breast. Her color grew ashen. The little Barbara, sensing that something was wrong, and having by this time completely forgotten Nan, nestled into the featherbed, and stroked Elizabeth's cheeks with her stubby fingers.

The household was clouded with gloom. Herr Huber sighed deeply for Diane, and his heart ached at the pallor of Elizabeth. Evenings passed like the silence of eternity, and Stiegel pushed away his manuscript music and tried to read. But he could not concentrate.

One night as he climbed into the bed beside Elizabeth, he felt her soft sobbing again, and felt that he could not endure it.

"I want Diane," she whispered feebly.

He groped for her hand, and warmed it in his. "God

knows I want her too," he admitted to himself, and he caressed the soft flesh, while the image of Diane, flaunting her yellow ribbons, whipped his mind.

The days passed in feverish activity, and the nights in restlessness. Between broken patches of sleep Stiegel heard the starved cry of the little Jerusha, then the smacking of tiny lips, and the moaning of Elizabeth as the relentless small chin dug into her tortured breast. Sometimes she put the infant between them and he could feel the movements of the swaddled bundle and the cuffing of the miniature fist. Sleeping in her trundle bed close to the cradle, Barbara was peacefully insensible to it all.

Stiegel tried desperately not to think of Diane, but the very silence of the house seemed to shriek his loss; it was a relief to get out to the furnace, and he found himself rising earlier and leaving the house in the gloom before daybreak.

It was about a week after the disappearance of Diane that the family became really alarmed about Elizabeth. Now that the last snowfall had been broken through, curious friends came to make their "setting up" visits, and Elizabeth languidly listened to their chatter and advice. The "groaning beer" stood untouched at the table by her side. Her new diamond ring, grown loose on her finger, jingled against the ruby. The pain leaped from her eyes, and finally guests were not allowed to see her. Barbara, who covered the house like a busy ant, tottered in often to see her new relative.

"Oosha," she announced, poking an inquiring finger at those glossy live toys in the cradle called eyes.

It was almost dark one afternoon when Stiegel, who was in the charcoal house, was confronted by Frau Habicht. She held her petticoats up high with one hand, and with the other clasped a shawl which half muffled her excited, wrinkled face.

"Quick. Cyrus has gone for the surgeon. 'Tis a wonderful change has come o'er the young mistress."

Stiegel fled to the house, and as he entered, he heard Elizabeth's breath escaping in long groans. Her whiteness as the baby suckled brought the sweat to his forehead.

"Take the child away," he thundered, "pox you, can't you see it drains the life from her?"

Frau Habicht flew with the enraged infant under her shawl, and Stiegel found himself alone with his wife, for the Hubers were wildly preparing poultices.

There was an ominous silence, broken by the crash of snow from the roof.

"I . . . don't want . . . to die," moaned Elizabeth, piteously.

"Ach no, Liebling, we shan't let you," panted Stiegel, and found her hand as cold as his own.

"My babies . . . Heinrich. They are . . . so new. . . . They are . . . so sweet."

"You are but a little child, darling. . . . You couldn't die," he said bravely, but he was seized with panic at the thought.

"Jesus said, 'Suffer . . . the little . . . children. . . .' Heinrich, it wearies me so . . . to keep breath . . . and it frights me . . . to stop. . . ."

She turned her eyes to him, gasping, pleading. He caressed her lips lightly with his own, curiously terrified and repulsed as he felt the rush of her labored breath. Diane filled his consciousness, and the sensual coaxing of her lips. He recalled the mussed black hair under his finger-tips, and agonized with self-reproach, hid his face in his hands, shrinking from death.

The house was stirring now with hurried noises, doors opening and closing, footsteps treading stairs, sobs, whisperings. . . .

"Heinrich . . . say . . . you . . . love me!" gasped the girl, trying to raise her hand.

He dropped down on his knees beside her.

"I . . . love you!" he whispered, burying his face in the quilt. The thin cold fingers in his hand relaxed.

THE HUBER household lay swathed in the deepest
mourning. Pictures and mirrors were shrouded in flowing
black. Food came to the table, cooled, and returned untouched to the kitchen. Frau Habicht wept and claimed
that her eyes were red because she had caught a bad cold.

Stiegel, driven to town by Cyrus, shopped for the family.
For himself and Elizabeth's parents he purchased night-
clothes of black taffeta, black hair brushes and slippers. He
ordered dozens of pairs of black gloves to give grief-
stricken friends, and mourning rings of engraved onyx for
the chief mourners. His own ring said: "Death parts united
hearts."

Elizabeth's death had come upon them so suddenly that
they were all unemotional and dazed.

Herr Huber sat with his Bible before him, but he did not
read. In his very piety he was questioning God. Now he
had written in the Bible: "Elizabeth Huber Stiegel, died
February 13th, 1758, ten minutes to five."

The brunt of the funeral fell upon Stiegel himself, and
he was grateful for being kept busy. He did not like Frau
Huber's eyes upon him. Everything she said or did seemed
to mock him, as if she must have seen Diane's engageants

falling softly over his hand those winter evenings. She had become suddenly hard as flint, this busy, kindly little hausfrau. When one of Elizabeth's bridesmaids asked the honor of making a family tree from Elizabeth's hair, Frau Huber cut the locks from her child, stonily. She pushed Barbara from her, and the tiny Jerusha sobbed herself to sleep in a neglected cradle.

Stiegel, stealing away from the condemnatory eyes of his mother-in-law, rocked the cradle timidly. Once, he lifted the baby in his arms, and frightened at its softness, laid it awkwardly back in its nest of covers.

On the day of the burial the furnace lay smoldering and footsteps were hushed. But the house smelled spicy with Frau Habicht's freshly baked cakes and burned sugar. Elizabeth lay like a delicate Valentine in her coffin. It had been tenderly covered with homespun, and her weary little head rested on a goose-feather pillow, her face covered with lace. All the shavings and sawdust of the home-made coffin had been carefully placed within it, for it was a known fact that if even a speck should be brought in loose about the house, another death would ensue.

Shortly before their friends were expected to arrive, Stiegel went into the parlor, alone, to look at Elizabeth.

" 'Tis all my doing," he reproached himself, trembling. "The shock of Diane's going has killed her. . . . We killed her together—Diane and I." He did not like to admit these thoughts even to God, but they repeated themselves over and over in his tortured mind.

As he stood there apathetically, he heard the white satin tread of Barbara's happy feet. He lifted her up to his shoulder, and with a playful snatch she bared the face of her mother.

"Peek!" she laughed, and held the lace out to Stiegel.

"Go away!" he stormed fiercely, dropping the child, and shrinking from the lace which lay in his hands. His voice resounded through the silence of the house, so that he shrank from himself. It seemed to him that Elizabeth stirred.

"Forgive me," he whispered brokenly, "if there's . . . forgiveness in Eternity. . . ."

Elizabeth's bridesmaids were her pall-bearers. They wore no hats or bonnets, but long veils of white gauze, for Elizabeth was the bride of heaven. The cortege of a hundred or more people on horseback moved slowly through the woods to the Brickerville Lutheran Churchyard. Gay snow flurries clung to the hearse-wagon and its burden, and the shrill wind of February escorted them to the country cemetery where Elizabeth was laid to rest.

The next day the furnace fire blazed against the sky and Herr Huber with unseeing eyes grew old in the chimney corner waiting for God to speak. His Bible still lay on his knee, unopened. Frau Huber's keys dangled from her side and her lips, in a thin line, did not move. Cyrus, sniffling openly, delivered the mourning gloves which had but just arrived, and Stiegel, at night, kneeling under the picture of the child at play with the birds, prayed solemnly to God.

The house was no longer endurable, and one day in early spring, Herr Huber said to Stiegel, "Magdalena and I think to return to our native soil to die. I shall deed my interest in the Furnace to you. Keep it bright . . . in memory . . . of her."

Herr Huber's announcement was like a legal declaration. It had been thought out carefully, though Stiegel had never had any inkling of the Hubers' desire to leave. The news left him bewildered. Now he would be rich, he thought, shamefully exultant. Rich, and alone. . . .

"But the children, what shall I do with them?" Stiegel stammered.

"I don't want to leave them," sobbed Frau Huber, searching for her handkerchief.

"Magdalena," said her husband stiffly, "we've talked this out between ourselves. . . ."

"I know . . . I know. . . . But I can't forget how little they are. Little, and no mother——"

Stiegel felt a lump rising in his throat, and he took the hand of his pudgy little mother-in-law and patted it.

"Don't worry, Mutter, that ——"

"Frau Habicht will mother them," interrupted Herr Huber, sternly. "She has had babies of ——"

"But she is deaf, and she's old," Magdalena protested, trying to live up to her husband's stoicism.

"But Heinrich is young," said Herr Huber slowly. "You will marry again, Heinrich. You are young. . . ."

The good ship "Myrtilla" which came into the harbor with clamorous bell-ringing, carried off the Hubers on its return trip. Stiegel, who accompanied them to Philadelphia, had planned to remain there for several months and become better acquainted with his partners. The Furnace was left in charge of a foreman of twenty years' experience, and the little girls, too young to be anything but indifferent at the family's leaving, were entrusted to Frau Habicht and a young German nurse girl.

"You promise me you will not let Barbara get any such little things into her mouth, like buttons, nicht?" Frau Huber pleaded as she left.

No sooner was Stiegel left to his own resources in Philadelphia than his spirits revived. He put up at the Coach and Horses which was continually alive with councils of all kinds. The city was filling with British regulars, for the king's response to America's appeal had not been an entirely altruistic thing. The redcoats gayly dotted the town, and then gathered to disappear into the wilds. They were to make short work of Ft. Louisberg and Fort Duquesne, of Diane's kinspeople. Other French colonies had already been scattered by the English as punishment for helping the Indians.

Stiegel wondered where Diane might be. It did not occur to him to fear for her safety. Instinctively he felt that she would be safe. Diane, who would be so heartily at home with the French! And who had managed the redmen in their own language. If only Diane had stayed. . . . And yet if Diane had stayed, Elizabeth. . . . Diane had not been meant for him, and he decided that he would forget her.

The night the Hubers left, Stiegel was invited to the home of Charles Stedman for dinner. Charles was sedate and retiring, the elder of the two Englishmen; Alexander, a man of fifty, was more prominent in the social whirl of Philadelphia. His arrogance was a pleasant thing to be favored with, and he seemed to become particularly attached to Stiegel. Homely, with large, soft features, he was utterly unconscious of not being as handsome as his new young German partner. From the moment of Stiegel's arrival, he had extended to him the use of his offices and clerks.

"To the new manager of Elizabeth Furnace!" toasted Alexander suavely as the ladies left the room after dinner. And he clicked brandy glasses with his brother Charles.

"To our young blood!" toasted Charles in return, and twirled the stem of his glass.

"You're very kind, both of you," returned Stiegel, mellow with wine and his new importance. "I am very grateful for your trust in me. I shall endeavour my best to uphold it."

"Alexander will see to that," remarked Charles drily, and Stiegel flushed.

"What do you mean, sir?" demanded Alexander, secretly flattered by this compliment to his shrewdness.

"You will keep him informed of his . . . liberties."

Stiegel laughed to cover his embarrassment.

"Now that I am your partner," he said, "I would like to

discuss with you my . . . liberties. My father-in-law was
an old man. With old-fashioned ideas. . . ."

"He made a deal of money," ventured Charles, nibbling
at a nut, "for all of us."

"Aye, the Furnace goes like a well-spun top. But it could
be spun faster," exclaimed Stiegel, filled with enthusiasm
over the plans he had been nurturing for months. "Twenty
tons of iron a week! Why, we could produce thirty tons of
iron a week, with new blowing tubs!"

"But the expense ——"

"Ach, Himmel, what is a hundred pounds, when we could
increase our output by half!" urged Stiegel. "Why, they
have been using blowing tubs in Germany for two hundred
years!"

"The Germans know everything," said Charles, with a
quirk of a smile.

"Stiegel is right," admitted Alexander. "The bellows is
outmoded, and the blowing tubs would give us an even
blast and better production. I think we would do well to
consider it."

Charles' smile broadened, as he gathered together a little
hoard of crumbs on the tablecloth. Stiegel was the sort of
person he did not like to encounter in court.

"I'll trust to your judgment, Alexander," he said. "You're
the one who understands the furnace business. How is the
new mining of iron ore?"

Stiegel felt rebuffed for the moment, but he was certain
that if he could win Alexander Stedman over to a few innovations, Charles would follow like a docile lamb. It was
just as well not to mention any further expansion tonight,
though. After all, the Stedmans had been used to dealing
with Herr Huber, a man of the Old World. Stiegel must
go slowly. He began to tell them about the new account
in Lancaster.

As they went out to join the ladies, Alexander said, "Lucy

is consumed with curiosity about you, Stiegel."

"I thought 'twas a settled thing, between Lucy and Robert Morris," ventured her Uncle Charles. "The way I have seen his eyes upon her."

"Lucy is a butterfly," her father laughed. "I have seen Robert quit the house a dozen times in a temper. But he always comes back."

"Red hair!" mused Charles.

"Aye, but that is not the reason. Lucy vexes them all. There is no one can withstand her, and there is none she can stand!"

Stiegel deliberated. This was a challenge he would have accepted in a moment a few years before. But Alexander Stedman was his partner, and there must be nothing to upset the amiable relationship. Least of all love. The thought of the injustice he had done by marrying Elizabeth without love continued to hover in his mind in spite of the stimulus of the city and new contacts. And though he had determined to forget Diane, this was impossible. There was quite enough to harass him, without Lucy. Yes, he was finished with love. From now on he would concentrate on his fortune and music.

But the following week Stiegel was invited to a turtle feast at the Stedman home in Walter Street.

Even Stiegel was taken aback by the glamour of the belle who greeted him in the drawing-room. Her hair was a lavish pompadour of gold, and staunch little curls rippled over the top and half hid her ears. Languishing in the gold netting of her hair were myriads of pearls. A polonaise of yellow satin bubbled over her hips in innumerable puffs, while beneath them a dozen stiff petticoats divulged laces and ribbons and embroidery. A heavy necklace of gold beads and rubies clung to her thin neck. On her long slim feet were red satin slippers, embellished with rosettes. A lace fan flickered between the curious appraisal of Lucy

Stedman and the ardent admiration of Stiegel; then the
girl slapped her fan together, curtsied, and welcomed him.

"'Tith a great delight to thee you, Baron. Reportth of
you have conthumed me with curiothity."

She led him to a sofa, and he found himself forever picking up her fan and then her handkerchief, adjusting pillows
to suit her comfort, and handing her Madeira, which she
sipped with great suavity. He had scarcely time to notice
that Lucy was homely—that her eyes disappeared when she
laughed, and her mouth became the center of wonder.
Fascinated, he watched the patch over the corner of her
lip. It was cut into the shape of a small star, and twinkled
about its planet with rare motility, seldom at rest. And by
this time, if Stiegel had noticed that Lucy was homely, he
did not care. He was thoroughly beguiled.

A party of prominent men was arriving; there was
Benjamin Chew, and Thomas Lawrence, the mayor of the
town. Alexander Hamilton and John Dickinson, lawyers,
came in together in argument, greeted Mrs. Stedman profusely, and fell to debate once more. To Robert Morris,
Lucy made a very particular curtsey. He was a sandy-com-
plexioned young man of twenty-four, and very tall. His
eyes, brilliantly blue, apprehended Lucy's elegance in a
sweep. He kissed her hand attentively.

"I cal'late we shall have nought but counting house now
that you and Tom Willing are here. Partners in boredom."

"I swear you shall not hear a word on commerce, Mistress
Lucy. The importations do bore you then?"

"Ah, not your fans and pomanders, Robert. The details. . . ."

"You would prefer we talk land." His eyes were teasing
her.

"A man's business is to be borne. But a hobby is insufferable, Robert."

"I have a passion for land," Robert informed Stiegel.

"'Tis the only trade for the modern generation. See how Philadelphia grows! So simple to own land, clear it of Indian tracks, and sell it to the Friends."

"I inhabit a land of all Indian tracks and no Friends," laughed Stiegel, emptying his glass of Madeira.

"The greater your chance, sir. Indian tracks are to be purchased for a flagon of rum!" His keen blue eyes sparkled with excitement. "Why, Penn's Woods would fit into your pocket for a handful of shillings. 'Tis the ——"

"Robert, do not intrigue the Baron. You are a maniac. Land is a barren thing. It frights me. It begets owls and . . ." Her fan trailed to the floor once more, and Stiegel and Robert Morris reached for it simultaneously. Stiegel thought his friend looked a trifle annoyed.

Then the meal was announced, a turtle feast for the men. There were great tureens of soup, baked turtle shell with its delicate clinging meat, and steaming vessels of terrapin stew. The turtle had traveled from the West Indies with a keg of limes especially for this purpose.

The more Robert Morris partook of terrapin and sack, the more eloquent he became about land. And as Lucy was not there to counterbalance him, he confided his ambition to Stiegel's ready ears. There was something alluring in Morris' plan; acres of land. . . . What could they eventually mean but power? The land about Brickerville, too, was rich. Farmland with sweet, black soil; woodland filled with the pine and beech and oak he needed for charcoal. There was no telling to what extent the iron business would grow, now that he had become manager.

"I shall buy land," thought Stiegel. "I shall need thousands more acres in the future. And it is fitting that I should have land."

He glanced about the table, over the great silver plate and fine china. It was wise to mingle with men such as

these, he thought. These were young men, like himself;
strong and dynamic, still independent of fate. Fate was
in their pockets now for a handful of shillings! He felt
powerful, excited, stimulated, leaning over the sheen of
linen, talking land to Robert Morris in the candlelight. The
men retired to a room in which was one of the few billiard
tables of the colony; the balls and ale rolled profusely, and
soon Lucy Stedman was a blur in Stiegel's mind.

The following afternoon, as he sat watching people
thread in and out of the tap room at the Coach and Horses
he remembered Lucy. It was a mild spring day, and his
thoughts must necessarily dwell on women. For the thousandth time he had gone over the tragedy of his brief,
married life with Elizabeth. They had never quite had their
chance, he and Elizabeth, with Diane there. He wondered
if somewhere Diane might be digging a new garden, her
eyes filled with eagerness. Where could she have gone?
How strange to think that he would never see her again;
that she had slipped out of his life as suddenly and dra-
matically as she had come into it. Well, she had given him
something no one would ever be able to take away.

He found himself looking for her under every bonnet on
the street; sometimes his knees felt weak as he saw a little
black-haired woman in the distance, and he would follow
her quickly, always knowing that he would not find her,
and yet never daring to take a chance.

Well, he must get over this frantic desire to see her again!

"I shall take a plate of tea with Lucy," he decided, after
a little hesitation, for there was something unexplainable
about Lucy which made him feel gauche and shy.

"I will tell her about my music," he pondered, "and if
she is alone, I'll hum a bit of the waltz to her."

But when he returned to the Coach and Horses with its
gleaming floor of mashed oyster shells, he had forgotten

his music. He could now enumerate a complete list of Lucy's beaux, and he remembered the tilt of her instep, and he saw the lavender lace ruffle bobbing on her neck with every ejaculation. He had been submerged.

9

IN THE MORNINGS Stiegel spent his time with busi-ness conferences and mail. It delighted him to meet all the customers whom Herr Huber had described in his droll manner, and to introduce himself as the new manager of Elizabeth Furnace, and invite them to dinner.

He waited anxiously for the mail which might bring him news of the children at home; Frau Habicht's letters were written in German, and read like an invoice. The sharp little vertical lines of her words were like the thousands of fine vertical lines in her cheeks, he thought musingly. Barbara had spoken of papa, she reported grimly. Jerusha could laugh aloud. When he read of them, Stiegel was swept with homesickness and a feeling of pity for the two little babies, and yet he dreaded the thought of return.

He loved the stir and sophistication of the city, the chal-lenge of sharp-witted men and fashionable women. In the afternoon he often sought out Lucy's company. Now and then he sauntered by in the late morning, and found Lucy lolling in the garden, her face masked beyond recognition, and her hands and arms protected from the sunshine with long gloves. Often he found her sewing on a purse which

she hid ostentatiously a few times. At last she made him
guess who might be the lucky recipient. He could scarcely
believe, he said, that these thousands of delicate little
stitches were to be for him!

Stiegel began to feel young again. It amused him to
divert her interest from the dynamic Robert Morris. It was
exactly what he had determined not to do before he met
Lucy. But he thought that Lucy was too arch to let herself
be hurt. She could well take care of herself. And she was
making a delightful game out of the affair. "Bob Morris is
smoldering; Lucy is flaming; and I am igniting. In all
events, it makes me a bit lighter-hearted, and I do not brood
so much over Elizabeth . . . and Diane."

So Lucy became very much of a habit with Stiegel. He
even met her, quite by accident, one Sunday morning in
the German Lutheran Church at Fourth and Arch Streets.
His eyes wandered frequently to the white horsehair hat,
and followed it out to the sunshine, where it drew a group
of swains as easily as the sun draws water. After church
Stiegel joined the Stedman family.

"Papa, 'tis certain the poor Baron will perish on catfish
and waffles at the Coach and Horses," pouted Lucy
"Mama, do we not have an extra joint of chicken for dinner?
And a new blueberry pudding from my very own receipt-
book!"

"My dear," smiled Mrs. Stedman, whose only unhappiness in life was to correct Lucy, "you quite forget you
have given word to your cousins in the country to take tea
with them."

"But tea is not dinner, Mama. You see, he is lonesome for
his babies. He droops a little. . . . We can doctor him with
a good table and send him back to the inn when we go!"

"Indeed, madam, it is presuming too much. . . ."

"Lucy's word is law, Baron Stiegel. You see, she is

offended a little. Lucy, my child, of course the Baron will
do us the honor. . . . That's a love."

After dinner was over the Stedmans reluctantly left the
charming company of the Baron, and his stories of the old
country. The day was remarkably fine, too warm to sit
indoors. Consequently Stiegel walked up and down the
more populated streets of the town, conscious of the eyes
of the storekeepers as they sat out on their benches and
marveled at his finery.

As he stopped to glance in the small window panes of a
mantua-maker's shop, he heard a vehicle creak to a stop,
and turning, saw a clumsy calash. A young lady poised on
the step, bewildered, for the street had been neglected by
the scavengers, and the gutters were glutted with mud.
The coachman, unperturbed by her predicament, deposited
her on the brick path which ran down the center of the
street and drove on. Dismayed, she gathered her petticoats
together, and put one toe out experimentally, like a shy
kitten. Stiegel, who had seen many women carried in Philadelphia from coach to walk, encountered the mud, and
lifted the lady over her obstacle before she had a chance
to demur.

She lifted her eyes to him painfully, and Stiegel saw that
she was very much embarrassed because the neighbors
were simpering. Then quite suddenly she said loudly
enough that she could be overheard, "Ah, it pleasures me
greatly to see you again. What good fortune that you
chanced to be passing! Do come in for a cup of tea."

Stiegel, being a gentleman, would not belie the lady.
Besides, she was lovely in a purple polonaise, and the sense
of adventure seized him.

When she had once closed the door of the house, she
faced Stiegel with resolution, her cheeks flushing hotly.

"Now, sir," she said solemnly, "if you would like to resume

your walk, there is a door out to the rear garden, and the neighbors will not know you did not want tea."

"Madam," he replied, bowing deferentially, "but I do want tea!"

The girl was still embarrassed at her own colossal nerve. If he had been a tanner or a wheelwright she would have laughed with him over the joke, but Stiegel's elegance made her tongue-tied. Her heart began to beat recklessly at the thought of having tea with this handsome young man.

Stiegel saw her confusion, and came to her rescue. "I mean it," he said. "My thirst is overwhelming."

She relaxed a little. "Oh, if you would *really* fancy staying. . . ."

Stiegel found himself in a plain little parlor, with a sanded floor and walnut furniture, certainly a contrast to the Stedman residence, with its handsome Turkey fashion carpets, carved and gilt sconces and Italian marble tables. Stiegel did not thrive best in a frugal atmosphere. Now he had an inkling that he was in the home of a Quaker. The street had been dotted with them. As he sat alone, waiting for the slow reappearance of the girl, he wondered why he had not excused himself in his chivalry and departed.

Eventually she returned, followed by a gawky maid with tea appointments. Evidently the best in the household had been mustered together, for the sugar pot was of silver, the milk jug of pewter, and a few pieces of delicate china were mingled with some ordinary pottery.

Then an amazing thing happened before his very eyes. On a little stove, Mistress Hölz set to melting chocolate and dropped into it half a dozen sausages; submerged and choked by the chocolate, they finally popped open, and the girl skilfully mixed the concoction with vigor, cut it up and served some to her guest.

" 'Tis the very kick of fashion," she confided, so Stiegel pretended he had often had it before.

They sat near the window, chatting. Elizabeth Hölz was an orphan, she said, and lived with her widowed sister, Mrs. Ege, who had two sons.

Stiegel felt warmed by the admiration of his hostess. Her eyes lingered on his finery as she talked to him, and she blushed if he seemed to notice her approval.

She was a girl of about twenty, Stiegel thought, plump and neat and pretty in rather a coarse way. Her features were large and even, and when she smiled he saw that her teeth were widely spaced, giving her a little-girl look which was somehow appealing.

She had donned a fresh cap and her brown unpowdered hair fell softly away from the starched laces and ribbons. The color came fitfully to her cheeks as Stiegel took notice of her, and she took his plate from him with a hand soft with dimples. He could not resist watching her eyes. They seemed almost the violet of her gown.

It was only the next day that Stiegel, bedecked in new scarlet, on his way to the Stedmans', found Elizabeth Hölz in the doorway of her home. He stood talking to her for five or ten minutes, amused to see the blushes which came and went as her eyes looked into his.

He saw that she was annoyed at the appearance of her two nephews, George and Michael, and did not know how to get rid of them tactfully. They hung about Stiegel, listening avidly to his conversation and scanning every detail of his dress with curious eyes.

George, the instigator, was a tall, thin boy of thirteen. His long, artistic fingers were bitten stubby at the ends, and continually played with something—fringe, a stray marble, or the flap of his coat. He leaned sullenly against the doorway.

Michael, his antithesis, was stocky and placid, a rather handsome little fellow although his front teeth were at various stages of entrance and exit. When Stiegel glanced

at him he smiled broadly and shyly, clinging to Elizabeth'
skirt with characteristic six-year-old timidity.

Stiegel was just about to walk on, when Mrs. Ege ap
peared.

"Tea-time," she announced blandly. "Oh—what
pleasure to find thee here, sir. Thee will share a cup o
modest tea with us, I hope? Michael, polish the gentle
man's shoes with spitballs."

Stiegel found himself submitting to their solicitude. Mrs
Ege, it was plain to be seen, was to be obeyed. She was ;
tall, heavy woman, with coarse black hair, and rather fierc
eyebrows; deep, vertical lines ran down her face, clos
to her mouth, and her voice had a masculine quality con
sistent with her appearance. The severe mode of Quake
dress seemed most befitting, and Stiegel smiled a little t
himself and thought she should have been the general o
an army, or at least a Lord Chamberlain.

Mrs. Ege was drawing the shutters now so that the su
would not come in upon him and fade his new silk camle
coat.

"May I have tea too?" asked George, sulkily.

"Of a certainty," said his mother, "thee talk as if te
were only for company!"

"Can I have tea?" proposed Michael, brightening.

"Run along, Michael," interfered Elizabeth, unable t
restrain her nervousness longer. And she whispered in hi
ear, "If you will stay out until the gentleman goes I wil
give you a penny for sweets."

When Stiegel at last left to make a belated call on Lucy
Elizabeth burst into tears.

"He didn't want to stay to tea again today, Anna," sh
cried.

" 'Tis small wonder thee are twenty-one and not mar
ried," retorted Mrs. Ege, brushing crumbs off of Stiegel'
chair. "Why, he is Baron Stiegel from Brickerville, witl

two thousand acres of land to his credit and just lately widowed."

"Two thousand acres!" interrupted George, his eyes narrowing into slits.

"Aye, and get thee to work, thou lazy tea-drinking boy," chided his mother. "Carry the tray to the kitchen—and return the silver tea-ball to the Tillmans."

"Well, he will never come again," sniffed Elizabeth.

"Did thee not hear me ask him for dinner, this coming Friday?"

"Anna, I'll not have him here for shad, at a penny a piece!"

"I shall take care of that, my lamb," consoled her sister. "Why, thou little fool, I shall even dress thee in a new farthingale to match thy eyes."

Elizabeth was comforted at once. "Oh, Anna, you *are* good to me. And . . . he *is* handsome. . . ."

"And rich," concluded Mrs. Ege. "I heard it from the shoemaker who knows the butcher who waits on Mrs. Alexander Stedman."

"But he could never like *me!*"

"A man with two children who need a mother? A man in the habit of having a wife?"

"Oh, Anna!"

Stiegel's life was now a round of pressing engagements. From his business appointments he hurried to lunch with Robert Morris, or young Willing. They invited him frequently to join the Mt. Regate Fishing Company, a group of the more élite and aristocratic young men of the town, which met every other Thursday at Robinson's Tavern on the Schuylkill River.

Also there were hundreds of plates of tea to be drunk. Stiegel had now met all the desirable young women, Mrs. Stedman said, at her receptions or at the Assembly. And he had painfully learned that he must drink one plate of tea after the other, suffocate or not, until he laid his spoon across the cup as a signal of saturation.

But after dancing and sipping tea with all the beauties of Philadelphia, he was still most entertained by the homely chatter and naïveté of Elizabeth Hölz and the sophisticated lisp of Lucy Stedman.

The small plump hand of Elizabeth fitted perfectly into the angle of Stiegel's arm, and they sauntered under the black walnut trees of the city, or had tea in the cool, plain little parlor. Sometimes they watched the ships come in, and Elizabeth would say,

"There, this is the ship that will bring you word of your opera."

"Do you think my old master has had it played by an orchestra as he promised?" Stiegel asked for the twentieth time.

"Oh, I am quite sure of it," Elizabeth consoled him.

"Then why have I never heard! After all the times I have written!"

"Have you thought to ask your uncle?"

"Aye, and he's scoured all Berlin to find him!"

"But the new score," said Elizabeth proudly. " 'Twill be far more beautiful than the first!"

Stiegel looked down at her fondly, and his fingers tightened on her arm.

She was a sympathetic little person.

Occasionally they rode into the country in a gig, or visited the Centre race track. (Lucy did not like the races. She proclaimed that she became 'dutth to dutth' long before her time.)

Lucy was amazingly popular. Her costumes were always ultra-fashionable and her diamond earrings scintillated with inimitable style. Before anyone else quite knew that Madame Pompadour was swathing her head in chiffons,

Lucy appeared in public bound up like an Armenian.

Stiegel was gratified at the look on the young men's faces when he escorted Lucy to a ball. The look quite plainly said,

"What chance have we with a Baron courting her?"

Stiegel and Robert Morris were together often; Morris found Stiegel developing a passion for land only second to his own, and sought out his company because of it. Lucy's name was seldom mentioned. Stiegel knew that Morris was inordinately jealous of him, and he was rogue enough to let the red-headed lover think that he was a serious rival for her hand.

One noon Alexander Stedman met Stiegel in The Spotted Cat, and Stiegel saw that his partner was preoccupied.

At last, over his flip, the secret came out. "Stiegel, you no doubt are well acquainted with my dear wife's fondness for you. Only last night she said to me, 'Mr. Stedman, 'tis an evil shame that the Baron must bide at an odorous inn. He is your partner, and 'tis surely befitting that he lodge with us and live in comfort!' What say you, Stiegel? You are a man of fine discrimination."

There was something in the approach of the invitation that reminded Stiegel of Herr Huber, and he wondered if being the guest of his partner would impose any marital obligation on him. However, there was no time to consider the question, and Alexander Stedman was already frowning a little because hesitation seemed insulting.

" 'Twould delight me beyond belief," accepted Stiegel, and that night he was once more the tidbit in a family bosom.

During the next few days, Elizabeth Hölz pouted a little. She was utterly neglected. The new violet gown she had had made lay impatiently in a chest, waiting for an occasion. George and Michael made her life miserable with insinuations, and alluded frequently to her being an old maid.

The very afternoon she and Stiegel had planned to wander out beyond Eighth Street to pick wild flowers, a colored servant superciliously handed her a note. It apologized:

"My dear Madam:
The fact that circumstances having fors'd me to trans-fur my logging from the Coach and Horses to the residense of Mr. Alexander Stedman has depryv'd me of your company to my sinseer remorse. My dear Madam, I hope you will parden my rudeness and will permit me to explane to you this evening my destitution. Believe me, Madam, your respectful and obed'nt
Servant,
Heinrich Wilhelm Stiegel."

"There, what have I told thee," chided Anna Ege, reading the letter. "Thou'rt too slow, Elizabeth. And if thee do not look to it quick, Lucy Stedman will have him. I am told she is ugly as mud, but all the men fight for her favor!"

"What more can I do!" wailed Elizabeth. "I talk about music and land till I am like to die!"

"Talk about love, then!" admonished Mrs. Ege. "Mercy, wipe thy eyes, and stand still! I must lace thee tighter than this for the new gown."

Michael, who was knitting suspenders for himself in the parlor when Stiegel arrived, was persuaded only with a shilling to go to bed.

"Smile!" whispered Mrs. Ege to Elizabeth as she shoved her toward the top of the stairs. "Make up for poverty with smiles!"

"'Twas all I could manage to get away," sighed Stiegel. "I had to belie my host and plead an engagement at the Bachelor's Club."

"It has been very dull," admitted Elizabeth, lowering her

eyes. And she thought of Anna, and went on boldly, "The time has dragged eternal."

Stiegel was touched, and he lifted one of her hands and kissed a dimple.

Elizabeth flushed scarlet. She was very pretty, thought Stiegel suddenly.

That same evening he ventured to kiss Elizabeth. He had escorted her to a wedding reception. He had kissed the bride, an uncommonly pretty little girl of fifteen, and his imagination was stimulated. Now, walking home slowly under the trees, he found that his brain tingled with punch. He stopped under the bough of a chestnut overhanging a garden wall, and impulsively tipped Elizabeth's face to the moonlight. Startled, she waited, until his warm be-wined lips found hers.

"Heinrich," she whispered, as frightened as if they had committed adultery, and he laughed at her gayly and took her arm in his again. He liked the feeling of her plumpness; she too, he thought, was virginal and unawakened.

Now that Stiegel lived with the Stedmans his routine was changed. Lucy rose languidly in the morning and took a few drams of brandy for breakfast, so that her appetite would not tempt her to increase the absurdly small waist. She then coaxed Stiegel to come into the garden with her, or drive to the shops, or sit beside her while she worked at some feminine task. She subordinated him always to her interests. He held the skein while she spun, or he fanned her while she read to him from Congreve, or he held her basket while she snipped flowers. She was always bantering lightly at his expense. It was a new experience, but he did not particularly like it. It was because she was not sure of her conquest, he thought.

One afternoon, as she was getting ready for a drive with Stiegel, Lucy chatted with her mother while she dressed.

"Lucy, 'tis not kind of you to flirt with Baron Stiegel so!"

"And why, Mama—tell me, pray!"

"He is papa's partner. 'Twill be very awkward when he falls in love with you."

"But I am going to marry him!" announced Lucy, filling her pomander with scent.

"Lucy! He has proposed?" asked her mother, in excitement.

"Do hush, Mama. Not yet, of course. 'Twould hardly be proper, and his wife only dead a few months!"

"But you said ——"

"He doesn't know it, Mama, but he's mad in love with me. Maybe I shall let him propose at the last Assembly!" Lucy picked up her mitts and pinched her mother's cheek. "Today, I shall let him kith me, Mama."

That was the afternoon that Stiegel kissed Lucy; they had let the gig come to a standstill, and the horse chewed lazily at the roadside grass. The kiss had not been a serious one, and it had not roused anything in him more than a normal exhilaration. He admitted to himself that he was disappointed. He was beginning to feel very lonely. He watched Lucy curiously all the way home as she talked, for her wide whimsical lips belonged to him now for the asking.

At night as he lay behind the chintz hangings of his four-poster bed he found himself strangely puzzled and emotional. He had begun to miss the idolatrous submission of his little wife, her soft fingers in the curve of his neck as he drifted to sleep.

And now, of late, he was beginning to feel restless. It was all very well, he thought, floating along in a Philadelphia spring, with tea and balls and indolence, but there was the Furnace waiting for him, and the two little children. Even in this short time he had almost forgotten how they looked. They couldn't be very happy there, alone with Frau Habicht. What they needed was a mother.

He thought of Elizabeth Hölz and Lucy, weighing one against the other coldly. Elizabeth would make the better mother, of course. She had been so dominated by her sister that she would be very gentle with the little girls. She would rock them and play with them, and teach them all the household arts herself. Elizabeth would lie passive in his arms.

But Lucy—she would always demand that he be her lover. There was something sensuous about her. He felt it when his hand touched hers, when her lips pouted for him, even when she sat still beside him in church. He could imagine Lucy stripping herself of her dozen filmy petticoats with a tantalizing air, and flaunting her nakedness before him. Her body would be ugly. And yet he began to want her, as he lay there thinking of her sensuality. He would always want her, and he would come to loathe her. She would be nothing but earth. Elizabeth was chaste, he thought. But he would rather have Lucy to wife. They lived in the same stratum of life, he and Lucy. She would know how to manage his fortune, how to furnish his homes. Her clothes would be the envy of Philadelphia, and his daughters would be raised in the society of men of capacity and women of wit and charm. Then too, business ties would be cemented. With the Huber and Stedman fortunes combined, Stiegel could possess thousands of acres of land. He would be the richest man in the countryside. He would have music—music enough to take all the loneliness and sting out of riches.

"What a pity I could not have loved one of them!" he pondered. "I have never loved a woman. . . . All I have known is lust. . . . And I want to know the beauty of love. . . . I want to know all things beautiful! . . . I shall never know love because I cannot get the passion for Diane out of

my limbs. We could have been so wild, so fearless together . . . forgetful of everything. I was a coward. She
would have released me. . . ."

An aching lump rose in his throat.

"How can she be gone out of my life, forever? It isn't
as if we had loved and said good-bye! Ach Gott, how I've
wanted her these months, lying to myself. And now she is
gone and I will take another woman to wife. There are so
many women in the world, pretty and soft—and yielding.
. . . But Diane—Diane had lips different from all the rest of
womankind!"

10

"Don't be a dumpish fool. Of course thee must ask him for the last Assembly," Anna Ege insisted.

"But . . . if he should say no!" Elizabeth protested.

"Why do'st think he has been walking thee in the woods, and dining here on catfish when he might eat turtle at the Stedmans'?"

"Do you think he . . . loves me?" asked Elizabeth with a little choke, and the thought of their one kiss filled her with confusion.

"To be sure. Don't be so sparing with thy eyes, Elizabeth. Let them speak out. Help the Baron to know his own mind!"

So Elizabeth gathered courage to invite Stiegel to escort her to the last Assembly on Society Hill.

"I shall sneak away at any cost," he told her gallantly. And it bothered him that he had not come out frankly and refused. He had a feeling that Elizabeth was too fond of him, and he realized that he must be tactful about letting her know that he would be marrying Lucy. He must simply see Elizabeth at longer and longer intervals until she must know that his interest in her had not been matrimonial.

Stiegel had no desire to go to Elizabeth's Assembly. It was merely a cheap understudy of the Old City Dancing Assembly which was an invitation affair, and which carefully excluded the goldsmiths and jewelers who danced the hipsesaw so vigorously with the glovers' and ropemakers' wives. The Assembly which Stiegel and his colleagues attended every two weeks from January until May was held in the store of Andrew Hamilton, and was an aristocratic institution which lasted for many years in Philadelphia. It was the proper place for young men to fall in love with the Mayor's daughter. Rheumatic papas and mamas were inveigled into cards while the younger generation tiptoed the minuet in the brilliant candlelight.

Lucy mentioned it casually one evening as she puttered with wax flowers. Naturally they would be going together to the Old City Dancing Assembly, she said, since Stiegel was a member of the houschold now. Stiegel was honored, of course. He had been trying to propose to Lucy for the last few days. Somehow, the thought always intervened that he had been treating Elizabeth shabbily, and that he was being too hasty and snobbish in neglecting her.

Alexander Stedman, at the escritoire, was absorbed in a sheet of figures.

Lucy tapered the petal of a rose, and beckoned Stiegel to drop the court calendar and sit beside her on the sofa.

"Heinrich," she whispered, "poor little Lucy is suffering dire neglect. You sit reading the news, or you stand gaping at Hogart's prints without seeing them. It's a woman!"

"Odd's life, Lucy," he replied, annoyed because she had guessed the reason for his abstraction. "A man's brain fatigues with business."

"Love and business both hide behind a serious mask— but sometimes business smiles! . . . That's what Benjamin

Franklin said to me one time at dinner (it was Thomas Lawrence's house). 'Sometimes, Mistress Lucy, business smiles.'"

Stiegel grinned. "You too far excel me in debates on love, Lucy. I'm all atangle."

"Ah, Heinrich, once you have kissed me. . . ."

"And you rebelled."

"'Tis the woman's way of assent."

"You mean you . . . liked my kiss?"

"Ah, Heinrich Stiegel, I did not half dream how modest you are. Saturday at the Assembly Robert Morris will ask me to marry him again. This time I think Robert means business! . . . He doesn't smile."

"You don't love him!" Stiegel said with finality.

Lucy shrugged her shoulders, and her eyes twinkled.

"I have fancied Robert for a long time. . . . He was the evening star in my sky—till the moon came up!"

"Lucy," Stiegel whispered, wondering if the girl had only been flirting with him all along, and suddenly taunted by the thought that he might not get her. "Lucy, you must tell him at once that you aren't going to marry him—that you ——"

"Stiegel," called Alexander Stedman, shoving his papers into the desk, and turning about abruptly. "I'm sorry I can't see this real estate idea as you and Robert Morris see it."

"I'm sorry too," returned Stiegel, pulling out his snuff-box, and flushing with the excitement of half a proposal. He glanced at Lucy under his lashes, and saw that she was putting her flowers in their work-box with a fit of temper. "Robert Morris says buying land now is like finding a purse with a thousand pounds in it!"

"Morris is too sanguine."

"He's gathered in all the property about Philadelphia with which he can safely speculate!"

"Ah, but that is the point. Is it safe? Morris is a rash reasoner. He'll die starving with all his land, that I'll warrant!"

For weeks Stiegel had tried to convince his partners that there was money in buying land. The thought of the virgin woods adjacent to God's-Acre and the little towns creeping into their midst tempted him irresistibly. Robert Morris had said, boldly and generously, "What I shall be to Philadelphia, you can be to Brickerville."

"I shan't give up hope, Alexander," said Stiegel, coming over to him and offering him some snuff. "Some day you will see the ——"

"If you *must* talk land," scoffed Lucy, "I'll tell you what I think, Papa. Robert and Heinrich are right. They're young and they must prospect. Why are you and Uncle Charles so stingy with Heinrich? You have more money now than I shall ever be able to spend. I want Heinrich to have it!"

"Lucy, you know nought of business," returned her father, nettled.

"Nay, Papa, but I know ought of men!"

"My investments have been paying poorly."

"The very reason for you to humor Heinrich, Papa. If you are losing money now, and you lose money then, it is all of a piece. And I'll warrant when Heinrich Stiegel owns land it will turn to gold!"

Stiegel stood fingering his snuff-box, a little embarrassed that Lucy was pleading for him so openly.

"Even if I should give my consent, there is Charles," mused Alexander Stedman.

"Oh, I'll manage Uncle Charles," laughed Lucy, and tripped from the room with picturesque confidence.

Stiegel found no opportunity to speak to her again seriously before the Assembly. He was nervous in spite of his assurance now that she wanted to marry him.

The Old City Dancing Assembly was an orgy of color.

The brilliance shifted from gowns to music, slow-moving, the rooms mellow with the lighted tapers and the rapprochement of lovers. It was the end of May. The last Assembly, the last scene of love before it moved into the moonlight under the willows.

Lucy was a vision of loveliness in blue satin, pearl-embroidered with flowers. Stiegel watched her lips as he bowed to her in the minuet, and her smile was coaxing. He saw Robert Morris glowering at them from a corner, his arms folded and his foot tapping the floor pertly to the music. They must escape Robert at once.

Every gesture, every sweep of Lucy's fan was meant to keep both men dangling in doubt.

Stiegel saw a matron go over to Robert Morris, and he took advantage of his rival's preoccupation to lead Lucy deftly off the floor and out of sight before the dance was over. They found a small, unfrequented room, and Lucy settled her numerous petticoats on a settee.

"Your patch is askew tonight; it belongs on your lips," he chided.

"Then you know not the secrets of the patch, Baron," she whispered. "To the left cheek, you are a Whig; to the right, a Tory. 'Tis only the coquette who scars her lips. And 'tis only passion that wears the patch at the corner of the eye."

She opened her blue enamel patch box, and saw in its little mirror that her patch had not loosened. "The hearts of a hundred men flutter tonight because Lucy is no more a coquette. Each one thinks, 'It is changed for me!' "

"Lucy, let the patch be where it will, you are an infernal coquette."

"Nay, Baron. The bee wanders from flower to flower only because it has not found the sweetest one of all!"

His fingers tightened on her jeweled hand, and she turned to him impulsively, her eyes narrowed. They seemed unusually bright, he thought.

"Lucy, we have both had enough of this banter. I want to marry you. You know that, don't you, Lucy? You know it, yet still you make it hard for me. . . ."

For a moment he hated himself.

"Heinrich. . . ." she sighed. "Heinrich, at latht I know love!"

He held her close to him, and he felt the sensuous warmth of her languor. It stirred him, and he kissed her lips; they were dry and strangely immobile. But he kissed her again, passionately. She was going to belong to him. . . .

"I want you, Lucy," he whispered, and he released her lips for a moment and looked down into the slits of her eyes that seemed the burning green of a cat's eyes in the dark. She lay limp against his shoulder.

"You are not well, Lucy," he exclaimed as she sighed and closed her eyes.

"Nay. And it wherrits me a little—the poplar-worm that fell on me today as I strolled."

"It could never have bit you. You'd have fallen ill ere now."

"It is only fancy that I feel ill!" She shook her curls defiantly. "The ballroom is so a-taint with musk and hot perfume!"

"I shall advise your mother," offered Stiegel, alarmed.

"Nay, she would make me keep chamber for days!"

He touched her cheeks with his fingers, and her lips. They seemed parched, and hot. He held her close to him once more.

"Lucy . . . when will you marry me?"

"How eager you are!"

"That is no answer."

"Heinrich—fan me!" Her hand dropped heavily from his lips.

"Lucy, you *are* ill! Tell me at once. What is it?"

" 'Tis the musk . . . chokes me . . . and the world is full of musk tonight. . . . I think it even drifts down to the wharf from the other Assembly on Society Hill."

"The . . . the other Assembly! Tonight too!"

"Aye, when we swing our last, so must they swing their last. Were we to dance in the rain, so would they!"

"You are not cozening me!" Elizabeth was waiting for him!

"Nay, to what purpose? Heinrich, a dram or two. . . ."

Stiegel hurried off to where the "treat" was being served, and procured some Madeira for Lucy. Besides being worried about her, he was confused and humiliated. He pictured Elizabeth, drooping with tears because he had not appeared. It was already nine o'clock, and he had so benevolently promised himself for her last Assembly.

As he stood waiting for the wine, he wondered how he was going to get out of this mess. A dozen plans jumbled themselves in his mind; to get Lucy home; to come back to the dance; to pretend to Elizabeth that he had forgotten, or had never been told the date of the other Assembly. It was scarcely feasible to propose marriage to one girl and leave her to go off to a ball with another! And yet that was the very thing he would have liked to do. Now that he knew Lucy was going to marry him he felt magnanimously sorry for the little Elizabeth whose violet eyes had kindled at his smile. She loved him, of course, and he had been thoughtless and brutal. Well, it would be impossible to explain to Elizabeth. Nothing but illness would condone such manners. Illness. . . . He would send a note to her at once, saying he had been taken ill, and until now had hoped to come for her anyway! At least he would not break her heart without a little warning. . . .

He hurried back to Lucy. She sipped her wine with annoying precision, her elaborate coiffure resting on Stiegel's shoulder. The gay bouquet of flowers in her bosom bottle rose and fell quickly with her heavy breathing. He would never get the note sent off!

She rose to her feet as the music began again, staggering a little.

"Robert'th reel. He'll be hunting me like mad. Heinrich, you mutht be the one to tell him the ——"

Lucy melted into his arms, and all at once she felt awkward and leaden, and had fainted. Stiegel laid her on the settee, propping a chair up close to it while he ran off for help.

When he came back with her parents she had been seized with convulsions. A crowd gathered hastily outside the door of the room, and someone fetched Lucy's wraps while Stiegel called for their carriage. Robert Morris carried her to the street, and the commotion gradually settled again into the gayety of the reel.

Once they were home, Stiegel hurried off for the doctor. As the servant lighted him through the street, he was torn between the images of the two girls. Lucy had partly revived, but was tossing with fever, tortured with thirst and crying out at the pain in her head. Now it was too late to send a note to Elizabeth. Her eyes would be stained with mortified tears. She would never accept his apology. When she heard that he was to marry Lucy she would be certain the insult had been deliberate. Well, perhaps he had never been much of a gentleman, sneaking off to see Elizabeth as if she were some common whore.

Elizabeth waited expectantly for Baron Heinrich Stiegel. Her waist was pinched in to look like the slender green stem of a flower; she billowed with lavender ruffles; her hair was powdered and curled, and after she left the house and Anna's keen eye, she would use the scent which she had hidden in her pocket. She was either "new" or "borrowed" from top to toe, with Maggie Tillman's bosom bottle (for of course Baron Stiegel would bring her flowers), and

Tabby Turner's fan, made for Tabby by the fan-mounter to whom she was engaged. Even Grandmother Whitsun had been in to see Elizabeth on display. There would be eyes behind every curtain in the street, to see her swept off by the Baron.

"Michael, do not come so close to me with your molasses bread!" warned Elizabeth. "Anna, I am like to die with these stays!"

"Get thee to bed, Michael," cried Anna. "And do not dare show thy dirty face at the stair-rail when the Baron comes. George, remember, bow when thee open the door, and offer to hold his hat."

"It is half after eight!" wailed Elizabeth. "Anna, think you he could have forgot?"

George began to laugh at the delightful possibility.

"Stop, you little clout," ordered Elizabeth, stamping her foot. "Can't you see I'm all unnerved!" And her dimpled hands in their borrowed gloves itched to slap him.

"Luddy, thee go off like touchwood," reprimanded her sister. "No, *do* not sit down, after I have ironed thy petticoats for hours."

"But I must do something!" cried Elizabeth. "I can't stand here to eternity. . . ."

"Perhaps the chariot has broke down, Lizzie," comforted Anna, in a moment of understanding.

"He could send a messenger!"

George yawned in his corner.

At nine o'clock Elizabeth paced the floor, her feet aching in the new red leather shoes.

For weeks she had been in a state of delirious hope that Stiegel might propose to her. What she wanted was the sort of life she heard about through the fishmonger or the poulterer who occasionally got blinding glimpses of a Stedman or a Hamilton in action. She was tired of making her own clothes and of cleaning Anna Ege's house. Anna had never let her marry. The young men who came along were not good enough for a Hölz, she said. Only the week before, Elizabeth had triumphantly refused a handsome young tanner, because of Stiegel. Now perhaps she would not have a chance again. It was Anna's fault for leading her to believe that Stiegel was vulnerable.

"You have bragged to every shopkeeper in the row that I am going to the Assembly with Baron Stiegel," she cried through a torrent of angry tears. "And now I shan't be able to show my face in public."

"Not if thee cry it purple!" retorted Anna. "Look, thee are dripping tears over thy new farth ——"

"What does it matter! I shall never need it. I shall never use it again, and we will dine on penny shad for months. . . ."

"I told thee to ——"

"Aye. To use my eyes, to use my dimples. He has been mocking me the whole time I have simpered at him! I'll warrant he's at the other Assembly this very moment, making love to that Lucy Sted ——"

"If thee had looked sharp, 'twas like a ripe plum falling into thy lap, thou little fool!" Anna had made no mean sacrifice to attach Heinrich Stiegel to the family, and she relished months of penny shad no more eagerly than her jilted sister.

"Now I shan't e'en af-f-ford a flowered bonnet f-for Easter!" And Elizabeth began to tear her new clothes from her, feeling somehow that she would be inflicting vicarious punishment on Stiegel if she ruined them.

Her feeling for him had shifted in two short hours from idolatry to hatred.

"If he ever c-comes to the house again I'll not speak to him; I'll s-spit at him!" she sobbed, throwing herself on the bed.

Suddenly there was the sound again of hoofs on the

cobblestoned street; George flew down to the door; Anna Ege ran for water to bathe her sister's swollen eyes; Elizabeth fumbled wildly for the petticoats she had shed in a heap on the floor.

A chariot stopped before the shop next door, and a coachman got down from his box to straighten the plume of his horse, lifted his wig a little to scratch his head, and mounted again to drive off.

George Ege began to snigger, stuffing his handkerchief into his mouth to keep his ears from being boxed.

Lucy's illness was not attributed to the bite of the poplar-worm, which was always dangerous and sometimes fatal. The doctor seemed puzzled. Stiegel was not allowed in to see her the next morning. He felt miserable and worried about her recovery, but no one in the Stedman household seemed to be thinking of him.

"When Lucy is quite well again, I will go to Elizabeth and tell her the whole truth," he thought. "She will not believe me, but at least I shall feel more honorable."

Meals were solemn affairs. Mrs. Stedman, sedate in her stiff Mercury cap, presided at her twifflers but did not talk. She merely asked at the proper moment, "Will you have another help of turnip, Baron?"

Stiegel adopted the mood of the household. He became solemn, and turned to the score long neglected in the drawer of the escritoire. He hummed minor tunes, and set them on paper. He practiced softly behind closed doors, and felt strangely as if he were living an interlude.

On the third day of Lucy's illness, the family became alarmed. Lucy had continued with vomiting and a fever which made her rave whimsically of Stiegel. Mrs. Stedman looked at him as he sat rigidly at dinner in her fine Chippendale chair. So Lucy had fallen in love with him!

"My dear," asked Stedman, who had just come from

Dickinson's office, "what says Doctor Rearsley of Lucy now? Devil burn him, does he not say 'tis the stomach?"

" 'Tis not the poplar-worm, he thinks. There is a rash today, but 'tis not the same. It creeps from her hair into her face. It aches her eyes. . . ."

She looked at them, afraid to meet their gaze.

Stedman leaped up. "Abigail," he burst out, sinking into his chair again with a groan, "I prayed you to inoculate her for the pox!"

Mrs. Stedman turned ashen. "Inoculation," she cried vehemently, "is a distrust of God's over-ruling care, a distrust that he procure us a possible future good!"

But Stedman had fled to seclusion, and the tirade ended in strange sobs.

Stiegel felt himself wild with terror, not with fear for Lucy, but with fear for himself. He thought of her suddenly as a loathsome object. The rash would surge through her straggling curls, and cover her large mouth with sores. The fever would whip her into delirium, and unsatiated, would break out into the household, hunting further victims. It was not just death. It was more formidable than death. He imagined the nauseous odor creeping down to him from the sick room, and rising in the fumes of the soup.

Stiegel left the Stedmans that night for an obscure little tavern called the Crooked Billet, which harbored sailors, many of whom were pock-marked. He had left graciously enough, not wishing to impose upon the Stedmans in time of illness, he said. He stared out upon the boats of the Delaware, and listened to the rough laughter of the pig-tailed seamen as they drank themselves riotous at night. The "weak women" too, who hovered in groups of two's or three's about the wharves and who did not dare appear in town, seemed to attach themselves to him magically. They clung like barnacles, but he laughed, half-tempted, and told them he was ill with the pox.

He abhorred himself. The glamour of velvets and gold watch chains was gone. He felt himself naked, waiting for the infliction of the dread disease. He had kissed Lucy's lips again and again. How could he escape? He was in-oculated for small-pox and lay alone through days of a mild attack, afraid of disfigurement, and yet more afraid of death. It was only through these long hours of staring at the whitewashed walls that he knew how much he loved life, how much he wanted from it. He wanted from it all the beauty that the earth held: he wanted passion, and he wanted fame—success, music, acres of virgin forest to call his own. He wanted sons—and he wanted beauty about him in little things. Crystal, and velvets against his skin. It seemed as if all his senses had only begun to waken; and he wanted love. Supposing he should live to a doddering, scarred old age and never have known love!

There would be Lucy, marked with pocks, and he would have to kiss her thickened lips, would have to lie with her, while his heart cried out against her. She would be help-lessly embittered, loathing herself and her fate. No man would look at her; and she would not endure neglect. All her light froth would be turned to venom, and she would not even be the ornament he had bargained for. God wouldn't do this thing to him! God wouldn't do this thing to Lucy! If God was merciful to all of them he would give Lucy death. . . .

At last, weak from fasting and torturing himself with these nightmares, he wandered out to the shops in the early morning, before society was up. He bought gifts for Lucy, fans, lace aprons, extravagant ribbons, a tortoise-shell patch box. He was filled with shame at the fear he had of her recovery, at the ugliness that filtered through his mind. To Elizabeth, too, he sent violets, and a letter to tell her of the tragedy. He would come to explain everything to her, he said, when he was certain of his own safety.

The first night he was able to be about, he walked unsteadily in the early evening to the Stedman house. He whispered with the negro maid who answered his knock—his heart pounding so that he felt she must see his terror. Mistress Lucy had become delirious. The fever had returned, and the sores which covered her body were crowding the breath out of her throat. Mrs. Stedman, too, had succumbed to fever. Mr. Stedman was confined to his room. The household was in a turmoil. The help had fled, indentured servants and all. A negress, a desirable maid because she had had smallpox, alone remained. She came to the door now in a filthy apron, an apple she had been paring still in her hand. Stiegel looked beyond her into the hall. A fashionable Persian carpet had been rolled into a heap and laid aside as an ornament is put out of the way; the marble-topped table was flecked with dead lilacs; the gilt sconces were spattered with candle grease which had long since overflowed; and an ordinary dip burned lazily in a Betty lamp on the table.

Sickened at the ravishment, he turned into the garden. The weeds rose unconquerable in Lucy's tender young flower beds; only the fruit trees of the little orchard came forth unafraid with a luxuriance of blossoms, sweetening the warmth of the night, and looking in the twilight like the white mist over a river.

It was the first time that Stiegel thought longingly of his home and his babies. He was so homesick for every familiar tree and stone that tears of hunger came into his eyes. The orchard would be breathtaking, and the flowers coming up in Diane's Garden of Eden! His little girls would be sweet and shy. He should only have thought of the woman who would have made them a good mother. He wanted to see Elizabeth again, with her fresh clean skin, and her cool pansy eyes. Clean, that's what she was.

Her cleanness would chasten his thoughts, would make him feel something of a man again. He had been groveling in fear and self-abasement as a sow grovels in mud.

If Lucy should live he would marry her. He shuddered, halting below her window as he left the garden.

"God," he prayed, "have mercy on her! She could never face it, pocked and bald!"

11

Lucy was buried ignominiously the day she died. Two weeks later, her mother was laid beside her and the house was scantily disinfected with vinegar.

Alexander Stedman, who had suffered a feeble attack of smallpox after inoculation, was blinded by the world much as if he had come out of a darkened theater. He felt himself an old man, sitting among his business friends at the tavern like a disembodied spirit.

"Stay on with me a while, I beg of you," he urged Stiegel one day.

"I have been gone too long now," Stiegel replied. "I only heard in the mail this morning that my head founder has been badly burned. And my children's nurse girl has run off and married." The truth was that he was too repulsed with the thought of the morgue-like house which had been so gay with Lucy's chatter.

"I have changed my mind . . . about the land," said Stedman slowly, caressing one hand with the other, as he did constantly now.

"You want the firm to buy land after all!" exclaimed Stiegel, trying not to show his fervor.

"Lucy . . . wanted it that way, you know."

[138

"But you must not do this thing against your better judgment!"

"You would have been my son, Heinrich. . . ."

Stiegel winced.

"I have talked it over with Charles. He consents to our buying unlimited forest land about Brickerville."

"Don't do this thing just for me, I beg of you," cried Stiegel, guiltily. He felt that much as he had wanted his partners to put in the money for land, he could not accept their cooperation on this basis. The speculation would make them all rich, rich! And he had prayed for Lucy's death. He was filled at the same time with temptation and shame.

"Lucy raved of you day and night."

"She promised to be my wife—the very night she was took ill." Stiegel took out a little silver ball of nutmeg, and grated the spice into his wine. He didn't want to meet the eyes of Alexander Stedman. He felt a fiendish desire to cleanse his conscience, and cry out, "I didn't love her! I prayed God to take her."

"And so I have asked John Dickinson to meet us in his law office and draw up the agreement."

Stiegel found that he could not answer. He had loved neither of these women who were the source of his riches. Both had loved him. Both had died to give him wealth. He had thought to come here to America and to make his fortune with his music, with his soul. How young he'd been! How much he had learned in these few short years.

Well, now he would marry Elizabeth Hölz—and she was poor. The children must have someone to take care of them properly, as daughters of his deserved to be raised. And Elizabeth would make a good mother. . . . He did not love her either, of course.

Alone, after dinner, he lolled in the kitchen of the Coach and Horses watching the bow-legged turnspit dogs twirl the sputtering roasts on their strong hempen strings. He remembered thinking when he came to Philadelphia that he had fate in his pocket. Now he had even more than when he came, with the promise of business expansion, and a pretty new wife for the asking. But he felt no more victorious than these poor little dogs. What was the matter with him, he wondered? Certainly he had learned to forget Diane, hadn't he? Was it just possible that one does not get everything one wants out of life, after all? Or that if one gets it, it may not come the way one likes?

He went directly to Elizabeth's house and asked her to marry him immediately, overwhelming her with the suddenness of his ardor.

" 'Tis great good fortune that you love me," he said, with something of gentleness in his voice.

"Ah Heinrich, mine is the good fortune! I think I am in a dream. I am not fine enough by half. . . ." There was an invasion of happy tears.

"You shall be the finest woman in Pennsylvania," he predicted magnanimously. "Why, the Governor's coach will be a scavenger cart beside our own!"

She stood there, laughing and crying. He felt so carefree and so happy again with the horrible weight of Lucy's illness off his mind. He kissed her dimpled hand, and a feeling of satisfaction filled him. He would not have to worry about his household now. Here was a competent, affable woman who would be contented rearing his children.

If Elizabeth knew that she was Stiegel's choice only because Lucy was dead, she did not complain. Rumor had brought to her quickly the story of Lucy's illness at the ball. Stiegel had deserted her for Lucy the night of the last Assembly. But she was in no position now to demand an explanation. It was quite enough that he had asked her to marry him. The bitter memory of the night of the Assembly Ball lingered faintly in her mind, and she could no longer tell what part of her acceptance was for love of him, and what for the sense that the luxury he would bestow upon her was a rightful amends.

" 'Twould be folly to buy thee very much," decided Anna Ege, "the man as rich as he is! 'Twould be like throwing water into a well."

"But I shall want to look a lady. I can't be shabby when he is so grand!"

"Well, cast thy violet eyes at the shop-windows as thee pass by. Now is the time he will buy thee all the gowns of Philadelphia."

And Madame Ege knew a buyer when she saw one.

Each time Stiegel thought of the house at Elizabeth Furnace it took on a more somber aspect, so lugubriously hung with crepe. The new wares in the shops became irresistible. Elizabeth's eyes grew large in unbelief at the costly and elaborate furnishings he chose on their shopping tours. He thought her hesitation sprang from her years of poverty. She would make an economic wife, not wanting everything she might see.

Elizabeth clung to his arm more tenaciously after each purchase, as if all this must be an air castle soon to dissolve. And Anna Ege, who accompanied them as often as possible, said artfully, "But thee must not go in debt for Elizabeth, Baron Stiegel; the things that thee buy are only fit for royalty!"

Whereupon Stiegel would react as neatly as if she had pulled the string to a puppet.

"This snuffer strikes your fancy, Elizabeth. 'Tis yours for a covetous look of your pansy eyes. Do you think Barbara would make tea in this miniature pot? She is two, sir, but uncommon smart. The painted floor cloth would do well for your bedroom, Elizabeth. The plaster bust, 'tis one of the King Richards. I favor the sturdiness of chin. 'Twould do well in the hall. . . ."

They visited James Rivington, too, in their artistic pillage of the town. He advertised "A great collection of wrote and printed music in stock from England and Italy," and he shelved a miscellany of fiddles, hand-organs, Hautboy reeds, and bagpipes second to none.

The hunchbacked old man peered curiously at Stiegel and the beribboned young woman. His eyeglasses were home-made of lead and window glass, and were held on by bits of twine, fastened to rings which encircled his ears.

"I shall buy four fiddles," announced Stiegel, who had just conceived the idea of transforming his workmen into an orchestra, "a pitch pipe, three German flutes, a French horn . . . a violoncello. And fiddle strings—a quantity of each. Some smatterings of bridges and screws. Aspasia (it was the name by which he addressed Elizabeth in his billets-doux), my own men shall learn my scores!"

One day at the mantua-maker's, Elizabeth laughed at Anna when she chose a flowered taffeta for the wedding, for Mr. Ege had been of the orthodox school of Quakers.

"I was always of a mind that poverty and Quakerism are cohorts." Elizabeth would never have dared talk to Anna this way until recently, but she had gained prestige in her new role.

"Thee are an ingrate," retorted Mrs. Ege, her conscience twinging. "Thee knows well enough I am inured to my dear husband's beliefs through marriage and not through disposition. But even now 'tis only for thy happiness, Elizabeth, that I submit to flowered silk. Thee cannot believe how it disgruntles me."

The marriage took place in the summer. Stiegel had delayed as long as possible telling Alexander Stedman his plans. The children needed a mother, Stiegel had told him, which did not interfere with love coming but once to a man, as Stedman must well know. It was hard to tell what Alexander Stedman felt as he listened to the news, caress-

ng one hand with the other. Stiegel thought the day would
never come when he could leave Philadelphia with its
haunting ghosts, and its memories of harrowing fear. It
seemed as if the whole world were opening wide again
to greet him. His apprenticeship was over, thank God!

Three days after they had set out with the mail, Stiegel
and Elizabeth and two new Negro servants arrived at Elizabeth Furnace. It was Sunday, and the grounds were deserted. The cold evening in the woods seemed to have shut
up the house like a cocoon, and there was no one to greet
them as they dismounted from their horses.

Elizabeth, bedraggled from her long journey, looked
about her into the darkening woods, and felt a sudden
chill of homesickness. For weeks, she had hugged the
thought of the elegant mansion that was to be her home,
and now that she encountered it, it seemed haughty in its
very massiveness. The shutters were closed, and the house
was gloomy in the drab twilight.

Stiegel, irritated beyond words, gave a curt "halloo." No
response. He tied the horses to the hitching-post, and
climbed the stairs to the house. Elizabeth followed him
gingerly with hurried, disastrous little steps, her russet
shoes taking ill to the smattering of puddles on the walk.
They stood together, gazing long into the kitchen in the
ell. A mammoth fire was inflaming the pots and kettles like
flint and steel, and over the fireplace and across the ceiling
of the room on long poles hung strings of dried apples,
peppers, and rings of pumpkin, like a Hallowe'en orgy.
The steam of soup rose from a brass pot on a trammel.
Near to it, his large nostrils inhaling the perfume, sat
Cyrus, scraping corn on the fire-peel. Barbara, a wiry rep-
ica of her mother without the pinkness, played with the
cobs, occasionally carrying one over to the lap of Frau
Habicht, who sat pegging. In the cradle on the hearth was
Elizabeth Jerusha, a bland, beautiful infant, sucking like a

gourmet on a salt spoon of silver.

Elizabeth and Stiegel looked at one another. They seemed intruders. Stiegel rapped, vociferously, for he had tried the door and found it was barred.

Cyrus peered at the window, and in his own time shuffled to the door.

As Stiegel burst in, much to the amazement and joy of the servants, little Barbara in her high heels clutched the skirts of Frau Habicht and glowered on him. The old woman picked up a tin horn, a Tyrolese masterpiece three feet long with a strainer on the end, and held it expectantly to her ear.

"Guten Abend, Frau Habicht. Haven't you received my letter?"

"Nein, the Post hasn't come for weeks!" Her thousands of fine wrinkles settled into a frown as she darted a prejudiced glance at the timid strange female.

Stiegel, scarcely aware of her answer, ordered the bedroom to be made comfortable at once. He turned to find Elizabeth picking up Barbara. Outraged at the presumption, Barbara screamed in true fright, releasing her small fist on Elizabeth's forehead, and knocking her hat awry. Elizabeth dropped her like a spitting cat, and the child flew to Frau Habicht and hid in her skirts, crying.

Elizabeth was humiliated, and turned away to the cradle. Jerusha stared up at her critically; the silver salt spoon was motionless in a puckering mouth.

Stiegel, cautious with experience, leaned over the child in her swaddling clothes and faded shawl. For a moment she flouted them both with stormy eyes, and then rather timidly, like a mouse cribbing cheese from a trap, she touched his rhinestone coat button with a pudgy finger. The thing glittered enchantingly. So their friendship began.

But Elizabeth was hurt. It was all she could do to keep

the tears from streaming down her face. The trip had been long and tedious, and it was the first time in her life she had been away from home. She had expected servants overjoyed at their homecoming, and the mansion shining in warm candlelight to welcome her.

Stiegel felt vexed that she should have such a desolate impression of her new home.

"Come, Elizabeth," he whispered, "in a few moments you will be in your very own bed—and I shall comfort you, Madame Stiegel. And in the morning the sun will shine, and the children will love you too!"

The house, unused, was still shrouded with black draperies, and the rooms, silent as a mausoleum, clutched them with formidable chill. They spoke softly as they tiptoed up the stairs, in reverence to the dead. Elizabeth, shivering, threw Stiegel's great coat about her and crouched before the fireplace in her bridal chamber while Frau Habicht, with the natural resentment of an old servant toward a second wife, glumly placed a warming-pan in the bed where Elizabeth, her darling, had died.

Stiegel was filled with emotion. He went quietly about the house, prying into dark corners, absently touching a quill pen or a bottle, his mind surging with the ghosts of those who were gone. In the hall he held his dip high before the portrait of Diane, who looked down at him patronizingly. She had been waiting for him to stop there, and her scarlet lips curled and said, "Bon soir, m'sieu. After a journey you will always come back to Diane!"

He choked with that dim, long-ago passion he thought he had flung from him so airily as he watched the dogs in the Coach and Horses. Holding the candle close to her throat, he gazed into her black eyes, with their menacing brows, and flinched, his brain muddled by her scrutiny. He was smelling the incense now of her yellow flower garden in July.

"Who is she?"

The lips of Diane moved, and he was so sure she had spoken that he was startled at Elizabeth's touch on his arm.

He returned slowly, stupidly, to her world.

"The foster child of my wife's father, Herr Huber. . . . Stole by the Indians."

He snuffed Diane out of sight, and turned to Elizabeth as if she were the stranger, leading her abstractedly up again to the chamber where the child was still at play with the birds.

12

N THE PARLOR TABLE there was now a new family Bible which had been drowsing in one of the deerskin trunks that came over on the "Nancy." It was a tooled leather volume containing a treatise in German on the elements of religion. On two blank leaves between the Testaments were the names of the Stiegel family, in a lacy German script, and the Baron now wrote in "Elizabeth Hölz Stiegel," with adequate margin for the offspring she would bear.

Although fundamentally Elizabeth was not a timid person, she was terrified with the catarrhal "he-hem" of Frau Habicht. She wilted before the eyes of the German tyrant, knowing full well that the old lady hated her, and Frau Habicht, who soon guessed her prowess, took unfailing advantage of the bride.

Elizabeth felt awkward with the children, too. She had helped to bring up Michael and George, but had had no compunction about cuffing them when they defied her. Barbara and Jerusha were active youngsters, spoiled and in constant mischief. If Elizabeth tried to discipline them they ran to the protection of Frau Habicht's apron strings. Elizabeth was puzzled. She had supposed that the children would respond at once to her broad smile and pretty clothes. Before she came to Brickerville she had pictured a sanguine family life awaiting her. The little girls would adore her and she would pet them and dress them as no other children in the community were dressed. They would call her mother, of course, for they were too young to remember anything of the flower-like Elizabeth Huber of whom she was so jealous underneath her smile. It had never occurred to Elizabeth that she might have to earn their affections with tireless effort. It hurt her pride that the children were indifferent to her, and she tried with devious means to hide her failure from Stiegel.

As the fall wore on, she became plump and roseate, and the church at Brickerville winked its eye, and said, "Surely, by May. . . ."

But Stiegel's son was not born that year. It was only the sumptuous food of the mansion which had gone to Elizabeth's waist—the gravied fowl, the thick cream, the casual plenty. It was with more or less relief that she greeted the activity of the springtime; she delved into the chests of clothes which had seemed forbidden to her till now, like Ali Baba's jars. As the mistress, it was her duty to put pepper into the blanket chests for moths, and shake out the clothes. She fingered gingerly the delicate pink hoopskirts of Elizabeth Huber, as if they might mysteriously bring her the same somber fate.

Stiegel, absorbed in his business, spent his spare time in riding about the woods. He bounded his land with a fence, being careful to lay the lower rails when the horns of the moon were up, and finishing the job when the horns were down, according to the German belief thereabouts. The Italian and English gardeners he had brought from Philadelphia were fighting like two strange cocks, and producing the most luxuriant of hedges and arbors and pergolas, inspired by rabid competition. The spring was blooming in no ordinary way in God's-Acre. The Italian gardener, ploughing up a patch of weeds near the carriage house one day, met with inexplicable wrath on Stiegel's part.

"Hold that spade, pox you," cried Stiegel. "Have you no respect for a garden but it be your own?"

"Noughta but weeds," flamed the artist.

"Everything yellow and orange," Stiegel told him. "Buttercups, pansies, sunflowers. The herb garden will do just as well behind the stable under the oak."

It was about this time that Madame Ege and the boys were cordially invited to spend the summer with the Stiegels. May found them installed at Elizabeth Furnace and thoroughly acclimated.

With the first scowl of her great forehead Mrs. Ege had sent Frau Habicht cowering to the lower domains. In a week she had taken the reins in her calloused hands. The linens had been examined and sorted. The great cone of sugar was cut by her hand alone. The keys to the wine cellar dangled from her waist.

"Thee must not do these things," she said to Elizabeth, who felt a little unnecessary in her own home. "What are all the servants for? That lazy Anne you and Heinrich brought from Philadelphia isn't worth her salt. The noddleheaded nigger! Thee must become better acquaint with the people of the town."

At the end of the summer, as Elizabeth and Stiegel were undressing for bed one night, Elizabeth said, "Anna's chest is surprising better since she is with us in the country, she says."

"That is good news," replied Stiegel, his mind on the French and Indian war, which still hung in the balance. "I saw in the news that——"

"I feel she should bide with us till she is quite cured, don't you, Heinrich?"

"Oh, if you wish it, my dear. . . . But the boys, they must continue their school!"

"Oh, Anna has already inquired of John Cramer, the schoolmaster." Elizabeth flushed; she hadn't meant to admit Anna's presumption.

"It seems all settled without my blessing," smiled Stiegel.

Elizabeth was annoyed with herself. She always meant to use Anna's tact as a pattern, and invariably she fumbled. As the winter wore on, she said to Stiegel, "You cannot think, Heinrich, what Anna saves us with her thrift! 'Twas only yesterday she beat Anne for spilling the sugar all over the cellar floor, and she ——"

"Beating the servants is your work, not Anna's," said Stiegel severely.

"But I was in Brickerville again," Elizabeth said quickly, hoping to divert him. "Mrs. Eggleston was having a party. And what do you think, Heinrich, she served me tea in a cup so cracked that the tea leaked out on the saucer! Such airs the woman has! And her gown patched under the sleeves, too."

Madame Ege's last belonging was moved from Philadelphia to Elizabeth Furnace the following fall, after she had been a guest over a year. Now Elizabeth felt she had a legitimate excuse for keeping her sister and nephews with her.

"Heinrich, do you not think Anna will make us a splendid housekeeper when the . . . the baby comes?"

"You want her to stay on—for good?" Stiegel asked.

"Think what she can do for me!" pouted Elizabeth. "I shall be distracted with a child!"

Stiegel thought of the Huber household, and how it had hummed all day long with activity—how Frau Huber herself had made the candles, feeling that no servant would get them white enough, and how Elizabeth had gotten out of a sick bed to make him cherry pudding.

"Think what we can do for Anna Ege!" he returned sarcastically, but the sarcasm was utterly lost on Elizabeth.

"Oh I knew you'd see it my way!" cried Elizabeth. "It scarce seems fair for me to have such grandeur and for Anna to starve!"

"You mean you were like to starve before we married, Elizabeth?"

"Ugh . . . think of the shad and tomatoes—tomatoes and shad. . . . 'Tis small wonder Anna has pains in the chest!"

"By all means," said Stiegel chivalrously, "we must rescue Anna from shad!"

Jacob Stiegel was born the following winter, and he slept in the cradle which had harbored the pinkness of Elizabeth Huber. Barbara resented his invasion. She had been raising her doll in the cradle, and yielded to Jacob's charms only when George promised he would whittle a miniature cradle for her.

Elizabeth, proud of having borne an heir to her aristocratic husband, was the plump, nursing mother of tradition. Brickerville came to pay its "setting-up" visit. Brickerville liked Elizabeth. She was gayly superior, as indeed they expected her to be. It made her social acceptance of them all the more of an honor.

The winter was a bitter one, and often the snow banks were piled so high that days passed before the roads were broken through by the farmers. The family, in exile, lived in complete comfort. The boys exulted over the holiday from school. But when Sunday came and there was not even the small excitement of attending church, they were peevishly bored.

On these Sundays, Stiegel, the patriarch, gathered his men together with solemnity and held a little service. They huddled bashfully in the best parlor and listened to the impromptu sermon of their master. Their voices trembled in shy cacophony while Mrs. Ege, a veteran artist on the harpsichord, blatantly performed, and George and Michael gazed out longingly for first signs of the spring influx of birds. At night they sat about in a group singing Conrad Beissel's sanctimonious hymns.

Stiegel worked hard these days. He rose at five in the morning, breakfasted before the women, and was about the furnace to see the dawn ushered in. He was popular with his workmen. They lived on the grounds in little cottages, each complete with its own garden and well. He was always kind to them, if a little dominating. Sometimes he took his violin out to them at the noon hour, and played some of the old German favorites. But he only worked at his score intermittently.

And yet he was not unhappy. For several years nothing had happened to break the even tenor of his life. Elizabeth and Anna Ege managed the house very well between them; he did not care much how it was run as long as they retained the standard of elegance he demanded. Barbara and Jerusha were lavishly dressed. Elizabeth was not overly affectionate, but she was good-natured and pretty.

As the spring flowered, Stiegel became absorbed once more with his plans for expansion. And fitting into them came a meeting with Adolph Gross of Lancaster, the frisky little rope-maker who was an old friend of his mother's cousin.

One evening while Stiegel was visiting his mother, Gross stopped in to have a glass of sack.

"What do you know of Charming Forge, Herr Stiegel?" he asked amiably.

"Charming Forge . . . 'Tis the bloomery forge near Wolmansdorf, run by Herman Coxe, nicht?"

"Ja, and he would sell it to me." Gross rolled his eyes. Stiegel raised his eyebrows. If there was a bargain on the market, why shouldn't he, and not Gross, benefit by it?

"What does he ask?" inquired Stiegel.

"Fourteen hundred and fifty pounds."

"Ach, Himmel, but that's robbery, Herman."

"My nephew is a journeyman nailmaker, and he says the place abounds in rich woods and streams. . . . Only one stack and hammer, but a new anvil for nails, and a new bellows."

For a long time Stiegel had wanted to invest money in a forge, to supplement the type of output of the Furnace. Now he poured more sack into Gross' glass, and urged upon him another of his mother's anise-seed cakes.

"Will you buy the Forge?" he asked warily.

Gross laughed heartily. "If I can buy it with wishes."

"You mean you—you'd like to buy it?"

"Ach, I would like the money that flows in from the iron, but it is so far from here, nicht? And I couldn't go so far from my friend Frau Stiegel and her good little cakes!"

Frau Stiegel, who was sweeping up the hearth, ignored him. She had an idea that Gross' interest went farther than her good little cakes. And his constant chuckle annoyed her.

Stiegel watched the by-play with irritation. "With a good manager at the Forge you would not have to leave the good little cakes!" he said.

"Ach, but such a funny lot of men there," Gross went on, his face comically full of crumbs. "The chafery man's an Indian, and the hammerman's a slave, Negro Jim. Then, with the indentures ——"

"With the right manager, it's all one nationality," said Stiegel blithely. "And you could appoint me manager."

Frau Stiegel gave a quick glance at this son she never could understand.

"Ach, *you* are the man to buy the Forge. You ——"

"I'll go into partnership with you, Herman," offered

Stiegel facetiously enough so that if Gross did not want to, he need not take the offer seriously.

"Gut!" cried Gross, entangled with crumbs, excitement, wine, and the intoxicating presence of Frau Stiegel.

"Ts,ts,ts," spluttered Frau Stiegel, leaving them alone to their covenant.

A week later the two men made a trip to Charming Forge, to investigate the works.

It was about twenty miles from Elizabeth Furnace, located in a crook of the Tulpehocken River, a place to which he could ride frequently and oversee without too much trouble. The seven or eight men who lived in the low red brick tenant house ran the Forge in two shifts. The land was beautiful, and Stiegel was filled again with his old passion of acquisition. Watching the ponderous iron hammer which fashioned out the iron bars, he imagined two hammers working, or three, or four. He would install blowing tubs here too, and there was no reason why the output could not grow to two or three hundred tons a year. Gross' seven hundred pounds would be very welcome to start the project, and in a few years he would manage somehow to buy him out.

The partnership was sealed a few weeks later in Frau Stiegel's parlor with more sack and anise cakes, and Stiegel felt this new venture was a feather in his cap.

He visited the Forge often the first year. In the spring he encountered heavy rains and more than once walked through the sullied roads up to his satin breeches in mire. Again, after weeks of drought, with the sting of July or August heat in his face, he might smell a forest fire, and if he were close in its wake, he would be forced to stop over at the inn until the fire had satisfied its gluttony with century-old pines and oaks. During the winter the journey was always difficult, and sometimes he had to remain fretfully in an "ordinary" for days. But Charming Forge was adding to his wealth. And it passed the time quickly to make trips there or to the thousands of acres the company now owned. The household seemed to get along without him very well, and Elizabeth Furnace, run for years in an able and efficient manner, could almost take care of itself.

But somehow, if he was not unhappy, he was not quite content. In a few more years, he decided, he would settle down to his music again. At times when he knew he no longer cared to compose he felt guilty, and told himself that it was merely laziness that bred such mutiny. Often the stress of business crowded out the finer satisfactions. But where could one get without money?

Occasionally he found himself dreaming of Diane at night. His dreams were always passionate, and sometimes he wakened in the darkness, and lay breathing hard, sick with excitement. Time and again he swore he must get her out of his mind. She was out of his life and he would never see her again. It was inane to let her memory trouble him. For long weeks then he scarcely thought of her, burying himself in work and in plans for every kind of expansion.

But finally he had word of Diane through an unexpected source.

One of the events of the early summer was the annual visit of Chepa Rose, a trunk pedlar. He usually came staggering under the burden of two thin metal trunks which he had fastened to his back by a harness of stout hempen webbing. He was, by his own tale, "half Injun, half French, half 'Merican," and every year when he returned with a cosmopolitan smile which only such a mixture could brew, he admitted having a new "bebba." He and Diane had gotten along famously. She knew more French than he and she had joked with him in an Indian dialect.

He was a famous medicine-brewer, having killed or cured a great percentage of New England. He helped himself to the herbs from the kitchen rafters above Anne's astonished head, stirred a concoction in a kettle of water on the hearth, abracadabraed it, and produced a vilely bitter and effective cough medicine for Michael, who had decided to play Indian in the woods one day without any clothes on.

He offered Mrs. Ege two kinds of plasters for her bosom pains, the kind to stick, or the kind to crawl, following the course of the pain. He made a sample of most delightful orange ink, and presented it to Stiegel; he mended the harnesses and dilapidated tinware, made a teetotum for Michael and laid out a tantalizing display of tops, marbles, pin-wheels and popguns. He held sway under the great oak beside Diane's yellow garden. Everyone in the establishment visited him, even Frau Habicht, who, bleary-eyed and rheumatic, came from her kitchen to see if Chepa Rose had any new bitters.

For Barbara, George purchased some fresh ribbons and a new busk of wood which was carved with appealing verses. In the intervals of salesmanship, Chepa Rose did them a little jig, the way "the laddies (female) hornpip' uppa Bostong way." Again, inspired by their applause, he caricatured "The Orphan," a play which he had seen Murray and Kean perform in a Connecticut inn one night.

Michael was afraid that any moment this wonderful artist would disappear into thin air and leave him without entertainment for the entire summer, so he showered him with beer and cakes, and even sneaked him small glasses of Madeira. Needless to say, Chepa Rose's artistry improved by the hour, and he had less desire than ever to move on. Night found him floundering among his possessions under the great oak, singing about Maneto, the Indian God, and vaguely connecting him with the Demon Rum. In the twilight he was teaching Michael to make a broom. He was torn between instructing the boy and a desire to lead himself in song with a spoon of laurel he had carved during the winter.

Michael thought this the ideal life, and followed every movement of the man with envy. As soon as Stiegel would permit him, he determined to wear a red and white checked linen shirt, deerskin breeches, blue worsted stockings, and cowhide shoes. There was a small portmantua under the eaves too, a very dusty and negligible one, which would never be missed. He might gather something from each of the girls as a nucleus, ribbons or bosom bottles, and he already could make as good ink as his schoolmaster, John Cramer. He was magnetized by the idea as he sat there at the feet of his idol.

It was not until early evening that Stiegel found half an hour to devote to the hawker, whose interpretation of current events was always original and humorous.

He was feeling particularly pleased with himself that day. He had been thrilled by a feeling of power as he rode among the forests, and on coming home had written Robert Morris a letter about new expansions he had made.

Elizabeth had become rosy and plumper as she nursed Jacob, and sometimes Stiegel teased her about her weight.

"Come, we will see if Chepa Rose has new stays that will make you thin!" he coaxed, pulling her away from her sewing.

"Think you I would buy stays from a pedlar!" she scoffed.

"Don't be vexed with me, Aspasia. You are very pretty tonight in your osnaburg gown. Come, take my arm, and we will stroll down and see what Chepa Rose has for sale!"

She sighed and relented. Her feet were hurting a lot these days.

"He's dirty!" she condemned.

"But funny, Elizabeth."

Chepa Rose gave them his famous grin, exposing a few yellowed teeth, and began to throw his arms about and expostulate on the French and Indians and redcoats.

"Old news!" cried Stiegel. "What have you that's new?"

Chepa Rose hesitated a moment.

"Monsieur Wolfe take Monsieur Montcalm and go pht!"

"Two years ago!"

"All over, everyone crazy with happy, uh? Diane she say ——"

"Diane!" Stiegel was electrified. He dropped Elizabeth's arm. "Where is Diane?"

"You have no see Diane?"

"Where is she?" Stiegel repeated tensely.

"Ah, Diane is beautiful, non? I say to her, 'Baron Stiegel, hees wife, pht!' And she light his eyes with fire, and say, 'Dieu Merci.' And she-um, smack kees, like Chepa Rose' sweetheart. . . ."

He rubbed his dirty brown hands together.

Stiegel bit his lips. He couldn't endure this chaff. He could feel Elizabeth stiffening beside him. But he was forced to go on.

"Where is she, Chepa Rose? I beg of you, tell me."

"She give me wine à Les Deux Poissons. And she sing ——"

"A barmaid!" cried Elizabeth, consumed with jealousy. "A lot the Hubers knew of the girl they thought was stole by the Indians. . . ."

"Ah, Diane a Conestoga. Diane do war dance like——"

"Where is Les Deux Poissons?" demanded Stiegel.

"Then I go back à Les Deux Poissons," went on Chepa Rose tantalizingly, "but Diane, she pht!"

"Gone?"

Chepa Rose nodded.

"Ach Gott!" It was incredible that she could be slopping wine and beer across an inn counter to earn her bread. That she would be toasted by teamsmen and drunkards, chucked under the chin, broached daily with invitations to sleep! Diane who was so exquisite and beautiful, Diane, who held

her chin so high, and her shoulders so straight. Struggling
for a living. And then a horrible thought occurred to him.

"She has not married—some sot!" he groaned.

"Non, non, non. She smile à tout le monde. She no
marry . . . no say she marry!"

" 'Twas probably too dull for her here," Elizabeth
sneered. "I'll warrant she ran off on purpose."

"Dull!" he retaliated. "The whole countryside was in love
with her. No place could be dull for five minutes with her
in it."

All the time Stiegel was saying these words he had not
wanted to say them. He seemed driven by some cocky devil
tonight. He saw Elizabeth's lips draw into an angry pucker,
and he knew that he wanted to hurt her. Why he wanted
to hurt her he could not say. But he did not relish the
thought of a scene.

"Here," he said to Elizabeth, tucking some notes into
her hand, "buy yourself some trinkets."

And he went back to the house, for he wanted to be
alone.

13

OR THE NEXT couple of weeks there was a long, sultry spell. The sun lay in apathy behind a gray sky. The lingering moisture of rain was suffocation, and the air smote the body like steam. Even the plants seemed to droop with inertia.

The children cried, fretful, and pulled at their garments. Elizabeth was quiet and seemed tired. She had been waiting on her sister Anna who was bed-ridden with Chepa Rose's new creeping plasters. Stiegel found himself searching for things that annoyed him, a dirty face on Barbara, the smell of bitters on Frau Habicht's breath, a candle stub left in a sconce. The thought of Diane in the Inn oppressed him terribly.

Each of them in his own world seemed to be waiting for a climax.

When the tenth day dawned with the same sullenness, endurance was low. Stiegel, having spent most of the day in the casting-shed, sauntered back to the house in the gloom of the late afternoon. He had driven the men hard today, ruthlessly. Now he craved his Chinese silk banyan as a man at the stake craves water, for his clothes clung to him like a stricken conscience.

"Heinrich," Diane said suddenly, as he reached the stairs of the porch. "Heinrich, mon cher!"

He staggered at the sound of her voice. She stood straight before him in a cheap cotton print, and she carried an oil-cloth cape, the relic of some luckless English soldier. Over her shoulder hung a large blue kerchief filled with clothes, and at her throat she had a bunch of wild honeysuckle. Beads were jumbled about her neck, and her feet were two squat mud pies in their moccasins. Her eyes gleamed brightly.

Stiegel leaned against the pillar in weak amazement.

"You—you've come back!" he said without meaning.

"Heinrich!" Her eyes were burning. "Is it true what Chepa Rose told me—that Elizabeth is dead?"

"Aye!"

"That is why I have come back," she said quickly, thrusting her brown hands into his.

He pressed his lips to them, praying for courage.

"Now at last we shall have one another, M'sieu."

"Diane . . . I . . . Diane, I have married again!"

She backed away from him as if he had struck her.

"You did not look for me," she cried sharply, stingingly. "Why did you not look for me?"

They were at cross-swords again, instinctively.

"I wanted to forget you," he said flatly. "You were wise to go away. We would have ruined our lives!"

"But you loved me," she retorted darkly.

"I didn't love you," he said tensely. "I wanted you. . . ."

"But it is the same ——"

"No, it is not the same!"

"You did not want me for a wife," she cried, her eyes like those of a wounded deer.

"Diane, I beg of you ——"

"What is it they can do I cannot do?" she stormed. "I can mend your shirts; I can make your cherry pudding; I can bear you children!"

"I can't say what it is," he answered, miserably. "You are wild and—and free. No roots. You're . . . different. You're ——"

"What's all this clack about!" called Elizabeth from the hall, and in another second she stood in the doorway.

She and Diane looked at one another like two wild animals about to leap.

"Elizabeth," said Stiegel, trying desperately to control his voice, "this is Diane. . . . I've told you about her. She has come back—to live with us."

"Non, non, non—I have not come back to live with you!" cried Diane spiritedly.

She saw the relief in Elizabeth's eyes, and appraised her with swift instinct. Fair and sweet, like a great chunk of cake. She would be able to rouse no appetite in him.

"You can't go out again into the world, alone," Stiegel told her quickly.

"I thought you had been stole by the Indians!" Elizabeth stammered.

"That does not mean I have been ate by them!" Diane's scar seemed to shimmer and vanish. "No, we make friends. I become a squaw of the Shawanoe tribe. . . . 'Twas not unpleasant."

Elizabeth felt the goose flesh creeping up on her arms. "You . . . you would . . . you're married. . . ."

"He is dead," said Diane. "I am weary of buffalo meat and sagamité."

"Diane!" Stiegel denounced her. He was furious. She would lie to a hitching-post, he thought.

"But how could you . . . give yourself. . . ." gasped Elizabeth.

"You talk as if Indians were not people!" cried Diane irritably. "They talk, they walk, they make their meals. They have children. They love their children. The children play. They breathe, like you. And the Indian chief, he is not afraid to love. He is tender to his squaw. He is strong!"

She looked straight into Stiegel's eyes, and they flinched.

"But Chepa Rose," Elizabeth blurted out, half credulous, "He said you ——"

"He found you at 'Les Deux Poissons'!" finished Stiegel, angrily.

"Oui. I have been many places."

"And now you have come home!" Stiegel commanded, his fingers gripping her arm tightly. He knew that if he let her go now he would never see her again.

"No, I will not stay!" insisted Diane, trying to jerk away from his grasp.

"Heinrich," began Elizabeth confusedly, "you will hurt ——"

But he didn't hear her. His eyes met Diane's with a mingled look of hurt and passion.

"Diane, please . . . you must listen to reason. . . ."

"Where is Herr Huber?"

"Gone to Germany ——"

"Oh!"

"You were his ward. Now you are my ward. . . ."

"This is your home now?"

"My home. Your home. . . ."

She leaned against the pillar of the porch, and smiled equivocally.

"I will stay—tonight. . . ." Diane compromised. She turned to Elizabeth, flashing her a smile.

Stiegel stalked into the hall, climbing the stairs, each leg a thousand-pound weight. He sank onto a chair in his bed-chamber. Soon Elizabeth confronted him, lighting the candle on his shaving table.

"She frightens me," she whispered. "She's so—so wild. I

couldn't live with her here in the house!"

"It is our duty. . . ." said Stiegel briefly. He pulled off his shirt and changed to fresh linen. His hands were trembling and he kept moving so that she would not notice it.

"But she's so strange. . . . Why is she so angry, and why has she come back if she must go at once?"

"She thinks you resent her. She sees you do not like her. You must be very genial tonight. Remember, this is the first thing I demand of you, Elizabeth!"

She bridled at his tone of voice.

"You are in love with her!" she accused him, remembering his talk with Chepa Rose.

"When Elizabeth died, I married you, not Diane!" he evaded.

"You did not know where she was!"

"I did not look for her ——"

He took Elizabeth in his arms and kissed her so passionately that she was staggered.

"I did not even look for her. . . ." he repeated.

Her heart bumped madly with a strange new thrill at his touch.

"I'll—I'll do what you wish, Heinrich."

"She knows how to nurse the babies; she can sew, and cook and spin; she will save you a thousand steps!"

And Stiegel turned to his dressing again.

Diane stayed that night, and the following night. She would go away soon, she thought. Life so close to Heinrich was agony, but it was so new again, and it was sweet agony which she would have the strength to battle for a while, at least.

Converted to civilization once more, she was still a strange contrast to her contemporaries. She wore her hair primly parted in the center now, and combed back, and she wore her old gold and yellow garments again, almost with insolence. She laughed annoyingly at Madame Ege's suggestion of using buttermilk on her skin. Madame Ege had a stern respect for Diane, whom she failed to intimidate.

She was with the Ege boys constantly. Boldly, they gathered wild honey from the trees, or disregarded snakes in mountain thickets, coming home with kettles of virgin huckleberries. They prowled about the woods once a month, gathering twigs and dried flower stalks for wash day. Diane, her strong fingers nimble with George's Bardow knife, fashioned whistles of chestnut or willow, and bows of hemlock. They speared fish excitedly, or sat sometimes by the brook in silence, with birds' claws for hooks. When her finger was gashed by a thorn, Diane laughed merrily at George's dismay, and bound it up tightly with green grass.

George, seventeen, was curiously stirred by this faunlike young woman. He had never known anyone like her. He became reticent, moody, gazing at her for long stretches at a time.

Diane was amazed at the orchestra which Stiegel had formed. During the summer, he rehearsed his men under the trees before twilight. Some of the men had never touched a musical instrument before he taught them. Most of them loved music instinctively, and attacked their instruments with innocent vandalism. The few more aesthetic workers were outblasted by their sanguine comrades. To Stiegel's sensitive ears the attempts were often hopeless.

Diane, leaning against an oak, loved the noise of it all. She watched Stiegel snap his baton in two (a tree branch), and wail like an exorcised dog.

" 'Twas not so bad, M'sieu; ere long they will be playing the score."

"Never!" exploded Stiegel.

"But why never? It has been played all over the world, n'est-ce pas?"

"It was lost," he said briefly, and picking up his violin, began to play.

"Heinrich, you do not write music now?" Diane asked, wrinkling her brow. "Oh, but then you cannot be happy!"

"Some day, when I have time, then I shall write again."

Diane clasped Jacob's hand tightly in her own; Stiegel's indifference to his music dismayed her. Music had been a part of him. . . .

"Come," she said, picking up the reluctant child. " 'Tis time for supper. We will play bird and worm."

One evening in fall, the entire family had gathered in the parlor for prayers. As they finished, Jerusha began to putter with trinkets in a large pocket, a foot square.

"What have you, Rushy?" asked Diane.

Elizabeth, who was knitting some initialed mittens for Jacob, dropped her work and examined the toy.

" 'Tis but an old pocket she has found today when I ransacked the attic," she announced.

" 'Tis. . . ." Diane dropped to her knees, and fingered the articles it contained. There was a tiny pocket-glass, or folding-mirror, and a comforter, or little box to hold as a hand-warmer in a muff. A strong-waters bottle, a little Bristol barrel-shaped flask, was of yellow and red flowers. Diane shook it, and the rum gurgled in its belly.

" 'Tis Lizzie's; 'tis your mother's," exclaimed Diane, gathering the things together while Jerusha let out an infuriated scream.

"Living jingo, Rushy, where have you dug up that?" Stiegel inquired.

Jerusha, still trembling with rage, pulled at the pocket, and Stiegel, giving her a smart rap on the shoulder, seized the needlework in his hands.

"The day we rode to the Fair, Heinrich, she lent it me because I had none, do you remember?" Diane was excited.

" 'Twas the night Shoe-Pegs-Meigs filched an oat bag from Stichler's sleigh for his horse, and found the next morning it was filled with shoe-pegs to be sold at market!"

Diane's eyes filled with mirth, and her laughter rippled briefly. Each holding onto an end of the pocket, they were simpering like lovers who recall a certain apple tree in May; the little audience watched them without moving. In the absurd silence, Diane turned and faced them, as if she seemed amazed that they existed here, these strangers.

"Had there been a will," said Stiegel so low that the others could not patch the words together, " 'twould have gone to you. Take it, Diane."

Elizabeth paused over her knitting, but her eyes did not meet those of her sister, Anna, who shrugged, as much as to say,

"And thee let this thing go on under thy very nose!"

The first break in the even tenor of the household came one evening when Elizabeth invited Stiegel to see the great star-patterned quilt which eight women had been working on all day in an upstairs room. It was the fourth day of a quilting-bee, and great strides had been made. Stiegel, in good humor, examined the embryo quilt in its frame, lauding Diane and Elizabeth, who were comparing the stitches of their neighbors.

"This patch, this heavy brocade of scarlet and gold thread, 'tis vaguely familiar," he pondered, taking a pinch of snuff.

" 'Tis only an old cloak, half ate by moths," replied Elizabeth, picking up a little cloud of threads which had gathered on the floor.

Stiegel snapped his snuff box to with furor.

"A cloak! Not the baronial cloak of my uncle! Slashed to patches. . . ."

Elizabeth shrank before his wrath.

" 'Twas half rotted," she whimpered.

"Rotted . . ." he raged. "I thought to wear it on my next journey! Hundreds of years old, to lie pinned to a star. . . . 'Twas for my son to wear after me. Pox me for a fool!"

Elizabeth, already sobbing from the insult and shock of this sudden invective, ran to her room.

Diane smiled slowly and blocked the doorway, watching the storm in Stiegel's face, and met the eyes as tumultuous and coldly blue as ocean waters in tempest.

"You are handsome, enraged, Heinrich. . . ."

14

For WEEKS Stiegel shoved the thought of his infatuation for Diane out of his mind. There was something hereditary in his resistance to temptation. He had come from a strain of phlegmatic, ethical people. He was like a stone in a tower, which the wind does not easily shake loose.

And he was always busy.

"Good morning, Diane," he said for weeks, without a glance. In the evening he mumbled "Good night, Diane," tonelessly.

Diane coaxed again to help him with designs for the stoves, but Stiegel was firm. He had engaged an artist now who did most of the technical work. Stiegel was miserable, but he had never definitely admitted the fact to himself. He was in constant fear that Diane would run away, for he knew now that her love was an all-absorbing thing. And he knew that his seeming indifference crushed her. He did not let himself look into the future. He worked as hard as it was humanly possible for him to do. Exhaustion was a sedative.

But one evening he came upon Diane alone in the back parlor. She was waiting for Robert Klingerman to come for her for a sleigh ride, and Elizabeth was putting the children to bed.

Diane picked up some toys which Jerusha had left before the fireplace. She was wearing one of the new outfits which Stiegel had asked Elizabeth to buy for her, a scarlet gown which matched the fur-lined capuchin she had slung over a chair. Her lips were scarlet too, in sharp contrast to her dark skin, and she smiled at him softly.

"Diane," he said simply, taken unawares, "you're . . . lovely."

"I never thought how I looked, until I first came here," she replied. "Then when I saw you, Heinrich—I wanted you to think I was lovely!"

He straightened a Dresden figure on the mantel.

"You are still afraid of me, Heinrich."

"I am afraid you will go ——"

"I try to go . . . but if I could never see you, Heinrich!"

"Promise me you will not run away again," he said quickly, for he heard Mrs. Ege's heavy tread on the stairs.

"How can I know what I will do?" cried Diane half under her breath. "I am human. You have Elizabeth. . . . I have no one. . . ."

"You will find someone ——"

"Non, non, non!"

"You will forget me."

"Non!" Diane clipped the word off sharply as Mrs. Ege entered the room.

Mrs. Ege raised her black eyebrows menacingly. "Thee must not wrangle, my dears!" she said warily.

Later in the evening, she recalled the scene to Elizabeth.

"Thee must not drink so much tea in Brickerville that thou'rt blinded," she intimated.

"Blinded?"

"Aye, Diane is beautiful—and Heinrich is just another man!"

"Do you infer . . ." spluttered Elizabeth.

"I infer that she's well aware of his charm!"

"'Tis only natural," Elizabeth expostulated. "A barmaid out of the woods; but she means nothing to Heinrich."

Mrs. Ege shrugged tantalizingly.

"He did not even look for her when Elizabeth died!" Elizabeth thought of the passion Stiegel had put into his denouncement the night that Diane returned; and the kiss with which he had sealed his words.

"Her eyes grow very large and black," mused Mrs. Ege irrelevantly.

All that night Stiegel thought of Diane, her eyes radiant as they looked up at him. He had wanted to go on the sleigh-ride with her, had been snappy to Robert Klingerman when he came into the hall. If he did not love her—and he thought of love as some fine, spiritual experience he had always craved and never known—why was it that she forever filled his thoughts? Hadn't he had enough of lust in his life? It was incredible that a man of his stamina and standing should give vent to these adulterous thoughts, should constantly be possessing the girl in his mind! Was it that he might have loved her, if only they had been given their chance? Was it possible that they might have found together the poignant joy which he knew could exist between a man and a woman? Why must he feel capable of this thing, and be denied it, forever? He was no schoolboy. He was thirty-two, and life should be at its fullest, he thought bitterly. He had known when he made her stay with them that soon he would want her again as hungrily as he had wanted her before she ran away. That it would only be a matter of time after watching her scarlet lips and her lithe brown body. And he had pretended it was duty!

Why couldn't he be honest with himself? Where would the thing end?

He watched Elizabeth as she mended socks, and the intensity of his gaze made her look up at him, and smile, a little doubtfully. He'd better come to his senses. He was married, and there were children who must depend on him and look up to him! It was only natural Diane should rouse him to passion—must rouse any man to passion, with her flaming beauty. He would go off to Philadelphia at once, until this fever had passed away, and when he returned . . . well, perhaps he would be able to think more clearly. To give in to himself and Diane would mean stark tragedy for them all. It was too naïve to believe that he could carry on an affair with her and not have his madness felt in the very atmosphere of the house. It would be better by far to take some common whore on the streets of Philadelphia, to glut himself with this degrading passion and come home clean, in mind at least, to Elizabeth.

"You are having trouble?" asked Elizabeth, coming over to him, and dropping on a stool at his side.

"Yes."

"That foreman ———"

" 'Tis not the foreman," he said, stroking her hand. "I must go to Philadelphia to open a new account of fire-backs."

"But cannot you wait till word comes that the coach is arrived in the city?"

" 'Tis well on the water by now, I'm sure. I shall wait for it in Philadelphia, and bring it home!"

"How exciting it will be! The grandest coach in the whole of the country!" cried Elizabeth.

The second day following, Stiegel left in a light snow-fall for Philadelphia. He found the city in an uproar. Pamphlets fluttered around on inn tables and shop cases, and newspapers were going rabidly colonial. Nothing was talked of but the injustice of the new taxes. The high tension of the town stimulated him. He unpacked his clothes at the Coach and Horses with keen anticipation. This was what he'd needed. A little mental spur. Why, in a fortnight he'd have found his equilibrium again!

As he lifted his stocks from his portmantua, something fell, and he picked up from the bed the little glass violin which Minnie's father had once made for him in Cologne. He chuckled, remembering that Jerusha had been playing around him as he and Cyrus had packed.

He fingered the little piece in warm remembrance of his salad days. The glass factory had always fascinated him. The men had seemed to twist and turn the molten glass and shape it with magic.

Minnie had wanted him to become a glass-blower like her father. It would have been fun, thought Stiegel, turning the violin over and over in his hands. The fine threads of glass which had been the strings had long been broken, and one of the little brown tuning pegs was chipped. Stiegel stood the violin beside his brushes on the highboy; it was pleasant having the little violin here with him in this strange inn room. Glass, thought Stiegel, has a mysterious, feminine charm.

He was invited that night to have dinner with Alexander Stedman at his home. The house had slouched into melancholia. Whatever needed polish was a little dull; even the mirrors were cloudy, as if they refused to reflect an iota of the radiance and bustle of Lucy's short reign. The colored, pock-marked girl who had ushered the two unfortunate women out of life was now expanded into a robust, slovenly maid of all work. She dominated her master with a lazy glance or word, and with senescent lack of resistance he obeyed the roll of her blurry dog eyes. It did not occur to him to curb her. He had paid a neat sum for her when he purchased her from a Newlander, and if his cornstarch

pudding was lumpy, he sighed that he was irremediably
bound by Fate.

The two men lingered over their wine, debating the poli
cies of the day.

Stedman, a valiant Tory, toyed with a lusterless silver
spoon.

"But how *can* the mother country protect us with troops
if there be no wherewithal?" he argued.

"They give us protection of body, not of soul, sir," de
fied Stiegel, thumping the gray damask with his fist.

"The soul lies in the body!"

"But 'tis an outrage to tax us without representation."

"The colonies are a stubborn lot of children, Stiegel, who
rebel at the natural counsel of a parent."

" 'Tis for us to decide the sum we can afford. Protection
fooh! We pay for the protection of England herself. 'Tis
only for her own interest she guards us so careful. Frighted
that our bounty may fall into the hands of her enemy, la
France!"

"You have had your chance to defend yourself. There is
not a noddle amongst you knows how but Franklin, and
you disregard his policy."

"But if only duty on English goods was not so exorbi
tant," Stiegel went on, touching the sore spot of the day.

"The rich can pay the price; the poor do not know the
difference in quality between English and American
goods."

"England had better beware," warned Stiegel. "With a
little practice America will out-wit her in all her manufac
tures."

"Fooh! Impossible; how could some little upstart in
America produce a Bristol punch bowl of that quality?"
asked Alexander Stedman, pointing to a dusty glass bowl
on the buffet.

"I could!" cried Stiegel, confident with wine. "It takes

a love of beauty,—that's what it takes. Caspar Wistar had it. And now that he's dead his love of beauty lives on in his Wistar ware! Stiegel ware. I'm going to make glass. I've always wanted to make glass, since I was a boy!"

"You jest, of course."

"Nay, I've never been more serious. Think on it—blues, reds, amethyst. . . ."

" 'Tis scarce the time to go venturing in glass," said Alexander Stedman, drily, and he motioned the maid not to give Stiegel any more wine.

"Nay, 'tis the very time. What better moment to give American glass to Americans than the hour when the colonies spurn all products from Britain? The pillories are bursting with the desperadoes who would thrust English ware down our throats. Pox me, the Glass House will flourish like paper over fire, or I do not call myself Henry William Stiegel!"

And the next morning, as Stiegel wakened and his eyes lighted on the violin, he thought, "There will be no harm in the trying! Another fortune in glass. . . ."

The idea grew into vast proportions, and Stiegel was avid to get the business started. The fact that Alexander Stedman had tried to dissuade him held no weight. Stedman had turned sour on life in general, thought Stiegel, and then with their difference of political opinion and Stiegel's marrying so soon after Lucy's death, there was bound to be a strained feeling between them.

In glass he would find beauty; with glass he could create again! He would throw all his passion into a glass factory, and he would be able to live in the same house with Diane, at peace with himself once more. If only the coach would come, he would have no qualms now about returning home.

He had enough business to keep him pleasantly occupied. The supply of shoes in the General Store of the

Furnace was depleted of large sizes, and the "purges" and "vomits" on its medicine shelf were running low. Her Huber's Bordeaux claret was gone; in fact, the whole wine cellar needed padding. And the workmen were clamoring for more beer and rum. There were trenchers to be bought for the new colliers' huts, and lists of purchases to be made for Elizabeth, varying from buttons to spice. The black smith at the Furnace, who had so skillfully made axes chains, hoes, locks, and all manner of necessities, had died the month before of lockjaw, and Stiegel wanted to inter view some young indentured immigrants with experience from Germany.

He succumbed to the gayety of the winter season, and went about with Robert Morris everywhere. The As semblies, balls, dinners and skating parties kept his mind away from home and Diane. He felt invigorated in the frosty air; sometimes they roasted a whole ox over a blanket of sand on the thick ice of the Delaware, or stood about red-nosed, clapping their hands, and waited for the horses to be off in a race down the river.

Sometimes, too, he and Morris skated alone under the six little bridges of Dick Creek—and as usual did not talk politics or of women, but of land. Now the subject seemed dull to Stiegel, and his imagination wandered off to glass while Robert expatiated on the latest real estate bargains Stiegel did not mention either to Robert Morris or the Sted mans that he was visiting wholesale glass houses, making contacts with merchants, and obtaining all the information possible on the problems of starting the glass business.

At last, after five weeks, Stiegel received word from the wharf that his coach had arrived on the "Myrtilla." He had engaged a coachman and ordered for him the finest livery And he left word with the man that the coach must call for him no matter where he was, as soon as the coach and horses and coachman were once a unit.

At the time, coaches were a rarity in Philadelphia. The Chief Justice and the widows Martin and Lawrence were the only ones who owned them. Thomas Willing and another man owned landaus. There were some eighteen chariots scattered among the élite, and not more than a dozen chairs. Stiegel thought with great elation of the place he held in the social world of the new country.

One Sunday morning in March Stiegel was attracted by an uproar when he ventured from church after the service. He thought at first, startled, that a new English officer had been cornered. Crowds of people were milling about in the street, stamping their feet upon the pavement to keep warm. They jostled and elbowed as the congregation moved out slowly with morning greetings. They hemmed in the worshippers. There were joiners, and tanners, mantua-makers, and fan-menders. There were little girls with cloaks thrown hastily about their shoulders, business potentates with gold-headed canes, and boys with sleds. There were débutantes, at whom Stiegel smiled benevolently, and who whispered to one another, "I have danced a minuet with him."

His coach was there, in the middle of this throng of people, waiting to carry him off. For a fraction of a second Stiegel halted, disconcerted. He had scarcely counted on such notoriety. As he brushed his way to the coach door he had a feeling that people sidled close enough to him so that their garments touched his. He was at once abashed and flattered and excited as the door clapped to.

His coachman, in scarlet and buff livery, came to life and lashed his whip with silvery ease, guiding the four bay horses from Virginia as if he were entirely oblivious of their immaculate pacing and long switch tails. Indeed, he seemed to hold his reins as Pope Pius his prayer book, his eyes on the glistening harness, his devotion to his cause supreme.

The coach was the color of thick fresh cream, globular and capacious. So embellished were the panels with muscular-limbed cupids and festoons of flowers that one half expected to see the exquisite little face of Madame Pompadour peeping out from under the blue shutters. The cream wheels with their gilded carving swirled the Baron over the partly frozen puddles.

Stiegel's heart pounded with the joy of possession. A pity his coach was only taking him back to the inn for a dinner of rack of lamb.

A weather prophet might have told Stiegel not to attempt a journey now to Brickerville, but the only oracle was a dull, glowering heaven. He started the trip home with a good deal of pomp. The acquisition of the coach was a definite step in his ladder of success. He was a rich man and he wanted people to know it.

The second day of the journey there was a light snowfall and the coachman continued "fanning" the horses. In the afternoon the clouds dropped as low as the tree tops, and flung into their faces a revelry of snow. The coachman's virgin costume of crimson and buff was covered with an oilskin cape; the horses' ears were peaks of white, and the precocious cupids, blanketed with a thin sleet, froze in unconscious action.

Stiegel, a ball of bearskin in a corner of the coach, sipped drams from a bottle. He had ventured once or twice to raise a shutter and give orders to his man, but a merry gale slapped him in the face. The road was rutty and hard, in spite of the snow, and even among his velvet cushions and new springs he was bounced into an irascible mood. The storm was frisky, and the vehicle lurched like a drunkard.

Toward dusk they followed a Conestoga wagon for a while. Stiegel hung out of his coach to look at the gay circus accoutrements. It was painted bright blue, with side

boards of vivid red, its great calash bonnet a dazzling white.
A bell-team of seven horses jingled before it, flaunting ends
of colored ribbons as gaudy as a handful of confetti. But
soon the phenomenon had tinkled out of sight.

It was the hour of day which is trebled in length by
hunger, stiffness and mental fatigue. The darkness came
early with the intensity of the storm. It seemed to Stiegel
that all the joy of life was condensed in a glimpse of roaring fire, or even a steaming dish of tripe which he ordinarily
scorned.

Now that the novelty of the coach had worn off, and no
one was near to admire it, he felt incensed at the weather
and essentially bored. It was strange, he thought, the new
feeling of self-assurance the coach had given him. A feeling
of power. How ecstatic Elizabeth would be with the coach!
She had come to him just before he left, tears in her eyes,
because Mrs. Eggleston had not invited her to her last
quilting.

"But you do not like to drink tea from a cracked cup!"
he had teased her.

Well, he didn't like to see Elizabeth unhappy over these
things. It was a reflection on him too that she had been
snubbed.

He was excited at the thought of seeing the family after
all these weeks. He had been right about going away.
Distance was a great healer of passion. And he must see
that Diane made a good marriage. With Diane married and
the new glass business to occupy his mind, there would be
no vestige of desire for her. He would see her tomorrow.
He would prove to himself that these things were true.

"I loathe her; she has no morals," he said under his
breath, and took another dram.

The coach, as if it had stumbled upon a boulder, swayed
momentarily on two wheels, and skidded suddenly to a
stop. Stiegel was in the act of taking snuff. He was hurled

onto the floor, with a shower of tobacco in his face. The door beside him was thrust roughly open and a voice bellowed, "Stand and deliver."

He rolled out into the storm, blinded with the onrush of snow and the sting of snuff in his eyes.

In the blur there might have been a dozen thieves—or only one. His pockets were being raped in a most professional manner, and he heard the blustering of the irate coachman. He was bandied about like a hornet's nest in the wind, his muff seized from his hands, his cape wrenched from his shoulders. He even felt the buttons being zipped from his coat—gold they were—and the silver buckles severed from his shoes. It was all as fast as a whisk of the tempest; he had a blemished glimpse of a loo-mask with eyes shining through it—and the next moment, bereft of any portable valuables, he found himself shivering on the step of the coach, the flakes pelting him in the surly dusk.

That he should be so debased enraged him more than the actual loss of his properties. He crawled into the coach like a mutilated tortoise pulling in its neck. Then he heard angry voices—the coachman muttering curses. He stuck his head out of the window, his eyes watering and smarting. He could barely discern two figures on horseback unhitching his thoroughbred bays. Lunging out into the snow, he remonstrated, and met the gleam of a gun before his nose. The coachman had been reminded with the butt of it that his opinion didn't count, and was staggering into consciousness again.

They stood there, the two of them, paralyzed by the speed of the highwaymen, for the latter were now two specks of black melting into a haze of blue-white. The two strange horses which were left champed about excitedly. They were hungry, scraggly-looking black mares, frightened at their desertion.

The roads had become black in a moonless night, and the coachman harnessed the horses and ploughed through the drifts, guessing boldly at the road. It was only with great perseverance that they managed to reach a drover's inn long after dinner. The Conestoga wagon was under the shed.

Stiegel dismounted from his dishonored coach, infuriated and bedraggled.

"I want a room," he told the innkeeper sharply.

The man shook his head. "We be chuck full. Ye can share a bed with the last drover as come in. The others be full."

Stiegel was inflamed. He had had to share a bed with a strange gentleman more than once, but to sleep with some stinking drover!

He was very tired. He nodded assent.

He took the dip which the innkeeper gave him and went in to the draughty little room. A great hulk of a man filled the bed, and his trappings were strewn about the chair and floor. He snored loudly, with fancy little variations.

Stiegel undressed, looking about him with great distaste. The stale smoke of a stogey cigar filled the air, and Stiegel gingerly picked it up, turning it over curiously in his hands. Partly smoked, it was still almost a foot long. On the lowboy was a wallet of bread, and a package of cheese and jerked bear's meat which smelled strong and putrid. Stiegel cursed his luck, as he blew out his candle and crept in beside the caravan driver. There was a small sliver of space for him to sleep in, and he gave the driver a few kicks with his stockinged toes. The man lurched, half crushing the breath out of him.

The room was icy. Stiegel hated admitting to himself that the sweaty body heat of the man was welcome.

He lay there wretched; it was unbelievable that his journey could come to such an ignominious ending. He might be forced to remain here at the inn for several days until he could take roads freshly broken out by some farmer's oxen. He thought a little shamedly of the triumphal entry to Brickerville he had been planning, and how an ordinary thing like snow had defeated him.

He had deliberately meant to show off, and he had been thinking that he would be very magnificent in the eyes of Diane. He had supposed he would see her again tomorrow. Now that he knew it might be several days before he reached home he felt he could never endure the long restless, endless hours here before the fire. How scrupulous he was, how Christian. How blandly he had been able to lie to himself about his infatuation for her, when he could not see her. And now that the snow had snatched her away from him. . . . She was still an integral part of his life, like his breath, he thought strangely.

It would be best to leave the coach at the inn to be bathed and stabled till after the thaw! How disappointed Elizabeth would be!

And Diane. How she would laugh. "But it is so *fun*-ny!" she would exclaim. "The great Baron . . . spilled by bad men into the snow!"

Damn her!

15

WHEN STIEGEL announced to his family that he was going to manufacture glass, there was general enthusiasm.

" 'Twould be perfect pouring cream from a garnet pitcher," Elizabeth cried, "and will you make me a cornflower perfume bottle for my glove?"

"You are a little beyond me! Practical things—green glass bottles, my dear, for a start."

Stiegel turned to Diane. "Now you shall have to help me again. I shall need you to design punch bowls and plates."

Her eyes lighted, but she did not answer.

"You do not like my new business," he accused her.

"But your music!" she said softly.

"I must keep you all in the kick of fashion," he laughed, but he was annoyed. Of course in these last years he hadn't been true to himself, to the sanguine young German boy who had come over on the "Nancy." He couldn't compose music when he wasn't happy—he wanted to tell her that. He wanted to pour out his heart to her, to tell her that he had gone away to forget her, and had failed. And that if he seemed indifferent and cold it was because it helped him a little to keep his balance.

He went into the new project of glass-making with all the vigor of which he was capable. Before two weeks had passed the little Glass House was going up, not far from the furnace along the creek. It was to be a large room, square and lofty, with an earthen floor, and a circular furnace in the center. Adjoining was a smaller room where his furnace-pots would be made. As it often took from one to two years to make a pot, Stiegel had ordered a crucible of English Stourbridge clay from Philadelphia to begin his experiments.

Silica for the glass came from Juniata County, and other ingredients arrived from various sources—soda, red lead, potash, saltpeter and manganese. Although he did not need all of these at first, he would want to experiment with finer things when the bottles were satisfactory.

For a while he would produce nothing but window panes and bottles. There was a large demand for both in the colonies—for bull's-eye window glass and transoms, and bottles ranging from pint to gallon sizes.

Stiegel advertised for only three glass-workers, a "gatherer," a "blower," and a man to handle the pontil rod. For he had decided on John Dickinson's advice to begin the business modestly with one fire-pot and one "chair" or crew.

Michael spent his entire time giving moral support to the erection of the Glass House, coming to meals with detailed reports of its growth, and recounting how he had terrified the carpenter by hiding in the ash-pit.

"I'm going to be a glass-blower!" he told them with enthusiasm. "Look, I've got lots of wind!" And he blew his cheeks into a round red ball.

"I thought thee wanted to be a collier," Anna Ege reminded him.

"Ah, what would Chepa Rose say!" teased Diane, whereupon Michael looked woefully puzzled and everyone laughed at him.

At the first tinge of autumn glass-blowing was begun. For a week or more the glass-blowers had been settled at the Furnace, cleaning out the Glass House and arranging their tools. The new furnace was stoked with great fanfare, the pot was charged with its mixed materials on Friday, and by Monday morning the word was relayed by the workmen via Michael to the excited household that the "batch" was red-hot and ready for blowing.

"Hurry, hurry!" shrieked Michael. "They're ready!"

And he ran back and forth from Glass House to mansion a dozen times trying to get the family collected for the ceremony of blowing the first bottle. Finally he had them corralled, and they huddled into a laughing group, flushed with expectancy and the stifling heat.

Stiegel watched the process with the thrill of a new father.

It was fascinating. Benjamin Misky skillfully inserted the heated end of his blow-pipe into the glowing clay pot, twisting the stem like taffy candy until it was covered with a lump of cooling metal. Then he rolled the parison on the marver until it had the long shape of a bottle.

"Me too, me too!" cried Jacob, bouncing in Elizabeth's arms, and trying to lurch toward the man.

Michael squealed. Christian Waltz, with all the solemnity of the Pied Piper of Hamelin, was blowing now into the ball of glass, creating an ethereal bubble of fire.

"His pipe is so long!" Michael shouted, his eyes following the pendulum greedily as it swung from side to side. "*Look!*" as it rotated rapidly.

"Shut thy mouth and watch!" cautioned his mother, but he continued to jump up and down.

Barbara clung timidly to Diane's skirts as Christian

Waltz leaped to the chair, his cheeks like a balloon, the pipe hanging down with its dangling bulb.

"I shall coax Heinrich for a new punch bowl for the holidays," whispered Elizabeth to her sister.

"Whew!" returned Anna, mopping her face, "I am all asweat."

Now Christian Waltz held his bulb high in the air, while the third worker thrust his long pontil rod into the blown end of the bubble, rolling it like dough on the long chair arm, and then deftly removed the blow-pipe. There was the quick snipping of shears, shaping and cutting the glass.

Then the first green bottle gleamed clear in the firelight, and there was a din of shouting and applause.

Diane's eyes never left Stiegel. Standing motionless, with his arms crossed, his face was filled with the passion she had been struggling to rouse in him for years.

The glass was a beautiful new mistress who had come between them.

Stiegel had long dreamed of creating a town that would be all his own, and calling it Manheim for his beloved Manheim in Germany. It would be a little model of propriety, and he would fashion it after the plans of the old Manheim, plans which had lain in his trunk all these years, not quite forgotten. It would be an ideal place for the Glass House, he thought. The property he had in mind was about eight miles away, a lovely little plateau surrounded by woodland, and adjacent to thousands of acres owned by the Stedmans. Thomas Lincoln of Lancaster would be the very man to survey for him.

It was only natural too, that Stiegel should build himself a mansion within the new demesne. The image of it had long inflamed his imagination. He scribbled plans at the desk, while the others went about the ordinary job of living.

He found that he was contented only so long as he was too busy to think, and he threw himself into his new plans with almost inhuman energy. He had built for himself a place of envy in the community. The Furnace was prolific in returns, exceeding his most ardent hopes. Charming Forge was leaping to growth as unconsciously as a frolicking puppy, and by early winter one could hardly call the glass-making business an experiment any longer. He was surrounded with luxury and deference. And yet he was always driven onward toward greater accomplishments, toward new satisfactions.

In the early spring the Stiegel household, as resilient as a rubber ball, added another member to its circle.

Stiegel came upon Diane one day as she was pulling weeds from her yellow garden. It was seldom that he saw her alone. He stopped to watch her, and she pushed back a wisp of hair with muddy fingers.

"My brother Anthony comes in a fortnight to run the Glass House. He is three and twenty. You will like him, Diane."

Diane halted, gazing up at Stiegel despairingly. "I shall loathe him!" she promised. He was trying to dispose of her! She still clung to the edges of his conscience!

At night she drifted into thought of Stiegel before she slept as regularly as a pious woman prays. "I am floating about like a lily plant in a pond," she reflected, "and one day I shall take root." She thought of him separate from social bondage, separate from conventions. Some time he must realize that he formed her entire world—that other attachments were minor and transient. He seemed almost to disregard her in his complicated routine. They were all so many particles of dust in the hurricane of his ambition. Sometimes she became almost frantic with the senseless drifting of her life, the inevitable household tasks, the stentorian Mrs. Ege. She was not unduly jealous of Elizabeth, for Stiegel's wife seemed no more essential to him than a capable automaton. He was concerned only with expansion, expansion in all he did.

As Diane and Anthony first met Stiegel watched them with a feeling of mingled curiosity and jealousy. Anthony would fall in love with Diane, of course. Diane might fall in love with Anthony.

Diane rested her eyes on the newcomer with a faint tinge of scorn. Anthony had heard of Diane for years, of her wit and beauty. He mustered courage to end the little bow he made with a sweep, and backed against a small table, so that its bric-à-brac shivered and clattered. Diane laughed, and he flushed a dark red.

Diane was true to her promise. She did not like Anthony, though he was not unlike Stiegel in feature and physique. He was pale, tall and aristocratic. But he lacked poise, and when Stiegel was near he became awkward and silent. Diane had an instinctive distaste for the daunted, and imposed upon him shamefully. She beat him at backgammon and cribbage. And she was very gay with him, drawing him out of his shyness and then taunting him. She treated all her lovers with gayety and so slight a tinge of scorn that they thought it was repressed emotion. It was inevitable that Anthony should worship her with a painful, premeditated devotion.

As the weeks went on and he took the management of the glass-works conscientiously in charge he began to fit quietly and unobtrusively into the household routine. He went off into corners and read, or hobnobbed with the boys.

George Ege, almost six feet tall at eighteen, inherited Diane's antipathy for the newcomer, but with obvious masculine reason. He was inordinately jealous. He begrudged Anthony the very contempt Diane gave him, so well cloaked was it with effulgent wit. His fingers lingered on her arm as he held thorny branches high for her in the forest paths. His eyes coveted her with the crudity of half-man, half-boy; he imitated the manners of his uncle, and practiced their inimitable grace. He grew moony-eyed when her eyes lingered quizzically on the lips of some gallant, and became infantile and pouty when Stiegel saw this and sent him to the mill to have cocoanuts ground into chocolate. George was in need of a change, Stiegel remarked one day, and they must think of sending him off to college—Yale, the New Jersey College at Princeton, or any of the gentleman's schools he preferred.

But when Martin Grenier, one of the new glass-blowers, came to Elizabeth Furnace, Diane at last met her equal.

He first saw her as she swung the top-heavy Jacob over a patch of herbs, plopping him onto a mat of moss. She leaned against the tree and breathed quick laughter with the exertion.

Martin Grenier had been at Elizabeth Furnace only a day. He had left his workbench for a moment, blinded with the white shimmering heat of the melting pots. A short, swarthy Frenchman, he wore loose trousers, slippers, and a tight-fitting woolen shirt. Swinging his pucellas in his hand, he stared at the two, and he felt a sudden lurch of his senses as Diane saw him and smiled. He hopped disrespectfully over a hedge and approached her. He had never seen Mistress Stiegel and this might be she. Like Diane, he was not afraid to make an occasion.

"Mistress Stiegel," he murmured half questioningly, with a deep bow.

She looked at him curiously. He was delightfully handsome, except for a very slight cast in one eye.

"Non, non, non; Diane."

His smile flashed suddenly at his discovery. "Ah, Mademoiselle, vous êtes française tambien."

"French, Indian, American—pot-pourri."

He sat boldly down on the ground beside her. They talked until Anthony was standing above them.

"He dare not dismiss me," informed Grenier with a swing of the tongs at Anthony. "I was the best glass-blower at Wistarberg."

"Then you take unfair advantage," retorted Anthony, as the man leaped over the bushes again with agility, and disappeared without looking back. He turned to Diane.

"Uncivil," he apostrophized.

There had been something almost insulting in the possessiveness of Grenier's last glance at Diane. Yet her eyes lingered on the doorway of the Glass House which had swallowed the Frenchman, and they were amused, roused.

She turned on Anthony with quick comparison. The antithesis of Grenier; a tiger and a shy, timid buck. They sickened her, suddenly, the amorous lot of them. She turned and walked away from him, leaving Jacob on the moss pursuing an ant. She wanted Stiegel. Wanted him with all the ardor of starving years. She fled into the rose garden, and Anthony, with the blind indiscretion of a man in love, thought this an invitation, and followed her.

"Diane, you must have seen. . . ." He touched her shoulder with great, diffident fingers.

The touch was ravishment, with Stiegel in her heart and mind.

She pushed him from her, her eyes branding him with abhorrence.

"I hate you, Anthony Stiegel!"

In another week, Grenier was making love to Diane, too. She played with him as a cat with a mouse; she languished in his arms, charmed by the fieriness of his passion, and plagued him with hope. She met him secretly in the evenings, and closing her eyes, pretended that his lips were Stiegel's, finding the dream painful and unreal. He wanted to marry her at once, before he left the Glass House in

April for the summer vacation. She laughed at him.

"Sacrebleu!" she exclaimed. "But you are afire like the furnace!"

And yet when he left, she missed him. He was a beautiful lover, she thought, and somehow so much like herself that she did not really mind his love-making. If I do not watch out, she thought, he is going to give me trouble. He feels for me what I feel for Heinrich. Some day we will claw one another to pieces!

It was toward the end of the summer that Jerusha took ill, and that tragedy stalked through Elizabeth Furnace again.

Stiegel himself had just recovered from an attack of influenza. He had worked at high tension through the entire summer, and he was thin and irritable. When Jerusha hung her head one day and said she did not feel well, she was bundled to bed and treated for influenza too.

Diane stayed with her constantly, for the child began to toss about with fever. Jerusha was her favorite of the children. She had dark, curling hair and impish brown eyes, and nothing of Elizabeth Huber about her.

It was shortly before noon the second day that the family became alarmed. Stiegel had just come in from the barns and was pouring water in his washbasin when he heard Diane's voice cry out in fear.

"Heinrich—Heinrich!"

He ran into Jerusha's darkened room, and Elizabeth, coming up the stairs, hurriedly followed him.

"Something's wrong!" cried Diane, leaning over the child who jerked and twisted with convulsions.

"Tell Cyrus to get the doctor!" Stiegel said briefly, his hand trembling as he touched the hot face of Jerusha.

Elizabeth and Diane looked challengingly at one another. Ever since Diane's coming, Elizabeth felt that the children loved Diane more than herself.

"You go! When a child is sick she wants her mother!" Elizabeth said quickly.

"Bête," exclaimed Diane under her breath, and flew down to find Cyrus.

Stiegel went back to his room, and sank into a chair. His fear was so intense that he dared not even express it to himself. His mind was jumbled with visions of Lucy, her fever, convulsions, and the sores that must have been one festering whole when she died. He remembered the warm musk and candlelight of the Assembly . . . Lucy lagging in his arms. But the child could not have the pox, he thought. This was influenza. She was merely tossing about because the fever was high. . . .

When they were called to dinner Diane said she would stay with Jerusha till the doctor came. Elizabeth weakly demurred. She had stood her ground before, and now it was fitting that Diane should stay with the sick child, and that she, Elizabeth, should eat the food while it was hot.

"Diane, you must not be in the room with Jerusha," Stiegel whispered to her. "I shall have Anne come till the doctor ——"

"But why, M'sieu? If she should wake and find me gone ——"

"Diane, do not question me! Today you must do as I say!"

She cocked her head.

"She does not like Anne!" she insisted, and laid a cool hand on Jerusha's forehead.

But Cyrus was unable to get the doctor, who was away on a fishing trip. For two days the household was frantic. Jerusha's fever was worse, and she began to call out in her delirium. Stiegel had forbidden anyone but Anne to enter Jerusha's room. It was not until Sunday morning that the doctor arrived. Stiegel was reading from the German Bible at breakfast.

The rest of the family, unmindful of the agony which Stiegel had been enduring the past two days, listened with accustomed calm. Diane, pulling the petals absent-mindedly from a calendula, thought of the rash Anne had noted on Jerusha's forehead. And Diane felt restless at the slow droning of Stiegel's words. He went off like touch-wood, she thought. He had been bled too much. And he was thin. She watched his fingers, as they toyed with the corner of the page; how beautiful they were, she thought, how strong and beautiful!

Michael, with typical male lack of concentration, squirmed, fed pie to the dog, and at last pulled surreptitiously from his pocket a boat which he began to whittle under the table.

Stiegel looked up and saw the spasmodic motion of Michael's bent shoulders. The boy smiled beatifically at the deep furrows of his mother's forehead.

With a scowl, a foreboding hesitation, Stiegel rose. "Michael!" he thundered. Then with a condemning finger he flipped the pages of the Bible and read the first innocent verse his finger touched:

"Cast thy bread upon the waters; for thou shalt find it after many days!"

"Michael Ege, you will learn to fear the word of God," said Stiegel, his voice worn. "You are chased from our sight for the day. You who put a boat before God, you ——"

His eyes lifted to those of the doctor, who stood in the doorway of the adjoining parlor, and whom Cyrus had shown upstairs earlier, not wanting to interrupt the family service.

"The pox," said the doctor, laconically. "No time to waste."

Stiegel stood transfixed.

"Smallpox!" screamed Elizabeth.

Mrs. Ege's face set into stern ridges, and George backed

against the buffet, horror-stricken, chewing at his nails.

"Jacob, my Jacob . . ." cried Elizabeth, wringing her hands, unmindful of the teacup she had sent splashing to the floor. "Jacob will get it. . . . We will all get it. . . . We will die. . . ."

"Who will nurse her?" asked the doctor, of Stiegel. "Her mother?"

"We will get someone from the village . . ." broke in Elizabeth wildly. "The Wenrichs' nigger . . . she's had it. . . ."

Diane leaped to her feet, tossing Elizabeth's words back at her with a sort of fiendish joy. "When a child is sick, *she wants her mother!*"

"But I am not her mother . . ." gasped Elizabeth, her face a milky white. "I am *Jacob's* mother. . . ."

There was a brief, electric silence.

"We must not endanger the family," the doctor ordered. "The child must be moved at once to one of the outbuildings ——"

Diane tossed her calendula onto the table, and Stiegel, terrified, gripped her arm so that she could not leave the room.

"Where are you going?"

"I am going to carry Jerusha out of the house."

"You've lost your mind!"

"I'm going to nurse her."

"Oh God no, Diane!"

She yanked away from him, her sleeve ripping with a snort, and the family sat paralyzed, watching the drama which was being played before them.

"You love Jerusha!" cried Diane. "I can save her!"

"But *you*," groaned Stiegel. "Oh God, I beg of you, Diane ——"

"I am not afraid!" she retorted, straightening. Then softening at the sight of his anguish, she touched his sleeve.

"I am not afraid, Heinrich," she repeated softly. "But Jerusha, she is so little . . . she will be afraid. . . ."

Unable to talk, he seized her hand, and the tears dropped on her fingers as he kissed them. Diane would do as she wanted to do, he knew.

"Anyone," he thought crazily, "anyone but Diane. . . ."

He fell into his chair again, weeping freely into his hands; for a moment there was silence.

The doctor laid his hand on Stiegel's back, knowing the living death of the days ahead, and wishing that in some way he might give him strength.

Elizabeth's sobs were the only sound, until two scrapping robins skirmished about the leaves of the nearest tree.

Michael's eyes followed them enviously from branch to branch.

"Uncle Heinrich . . ." he said in a small, humble voice. "Did you chase me to my room—or may I go down to the sawmill, if I keep out of sight?"

16

URING THE NEXT few weeks the household was in
a state of utter chaos. Jerusha was moved down to the cottage of one of the colliers who lived across the stream, and Diane entombed herself with the little girl. The protests of the family were of no avail, and at last the doctor had said, a little brusquely, glancing at Elizabeth, "Aye, Stiegel, but *someone* must nurse the child!"

When a ghastly fortnight had passed, it was fairly certain that no one in the household would be ill. Jerusha had only a modified case of the smallpox. She would recover easily, the doctor said, with little, if any, pitting.

Stiegel went off by himself for long walks or rides in the woods. Jerusha would be well, but Diane's safety was no more certain than at the onset of the dread disease. Every exhausting moment she spent with the child she was more liable to succumb. Half a dozen times a day he stopped at the cottage, looking into the square-paned windows and terrified that he would see a rash spreading over Diane's mellow skin. Always she smiled at him, making little signs to show him how well Jerusha was getting along. Some-

times he found her reading, or doing a pantomime, or
dancing and singing for Jerusha; at night, before he
dropped an Almanac or dish of apple tart for Diane at the
cottage threshold, he watched her for long moments as she
sat in the candlelight, her hands folded before her, staring
at his sleeping child. Always he dreamed of them; that
Jerusha had suddenly turned worse and died; that he was
following the rumbling wagon hearse to the cemetery—and
the rumble filled his head; that Diane met him in the barnyard, her pail full of frothing milk; that she curtsied, but
he was sickened to see her head bald and fully of ugly yellow sores; and the dream which kept repeating itself during the crazy weeks was that of Diane, lying naked and
beautiful on the grass beside the brook. Then while he lingered beside her, he saw the little sores begin to come.
They came slowly, insidiously, like pin pricks, growing
into patches, festering while he watched, bursting, covering her, a thick yellow mass of smear, until, screaming—he
would waken in the dark, and find Elizabeth tugging at
his arm. Sometimes he thought he could not endure the
endlessness of it all; his thoughts were so inchoate that he
began to let the business run itself. If he appeared at meals
he could not eat. His mail lay unanswered.

Elizabeth, haggard, tried in a dozen pitiful, ineffectual
ways to divert him.

"But the danger is gone!" she reminded him. "Jerusha is
getting well. Jacob is safe!"

Often he turned from her, not bothering to answer. His
new love for Diane was so poignant, so deep, that when he
thought of her he was unable to bring ordinary words to
his lips.

In September Grenier returned, and when he heard of
the catastrophe he turned on Stiegel with fierceness.

"You are letting her nurse the pox! You—murderer!"

Yes, he was a murderer. He had let her give herself up

to his child because she loved him and because it had been easy. And now that she might die, and it was too late, he could see that he really loved her.

One night he determined that he would go down to Diane's cottage after dark. Jerusha would be asleep, weary with her first hours of sitting up in bed. At last he would hold Diane in his arms again. What did it matter now, now when he knew so plainly that he loved her? This was not only lust for her body. This was lust for her soul. Whatever might come to them in their sin, whatever shame or humiliation, there would be the joy of suffering together. And if she should fall sick and die—at least they would have had tonight!

Trembling, his pulse racing, he left the house without a lantern, following the road down to the collier's cottage. The sharpness of September nipped the night air, but all the familiar sounds of the grass and the glow of the fires gave him comfort. The cottage, with its little fenced-in garden, shone vaguely white under half a moon. He strained to see the candlelight, beside which Diane would be sitting.

How cruel he had always been to Diane! How he had held off her love with a smug complacency, as a thing which he might have when it suited his fancy. And how she had wasted years waiting on him and his children, while he had played with temptation, proud of his sanctimonious virtue, and yet weak and selfish enough to want her near him. During these long weeks of suspense and agony he had come to know her strength and beauty. And now he wanted her so much that no fear or ambition or godliness could possibly swerve him.

As he approached the place, he saw that it was entirely dark. He stopped for a moment, uncertain what to do. Diane must have been exhausted and gone to bed immediately after supper, he thought.

Then he was suddenly conscious of a mumbling of voices, and he knew at once that it was Martin Grenier in the garden with Diane. Stiegel felt angry, daunted. He went on a few steps, until he could hear word for word.

"Diane, the huntress," Grenier was saying bitterly. "Hunting the hearts of men."

"I don't hunt them, M'sieu."

"You have not so much mercy in your heart as the Mother Mary in her footstep."

Diane laughed.

> "*Je vous aime,*
> *Je vous adore!*
> *Que voulez vous plus encore?*"

she taunted.

Stiegel saw Martin Grenier get up and pace before Diane on the gravel walk.

"Mon Dieu, I could kill you!" he cried. "I am mad with love for you—and then you jest!"

Diane did not answer.

"Some day I will show you the meaning of love," Grenier went on, stopping sharp before her, as if he would fling himself at her feet.

"I know the meaning of love," she said quickly.

He dropped on the seat beside her again, pulling her to him, clinging to her lips.

Stiegel snatched at a handful of leaves from the bush, crumpling them in his fist.

"I will show you how exciting love is—how beautiful, ma chère."

Stiegel turned away. He could endure the gushing sentiment no longer.

He would go on down the path, wait until he saw Grenier leave, if it should take half the night, and then come back to her. When the Glass House closed he would dismiss the damned little Frenchman for good.

He stumbled down to the brook, and felt about for an old tree stump which he knew to be there.

How could he bear to wait here and let Martin make love to her? She might be willing to give herself to Grenier. She had no morals. Time and again he had told himself that Diane had no morals. So that she and Stiegel might only have one another there was no exile, no punishment she would not endure as a result. He knew this as well as if she had told him in so many words. And yet she was willing to listen to Martin. . . . He could not understand her. He could understand himself even less. After all the years of painful virtue he had come to think this weakness would be right. And now he had sneaked down to her in the dark, like some prowling tomcat. Needing her strength because he was suddenly crushed with the truth. Never thinking of consequences, only so long as her scarlet lips might belong to him. It was always himself he had thought of, how their love might affect his name and fortune, not what their consummated love might mean to her. Tonight was no different. For himself he had finally decided to take all risks, but he had given no thought to Diane. And yet why should he hesitate when she herself had no fear of the future?

His reasoning went in circles, like the silver whirlpool that spun around and around in the water, and he began to loathe himself wholly and keenly.

No morals—and yet she had been willing to die for him and his child.

The cottage was still dark. The damned little Frenchman would never go. Diane had not seemed resentful. Grenier was handsome, virile. The same blood flowed in their veins. And he loved her and wanted to marry her. Perhaps if she had been given a chance she might have loved him too, might have bestowed on him the luckless passion she kept in her heart for Stiegel. Perhaps even now in her loneliness she was yielding to him. . . .

For a long time he sat there, wretched with the conflict that was so new to him.

Diane had a right to passion. Diane had a right to happiness. He and Diane could never know happiness. If he went to her tonight, she would become his mistress. How could he ask her to give herself to him, always fearful of disgrace, always cautious of a love which should be open, always miserable with the thought of Elizabeth lying in his dutiful embrace? How could he ask her to share this greater loneliness than they had already known?

"God—that isn't what I want for her!" he groaned, starting back on the thread of path toward the mansion. "I've got to think of her for once. . . . Got to look at the future coldly, without passion! She loved me enough that she was willing to give her life for my happiness. I'll go off somewhere again. I've got to go off somewhere. . . . Got to give her a chance. . . . Europe, Germany, England. I will say I am going to Bristol to get glass-blowers for the Glass House. . . ."

If he should go away, if he should stay long enough, six months or a year, perhaps, Diane would forget him. She was young and emotional. He thought of her gay in a little white cottage with Grenier, whistling as she mended his shirts, weeding out her patch of flowers, radiant with life.

Stiegel paused at the beaten track of weeds which turned off to her cottage. Martin must have gone. There was no sound of voices, and soft candlelight came from the window, shining on the heavy dew of the grass. Diane would be thinking of him. . . . If he went there just this once. . . . It would mean so much to them both! The sort of ecstasy he had always known existed somewhere; the sort of beauty he had always dreamed of . . . and then he would go away!

But she would know then that he loved her, and while

he was gone she would only be waiting for his return. It would be futile going away.

He drove himself on up the path toward home, hating himself for his new-found courage. This would be the first decent thing he had ever done in his life, he thought bitterly. But she had not been afraid to risk her life for him. If she was safe—if God was going to respect her bravery—the least he owed her was a chance to forget him.

"Yes," he said grimly, "I am going to Europe."

The day after Diane and Jerusha were reinstated in the house, Stiegel announced to a dumbfounded family that as soon as he could make arrangements, he was going to Europe.

Elizabeth fell onto a comfortless shoulder, wailing of whole shiploads being thrown overboard with the pox, and swallowed by storms at sea.

Michael shrieked, "Maybe you'll meet pirates!"

Mrs. Ege ts-tsed her disapproval, and Diane asked, with an effort at composure, "How long shall you stay?"

"A half-year at most," he lied.

She jammed the silver knives into the mahogany knife box on the buffet.

"To get yourself a new baronial coat?"

Her retort cut him deeply. "To learn the business of glass-making," he said coldly. "To visit Bristol; to bring back the best glass-blowers in Europe. To learn to make Stiegel glass that will make the imports look muddy!"

"But Heinrich, 'tis almost winter—and the sea!"

She was terrified at the thought of the little vessels which teetered for weeks on a ruthless ocean. She was closer to tears than she had been since she lost her father. Unashamed, she gripped his sleeve with pleading fingers.

"Heinrich, I pray you, do not go!"

"Diane—while I am gone—you will nurse my little Jeru-

sha faithfully, won't you? It will be months before she is
strong."

"Need you ask?" she answered, and turned away from
him.

"I mean, you will not go into the woods and be stole by
the Indians again?" he asked, definitely.

Their eyes met in understanding.

"I will be here, when you come back, Heinrich. . . . I
will be very careful—of the Indians."

A few days later he drew one hundred and twenty
pounds from the general fund of his business and started
on his journey to Philadelphia where he took the stage-
coach to New York. For weeks there was no news of him.
Finally a letter arrived from New York to his brother Anthony:

" 'Twas a most dust-laden Journey of fitful Charakter.
Howbeit we did encountre Rivers of Mud ere we arrived
at New York. The Driver bellowed Now Gentlemen to the
right and Now Gentlemen to the left and as a Company we
did lene in the prescribed manner. Yet e'en with this obe-
d'ence we nigh o'erturned in deep Ruts more than once.
In one spot alone had we difficulty not being light enow
to pull out of the Mud. The Driver ordered all to abandon
the Coach that he could rescew it from a mirey Grave but
two Ladies refewsed as they would not besmirch there
Ancles and were the first to complain that the Driver pulled
forth a Sigar and deserted our Plite. Why did we not move
they said and he made reply we should have to bide till the
Mud dried out! The Ladies then took to the Mud and the
Ancles were full gainly. My visit with the Messrs. Stedman
was not too amiable. They do not favor the Glass exploit
nor the journey abroad. The travel by Coach is a constant
dramming for sake of warmth.

The City of New York is of colosal size of two or three
thousand Buildings and from sixteen to seventeen thou-

sand People. It is direful irregular in Plan with crooked
narrow Streets but rather well pav'd adding much to the
advantage of Carriage.

The Houses are Dutch with Gabels to Street and spa-
shous and more modern of four to five Stories high of hewn
stone or brick and white Holland Tiles, neat but not grand.

The Inns have been but middling with Bed and two
Meals for twenty-five cents, the Driver with corn husk Bed
and two Meals for ten cents. My Vessel has not yet come to
Port and this is the third week I await to sail.

Anthony, I forgot to mention to you before I left the
Slag is too dark and is low in graphitic karbon. I advise you
go yourself to the Mine and ——"

The letter was read and reread among the family, and
passed around to friends until it was dog-eared. Diane
pored over it, memorizing each word, so that she could repeat the letter to herself at night, before she slept. She was
grateful that he was safe.

The next letter, arriving months afterward, mentioned
nothing of his homecoming, but was filled with bits of
nonsense:

"It is rumored that Madame Pompadour suffers an Ail-
ment and will not be long in Rain. Paris is gay as a Dream
and I must quoat Benjamin Franklin who says of the Ladies
There is no gradual diminution in color from full Bloom of
middle cheek to faint Tint near sides but Color is the same
in each Face. Perhaps a Hole is cut in Paper and lade on
Cheeks and Color dipped on with a Brush. Paint Powder
and Paches are generaly used my dear Ladies in the most
fashonable Circles though in France I must say there wooly
white Hair and red faces make them look more like Skinned
Sheep than human Beings. I have made more than one
Purchus for my Darlings and will make Elizabeth Furnace
the envy of all Paris when I come home laden with things
of the Mode.

I now sail to Bristol and must forget Lady Style and cort
Sir Glass. My dear Wife and Children are in good health
I hope and my many Wards of all sizes and varieties——".

George, who assumed much of the social responsibility
of Stiegel while he was gone, became definitely a man. He
read to the family from the Bible morning and evening.
He coaxed various wearing apparel of Stiegel's from Aunt
Elizabeth for a short loan. He led the family into the pew
on Sunday and made an altogether magnificent understudy. He resented Anthony's responsibility, treating him
shabbily.

And Anthony, silent and unswerving, plodded on, seeming not to notice the insult, seeming not to fathom Diane's
mockery.

"Will you come for an amble in the woods, Diane?"

"Nay, 'tis too warm."

"But I have seen snow flurries this very morning!"

"Ah, then 'tis too cold. Too warm and snug here by the
fire; too cold without."

"A set-up at backgammon, Diane?"

" 'Tis indifferent fun. I do not like to win always."

He fingered the lace which made ridiculous his large
hands; they looked like lobsters squirming for freedom, all
claws.

Something about the sudden droop of his eyes reminded
her of Stiegel.

"Come then," she added, "promise to pay attention to
the game, and mayhap you will be the victor."

17

VER SINCE Diane's sacrifice for Jerusha, Elizabeth
had treated her with cold indifference. Stiegel had never
once condemned Elizabeth for her refusal to nurse his
child, but she knew that in his heart he disdained her for it.
She began to be jealous of Diane. And she loathed the girl
for her ridiculous courage. Diane was too ignorant to know
to what danger she had exposed herself, Elizabeth thought.
She was an exhibitionist; she was in love with Stiegel and
she had merely wanted to show off before him. A thousand
little memories came back to haunt her, times when Diane
had only lifted her eyes to meet his, or had brushed his
sleeve as she passed him in the hall. She had been unconsciously jealous of the dusky beauty which was so striking
a contrast to her own meagre prettiness. And Diane's tiny
waist had always aroused her envy, too.

Elizabeth visited the mantua-maker's and ordered a
whole new winter wardrobe. Now that Stiegel was gone,
she ignored Diane's needs. Diane was only an elevated
servant anyway, an orphan who had climbed to her present
position by her brazen wits, and there was no telling to
what height of insolence she'd go if she were constantly
given gifts worthy of the mistress of the household.

[206

It had incensed Elizabeth when Stiegel asked Diane to take care of Jerusha. And now that he was gone, the women began to have disputes frequently over the child. Elizabeth was irked that the little girl always called for Diane when she wanted help, or came running to her to share her joy. If Elizabeth bought her a new doll, Jerusha politely thanked her and sat her on the bedroom shelf, dragging around the one Diane had whittled out of wood and dressed with scraps of goods. Jerusha kissed Elizabeth punctiliously when she was asked, and was very careful not to slap at Jacob in front of his mother.

One damp February day, Elizabeth said, at the table, "Diane, have Jerusha ready at four. I am going to take her to Brickerville with me for a dish of tea. See that her curls are even."

Diane, broiling at the dictatorial manner Elizabeth had adopted since Stiegel's going, answered, "It is too damp for her to venture out today. She has been coughing, of late."

"I shall decide that," retorted Elizabeth. "One would think from your talk, Diane, that *you* were the mistress of the household!"

"Heinrich left Jerusha in my charge!"

"To dress her and wash her, of course."

"Oh please, Nan," cried Jerusha, "I want to go to Abigail's. She has a doll's house."

"You are not well enough yet, Rushy," and Diane walked arrogantly from the table.

At four, Elizabeth came from her room, beribboned and scented. But Jerusha was nowhere about. She hunted out Diane who was unconcernedly beating up a batter in the kitchen. Elizabeth faced her with consternation. She would make Diane dress the child, although it was late and the coachman was waiting. "I shall show her who is the mistress here," she determined.

"Where is Jerusha?" she demanded of Diane.

"I have not seen her."

"But I told you to ——"

"Here are the blueberries," said Frau Habicht, shoving a jar of fruit across the table to Diane.

"You have defied me on purpose!" accused Elizabeth, reddening with rage. "You have hid her. . . ."

"I have only obeyed Heinrich, across the water!" retorted Diane.

And from then on, the two women were consciously at war.

Diane turned to the household drudgery with vim. Mrs. Ege had dyed all the worn silk gowns in sight, and it fell to Diane's lot to ravel them, wind the silk on a bobbin, and weave it into cushions. Sometimes, finding the house unbearable, she took Barbara out to the barn to visit the cows, soothed at the smell of the hay and the fresh steaming dung. Or they stroked Stiegel's favorite horse, and fed him sugar stolen from Mrs. Ege's sugar cone.

Repressed during the day, at night and on Sundays Diane became hysterically buoyant for the parade of lovers who came. Anthony was morose, thin; young Klingerman, fretful, poetic; George Ege, pouty, and sprawly-legged as a young heifer; and Grenier, dynamic, eloquent. Diane kept busy tempering the atmosphere. The lovers were always meeting, and numerous others besides, who drifted in from Lancaster and Brickerville, drawn by the tantalization of indifference. Mrs. Ege called Elizabeth Furnace the Marriage Mall. She could afford to bluster, for she supposed George was dreaming of ships and duels and manhood, and she was far too busy seeing that Elizabeth did not mismanage her own household.

One night the kitchen fire went out, through Frau Habicht's carelessness. Anne, her eyes luminous as an owl's, refused to go to Cyrus' cottage to bring back a torch.

"Soon's de dahk come on," she quavered, "de lines and tigahs pattah nigh de kitchen do', a-callin' to de ghosts ob de beahs I've cooked."

Diane, giggling, volunteered to go, and took from the fireplace an old ship's lantern, two feet long, replacing its stub of a candle. She had gotten only as far as the stable, sure-footed even in the blackness, when she heard George's voice. "Diane, pray let me go. Fancy if the Indians are prowling about. They have too great a passion for you."

"I do not mind the dark, George. 'Tis restful."

" 'Tis not a woman's work," he argued, feeling for the lantern, for the moon was down and the night was murky. "Come, give it me, Diane."

His fingers fumbled against hers, and closed on them. He pressed her hand to his mouth.

"George, you must not do this . . ." warned Diane.

"I am twenty—and you treat me as a child," he fumed.

"Twenty. Ah, but I am six and twenty!"

"No matter," he said huskily. "You are a woman. I am a man."

She smiled broadly, because he could not see her. She would have Stiegel send him off to school when he returned. This tutoring in Brickerville did not keep him busy enough.

"A man, indeed," she sighed. "With all a man's weakness."

"A man's passion, Diane."

"The twain are one. Come, George, save your kisses for youth and beauty. I shall be here making tasks forever and a day. Listen to the horses champing in the stable. That new mare you ride ——"

And she led the way quickly, surely, bantering to arrest his seriousness. Her hand felt moist where he had pressed it to his mouth; the thought of his immaturity irked her.

When they returned, Mrs. Ege was waiting at the kitchen

fireplace to light her dip, and she glowered at George.

Diane, whistling, left him to the mercy of his mother.

"Thee have been gone long enough!" she complained.

"We stopped to look at the horses."

"They won't be there on the morrow, I'll warrant!"

The boy started the kitchen fire with his torch.

"The dark is an evil breeding-place—remember that, George Ege!"

"Oh, let me alone," he cried petulantly.

"And Diane—she would bring a stone to calamity—if it but had breeches!"

The next day Diane and Michael had a race down to the Glass House, to tell Anthony that a stranger from Lebanon was waiting at home to see him on business.

The message delivered, they stood panting in the doorway; it was almost impossible to get one's breath back here in the hellish heat. It seemed to screech like Bedlam, burning the nostrils, flailing the flesh.

Diane watched the men a moment before they were conscious of her. Martin Grenier's cheeks were scarlet and ridged with sweat, his eyes swollen.

When he saw her he passed the sugar bowl he had just finished to an annealer, and seized a gourdful of water from the pail which the water boy passed to and fro to relieve the burning thirst of the men. Michael dashed past them, to the out-of-doors.

"But you are beautiful today, Diane," Martin exclaimed, his eyes devouring her.

"Only today, M'sieu?" she teased.

Grenier pressed her hand to him, and she shrank at the touch of his sweated shirt.

"Toujours, Diane; toujours!"

Benjamin Misky smiled at her broadly, and she pulled her hand away from Grenier, and cried, "Au revoir!"

He drew her impulsively into his arms, his blazing, bloodshot eyes possessing her as he kissed her.

Benjamin clapped his applause, and the attention of the other men was drawn to the love scene.

Diane, infuriated, half blind with rage, struck out at Grenier, smashing at his eye, and tore from the building, the shouts and laughter of the men ringing in her head long after she was out of earshot.

That night Martin tossed wretchedly in bed, wondering what he could do to assuage Diane, and cursing himself for his impudence. His eye had swollen painfully and throbbed without cessation. He had asked her innumerable times to marry him, but she always answered him lightly that she was not yet ready to marry! Since the melodrama today he had gone twice to the house to apologize, but she had refused to see him.

If only he could give her something she wanted—something so fine that Baron Stiegel could not even buy it for her!

Strange how his thoughts always turned to glass as the most beautiful thing in the world. How he would like to immortalize his conception of Diane in beautiful glass—a bowl so exquisite that no one would believe he'd made it! His imagination began to work excitedly.

Martin had been imported to America by Richard Wistar's manager. During his apprenticeship among the Irish workers at Nailsea he was famous for getting miraculous variation of color. His talent was so subtle that many of his results had been attributed to chance. But Martin had come to America with several secret formulae. And when Stiegel heard of him, he was not satisfied until he had lured him with exorbitant wages.

In a French chateau Martin had once seen a blue glass bowl which the housekeeper said had been stolen from King Alfred by a soldier whose paramour fancied it. It had been minutely etched, a glorious unattainable blue, with the coat of arms enameled in infinitesimal beads. Martin had stood reverent before it, memorizing the exotic detail. Now, in the darkness, he saw the bowl again on a burnished mahogany chest, one of a thousand treasures in a cadaverous chateau. It was the most beautiful glass he had ever seen. He would duplicate it.

He jumped out of bed, dressing feverishly in the dark, and found his way to the Glass House, cherishing the bowl in his mind with the same feeling for form that a poet has for rhythm.

Four or five hours were the limit that he was able to work in a day. The intense heat and glare of the Glass House were almost beyond endurance. Only last summer he had been threatened with glass-blower's cataract. To make the bowl for Diane he would have to work at night. It would be torture for his eyes. . . . How inconceivable to be blind and not be able to see Diane!

Well, if he made himself a blue glass ball and hung it in his window, as they did across the water in French Rank, he would probably be able to ward off the evil eye.

In the early glass factories there were receptacles where bits of discarded glass were thrown, the blowers being allowed to have these for their own utilization. Excited, he gleaned bits from the discarded glass, and tossed them into the red-hot cavity of the pot of fire clay. He worked with vigor, melting and mingling his materials as if they had been the weak arguments of Diane against his courtship. He thought of her constantly while he worked. She was beautiful; mon Dieu, but she was beautiful. The bowl would be beautiful. He watched the molten mass avidly, skimming the impurities from it. The color would be fire, like the spirit of Diane. . . . It would be superbly beautiful, he told himself over and over, like the spirit of Diane —and he would fashion it to suit his will!

All through the early March nights, while the other workers amused themselves or slept, Martin Grenier went alone to the Glass House to make perfume bottles for the pleasure of some very special ladies—so he said.

It was very difficult working alone, handling both the blow-pipe and "punty" himself. Night after night he was dissatisfied with his nucleus, and remelted the bubble, refining it, adding secret ingredients, until he was afraid it would become crystalline. Strange that he could not get the blue of Alfred's bowl as he saw it in his mind's eye. And he was not going to be satisfied with any other.

Diane had accepted Martin in her good graces again long before the bowl was finished. He decided that he would give it to her as a parting gift when he left for the summer.

The spring balm had been almost unbearable at the Furnace. Grenier, a tired, strained expression on his face, had loitered more frequently in the doorway of the Glass House, where he could see the Yellow Garden.

One day Anthony came to him, in a flurry.

"Have you seen a letter about from my brother? 'Twas most important."

Grenier shook his head, and Anthony made a thorough search of the Glass House. In the meantime Elizabeth, Mrs. Ege, and Diane hunted through the house.

"I saw it here on Heinrich's desk this very morning," said Mrs. Ege.

"Do you think Jerusha or Barbara have run off with it? I asked them. . . ." said Elizabeth.

"Jacob!" exclaimed Diane, victoriously.

"Jacob indeed," spluttered Elizabeth. "A mere baby."

"But with hands! And legs . . ." laughed Diane tantalizingly.

"If only I could remember . . ." mused Anthony, stopping, his forehead wrinkled.

"Remember what?" asked Diane.

"About the Philadelphia property. . . ."

"Oh, he said, 'Write to John Dickinson at once Anthony conserning the Proppertie we spoke of on Mulberrie Streat. I shall have Bizness more frequent in Philadelphia and feel a Man of my Posishun should have a Home there among my Partiners, but . . . but . . . tell him not to purchus ased Proppertie for more than five hundred Pounds—five hundred Pounds. . . .'"

Anthony stared at Diane.

"You know it as well as if you had wrote it," he meditated, and as he looked at her, a queer sick feeling of presentiment came over him.

"I have read it," said Diane.

"But the amount—if only I could be sure of the amount. . . ."

"'Twas five hundred pounds," insisted Diane, and she avoided Anthony's eyes and began to search some more in the pigeonholes of the desk.

That evening Elizabeth remembered after she was in bed that she wanted to tell Diane to pick dandelions for wine in the early morning. Slipping into her nightgown, she puttered across the hall, and opened Diane's door without knocking.

Diane was sitting at her dressing table reading a letter, and as Elizabeth entered she jumped up and involuntarily crushed it behind her. Diane's hair was hanging long and black over her shoulders, and she seized her brush and began to brush it.

"Diane," and Elizabeth's voice trembled. "You have Heinrich's letter."

Diane knew in a flash that it was useless to lie, and she was furious with herself for having acted the part of a thief.

"Aye, I have it," she said, handing it to Elizabeth. "I

only found it before I came to bed, stuffed in the wood box."

"Why did you not bring it to me?"

"I wanted to make sure of the five hundred pounds ——"

"Anthony will do that!" Elizabeth snatched the letter, and forgetting her orders for Diane, started for the door. Then she turned, her face white. "You were going to keep the letter!"

"Fooh! What would I want with a letter," cried Diane, coloring in spite of herself, for Elizabeth had taken her unaware. "A mess of paper and ink!"

"I don't care what you say, you were going to keep it! I don't know how I know, but I know it! You lie to me— you lie to all of us!"

Diane looked at her with fire in her eyes. "I knock on a door before I enter!" she said scathingly.

Elizabeth slammed the door and went back to her room. The whole episode had upset her badly. She had begun to hate Diane with a hatred that was unexplainable and greater than she had ever felt for any one in her life. Diane had sewed for her, nursed her child, pickled parsley, samphire, and fish in season. She had never for a moment been lazy—helping to milk the cows and working in the vegetable patches. She had even been willing to sacrifice herself for Heinrich's child. That was it—Elizabeth knew it herself—Diane had made her insignificant in the household, small. Elizabeth was an elegant piece of bric-à-brac, and not even Brickerville seemed impressed any more at her appearance in the coach. She had supposed when she married that life would be a whirl of balls and adulation, that being married to Baron Stiegel would carry her along forever in a cloud of glory. Just since her husband had gone, several people had avoided her in Lancaster. And she had not been included in the Christmas Assembly there which they had attended ever since their marriage.

She got into bed again and started to cry. Nothing seemed to be going right. She knew instinctively that Diane had lied to her. Why would she want to keep Heinrich's letter? He had made no mention of Diane in it—in any of his letters. Diane *must* be in love with him. She had suspected it before, and Anna Ege had intimated it many a time with her arched eyebrows, but had wisely kept her tongue. Elizabeth felt suddenly overcome with jealousy. It was incredible that Stiegel would pay attention to Diane's wiles. He had never had any feeling but duty toward Diane—she was confident of that. He had deliberately been contemptuous of Diane in front of her. And of course, if he had been at all infatuated with the girl he would never have gone off for so long a time. And yet she could not altogether quiet her suspicions. For weeks before Stiegel had left he had not come to her. It was not like him. He had always been passionate, gay and coaxing. But he had been ill. And before she was well, Jerusha had driven him half insane with worry.

She wondered where he might be tonight—if he might be dining with royalty in some old baronial hall. He seemed very far away. The woman beside him would be little, with sparkling black eyes and hair. She would lift up her wine to him and embrace him with her glance. Perhaps she would even look like Diane. A miniature waist. . . .

Elizabeth bit her lips. She would begin to diet tomorrow. But tomorrow noon there would be huckleberry tart. She would not begin tomorrow noon;—tomorrow night.

18

MARTIN GRENIER, at last finished with the bowl, hid it in his room among some old clothes. And it was not until April came and the Glass House closed down that he gave it to Diane.

She had forgiven him his impudence and reinstated him as the most likely of her lovers. But now that it was the night before his departure, she listened to his love-making with abstraction. She was bored with the evening, with the twilight which challenged contentment. Another letter had come from Stiegel, and there was still no mention made of his return. The time since she had seen him seemed infinite; surely he could not be home before Christmas—and it was only spring! She thought in desperation of her fruitless years at Elizabeth Furnace; gardens, babies, lovers. She had not lived. She had merely been watching life go on about her.

"Heinrich loves me," she thought feverishly as she submitted to Grenier's ardent kisses. "But I have never really roused him. No one has ever really roused him. He is in the fortification of his dreams and of his ambitions. . . ."

"There is nought in the world so soft as your kiss—so thrilling as your breath on my cheek, Diane. . . ."

"Ah Martin, you must come down to earth!" she admonished. She was no longer amused by his passion.

They had gone down to the same rotting log where Stiegel had sat the night he waited for Grenier to leave Diane.

"But Diane, while I am gone . . . I can think of nothing but you—how you smile, how you laugh—how your fingers look in the earth. . . ."

"But I do not love you!" she cried emphatically. She felt choked with tears which sprang forth in unexpected laughter.

"Diane—do not mock me!"

"Non, non, non, mon cher. I do not mean to mock you. I cannot say what I feel. So . . . so tired. . . ."

She closed her eyes, and leaned back into the coolness of new leaves, resting against a tree trunk.

"But Diane . . . surely when I hold you against my heart . . . and I feel your heartbeat fast against mine . . . *you* must feel something. . . ."

"Non—not for you, Martin . . ." she said wearily, benumbed by his unctuous declarations.

"Some day you will learn to love me. Say it, Diane! I implore you. . . . I have such mad hope for you, Diane. I have already a betrothal gift . . . it is very rare. . . ."

He clung to her lips for a moment, and then bolted away. She dropped down onto the fallen log, unmoved, but bewildered and half curious.

A gem, perhaps from an Egyptian tomb! Why, she had not said she would marry him! She would never marry. The uncanny Indian ceremony had not been a marriage; it had been a stratagem of war, beyond her power. Suddenly, filled with restlessness, she took off her shoes and stockings and holding up her skirts, began to paddle in the brook, shocked alive once more by the deliciously cold April water.

"Elizabeth!" she thought. "How glad she would be to be rid of me. If it is simply to spite her I shall never marry. . . . Ugh—how long and curly and black is the hair on Martin's chest! I should suffocate with cologne, lying in Robert Klingerman's arms. And Anthony—he would always ask permission to kiss me. Fooh! They make me ill. Why is it I have seen Heinrich sweat—I have seen him with his face black—I have seen him sick, with his beard long— I have seen him ready to kill me—and yet I love him the more for all of this. . . ."

Martin Grenier, his eyes panther-like, held the bowl triumphantly before her. The beads of enamel on the coat of arms gleamed like tiny jewels.

She left the brook, regretting the delightful feel of mud oozing through her toes, and plopped down excitedly on the tree trunk.

She turned the bowl about, bewitched. Martin held it before the lantern he had brought back with him, and she exclaimed at the effulgence of rich blue.

"Ah, c'est trés, trés beau!" she cried. "And 'tis very old!"

Pride in his workmanship struggled for a moment with the temptation to augment the worth of his gift.

"Stole by a French soldier for his paramour. Stole from the halls of King Alfred."

She was almost afraid to hold it now. "And how came it to you, Martin?"

"I suppose I'll never know! Tradition lies. A family treasure for generations. The lady bore her soldier a child, mayhap, for the gift. Hence my heritage—my love for glass. My love for beauty—for you, Diane!"

"What a pity 'tis nicked!"

Grenier shrugged his shoulders. His heart was pounding with joy. He had come to love the bowl ardently.

"I want you to have it . . ." he declared, holding it again before the lantern.

"But the lady bore her soldier a child. . . ."

"Diane ——?"

"Non, non, non . . . I should be afraid of breaking it!"

"But it belongs to you!" he insisted. "I charge you with the keep of it—together with my heart."

She picked it up again, fingering it gently. It had an old, worn feeling. She wanted suddenly to share this discovery with Stiegel.

"How he would love it!"

"He —— "

"Heinrich. He must have everything of beauty within reach! He would want it!" she mused. "He would want it very much."

"Diane, promise me you would not give it him!" cried Grenier jealously.

"Non, non, non, of course I shall not give it him!" she asserted, excited at the thought that was blossoming. "He will want it very much—but he will not always have everything he wants, non. . . ."

Stiegel would want the bowl and it was hers! She rose and picked up her shoe. Grenier began to lament the long summer when he would be forced to rest his eyes on a cool New England farm. He could never bear the long separation until the fall. Diane listened to him as a child to a geography lesson. He was handsome, vital, but somehow he failed to affect her. She suppressed a yawn.

"Tonight I shall see moonbeams through enchanted glass, Martin. How beautiful it is! Merci, mon cher!"

"Diane, don't go," he coaxed, stroking her hair, "I want to hold you in my arms till eternity. . . ."

She lingered in his embrace a moment, with a sudden feeling of remorse that he loved her too much. Then she slipped away, the bowl in one hand, and stockings, slippers, and muddy skirts in the other. She was eager to examine the exquisiteness of the bowl alone.

Maytime had come round again, the sensuous season of blossoms and odors of earth, timid hues of pink and green, and virgin white. The gardeners moved slowly about their work, like worms crawling out of a silk nest. The grounds bloomed with grottos, arbors, and shady summer houses. Vines went adventuring over old stones. Elizabeth painted flowers and led her needle through a labyrinth of daisies on a pocket. Barbara worked under the oaks on blossoms of shell—ornaments of the future to be preserved "sous cloche." Stirred with the wakefulness of things, Jerusha gathered violets, long, odorless and lovely, and bunched their wilted heads in a mammoth vase on the dining-room table. Jacob, in fits of perturbation, beheaded tulips, irises and the first pinks. And Diane labored lovingly in her Yellow Garden. The yellow tulips had lived and died, but small shoots of green were thriving under her careful hands.

She felt more at peace now that summer had come. It was easier to evade Elizabeth, whom she knew hated her intensely. And now it would only be a month or two before Heinrich would sail, he had said in a letter to Anthony.

One evening after sundown George came over to her, as she took a few stitches in her black lace mitt.

"Come for a stroll in the garden with me, Diane."

Diane, smiling to herself at his dictatorial manner, acquiesced, putting her small brown hand through his arm. She trotted along beside him, amused at his swagger. He was indeed the gentleman. His hair was a silky sheen in its new shower of powder; his ruffles emerged from his bosom as taut and pure as angels' wings; his thin waistline was buttoned tight in a lavender summer satin; his person smelled faintly of musk. He led her over the soft, tightly clipped grass to a sequestered corner under an oak. Diane smiled to herself. She had been led into the garden before, and never to talk of glassware or the sugar tax. She adjusted her petticoats over the bench, so that there was scarcely room for him to sit beside her. His fingers slipped over hers.

"Why is your heart so calloused?" he asked.

She drew away her hand. "So you led me into the garden to chide me," she said.

"I would have you know I am a man, Diane. You still treat me like Jacob."

"Sacrebleu! There is but one Jacob in the universe!"

"You dispensed with me on horse to Lancaster with Anthony as if I were a groomsman."

"Ah, so 'tis that which rankles. I thought you loved adventure."

"Adventure! Two days of swallowing dust! And being away from you, Diane. Every minute I was gone I thought of the others here, making love to you, touching your hand . . . kissing the hem of your skirt. . . ."

Diane burst out laughing. "How romantic! . . . But no one has ever kissed the hem of my skirt. I am a devil. They see it and love me because I am a devil. But my skirt. . . . Ah, cheri, *you* kiss the hem of my skirt and make me a saint, I beg of you. . . ."

He fell on his knees before her, grasping her dress, pressing it to his breast, and she thought she would let out a hysterical scream. George—George groveling before her! Why, when she first returned to the Furnace she had scolded him for bitng his nails, had helped administer to him sulphur and molasses! She began to think fast, half sickened by the mingled scent of phlox and overpowering musk.

George must be kept subdued. She must not have trouble with George, or his mother and Elizabeth would combine to accuse her of seduction. Heinrich would not understand. They would tell him things that were not true when he returned. Elizabeth would try to get rid of her—she was sure of that.

"Diane, I am horn mad with jealousy! Tell me you do not love Martin Grenier!"

"No, I do not love him," she consoled him.

She gazed up at the lovely white moon, and closed her eyes against his florid phrases. "Exotic passion . . . turbid soul . . . celestial love. . . ." He had been reading novels. But she must not laugh at him again!

"You are too cold to know love—too radiant and brilliant and cold," he censured.

"Mais non, mon cher, I am not cold. But you must not go on like this. There are so many reasons why. George, believe me, you must try to divert your thoughts. Perhaps some day I can explain. . . . Susan Eschbach would give the world for a smile from you! And when you keep on like this, it only endangers my happiness. . . ."

"You think my mother will not approve!"

"She would be joyed to gouge out my eyes."

"I'll show her I'm a m——"

"Non, non, non, George, there are so many things ——"

"My Aunt Elizabeth, she treats you like a beggar."

"I am a beggar, George. That is it. . . ."

He was leaning against the garden wall, dejected, fumbling with a vine much as Jacob might have done. She touched his arm with vague sympathy, and the contact seemed to release a spring in him. He leaned over and picked her up, his thick warm lips holding hers to long submission, while his fingers rambled frantically over her hair and the bows at her shoulder. At last he released her, and stalked from the garden.

She sighed, heartsick. She was choked with the futility of her own love, and the abject kisses of a cavalcade of lovers. Small stinging tears of anger clung to her eyes.

She would far rather have averted this outburst from

George. It seemed as if she had no friends left in the house-hold. George would begin to mope like his amorous prede-cessors. In a twinkling his mother would divine his secret, and would blame Diane. Even Michael seemed to have out-grown their romping together. He was at the age where he enjoyed a sense of abuse, she thought. The girls had begun lately to preclude Diane from their confidence, because she was twenty-six and might die any day from old age. She began to wonder how things could last this way, how she and Elizabeth would be able to live under the same roof. And the roof was Elizabeth's. Diane did not want to go away again. She was no longer so young and impul-sive. And if it was agony having known Stiegel's kiss, and never knowing it again—it had been greater agony when long months and even years went by without so much as a glimpse of him.

When she returned to the house a moment after George, she was met with a condemning silence. George stood be-fore his mother and Elizabeth, and he lifted his eyes sheep-ishly to Diane as she came in. Unwilling to be belittled before her, he turned and fled.

"And thee should not have gone into the damp with thy cold, either," his mother tossed after him.

"Diane, I will thank you to leave my nephew out of your scheming," Elizabeth remarked pointedly.

Diane stopped in the doorway.

"I have enough lovers that I do not have to angle for schoolboys," she retorted.

"Enough lovers!" cried Elizabeth. "Women like you never have enough lovers! I've watched you with them. You let them hang on with hope until they're ready to stab themselves. Anthony—look at Anthony! You have a heart like a cat. . . ."

"Merci," said Diane, infuriated. "Anthony, is he in love with me too?"

"Fooh, as if you didn't know!"

"He has never spoke a word of love to me, I swear it."

"He is too fine to have his heart broke by you——"

"He is dull," interposed Diane.

"And George, you will let him go his own way!"

"Shall I?" cried Diane. "All right, I shall, if you wish. I shall let him kiss the hem of my skirt every night at sundown. . . . venêt!"

Mrs. Ege opened her mouth to indict Diane, but she had escaped. From then on until Christmas the house was charged with tension so great that Diane often dashed off to her room alone to keep from strangling Elizabeth or Mrs. Ege. She tried frantically not to think of the future. Oh, if only Heinrich would come home! Surely he would do something to help her! Anthony pleaded with her to keep peace—not to answer Elizabeth when she wronged her. But it was like asking fire not to burn. The holidays were dismal, and the grand climax came one day in February.

Elizabeth, rummaging among Stiegel's indenture papers, discovered that Frau Habicht was now free. She had served her prescribed period of twenty-five years, and was entitled to her liberty. Elizabeth was delighted. She had never demolished her fear for the old tiger, and now that she was at last to be rid of her, the news seemed like a fresh sweep of breeze on a torpid day. Mrs. Ege, who was indulging in a creeping plaster, refused to break the glad tidings; she declared that Frau Habicht's room stunk and would speed her to bed.

"Diane, what more like than that *you* should go!" Elizabeth ordered. "*You* will be able to manage her, no doubt!"

There seemed to be no choice for Diane. Moreover, Frau Habicht had in the last few years harbored almost a liking for Diane. Whether it was because Diane was a relic of a happier and older era, or whether she admired the girl for her mettle, was an enigma. Stiegel and Diane had often laughed about the sudden change of heart, and attributed it to the mellifluent effect of the bitters.

During a recent heart attack no one had been allowed to pass the threshold but Diane. No matter how deaf the old tyrant was, her eyes immediately popped open at the sound of a strange footstep.

Diane was loath to go. She thought this Elizabeth's job, and did not like Elizabeth pussyfooting after her to listen outside of Frau Habicht's door. Nevertheless she went the following morning, thinking it the best time to find her rational. The servants' quarters were an L of the house beyond the kitchen, and Diane passed the curious eyes of Cyrus and Anne and one of the gardeners, Elizabeth close at her heels.

She knocked at Frau Habicht's door briskly, and going in, pushed aside her bed-curtains and opened the windows to let in some fresh morning air. Frau Habicht was still bound up in a woolen night-rail, and the room reeked of liniment, so that Diane felt almost asphyxiated.

"Hark you, in my straits I can't bide the air, miss. Shut that window."

"Frau Habicht, I have good news." Diane sat close to the invalid on the high bed and shouted, "You are free!"

"Free! That I'll tie to."

"Free, to . . . to leave," blurted out Diane.

"Heyday, 'twas my home before 'twas his." Frau Habicht picked up her long earhorn as if she were anticipating a battle.

"Then you . . . you do not want your freedom?"

"I live here; I die here!" She coughed violently to prove that she might fulfill her threat at any moment.

"Has your master nought to say?" asked Diane acridly.

"Nought! Hm, I've a swipe o' things the Mistress would ope' her ears to!"

"You can say nothing wrong of him!"

"Ja? . . ." asked the old woman cynically. "But *you*—das Gänzemädchen—she fondles the goose yet, nicht war?"

Diane, terrified at Frau Habicht's sharp conjecture, knew that any display of temper would be a betrayal. Her abomination of this shrewd shell of a woman flooded back, but she smiled placatingly as she went to the door. She wondered with her heart turning somersaults if Elizabeth could possibly have gotten the intimation!

As she stepped out into the dark narrow hall, closing the door behind her, she felt rather than saw Elizabeth before her.

"I had no luck!" she said briefly, walking on ahead.

"Stop!" said Elizabeth, and Diane swung about, though she could see nothing with all the doors of the passage closed.

"You . . . you *are* in love with Heinrich . . ." whispered Elizabeth. The words had been trembling on her lips for months.

"Are *you?*" cried Diane, into the dark.

"You want to get him like the rest, get him sick for love of you, you rotten little hussy, and then throw him ——"

Diane swung into the corner and slapped Elizabeth fiercely on the cheek.

"What if I *am* in love with him," Diane cried brokenly, and she felt Elizabeth lurching at her, felt her nails digging painfully into her forehead. She grabbed blindly, seizing Elizabeth's wrist, and with her strong brown hands pinned Elizabeth to the wall, panting.

"You get out of this house, you strumpet!" gasped Elizabeth. "You won't sleep another night under this roof. . . ."

"I won't get out! I belonged here before you. We all belonged here before you and your tribe. . . ."

"Let go of me!" groaned Elizabeth, tossing her bulk from side to side.

"Non, non, non—not till you swallow your words!" cried Diane.

She could feel Elizabeth's hot breath on her face, and she had a desire to crush her to the wall, to pummel her, to spit on her, to scream to her that she would love Heinrich till the end of time, that she would never let him go back to this mealy pudding of a wife who lived on his bounty and did not love him! Pansy eyes! She would like to scratch them out so they could never see him again!

Her fists tightened like wire on Elizabeth's wrists, and she threw her back into the corner and tore down the hall, almost afraid of her own murderous impulse. She flew to her room, looking like a harpy, and locking the door behind her, sank onto the floor.

"Holy Mother of God!" she exclaimed. "Another moment, and I'd have killed her! What will he say . . . what will he do . . . will he send me away . . . ? Oh God, I love him . . . why can't I have him when she doesn't love him . . . I can have him . . . I can have him if I want to . . . I will be a hussy; I will make him sick for love of me!"

She stared up at the ceiling. "I will have him . . . I'll lie in his arms in her very sight . . . I'll madden him . . . I'll do all the things I could have done these years to get him. . . ."

She rolled over, her trembling fingers twisting the flowered chintz of her dressing table. "I've been so good . . . so miserable—and now it will be sweet. Mon Dieu . . . not to dream of his kisses—to wake and find them on my lips. . . . Heinrich, Heinrich, I love you!"

19

ONE SHOWERY April day, Diane was pulling
some shifts from the clothes horse in the kitchen yard,
when the Indian in her felt rather than heard the reverbera-
tion of horses' hoofs. They were indistinct at first as far-off
drum-beats, increased like the quick pulsing of her blood,
and soon rumbled into near thunder with the appearance of
a carriage. She dropped the clothes on the mud-tipped
grass, running down the road in the rain, and headed
perilously into the path of the vehicle, her satin toes dodg-
ing puddles.

"Heinrich," she cried, throwing herself into his arms as
he alighted, and pressing her face against his newly bro-
caded bosom. "Heinrich!"

"Diane," he murmured eagerly, and quickly kissed the
lips upturned to his.

Cyrus was loping down the lawn now to meet his master,
and Jerusha was screaming from the window. Jacob took
the front stairs with a leap, crying, "What did you bring
me?"

Sweating men came grinning from the outbuildings to
greet Stiegel. He waved to them all, trying to duck up the
stairs to the porch. There was Barbara, squealing a little

and grown a foot taller; and Frau Habicht, miraculously recovered, rubbing her hands on her apron, and squinting her thousand little wrinkles into a smile.

Elizabeth was teetering on the top step, almost getting wet in her enthusiasm as she leaned forward to embrace him. Fat as a dumpling.

He turned from one to the other, excitedly, scarcely knowing where to begin, pinching Jerusha's cheek—how well she looked!—and crying to Anne, "Wait till you see what I've brought you!"

"Thou'rt pindling from thy long journey!" exclaimed Anna Ege, noting greedily the dark circles under his eyes.

"I've been seasick for weeks," Stiegel laughed, his eyes going back to Diane again hungrily.

"Elizabeth, how thee stand shaking, child," chided her sister.

" 'Tis the damp," cried Elizabeth, flushing scarlet, for this well-set handsome gentleman scarcely seemed to belong to her. She felt herself groping for words, self-conscious, abashed.

Stiegel was talking volubly of the sea, the ship, glass, London, Bristol, and glass again; and everyone was asking him questions, and putting more questions to him without listening to the answers.

"Glass of the most engrossing blue. . . . In London, young ladies at the boarding-school wear neat polished collars of steel and . . . brought Russian gauze to outwit mosquitoes . . . excellent; George the Third has proclaimed. . . ."

They surrounded Stiegel like turkey buzzards, each hungry for his share. All but Diane. Leaning against the harpsichord, her head tilted back, her eyes half closed, she seemed to be waiting.

But if they assaulted him like buzzards with questions, they now clung like leeches with anticipation when Cyrus and the gardener brought in the pigskin trunks.

Ghentish sheeting, dozens of colored lace mittens and aprons of exquisite finery tumbled out on the floor in search of owners. There were caps for Madame Ege, with sprigs of spangles on flowers, smaller, in the new mode, and a velvet bonnet of black, scalloped to suffocation. There was lutestring for new gowns for Elizabeth, and a Mogul ring of great antiquity, set with a mirror an inch wide. Elizabeth burst into ecstatic tears at sight of the English glass preserve pots, tazzas, a castor, and—grand finale—a Nailsea rolling pin with a ship on one end, an anchor on the other, and "Be True to Me" written across it in the glass. A trinket from each of Bristol's fifteen glass houses. Then there were splatterdashes and gem-like marbles for Michael; John Newberry's "Mother Goose Melodies" for Jerusha. There were layers of impersonal things—hair brushes, lasts for making shoes, liquid blacking and shoe brushes, carpeting for the stairs. Things were cudgeled into a corner in the excitement of the game. For Barbara there were pack-thread stays, masks, caps, necklaces, calamanco shoes, stiff coats of silk. For Jerusha, kid mitts, fans, bibs, ruffles, leather pumps and needlework stamped with proper pattern in London, to be worked with crewel at home. It was an orgy of elegance such as the old house had never witnessed before. The chairs, tables and harpsichord were overflowing. George's fine lace handkerchiefs and great silver comb were incarcerated on pages nine and ten of the Mother Goose book; Anthony's enamel snuff box lay in Madame Ege's bonnet, and his fob ribbons with clusters of delicately cut seals hanging from them dangled from the pocket of Michael, who hung on the edge of the commotion, like a warrior suffering from shell-shock.

Stiegel, standing for a moment to rest an aching back, chanced to look at Diane, strangely quiet in the seething tide which had swept her into its midst. He grabbed a small string of gold beads which had tumbled back into his trunk unclaimed and thrust it into her hand.

"For you, Diane," he confided excitedly, "I have brought a harp."

"A . . . a harp!"

"It is *beautiful!*"

She laughed hysterically, and felt smothered by the Babel.

"I cannot play . . . I cannot e'en play a harpsichord."

"But you will learn, Diane, for me—will you not?" he pleaded.

"Heinrich, mon cher!" She had seen Elizabeth's eyes darkly upon them, and she became suddenly very gay, clasping the beads around her neck, parading in the white Leghorn hat George had feverishly passed on to her. Heinrich was giving her what he loved best of all his gifts—music!

Stiegel, almost overwhelmed with business details after his return, did not notice at first that the atmosphere of the house was combustible. Rather, he was absorbed with the obvious growth of the children, the new grape arbor the Italian gardener had pampered, the foal of his favorite horse, the size of the wheat crop of the preceding year.

All during the long months of his absence, he had told himself over and over that Diane would forget him, that this would be best. It was what he wanted, the thing that would bring her ultimate happiness. And now that he was back again, only a glimpse of her running to him in the rain had made him weak, had given him a quick sort of twist in the pit of his stomach, a delicious emptiness in his head. He watched her furtively as she went about the house singing in her husky voice, her head back and her shoulders straight, as if she might have been in the woods holding her hands to the heaven, singing to the clouds!

Always that feeling of freedom clinging to her—of outdoors and freshness and fullness of Nature. He had not remembered that she was half so beautiful!

As he talked to Anthony at night, it was hard to concentrate on glass, the number of hogsheads that had been shipped to Lebanon, to Lancaster.

"I sent to Philadelphia for the English bricks for the Manheim house," said Anthony, as the two men lounged before the fire together.

"You say 'twill be done by fall?" asked Stiegel, his eyes on Diane's fingers as they helped Barbara with the fox and geese stitch. He imagined them plucking the strings of the harp, strong, graceful, sure.

"And the Glass House at Manheim," he went on, not listening for Anthony's answer. "You will have a job to oversee the men I have brought back for it."

Anthony knocked his pipe against the mantel slowly, and said, without looking up, "I am not going to manage the new Glass House, Heinrich."

"What? Why, it is the chance of a lifetime, Anthony. The business grows like a mush ——"

"Mutter is alone now," Anthony added quietly, and he was thinking of the ugly things the servants had been saying about Diane, the scandal about her love for Heinrich. What if she was meretricious and barbaric? These were the things he needed, he cried out to himself. He had been so good all his life, so unbearably good. And he had wanted her! And he had never even been able to tell her! Well, Heinrich would have her, eventually. He knew that from the way their eyes lighted on one another. And at least he would not have to be there to see it.

Stiegel looked at the curiously pale and unemotional features of Anthony and thought him a nonentity. Their relationship had at no time been an intimate thing, for age as well as temperament separated them. Stiegel, thirty-four,

in the vortex of his ambition, still looked upon the twenty-
four-year-old Anthony as an insignificant, aimless child. A
boy who was timid about Indians, and had not learned to
manage his hands, much less say to finger a snuff box with
urbanity.

A week later, after he had paid Anthony off, he called
him back to his desk, prompted by a vague, ineffable sympathy for him, and gave him a present of twenty-five
pounds for himself and old Frau Stiegel. And Anthony had
but kissed the small brown hand of Diane in the interval,
and said a composed adieu to her.

Stiegel's first inkling of the discord in the house came
when the harp case was opened the next day. The family
hovered about the big wooden crate, watching it burst
apart with a splitting sound, and finally when Cyrus lifted
the instrument in its green felt cover from the box and set
it beside the harpsichord, there was a mumble of surprise
and delight. The children danced about it; it was as tall as
Diane, and she rested her head against the gold leaf column
with a thrilling sense of joy and possession. This was a bond
between herself and Heinrich, a bond which no one else
would be able to understand but themselves. She touched
the raised flowers of gold, and caressed the strings softly,
so that they sounded like wind in the trees.

"Oh, Heinrich," she said raptly, " 'Tis very beautiful. . . ."

A little while later, Stiegel and Elizabeth went across the
hall to talk over guests who were coming.

" 'Twas very dear, the harp, I suppose," she said. Ever
since Stiegel was home she had been waiting to burst out
her hatred of Diane, and to demand that Diane be sent
away. But every time she approached the subject she had
quailed. Stiegel's casual manner did not inspire her confidence. She had watched him avidly for signs of infatuation of Diane. She had been wild with fear that she would

come upon them suddenly in one another's arms, and yet in some unexplainable way, almost greedy to have her fears verified. Then she could thrust Diane from the house before the very servants. As it was, she felt the subtle undercurrent of their love, and could neither analyze it nor touch it. She knew that an outburst on her part would only incense him. Soon she would have some justification to cry out her mind, and until then she would have to be content with this harrowing suspicion.

Stiegel felt at once the jealousy behind Elizabeth's remark, and said, "Aye, 'twas very dear. I was six hundred pounds in debt when I came home!"

"Six hundred pounds!" repeated Elizabeth astounded. "For a harp!"

"I did not say six hundred pounds for the harp," returned Stiegel, who had wanted to be malicious. "But even so 'twould be small return for the life she offered Jerusha."

Elizabeth colored and tried to cover her humiliation with a smile. He would never send Diane away; never, no matter what she would tell him!

Stiegel perused some bills which had just arrived. "You contracted some debts of your own while I was gone, I see. This is outrageous!"

"Heinrich, you remember very well you told me I should have everything to make me happy while you were away."

"I did not expect you to buy Philadelphia, Lizzie!"

She trotted over to him and tried to wheedle him with soft little kisses on his neck. He stared down at the desk. He wondered what was going to become of them all. Last night Elizabeth had been a lump of putty in his arms. Jacob was the only one who meant anything to her. She was primarily a mother, not a wife. Well, he had never asked for her love. Why should he want it or expect it, now?

Diane's harp became a sensation. People admired it with

awed restraint, not venturing too close to it. A few more
bold, including Robert Klingerman, plucked at a string
with taut forefingers, or endeavoured to pick out a popular
hymn with an experimental thumb.

Diane's master was an old goldsmith in Lancaster who
had been bred in Dublin. Stiegel had engaged him to come
to Elizabeth Furnace once a week for a lesson. He was a
round, red little man, with a round red nose, and a circle of
a mouth that drew up tightly when he played.

The first time he came he sat himself before the harp with
a flourish, his audience falling quiet in its respect for art.
Then tossing his ruffles back upon his wrist, he maundered
up and down upon the strings, tuning capriciously with his
right hand while he plucked out a little tune with his left
(a very special trick). Soon he was off in an Irish lilt, bolting down a quaff from the glass which stood beside him,
and this during the most tender and touching rests.

Barbara, her large blue china eyes concentrating on his
spry fat thumbs, stole up close to him. She clasped about the
waist an almost adult-sized doll which had been sent to
Elizabeth's mantua-maker from France, a "grand courrier
de la mode" which for six months had advertised the newest
fashions in the shop-window of the modiste and had now
been replaced by a newer and smarter courrier.

With mischief in his twinkling gray eyes, O'Harpigan
lifted the doll onto his lap, and with her mittened hand in
his, played an abridged Irish tune, singing soulfully into
her limpid face that she was the "Macushla" of his dreams.
Barbara hopped up and down with sudden lack of dignity
at seeing her favorite doll perform on the harp.

" 'Twas but a mite of a trick," he laughed, hugging the
unsuspecting puppet to his rather soiled cascade of ruffles,
and then bending her in a modest curtsey to acknowledge
their applause.

Then the lesson began in earnest, and went on all day.
It was a spasmodic series of lectures between O'Harpigan's
quenchings of insatiable thirst and "restings of the eyes."
Sometimes they lasted for half an hour. Sometimes they
amounted to only one aria played by O'Harpigan, his face
twinkling with bygone memories. He had quite forgotten
that Diane was there, now, waiting with restless brown
fingers to show her progress. Humming in snatches, he
accompanied himself, gazing mellowly at one of the pictures, his frayed lace engageant resting at last on the strings
moodily. Then again, he bustled in from a jaunt about the
grounds, and seating himself beside her, reminisced about
Dublin.

"Oi have yet to become acquaint with the human who
does not jest that *he* will play at the harp in hiven. Devil
burn it, Mistress, do they not banter in loike manner with
you?"

"To the man," agreed Diane, laughing. "Each one thinks
'tis the first witticism of the kind. 'What, you are learning to
play the harp? Practice for your angelhood, non?'"

Then the lesson would meander on again in a more
serious disposal of scales and arpeggios.

In the afternoon at his desk Stiegel could hear the droning of O'Harpigan's "one, two, three," and a tinkle of
strings. Diane would be sitting at her harp, eager, alert.
Had she fallen in love with Martin Grenier? With someone
else? He dreaded to ask. He knew he would never be able
to keep the fear out of his voice; and yet he had been home
from Europe a week, and he felt that he could not go on
much longer without knowing. Something had happened
to her, he was certain. Something exciting. Her eyes had
been quick, sharp; her laughter, mercurial. Perhaps tonight
he would be able to tell.

That afternoon George rode back to Lancaster with

O'Harpigan, and Michael appeared at dinner dressed in some of his brother's clothes, to the indignation of his mother, who trounced him out by the ear.

Diane giggled, and Anne, poking about the table with a dish of cottage cheese, snickered audibly.

"The size of George staggers me," said Stiegel. "And I thought when I first saw him his neck would crack in his stock, 'twas so frilled and starched."

Elizabeth passed the chives to him.

"He bats around a funny little ball with a stick and calls it gouff," she smiled.

"And won't use a bird's claw any more for fishing!" cried Barbara.

"Jerusha! Barbara!" reproved Stiegel, tapping his knife against the water glass. "Children should be seen and not heard!"

"And how often have I told you never to take salt except with a clean knife!" reprimanded Elizabeth, frowning at Jerusha.

"He wears a gold cane," put in Diane, "and dazzles Susan Eschbach so she can scarce see anyone else!"

"His father was a gentleman!" declared Elizabeth. "Anne, the pudding ——"

"But a Quaker, n'est-ce pas?" asked Diane.

Elizabeth had not spoken to her since their battle, and it amused Diane to challenge her in front of her husband.

"An educated man," went on Elizabeth, turning to Stiegel.

Diane snapped up the opportunity quickly. "George is of an age for higher education, is he not?"

Stiegel played with his fork thoughtfully; then as an idea struck him, he turned to Diane and said, "Would you like to see him at college, Diane?"

His eyes had said, "Has he been molesting you, Diane?"

Well, he thought, smiling grimly to himself at the comi-

cality of it, it was not George who had made her so gay,
at least!

"Heinrich, that is something for my sister Anna to de ——"

"Aye," interrupted Diane, devilishly. "I should like to see
him well preserved from temptation. He is like to stunt his
manhood here, in a coterie de femmes."

Elizabeth grew scarlet, and began to speak again when
Stiegel concluded, "I have thought of it long since. He
shall go to the New Jersey College at Princeton, or to the
Academy in Philadelphia, in the fall."

"Heinrich, you must admit that my sister will have something to say of ——

"But Heinrich will pay!" finished Diane, with audacity,
and went off to practice her harp.

"Heinrich," cried Elizabeth, with angry tears in her eyes,
"you will not believe what I have had to put up with while
you were gone. You would not stand ——"

"He's not in love with her, is he?" asked Stiegel in a low
voice, seeing that the little girls were whispering together.

"Of course not! But she has led him a merry chase, along
with the rest," Elizabeth cried. "She carries on with them
all so it's a disgrace, and Anna ——"

"Sh!" he warned. "Little pitchers ——" pointing to the
girls.

"Children. You are finished. Leave the table."

"Anne says she meets Martin Grenier every night of her
life, and no telling what goes on."

"Elizabeth, Diane is my ward!" So it *was* Martin Grenier.
He felt suddenly sick to his stomach.

"That's the very reason you should know these things.
What kind of influence do you think she is for the girls?
Little innocent girls. Loving and kissing every man who
comes ——"

"That's not true!" cried Stiegel, slamming down his knife
on the table.

"You're a man—that's why you're so blind! Of course she can fool you. Smiles and ogles and throws her body around. George ——"

"Elizabeth, I forbid you to say another word!" Stiegel jumped up in a rage, walking about the table savagely. "Anne, get out of here!"

"I won't stop till I've had my say," Elizabeth cried, bursting into tears. "She's a bad woman, and I have to live in the same house with her. And my nephew has to sit at the table with her and be tempted—just a young boy, a good boy. She'll get him in trouble. . . ."

"I suppose he'll have a baby!" shouted Stiegel, in derision, wishing he had the young scoundrel by the neck.

He went out onto the grounds; tramped over to the stable to pet his horse.

Diane wasn't like this. She couldn't be as promiscuous as Elizabeth had said. Of course Diane met Martin Grenier. She was in love with him at last; it was the way he had planned it, going off so this very thing would happen. Having her chance! A damned prude expression. Having her chance! If only he could be sure.

But it was only several days later that Stiegel received his judgment from Diane's own lips.

Robert Morris had come up to visit the Glass House before it should close down. A very elaborate dinner had been planned for him, with half a dozen people arriving from Lancaster. Elizabeth, in her powder mantle, was preparing a careful and exquisite toilette.

Stiegel was secreted in his wig closet. This was a recess in which every real gentleman had his wig powdered. Each Saturday, to be sure, the wig was recurled on small rollers of pipe clay in Brickerville, but for social affairs of the week, the barber officiated at home. Great cloths were wrapped about Stiegel's neck, and his face was protected from the onslaught by a glass cone, which he held dutifully before him as if he were inflicting on himself a dose of ether. The barber had a quail pipe, which was commonly used to allure quail. Through this instrument he blew the powder professionally though gaspingly, for this was indeed an exertion. The operation was only .half performed when Elizabeth could be heard sobbing.

" 'Tis my tooth . . . I am like to die!"

Stiegel, disconcerted, was oozing dust in the bedroom so recently "wung" or straightened, for guests.

"Has it a puff?"

"Aye," she sobbed. " 'Twill soon burst my cheek."

"Have you tried to prick it?" asked Stiegel.

Elizabeth, her endurance tried to the limit, leaned on the dressing-table and began to cry in earnest.

"Come, Lizzie," said Stiegel, patting her shoulder, while the barber stood by with his quail pipe like some outwitted huntsman. "Your eyes will be all stained with tears, and the guests will be here in a little while."

Cyrus, who was lighting candles, stopped for a moment before them, his long black face filled with sympathy.

"I knows a remedy," he condoled, and ran out of the room. In a few moments he returned with a frog which he kept caged in the brook for just this purpose.

"I don' know's he cures white teef," he adjured them. "But he sho do cure black teef, Marsa Baron. . . . Now, Missy Stiegel, I pray you, spit in he's mouf, muttah ovah he's head, suffah him to hop astray, and fooh! de devil take de toof-ache!"

This rather delicate and trusting operation was performed while Stiegel's wig was finished. But Elizabeth, who had not spit voluminously enough into the frog's mouth, perhaps, was unaffected.

"White teef," muttered Cyrus, fumbling under the bed and in the corners for the refractory frog.

Stiegel stood watching his wife, wondering desperately

what he could do to relieve her.

"You must lie quiet abed, then, Lizzie. Diane can take your place at table."

"I will sit at the table myself," she cried thickly.

"But you cannot sit there and cry. . . . Tunstall," he inquired of the barber, "can you pull teeth?"

The barber shrugged his slim shoulders, which meant that he was as good at it as the next fellow.

"Yes," cried Elizabeth. "Pull it! I can't stand the pain another second."

"Cyrus, get a hammer and nail. Quick. . . . *Diane*," Stiegel called, going to the door of the hall. "Come and hold Lizzie's head while the barber pulls. . . ."

"No, I won't have her touch me!"

"Diane," cried Stiegel, as Diane came running into the hall, unfastening the apron which she had put on to protect her gown while washing Jacob for bed. "Diane, better yet, I'll hold Lizzie's head, and you run for some brandy."

Elizabeth, wailing and shivering with fright and pain, sat on the floor, her head secure between Stiegel's knees; Cyrus held the nail against the tooth of the hysterical woman, and Tunstall pounded at it with a hammer.

Her cries could be heard all over the house, and when the tooth had been finally yanked from her bleeding jaw, Stiegel and Diane helped her over to the bed. Cyrus and the barber went mournfully out of the room and closed the door.

"Here, Lizzie, swallow some brandy," cried Diane, forgetting the feud which had been going on for months.

"Get out of here," moaned Elizabeth, pushing her away so roughly that the glass jerked and a spurt of brandy flew out onto her satin bodice.

"Try to rest," Stiegel cautioned her, "or you will be ill. Do not worry, Lizzie; Diane will take care of the guests. She will sit at your place at table and ——"

"I'll sit at my own place at table!" Elizabeth cried, the blood drooling thickly from her mouth, and Diane mopped it with a towel which she held in her hand. "I've stood her tricks long enough."

"Lizzie——"

"I have! All the time you were gone. . . ." She grasped the towel, choking and spitting into it. "I'm the mistress here! I'll sit at my own place at table. You don't believe me when I tell you these things. . . . She's in love with you!"

"Lizzie!" cried Stiegel again, his eyes blazing into Diane's.

"She's trying to take my place . . . to shove me and my baby out. . . ."

"Stop!" Stiegel clenched Elizabeth's arm so that she cried out with pain, and Diane drew herself up straight, her brain flying fast, terrified.

"You are in love with him, aren't you?" Elizabeth yelled, rolling from the bed and standing before them, dishevelled. "You came out of the woods—and you want the jewels I have, and the gowns and the coach. That's what she wants, Heinrich . . . and you are so blind you can't see it. I'm your wife—and she's got to get out. . . ."

She fell onto Stiegel's shoulder, and her words were muffled and jumbled. "I thought it—it was going to be different. . . . I wanted the children to love me. . . . I wanted you to love me, Heinrich. . . . All you care about is . . . glass, stoves, land. . . ."

He put his arm around her, and he loathed himself. He had made a mess of things. But if Diane loved him—now before it was too late. . . . He looked over at her with pleading. She was strong, straight. His fingers burned to reach out and touch the shimmering yellow silk of her gown, the curling, scornful red lips. . . .

Diane's eyes bored into his. He was pleading for himself, she thought, agonized, pleading for her to save him. To save his glass and his stoves and his smiles from the country-side. Pleading for her to free him. That was it. He was weak. He wanted everything from life! He could not bring himself to make a choice. She wanted only one thing. She laughed suddenly in contempt at the two of them standing there before her, and she said lightly, in utter amazement at her own words, "I won't burden you much longer! I am betrothed to Martin Grenier."

Stiegel felt Elizabeth sagging in his arms, and he would have liked to throw her fiercely across the floor. He hated her with all the passion that was in him, and almost afraid that he would do her violence, he rushed out into the hall after Diane; Robert Morris was coming down the stairs from the third floor, whistling and debonair, adjusting the ruffles at his cuffs.

An hour later, her cheek tight-skinned as a ripening peach, Elizabeth presided at her dinner party.

20

AFTER THE GUESTS had gone to bed, Stiegel and Elizabeth lingered a few moments in the parlor to gather wine glasses on a tray; the dinner party had been a riotous success, and Stiegel thought that every shriek of laughter would split his head. Martin Grenier! How gay they had all been with the news! Martin would be fierce in his love. Stiegel winced at the thought. Security! This was what he had wanted for Diane.

"Heinrich, don't you hear me or don't you want to talk to me?" Elizabeth asked. She had made up her mind that she would treat her tantrum before dinner as if it had never occurred. The news of Diane's coming marriage had made her exultant in spite of the horrible throbbing of her jaw.

"I have a headache," he said briefly.

"But it was a success, don't you think?"

"A vast success."

She picked up a handkerchief someone had left on the harpsichord, and smelled the scent. Perhaps it would be better if she gave some sort of apology for her behaviour. She went over to Stiegel, and putting her hands on his shoulders, turned her face up to be kissed.

245]

He looked down at her swollen cheek, and thought of the blood which had bubbled from her mouth. Repulsed, almost nauseated, he turned away from her gruffly.

"I'm sorry about tonight," she said, her voice trembling. "I was nigh mad with the pain. I don't know what I said. Will you forgive me, Heinrich?"

Forgive her! What else was there to do? What difference did it make, anyway? He turned to her, taking her firmly by the shoulders, and his voice was grim.

"Elizabeth, no one can take back words that have been said. But I expect you to apologize to Diane, and to be ——"

"How did I know she was going to marry him? The way she flirted. . . . George did not eat a bite of ——"

"You will apologize to her," resolutely. "And you will be pleasant to her the rest of the time she is here!"

"I will try, Heinrich. . . ."

"You will not *try*, Elizabeth. And you will *not* be sourly civil. You will be pleasant!"

She bridled at the peremptory tone of his voice. Stiegel did not often turn on her like this, but when he did she was afraid of him.

"If I've done her an injustice . . ." she mumbled, her fingers toying with the braid on his coat.

"Elizabeth, don't touch me! Go to bed. I'm—I'm all un-done, can't you see it?" he said, his voice breaking.

Rebuffed, she stood before him, tempted to run off again in another outburst, and yet beginning to see that she was a fool. Her hatred of Diane would be inconceivable to him. He must think her nothing but a shrew, never knowing how gnawing her jealousy had been. She was so relieved at Diane's betrothal that she could have screamed from the housetop with joy. Only a few more months and the girl would be gone. She would be living with a glass-blower in a little cottage, and have better than what she deserved. For Elizabeth there would be the new house at Manheim, and the gay social life of Philadelphia, opened up to her for the first time. She would be going to the Assembly at Andrew Hamilton's. She would see that the house on Mulberry Street was unequaled in splendor. Heinrich had grown away from the passion of their early marriage, but she would win him back again in a thousand little ways. It would pay her to be affable to Diane.

Heinrich obviously only felt duty toward Diane or he would not be consenting to this marriage. Poor Diane, she thought—it was quite natural that she should fall in love with Heinrich. He was very rich. Her heart began to flutter a little at her possession of him, and she paused in the doorway to look back at him before she went upstairs.

He had taken off his wig, and was running his fingers through his blond thick waving hair. What a beautiful figure he had, she thought. And how strong and handsome his candlelit profile looked against the dark shadows.

A harp string snapped in two with a startling rip, and she and Stiegel both jumped, staring at one another for a moment like strangers. It was almost as if Diane herself had suddenly laughed at them again.

Diane, alone in her room, was jubilant. She had been certain from Stiegel's actions tonight that he loved her. She had saved them all from destruction by a simple little lie. How surprised they would be if they knew she had no intention of marrying Grenier. That before the summer was over she and Stiegel would belong to one another. She laughed to herself, half breathless, a little hysterical at the quick turn matters had taken. In another week Martin Grenier would be gone. She was almost afraid of him. When she had told him tonight that she would marry him he had lifted her off her feet in a frenzy of excitement. But they must marry at once, he said. With Stiegel away his responsibility had been double, and he was nervous and thin and combustible. He tried to shatter her arguments with jealous impatience. She had been very foolish to give herself to Martin Grenier during the eternity that Stiegel was gone. He had been a beautiful lover, she repeated to herself, but she did not love him. It would not be easy in the fall when he came back to untangle the situation. But that was far off. That must take care of itself.

From then on, Elizabeth and Diane were hypocritically amiable to one another, anticipating their permanent separation. Elizabeth could have her jewels and her coaches, smiled Diane to herself. By the fall, Diane and Stiegel would be meeting in the woods. . . . Her whole body pounded with the thought of their union. It would all be very easy. Stiegel would dismiss Martin Grenier. Diane had simply found that she did not love him. That would be excuse enough. Among the family, she and Stiegel would be pleasantly casual to one another. She must be very careful not to rouse Elizabeth's suspicions again. The months, the years would go equally on. The liaison would be a great game of wits. The days would seem lazy and aimless, but to herself and her lover they would be thrilling.

It would not be simple to break down Stiegel's German impregnability. It was this intangible thing called conscience which it was so hard for her to battle. Essentially pagan, she had never bothered to accept the conventional God, feeling capable of managing her own affairs quite satisfactorily by herself. Only once before had she had the sense of her own powerlessness. One night when she was small she had run away from her home in Acadia and found herself on a mountain road, with a universe of black and silver trying hungrily to absorb her. Now again some outside force was trying to break her will of iron. Well, she would not let it. Morals were silly little rules which had been made by man. The only reason she had given herself to Martin Grenier and not to others was because his passion was strong and virile, and the others were weaklings. Stiegel was different still. He was her mate.

She tossed about her bed, restless with the balm which hung in the spring air. The flush brooks were overflowing into the rivers, and the birds were singing in the morning as if their hearts would break with love. Heinrich's heart had been broken too, today. She would heal it. He wanted to have the decision made for him—to be swept away by their passion so swiftly that he could cry out to his conscience, "I couldn't help it . . . I tried to be strong. . . ."

What she would do tomorrow and the next day and the next, she had not quite decided. But this time she would fight his conscience to the end. This time there was no timid Elizabeth, bearing babies and crying out for love that he couldn't give her. This time she would be harming no one who was too weak to fight back! There would be the preposterous betrothal dinner in another week. And there was the blue glass bowl. . . .

"Heinrich, Heinrich . . ." Diane's musing wandered, drifting deliciously into sleep and back again. "If there is a Hell, and we go there hand in hand . . . how sweet it will be . . . my Heinrich. . . ."

The betrothal dinner was set for the day the Glass House closed. The evening before, Diane met Stiegel on the stairs of the upper hall. He hesitated for a moment, and she smiled bewitchingly.

"Diane," he said awkwardly. "You . . . I hope . . . wait, I have something for you. . . ."

He went into his room, and came back with a bracelet in each hand.

"For me, Heinrich?" said Diane softly, filling up the awkward moment of silence as he held them out before her. "Oh, but these were made for a *lady*, mon cher! Not for a . . . a strumpet!" She laughed wickedly.

Chagrined at the reference, Stiegel paused, her slim

brown wrist in his fingers, and the bracelet half about it.
He had not been so close to her, so alone with her for
months; as she stood before him, small, her face upturned
to his, she seemed part of the haze of his mind, a haze of
blurring candlelight and shining stairs which curved beyond them. She was a soft brown like the hall at night, and
all that seemed clear in his mind were her coaxing black
eyes with their long straight lashes and the foolish daisy
chain about her hair.

"Diane, forgive Elizabeth her jealousy, I beg of you. . . ."

"Oh, her jealousy—that is all quite gone, M'sieu. She is
working for me a pair of the *most* handsome pockets. They
say:

> *'Cupid's arrow*
> *Hath hit true,*
> *It plights the love*
> *Of sweethearts two.'*

"Roses . . . all over the pockets, and *beaut*'ful big
thorns ——"

"Diane, you cannot think what heartache these quar——"

"I know, mon cher. . . . Elizabeth pulls my hair; I slap
her. We have a most wonderful time. . . . But you cannot
slap; you cannot pull. . . . *You* cannot even be heard if
you talk. Miserable, Heinrich, n'est-ce pas?"

"Diane," he said, clasping the bracelet with fumbling
fingers, "I want you to be . . . happy!"

"Oui, I know . . ." in a husky whisper.

He looked up, and caught the light in her eyes.

"Diane, you . . . you . . . do you love ——"

Elizabeth began to climb the stairs, puffing, and Stiegel
fastened the other bracelet on Diane's wrist, and lifted her
fingers to his lips in a quick flash.

"Law, 'tis hot," Elizabeth gasped, fanning her pink per-
spired face with her apron. "Most unseasonly. . . ."

"Elizabeth," Stiegel said tersely, "I have just given Diane my—our betrothal gift. See what you think of my choice."

Diane held out her wrists, and Elizabeth, trying unsuccessfully to keep the resentment from her fading pansy eyes, said nicely, "My, how *very* beautiful. . . . But Heinrich, do you think Diane will have occasion to wear jewelry like this after she is married?"

The bracelets glistened as Diane held them up in the candlelight. They were of broad gold, with a large yellow diamond in the center, surrounded by amethysts. They were more exquisite by far than anything Stiegel had given Elizabeth.

"Why not?" Stiegel returned abruptly.

Elizabeth was flustered and angry, and controlling her emotions these days was no easy matter. "A poor glassblower needs tables and chairs. A cow of his own, some pigs ——"

"Oui, oui, oui," cried Diane, delighted at the doltish turn of the conversation. "Do give me a cow, Heinrich! Do you remember—the last Assembly in Lancaster before you went to Europe, when we danced the minuet together? You said, 'Diane, you do not need these baubles. They are for the dull and old!' . . . Mon Dieu, there is Jacob calling for a drink of water again!"

Stiegel turned to Elizabeth hotly after Diane had hurried off.

"You see?"

But Elizabeth was not in the mood to have her extravagance and debts brought up again. She said coldly, "You were quite right, of course. 'Twill be something Diane will always have to remember us by!"

The next morning Stiegel passed through the kitchen as Diane stood before the fireplace, waiting for a large lump of butter she had tied there to melt drop by drop into a bowl of cake flour. Anne had gone to the cellar for apples.

"Here is a pence for the cake," he smiled, jingling some coins in his pocket.

"Nay, not for a betrothal cake, mon cher."

"This seems like a game today, Diane. So sudden, so. . . . Diane, Martin Grenier—do you love him, Diane?" He had been burdened with the question night and day; it seemed so crude, but somehow he must know, if he were ever to have any peace again.

"In de hayben ob de Lode . . ." chanted Anne, her skirt filled with apples as she shuffled up the stairs. Diane could easily have answered, but she seized on Anne's interruption as an excuse, and remained silent. Stiegel walked impatiently away.

He had no opportunity to speak to her again until she was dressed in her new Paris creation. The more intimate of Elizabeth's and Stiegel's friends had been trailing in all day with bandboxes and new bonnets. Diane had no friends. Her guests were rejected lovers and their fiancées and wives. The company was chatting, drinking punch, sparkling with wit and satin. Grenier, who had been standing with Stiegel and Diane, went off to find a cushion for a lady in a condition.

"His eyes consume you," remarked Stiegel, who would have been shocked to see that his eyes did the same. "It's a red letter day for Grenier."

"And for you, 'Baron,' " sarcastically.

He folded his arms, so that he would not shake the lithe shoulders in their rococo lace. He felt a sudden dire need to hear from her own lips the answer to the question he had been repeating all day. He turned his back to the room.

"Diane, do you love Martin Grenier?"

It was Cyrus now. "Marsa Baron, de dinna's all sizzlin' an' waitin'. De Klingerman boy, he's on de second decantah, and he's still sottin', marsa."

Stiegel, vanquished, looked at Diane in despair.

She laid her hand with its sparkling new ornament upon his arm and smiled up at him, amused at his childish vexation.

"Heinrich, is it not de trop to ask?" she said ambiguously.

After the meal had been served, Diane flew off to her room and brought back the blue glass bowl.

"My betrothal gift!" she announced in a ringing voice, and there was a buzzing of exclamations and comments as the guests crowded around her. She held it proudly before the silver candelabra so that the light shone through it and seemed to absorb the shining damask. Then she set it down tantalizingly before Stiegel.

He picked it up, and fingered it reverently. "Ach Gott, what divine blue!"

" 'Tis a favorite color with you, isn't it?" she remarked quickly.

He did not answer, examining the bowl with deep concentration. He felt a poignant hatred for the keen, swarthy little Frenchman.

"Monsieur Grenier is so *clev*-er!" giggled Amanda Powell, knocking over a full glass of red wine with her fluttering fan, and enjoying the commotion she stirred among the rescue crew.

"But he did not make it," returned Diane to a diminishing audience, for the accident was getting its due notice.

"Who then?" cried Robert Klingerman loudly; he was flirting painfully and outrageously with a Brickerville girl, and he wanted everyone to know it.

"Stole from King Alfred by a French soldier. His paramour fancied it. Handed down from father to son. . . ."

"The blood of a paramour in his veins," George muttered under his breath, but loud enough so that Robert Morris could hear him.

Robert Morris picked some moist grease from the candle, and rolled it into a little ball.

"Do you think the words of a marriage ceremony enter one's blood?" he bantered, and he thought, "What a suffocating Macaroni George is getting to be! And a little sour at the celebration, like the rest of us."

"I've never seen such tiny dots of enamel, Grenier," Stiegel said excitedly. "The crown and coat of arms are a lost art. Himmel, but it's beautiful! And look, this is no job of puttering, this engraving. . . ."

The bowl was being praised now in little whispers and murmurings, so that Stiegel's professional comments could be heard.

"Look at the ostrich feather!" cried a lady with good eyesight, leaning close over Stiegel's shoulder.

"There's an angel in flight engraved here," pointed out Diane.

"And see how the knight charges on his steed!" Grenier cried out, craving every atom of praise he could get.

He was very handsome in his scarlet and flowered waistcoat, thought young Fanny Eschbach.

"The ramping lion is of the house of Philip of Alsace," Grenier boasted.

"Oh, I see now . . . it's all of a symbol," cried Stiegel. "The great crown and arms of enamel are of Philip of Alsace. The others are of lesser men, in subjection. That's why they're engraved dim about the bowl, in confusion, I'll wager!"

The bowl, like a large pending soap bubble, pivoted in Stiegel's fingers. He followed the delicate tracery of stars, fleurs-de-lis, gaping fish, crosses, castles, and dragons. They had been engraved so minutely, so finely, in subordination to the king's brilliant insignia of enamel, that only on close scrutiny did they seem anything but an imbroglio.

"A pontil mark not unlike our own. . . . A pity the bowl is nicked."

"An aged beauty with a mole," laughed Diane.

"I would like to copy the blue, Diane," Stiegel whispered excitedly, as the group began to disperse, and Robert Morris got Grenier aside to talk to him about the treasure. "Give me the bowl for a time. It shall be safe in my hands."

"But the Glass House will be closed in three days!"

" 'Twill only be a matter of a few days. My color compounders have a genius for blue. And Martin Grenier, he can do anything!"

Diane shook her head obstinately. " 'Tis far too old, Heinrich. I'd never trust it to ordinary hands! You forget, 'tis my betrothal gift!"

"But Diane, it's a blue worth thousands of pounds," he went on in an excited undertone. "The subtlety . . . the . . . the rareness of it!"

Undaunted, stimulated, her eyes blazed defiance.

"Oui?" she said, elated with her success, and, picking up the bowl, carried it off safely to her room, and hid it behind the folds of the dressing-table chintz.

For the next few days, Stiegel plagued Diane for the bowl.

"Diane, I *must* have the bowl."

"I hardly dare touch it myself, M'sieu. 'Tis too old."

"Odd's life, but you have got squeamish, Diane!"

"Say what you will, but it's my one treasure, Heinrich. Martin would not forgive me."

"But 'twould be the fortune of us all if we could copy the blue. Have you no heart, Diane?"

"Martin has been working on it day and night, n'est-ce pas?" she asked.

"Plague take him, he's too love-lorn to see anything but a blaze! I want the bowl—in my own hands!"

Stiegel was determined to duplicate the color, and ordered his color-compounders to make up every conceivable shade of blue. He had always accomplished everything he

wanted with perseverance, and he knew now that if he kept
on long enough he would come upon the formula.

" 'Twould be wise to give up these attempts," she advised
him, knowing very well that this suggestion only strength-
ened his desire. "You have told me yourself there is inimitable art! That no paint will endure like the frieze at Pom-
peii! And no fluid will keep the corpse fresh like the
Egyptian mummy!"

Diane, casually examining her saffron-stained finger-
tips, smiled with exasperating levity.

"Diane, can't you see it's a passion with me to surpass
all the art of glassware?"

"I can scarce keep apace of your passions. 'Twas music
and the score, yesterday, n'est-ce pas?"

"A man's passions are . . . illimitable."

Diane shrugged her shoulders. That was exactly what
filled her with animosity. A man's passions were illimitable.
He had loved music, and stoves, and honor, and now glassware. He had loved these things more than he loved her—
all of them. She had never loved anyone or anything but
him. And her passion would never change.

But his eagerness for the bowl itself was just what she
wanted. After Martin was gone she would consent to let
Stiegel work on the bowl, but she would sit in the Glass
House long hours with him, if she should roast alive to do
it, and she would say of course that she would never trust
the bowl out of her sight.

When Martin Grenier actually came to say good-bye to
her, Diane was so relieved that it was all she could do to
hide her exultation.

"Diane, I can never wait through the long summer
months to hold you in my arms again," he cried, pressing
his lips to hers covetously, and she closed her eyes and
longed for the long summer twilights when he would be

gone at last. Autumn would come too soon. Why had she done this thing to herself and Martin?

"Diane, I'll not go to the farm. I'll stay here with you, at the Furnace!"

"Non, non, non, cheri. Your eyes. You might go blind with the heat!" she exclaimed in a panic.

"Now that I've had you I can never endure the separation again!"

"Oh, but you must . . . for my sake, you must, Martin!"

"Diane, come with me to the farm then!" he pleaded.

"Un feu d'enfer! The Furnace has made of you a habit, mon cher. Three, four summer months; 'twill not be long . . . then the feu de joie!"

She looked into his bloodshot eyes, and she was stirred by a combination of pity and fear again. She had never been afraid of anyone. The feeling was not comfortable.

"Martin, you have not yet the secret of the color for Heinrich?"

"No. . . . I think there's one chemical missing."

"You have not told him what you think it is?" she asked, disturbed.

"Oui. The dye called time." Grenier wished he had not fabricated so exotic a tale about the bowl. Stiegel had kept after him assiduously, almost fanatically. Several times he had been tempted to tell Stiegel how he had compounded the blue. Well, it would not do to make the thing too easy. In the fall, perhaps. Now he was not in the mood to belittle his gift. He was very tired, and it seemed as if the fires of the long winter had scorched his eyes, dimming them.

"If you philander while I am gone I shall kill you!" he raged, as he said good-bye, and Diane soothed him with kisses.

He left an antique seal ring with her, and some books of rare old binding made in a French monastery, handsomely illuminated. As soon as he was gone, Diane tossed them into a cupboard in the attic. She did not want to be reminded of him. All that mattered was that at last he had gone, and that she still possessed the bowl and Stiegel wanted it.

21

IN EARLY MAY the Manheim mansion was ready for occupancy, and the question arose of who would go there to get the house in order for the family.

"Perhaps your sister had best go; she will know just what supplies we will need on our coming," suggested Stiegel to Elizabeth.

"But I have not seen the house, Heinrich!" cried Elizabeth.

"You will not want to go into it with painters and carpenters still at work, my dear."

"Oh, but I can't wait to see the German spinet, with its black and white keys all reversed; and the English chafing-dishes and the wall tapestries and the Dresden china ——"

"I shall not be able to stay with you," he said. "The Stedmans are growling. . . ."

"Oh, that's all right. I shall take Jacob with me, of course, and the new indentured German girls." She hesitated a moment, and then added, "And Anna will be here to look after you."

She was not only referring to his cherry pudding. She knew that Anna's eye was even sharper than her own, and that Diane would not dare to take any added liberties with

259]

Anna in charge. Then too, it would be wonderful being mistress of her own kitchen in Manheim, and not having to be courteous to Diane.

Stiegel did not answer her, and she wondered if he resented the fact that she was content to be separated from him.

"I shall not be gone very long," she reminded him, her dimpled hand stroking his cheek, "with the wedding so close."

The new furniture and bric-à-brac which Stiegel had brought from Europe would be entrancing!

Stiegel turned away so that she wouldn't see the relief in his eyes. At least these last few months he and Diane would be free of her quibbling jealousy.

He accompanied Elizabeth to Manheim, which was no more nor less than a village green cleared out of virgin woods. The mansion itself overlooked the green, and even Elizabeth was satisfied when she saw it. It was forty feet square and two stories high, with a broad flat-railed platform surmounting the gabled roof. This, Stiegel had designed for his band. The dining-hall and kitchen, lovely spacious rooms, were outfitted with English china; the sideboard had ridden the waves to repose in that very nook. English tapestry of hunting-scenes hung in the large parlor, and the chimney-place was decorated with scriptural tiles. For months, workmen had been meticulously carving the wainscoting and doors.

The second floor had only a few bedrooms. The family would be decreasing with Diane getting married and George going off to school, and there would be the King of Prussia Tavern for the overflow of guests. Besides, Stiegel had preferred having a little chapel on the second floor in which to preach to his workmen.

The Glass House to be finished in the fall was fast taking shape, and a little inn was being built on the road which finally lapsed into fields. Cottages for the glass-blowers were beginning to spring up. There was a continuous sound of hammering and sawing; wells were dug; and an office built for Stiegel near the Glass House.

In the fall he planned to move his entire glass business to Manheim. It was growing miraculously, and he wanted it established here where he anticipated spending most of his time. It needed him now more than the Furnace, which had run as smoothly as the well oiled water wheel for years.

Sitting on a crate in the room which would be his office, he took from his pocket the letter which had come in the last mail from Alexander Stedman:

"I am happy to note your town of Manheim is thriving and I wish you happiness in the accomplishment of this your life-time ambition. However, the fact that you are planning to move the glass business only serves to corroborate my feeling that this comes first in your devotion, and that the iron industry is a secondary considerashun. As Charles and I are not benefitting by your artistic endeavours in glassware it is only natural that we judge a falling off of iron orders is due to neglect on your part; Warwick Furnace has had the biggest year of its history. . . ."

Stiegel shoved the letter back into his pocket. Partners, partners. Hadn't he informed the Stedmans that the cause of slack business last year was due to the freezing of the water power, so that the furnace was out of blast a month beyond its normal time? It was natural that orders should shift under the circumstances. The Stedmans were jealous, of course, because the glass business was so profitable; it was obvious from their frigid letters.

Going back to Brickerville, Stiegel tried to comfort himself with the thought of his prosperity. With the glass-blowers dismissed for the summer, he had settled down in his spare moments, which were rare, to sketching large perfume bottles, cream jugs, decanters and smelling-salt bottles. The whole family was enthusiastic about designing new glassware. Even Anne Ege suggested wine glasses of tulip shape, a water lily salver, a poppy punch bowl.

Robert Morris, whose fervor for God's-Acre and the surrounding land was second only to Stiegel's own, still lingered on, riding in and about the woods by day, and talking land at night.

One evening he slipped into his chair, with an air of excitement.

"Well, a fine lot of news that Chepa Rose brings with him!"

"Is Chepa Rose here?" cried Michael, slithering away from the table unnoticed.

"England's enforcing the Stamp Act in November!" cried Morris.

"No!" returned Stiegel, amazed. "I'll be damned if I'll pay hundreds of dollars for stamped paper for *my* bills of merchandise!"

"That's what a million others say. They've banded together in New York, and seized the Governor's carriage, stuffed it with the images of the Governor and Satan, and hauled it about town in a torchlight parade."

"Everything but our breath is taxed!" cursed Stiegel.

"Sons of Liberty they call themselves, and Chepa Rose says the whole city of Philadelphia is alive with excitement. . . . Pamphlets, meetings, tar and featherings. . . ."

Diane's eyes shone.

"The whole town's on the strictest lamb diet," Robert Morris ran on. "So wool can be used for clothes. The women refuse to wear imported cloth. Imagine Mary White in homespun, Stiegel!"

"But Madame Du Barry . . . she will be furious not to be copied—now she has just come to the throne of fashion!" laughed Diane.

"I've got to get back at once," said Morris. "Business has been bad enough. Now very like there will be no business waiting for me at all."

"I'm glad for every ounce of sugar I've smuggled in," cried Stiegel, the noodles remaining untouched on his plate.

"You'd better give up the glass ——" Robert Morris advised.

"Give it up! The very time to plow ahead! Gott! I can make glass equal to England's any day. . . . And ——"

"Look what people have got for smuggling! You're a fool to think England's going to approve competition in her glass business."

"You sound like the Stedmans," retorted Stiegel, who was determined in his course.

"I hope we'll never have to wear homespun," Barbara complained, thinking that Samuel Froelich's eyes upon her in church would surely not be so admiring then. "I don't like the prick of it."

The threat of the Stamp Act inflamed Stiegel more than ever with a desire to copy the bowl. This was the time for innovation. God knows, he could use the extra money. With all the expansion of Charming Forge and Elizabeth Furnace and the glass works, cash was a little scarce.

Diane still withheld the bowl, and for a long time Stiegel had not made mention of it.

Then, the evening after Robert Morris left, she and Stiegel and Michael came to the table before the others. Against all rules, she helped Michael to his food so that he might be finished quickly and return to the dam he was building.

"Diane," Stiegel exclaimed suddenly, and she thought he was going to scold her for this breach of etiquette, "you are a child and a fool about this bowl."

"I think you place the value upon it yourself, mon cher."

He was nonplused for a moment. " 'Twould bring me a fortune. You refuse me from stubbornness, Diane."

"You have no sentiment yourself; how could you suspect me of any! I dream of the bowl at night, terrified lest it break," she went on with a keen sense of enjoyment. "Then I dream that it has broke and wake up and vow I shall *never* let it go from my sight."

She glanced at Michael. He was assimilating German noodles, his concentration deep and complete.

"Heinrich, can't you see what this gift from my lover means to me?"

"You're lying," he thundered, and slammed down the silverware he'd been toying with. "The bowl means nothing to you! It means everything to me."

Michael, who had been struggling with a most unwieldy noodle, dropped his spoon upon the plate in alarm.

Diane met Stiegel's eyes, cold as the piercing light of the northern sky, and her heart pounded with jealousy. Stiegel did not care that she was going to be married. All he cared about was the blue of the bowl. Perhaps if he found it he would be more conscious of her—of the few months that supposedly were left to them. . . .

"Some day I'll give it you," she said, and as the thought grew in her mind that the summer was short, she compromised. "Heinrich, I shall go with you to the Glass House tonight with the bowl. I shall sit close to it, and knit."

"Gott!" he exclaimed, trying to hide his elation. "You treat me like a child!"

After dinner Stiegel and Diane went off to the Glass House. Diane, carrying the bowl, stepped carefully to avoid accident, and Stiegel, a little haughty over the whole affair, held her arm. Cyrus shuffled in the rear with the lantern.

A fire had been lighted in the deserted Glass House, and pots of hot metal stood ready for experimental mixture at

Stiegel's hands. The shop had an air of trimness; the marver was shining and immaculate, barrels of supplies were
covered; and pucellas, pincers, marking-compasses and
measuring-sticks lay neatly on their shelves in a summer
drowse.

Stiegel went to work with a vengeance, adding to and
subtracting from the batch with awkward fingers, swinging small colored blue bubbles from the blow-pipe, tense,
expectant. He seemed totally unconscious of Diane, as he
worked in the linen shirt which was fast wilting, his sleeves
rolled to his elbows. She sat there knitting, guarding, like
Madam La Farge. Occasionally she pushed the damp locks
back from her forehead, straightened her weary back and
sighed. The small panes of the Glass House had become
black now, with sharp red darts of firelight. Stiegel's satin
breeches and thick blond hair were dull rose as he gripped
the pontil rod. She watched the muscles of his arm coming
and going like ripples upon the water.

He turned to her once, suddenly.

"It's too hellish hot for you here, Diane," mopping his
forehead.

"Nay. Three of my petticoats lie home upon the bed."

They were silent again. Nothing but the crepitation of
burning charcoal beneath the pot, the click of Diane's
needles, the caucus of frogs in the creek.

Anna Ege came to the Glass House once or twice in a
great perspiration to see if Heinrich had had any luck, she
said. And during the evening she sent Michael and George
and Cyrus and Anne, at absurd intervals, on the same mis-
sion. If the heat had not been torment to one of her weight,
she would have stayed to chaperone Stiegel and Diane.
She did not like the idea of their being alone, although
Diane's over-anxiety about the bowl made her feel that
perhaps she had misjudged the girl. However, with Elizabeth gone, Stiegel's soul was in her keeping, and betrothal

or no betrothal, she still could not whole-heartedly trust Diane.

These nights of experiment were repeated throughout the following week, except when the weather was too hot, or a new batch of metal had to be made. Diane always knitted, and periodic inquiry was always made from the house. Each evening Diane laid the bowl with dramatic care at one end of the marver. It was iridescent, like a sulphur flame, she thought, and Stiegel seemed to become one with it in his utter worship.

She wondered if he could love any woman with the same abandon. His eyes gleamed softly with hope as he handled the bowl. He had never looked like that at Elizabeth Huber. She had never seen him caress Elizabeth Hölz. Her reminiscences drifted back to the cottage of Cyrus the night Stiegel had clung to her lips, and whispered, "You are maddening, Diane. . . ." Then there had been the same quest in his eyes.

But the bowl was his mistress now. She had not meant to come here to the Glass House and be totally neglected, playing second fiddle to a pretty piece of bric-à-brac. The heat irritated her beyond all expectation, as did Mrs. Ege's diligent surveillance from the house. The old fool, did she think anything short of God could swerve Diane from her purpose?

Stiegel worked till the clothes clung wet to his body, and the sweat poured in rivulets from his face. Although he seemed to pay no attention to Diane, he was acutely conscious of her. The whole matter of her engagement still left him in utter confusion. He was so deeply hurt at the thought of her marriage that his manner toward her was overbearing, curt. He was very madly in love with her; very desperate at the thought that in a few months now she would belong to Martin Grenier. But it was what he had wanted, he told himself over and over. Three months more and Diane would be married. Elizabeth would wear pink lutestring, and she would cluck about Diane and whisper to her connubial secrets with vague superiority—to Diane, who had known the love of a red man and lived with him savagely on the plains!

Diane had been trying to wheedle him into civility again, using all the propitiatory wiles she knew. She sparkled with wit among his guests. And yet she had been flirting boldly with Robert Morris since Grenier left. No sooner had the Glass House closed than she had gathered about her again a retinue of bachelors and widowers, who seemed perfectly willing to come to the house even if she were betrothed, and who gratefully accepted any crumbs of attention she gave them. Why did she do this if she loved Martin Grenier and wanted to marry him? And he could not bear the thought that she might be going into a loveless marriage. He knew if he talked to her about these things she would only lie to him, and also that if he unburdened his heart to her, he must tell her that he loved her.

He felt the shock of his thoughts like a sudden chill. The only way he would be able to face the long interval of summer would be to work so feverishly that he could not torture himself with suspicion.

He tossed a bubble back into the pot, and knew that Diane had stopped knitting and that she watched his swollen hands.

The experiment tonight proved no more enlightening than before. After two hours, when Cyrus came with a lantern for their departure, Diane folded up the knitting that had clung to her fingers, rammed it in the bowl, and went to the door, drinking in the cool May night hungrily.

"Maneto!" she prayed savagely, the stern Indian God rising before her, "help me to get what I want!"

The next evening it rained so hard that Diane and Sti-
gel did not venture to the Glass House.

The parlor seemed to be teeming with noise and con-
motion, and Stiegel was irritable. The experiments had b
come a fever, and he felt that soon he *must* come upon th
formula. He saw the blue of the bowl in the leapir
tongues of fire on the hearth; he saw a glint of it in the ey
of the innkeeper's child. Why was it so elusive, when
was so ubiquitous? And if Grenier was so deuced cleve
how was it that he had not been able to duplicate the colo.

Well, the quest would keep him from going quite ma
in the next few months. It would serve that purpose, a
least. God, life would soon be so empty that with all th
glassware in the world he would never be able to endure i

Diane began to play a song that she had learned, and I
listened to the low throaty tone of her voice as she ha
sang, half hummed. She leaned her head against the har
affectionately as she finished. She was beautiful, almo
part of the shadows of the room in her lavender taffe
gown. And unlike most beautiful women, she was n
thinking of how beautiful she was.

"Your progress is amazing, Diane," said George, watcl
ing her greedily.

" 'Tis simple," she replied in small boy fashion, whic
never will admit exertion.

Stiegel watched her for a moment. "And great gratific;
tion to me," he said.

"Why?" asked Diane.

"Think of the money he has spent on lessons!" Anna Eg
reminded her.

"That is not what I meant," rebuked Stiegel sharply.
meant that my business presses me so, I must get my mus
through others."

"You are not fair to yourself, Heinrich," cried Dian
pausing. "You must not put music so far behind yo

'sieu. It is a part of you. . . . It is *you!*"

"I have too many mouths to feed. . . ."

"Fooh! The mouths are bulging with gluttony!" She
•oked about at the family and shrugged her shoulders.
And yet you starve yourself! Come, get your violin."

"Oh, that reminds me," said Anna Ege quickly. "There
a bill I would like to show you. Two barrels of sugar for
ie Manheim house ——"

Her subterfuge angered him.

"Put it away for the morrow," he said decisively, and he
cked up his violin and began to tune it.

These few months were too precious to let slip by, im-
assive. They were something he must seize and hold in
s heart to remember forever. He did not care how Anna
ge might writhe, he would accompany Diane at night on
e violin, and they would have some of the simple happi-
ess that had been denied them over long years of im-
risonment. People! They were always surrounded by
eople!

Stiegel's fingers quivered mechanically on the strings, so
at he might watch Diane, her mouth puckered child-
hly, her fingers curved. He was happier for the moment
an he had been since he first came to America. They had
ways had so little of one another, he and Diane. And they
d fought, always. It was their love they had battled, not
ie another, Stiegel thought painfully.

He had deliberately transferred his powers of accom-
ishment to Diane. He thought of the scorn Diane felt for
s ambition. It was only tonight that he realized he had
en trying for years to build up an immunity to her by in-
ssant enterprise. Instinctively, he had not dared to pause.
id music was a deliberate pause of the most perilous
nd. It was a suspension of logic, an invasion of sentiment.
e wanted to tell her these things; he wanted to tell her
at it was only because he loved her so much that he had

been forced to crowd his beloved music from his life.

The memory of his early hopes filled him with home-sickness, and he felt suddenly careworn, spiritually emaci-ated. He had a queer hatred for his Stradivarius, as for a counterfeit friend, and began to put it into its case. Diane's hand paused on his arm.

The room was quiet. George and Barbara played chess in the corner, with absorption. He had not even noticed that the others were gone.

"Let us keep on," she coaxed him.

"Diane, I am six and thirty. By now I hoped to be famous."

"We all have hopes that die very young, Heinrich," she answered.

"I loved my music. . . ."

"Oui, M'sieu—but she does not make money for you! Heinrich, write me a love song—for the harp!"

"Love song," he answered scornfully, cut by her accu-sation, "I have wrote études, sonatas. . . ."

"You have begun them. For me, Heinrich, *finish* a love song—little and simple . . . and . . . beautiful. . . . Put in it the sorrow of one who has lost music—and love. And the joy of one who may find them both again!"

"An epic!" he said with disdain.

"Pourquoi non?"

22

MIDSUMMER had brushed Brickerville with her gaudiest paints, assisted by the Italian gardener. Hollyhocks sheltered all the outbuildings as well as the mansion itself. The beehives were hidden in beds of sunflowers back of the house, and the graded garden was brilliant with pinks, larkinspur, sweet williams. The lovely lush green of the lawns spread beyond the house to the creek, and petered into shrubs and berry bushes, and woods. Stiegel began to find cut flowers everywhere he was in the habit of spending any time. There were fresh Queen Margrets on his desk each morning; sweet-scented pease on his lowboy at night.

Diane whistled gayly at her work, and the fact that she was being happy without him was more than Stiegel could bear.

After lunch one noon he thought that Barbara and Jerusha looked particularly flushed and lively. Mrs. Ege had gone out to measure the fresh-picked currants, and Diane said, "Now, I think he shall be in good mind!"

Barbara's lashes dropped quickly onto her cheeks and her lips knotted in sudden shyness.

"We would make a trip to Lancaster," blurted out

Jerusha, "to our Grossmama. And . . . and there is
French dancing-master there!"

"We would be very mannerly," added Barbara, excitedl
now that the bridge had been crossed.

"We've never seen Uncle Anthony's wife, and he sa
Aunt Maria is very pretty!"

"The cherry preserving is done ——"

Jerusha ran impulsively to Stiegel and put her tv
chubby arms about his neck.

"Oh, please, sweet papa. 'Twould be *such* good fun. Ar
Grossmama would ne'er. . . ."

"Heinrich," interrupted Diane, craftily, "your moth
has always had no for an answer. 'Tis her due to have tl
girls, is it not?"

"I scarce trust them fifteen miles alone."

"George would be joyed to ride with them."

George thumped his wine glass down on the table, ar
glared at Diane. He was trapped.

Soon after sunrise a few days later, Barbara and Jerush
fluttered about on the lawn counting hat-boxes and sea
skin portmantuas. The girls cried a little with happy e
citement. They kissed everyone good-bye, and hugged Anr
as she stood goggle-eyed at their intrepidity. They woul
begin the journey side-saddle on their favorite horse
changing to the phaeton at times for a rest. The apoplect
coachman with the red nose held his reins tight and hig
ready for the electric "go." There were more good-by
and more good-byes, and first Anne detained the travele
by forcing on them a violin bottle of spirits of campho
and then Cyrus regaled the horses with sugar lumps–
voluptuous extravagance.

George glumly sipped at a stirrup-cup before h
mounted. Then most unexpectedly, he seized Diane's tv
hands in his own, kissed them warmly, and leaped into tl
saddle.

"Diane is betrothed, George," chided Barbara with vir-
ous indignation, and Jerusha snickered.

George reddened and Stiegel, with one glance at Diane's
ornful face, took a pinch of snuff and walked up the stairs
ay from them. Well, it served Diane right, he thought
th rancor. She had been flirting with George as well as
th other men all summer. And he was unconscionably
lous of them all, even of George, whom she obviously
thed. George had always been a furtive sort of person,
ushing against Diane as he passed her in the doorway, or
storing her fallen handkerchief so that his hand caressed
rs. Stiegel could not bear the sight of George pressing
ck kisses into her small brown hands. He could not bear
e sight of anyone touching her.

For a while the nights had been too unbearably hot to
ep the fire going in the Glass House. Now, in August, he
d started again his attempts to copy the bowl. On the
ght that the girls left, Stiegel thought the heat seemed
re excruciating than ever, and his temper was short.

"Diane, why do you come here with me?" he asked
sely.

"The bowl ——"

"Diane, you can't lie to me," said Stiegel, slipping his
t off. "We've lived under the same roof for years. You
n't give a damn if I smash the bowl to bits. And you don't
e Martin Grenier."

Startled, she opened her eyes wide, like a cat penetrat-
 the dark.

"Diane, is it . . . is it Elizabeth who is driving you to
rry Grenier?"

She wondered swiftly what stand she should take. It
uld never do to tell him yet that she would not marry
rtin.

"Heinrich . . . it is better like this, n'est-ce pas? Eliza-
h will no longer hate me. Martin will have what he

wants. You will have what you want—peace. And I shall
not be unhappy. I shall have my little cottage, mon cher—
my woods, my cow. . . ."

"But it is Hell to be married to someone you do not love!"

"I know, mon cher," softly, "but it is worse Hell ——"

"Did you get it?" cried Michael, tearing around the
hedge. "Let me hold the blow-pipe."

Diane repressed her desire to smack Michael. In a few
weeks Martin Grenier would return. She had shoved him
from her mind all the happy nights she and Stiegel had
played their harp and violin together. But now, soon, something must happen! What would she do if Martin returned
and Stiegel had not made love to her? She must not let the
days and nights slide on like this. She knew that he had
been working on the song for her. She had seen scraps of
music in his room, and found rejected bits of music in his
waste basket. One day she had unfolded one, played the
phrase over softly on her harp, and found the few notes
thrumming in her mind as she worked.

Michael had run out again. He was in and out of the
Glass House like a butterfly. Diane watched Stiegel struggling with the molten glass. The minutes ticked on, endless.

"Oh, Heinrich," she thought, "how can I make you know
that you love me! How can I prove to you that nothing
else matters? If you love me why are you not eaten with
jealousy, with passion, as I am? Why do you think I toy
with the simpletons that make love to me? Heinrich. . . .
If you were George I would blush and whisper, 'I love
you! If you were Martin, I would let you kiss my naked
breast. But you are Heinrich, and I must do none of these
things. Our love must seem to burst in you, mon cher. . . .
To be hidden and grow until it bursts and you must sweep
me along with *you*. . . ."

"I have it!" he cried in sudden triumph. "Ach Gott, I
have it, Diane! Thousands of pounds. . . . Look! See how

perfect it is!" He was down on his knees before the bowl, a bit of light blue in the blow-pipe. "Ach Gott, I have it at last. . . . How simple it was, how simple."

She was ill with presentiment, too ill to answer him. With shaking hands she dropped her knitting and sank onto the marver at his side. He flew about the shop hunting for a pen, and finally finding a quill and ink upon the shelf, scratched down the formula with trembling fingers.

"Michael, Michael, come here! Where are you? Run ahead and tell them I've found it. . . ."

At home, jubilant with victory, he pulled his violin from the cabinet and motioned Diane to sit at the harp.

Anna Ege and Michael joined in the excitement.

"Heinrich, thou art a great man!" applauded Anna Ege, who was thankful for more than one reason that the formula was found at last.

"Yippee!" shrieked Michael, leaping up and down. "Yippee!"

"Come to bed, thou night hawk!" cried his mother, "and I shall scrub thy ears!"

Cyrus flung open the shutters of the parlor, and the cool night air stirred the curtains and chased the candlelight like a ghost at tag. Stiegel and Diane were left alone.

His bow quivered on the strings, as Diane tuned somberly. She felt that the end of her world had come, and laughed at her own idiocy. What else might she have expected? She or the bowl would be of no more consequence to Stiegel than a bit of milkweed floating across his vision. And he had never seemed so precious to her as he did tonight. In his reckless mood he was graceful and chivalrous. He flung notes from his violin with flippant ease, and because she loved him so much, she began to hate him.

"Hurry!" he exclaimed. "The Viennese waltz. . . ."

"Why not the epic?" reminded Diane, with a little hollow laugh.

"You won't believe I have wrote one, Diane, but I have!"

"Play it," pleaded Diane. "I beg of you, mon cher."

"But it's not polished ——"

"No matter."

"I want it to be perfect."

"But I want it *now*, Heinrich," she demanded.

He hesitated, and then broke into a pensive melody. She sat enthralled. When he had finished, she whispered, "It says the very things I asked you to say; oh Heinrich ——"

"But I'm not in the mood of a dirge."

"It is not a dirge!" she cried. "It is a love song."

"But it does not sound right for you, Liebling. It must be gay, like *you*, Diane. I must transcribe it—a waltz—something light ——"

"No," she protested. "The first is more to my liking!"

But in spite of her, he began to change the music to three-four time.

Furious, she let the pedals of the harp snap up with a bang, and stood before him struggling for words.

" 'Twas to be a love song," she cried, "and now you have wrote it to the bowl!"

He was bewitched by her scarlet fury, and in the recklessness of his mood, seized her in his arms, and kissed her.

Diane tore loose from him, and struck his cheek. Then as the angry tears flowed down her face, she laughed hysterically and stormed from the room.

Stiegel wakened the following morning with a feeling of elation, and he jumped from bed to admire the little sample blue ball. As he dressed, his eyes fondled it, and his imagination formed objects of the beloved color—ink-wells and cruets alike.

The sun edged slowly over to the shaving-table where it stood, and suddenly he caught his breath, as if with sharp pain. The little ball looked green! He ran to the kitchen to hunt out Diane, his stock unpinned. Anne, who was toasting bread on a long fork, recoiled into the corner of the hearth, and the golden brown square whipped into a flame and became ashes.

Diane was waiting for the tardy Michael, and had stooped to pull a Canadian thistle from her garden.

"Diane, come quick. I must see the bowl."

Overcome with curiosity, she forgot her rage of the night before, and hurrying after his great stride, she unlocked the cupboard in her room. He snatched the bowl without further explanation and ran with it into his bed chamber It lapped up the sun and shone defiantly blue.

Stiegel dropped onto a chair and groaned, "Ach Gott!"

"You have not got it after all?" cried Diane, exultantly.

He did not answer.

Anne had burned her hand and was whining with pain in the chimney corner the entire morning. Diane made the cherry pudding herself. It was a masterpiece of perfectly proportioned cherries and honey. Stiegel seemed unaware of it, and most of it was devoured by Michael,—unhampered by the restraint of his mother who was in bed, with another attack of neuritis.

In the morning Diane had taken breakfast to her, and wondered why Mrs. Ege was always so much pleasanter when she was ill than when she was well. She picked up the rose that Diane had put on her tray, and frowning with the pain of the effort, smelled it.

"If I had only not gone from that blazing Glass House into the chilly night," she moaned, leaning on her "good side," and Diane put down the tray and smoothed out the sheets. "Thou art shamefully healthy, Diane. Like some wild animal. The household keys are there on the table. . . . Ugh!"

Diane whistled as she went down the stairs. "If only

more people had creeping pains more of the time," she meditated, "the world would be a happier place by far."

In the afternoon, the preserves which Diane was making stuck to the kettle, and she swore and hoped that the tell-tale odor would not drift up to Mrs. Ege. Would nothing go right today, she wondered! Cyrus had found a copper-head snake on the stones at the well, and a hog had rolled over on two of its litter and killed them.

At supper time, Cyrus came to Diane to report that Michael was missing. The table had been set for three, and Diane realized with a rush of excitement that she and Stiegel would be alone if Michael were late.

"But Cyrus, he was here a short time ago. He dipped his dirty fingers into my preserve, and I gave him a trouncing!"

"Don' know, Miz Diane. I done see Marsa Michael las' on the white farm hoss."

"Ah," cried Diane knowingly, for she had heard hounds in the neighborhood. "He has gone off to join the hunt!"

She was delighted. She prayed that Michael would utterly forget his appetite for once in his life and not return until the meal was over. She wore her favorite gown, a peach taffeta festooned with French lace and lavender velvet flowers. Over her supple brown wrists she snapped the bracelets Stiegel had given her, and fastened calendulas in her hair.

But when they sat at the table together, Stiegel seemed not to notice her splendor, and was silent and morose.

Diane felt desperate. She would not let these precious moments slip by like the desultory interval of an ordinary meal. She had told Anne to use the green glassware and new silver candlesticks. She became spirited, garrulous, so that in spite of him this supper by candlelight seemed a gay affair. By tacit consent they disregarded the scene of the night before.

"Heinrich, you are so sad, mon cher. . . ."

He smiled with effort. It seemed to Stiegel as if his failure to create the blue glass was symbolic of all the hopes and ambitions he'd failed to attain.

"You look like a *very* little boy, M'sieu, who would like only to cry."

He laughed sheepishly. "That is because tonight I seem to think of everything I ever wanted, and have not got!"

"Everybody in the countryside knows that Baron Stiegel has everything he wants!" she countered. He had not got the blue of the bowl. He had kissed her. He loved her. He had not got the blue of the bowl. . . .

"Diane, do not make light of my failure!" he begged, and as he helped Diane from her chair, he longed to pour out the jealousy and worship of her which seemed now to have got to the breaking point.

Tonight he snatched up his violin without waiting for her, and began to play the love song as he'd played it to her at first. It was an apology for the night before. She knelt on the sofa, and listened to him, her eyes clinging to his half-parted lips.

You are so beautiful, my Heinrich . . . she thought fervently. So strong and sad. . . . The way your fingers touch the strings . . . Your eyes half-closed . . . The light shining on your hair . . . Why do all these things do something strange and exciting to me, Heinrich? Why does it make my heart fly when you only sway a little?

"Non, non, non . . . don't stop, Heinrich!" she pleaded, jumping up from the sofa, half intoxicated with her thoughts. "Show me how to play it on the harp . . ."

"Not tonight, Liebling . . . I am too . . . restless. I want to walk in the garden—alone."

If she came close to him perhaps, in the dusk of the garden. . . . If he could feel how her blood was racing. If he could feel rather than see her beauty!

She put her hands in his impulsively, and he lifted them

gently to his lips, as if he were performing some sacred rite, and went out into the twilight.

She ran to her room for a crimson capuchin to fling over her shoulders. He was out there in the garden, treading back and forth on a gravel path, wanting her, suffering because he felt he could not have her . . . Well, it was too late now to babble of honor. . . . They must be honest with themselves at last. They must say in words, in caresses, the things their eyes had been trying for years to hide from one another.

Stiegel sauntered up and down on the flagstones, abstracted, treading on the mignonette which tumbled over their borders.

What if Diane were marrying Martin Grenier to escape Elizabeth? What if Elizabeth had driven her to this? Diane was no longer a child. She would know that running away would never solve her problem. Or Stiegel himself? Could it be possible he had driven her to it? Could she possibly think that she was a burden to him? Every day he felt more and more bewildered.

"Heinrich, my little gold watch with the doves—I must have lost it today in the woods." She ran up to him, her voice filled with excitement.

He listened to her with concern. "Oh, but that is a pity! Call Cyrus."

"Non, non, non. He is so clumsy, he would tread it into the earth. Come, M'sieu, you help," she begged, snatching his hand. "You gave it to me, Heinrich. . . . I shall fetch a lantern."

Stiegel was tractable. He took the brass lantern from her, and led the way into the blackness of the woods, prying into the new foliage of midsummer growth with a gnarled dead branch. Finally the path shrivelled into a thin cord, hidden at times in a density of underbrush.

Diane took the lead, holding back the lithe branches so

that they would not lash his face. "Come, 'twas through here. . . ."

Stiegel was irritated. He had not bargained for this maltreatment. The lace of his cuffs was shredded with thorns, and the brambles scratched mercilessly at his silken clad legs.

"We'll be lost," he remonstrated, setting down the lantern in a bed of skunk cabbage.

"Heinrich, I think I see it shining there."

Stiegel lifted the lantern and forged ahead through the tangle on to the path again, pushing aside the scalloped fronds of cinnamon fern with his stick.

"Oh, it was only a light bug, Heinrich," she laughed.

"You're horn mad to wade through the woods alone, Diane. Wasn't it just a week back that Cyrus killed a rattlesnake in our raspberry patch?"

"Fooh, snakes do not fright me," she boasted, but gathered her skirts more closely about her. The exquisite French lace clung to the briars, and Diane pried them apart ruthlessly, unwilling to stop. Her breath came so fast that she thought it would choke her.

"This is a hopeless task," protested Stiegel.

"Non, non, non. . . . We are almost there. Michael and I fish there, where the brook makes an opening. See, the path widens. . . ."

They reached the clearing at last. The water gurgled darkly past them. There was no moon. The night was sultry and the dampness rose from the stream and was suffocating.

Diane sank to the ground and leaned against a huge tree trunk which was gray and smooth with time.

"My hand. It's wet."

Stiegel placed the lantern at her side. Blood was diffusing from a long scratch. He dipped his handkerchief into the edge of the brook, where forget-me-nots spread in rich profusion. Then he bound it tightly about her wound, his petulance changing to solicitude.

"Does it pain you, Diane?" He dropped down beside her to rest.

"Non, non, non. Hark you, an owl."

"He is brave in the dark."

"'Tis not a hoot, Heinrich, but a wail. He bewails my loss."

"Your loss, what does it really matter, Diane?"

"Ah, mon cher—and yours? Some night perhaps you will dream the formula. Then life will be complete for you, n'est-ce pas?"

He made no answer, and her hand crept over the soft, damp moss until it rested in his.

"Heinrich, soon Martin will be back. Then what will become of our love?" Her voice was pleading, thrilling.

Stiegel crushed her hand to his lips. Diane still loved him! Beyond this his thoughts were vague. A small white flame began to burn within him.

He swept her into his arms, impassioned; he did not belong to himself any longer. He belonged to some fiery, impelling force within his blood.

"Heinrich, I love you. . . ."

"I love you too—unto Heaven . . . unto Hell, Diane. . . ."

Intoxicated by her kiss, he stroked her hair fervently, her cheeks, her lips, maddened that he could not see her beauty in this witching moment. He was obsessed with the anguish of losing her.

"Diane, you are all aquiver . . . like moonlight in my arms . . . beloved."

"I am too happy. . . ."

They clung to one another like vagrant leaves on a fast-flowing stream, neither fearing their course nor caring where the tide hurried them. Stiegel felt that he had only dreamed his life, and the weary struggle to crush this overpowering love. Babies, acres, riches, hopes—how nebulous and faint they were beside this ecstasy!

"Diane . . . Diane . . . Diane. . . ." he whispered.

There was no other world for him but this, where the tiny things of the wood twittered, and the leaves hung breathless, and forget-me-nots lived in the laughing ink of the brook. He would be there always, one with the opaque night, with the velvet moss—with Diane.

23

IN THE MORNING the sulkiness of the weather had given way to rain. Stiegel opened his eyes, and heard it on the eaves—tap . . . one, two, one, two—like the laborious poking of a child at the piano keys. He drew aside the curtains of the bed, and watched the drops shivering at the moment of their impact on the windowpanes—then merging, tumbling headlong. He . . . Diane. He thrust his head into the pillow, and lay there for a moment, heavy-hearted with guilt. He hungered for the sight of Diane, dishevelled in the lantern light, the calendula fallen crushed from her hair, its twisted, bruised petals lying on her breast. He was filled with the pagan spirit of Diane.

And yet in the familiarity of his room, the night seemed an hallucination. He rose, and aimlessly fingered Elizabeth's sewing box, with its dozens of neat little spools revolving about it. Its homeliness gave him a sharp sense of reality, and he fell on his knees at the edge of the bed, and prayed: "Oh God, pity my weakness. . . . I love her. . . . Help me to do what is right."

The house was still, somber. Anne sleepily served him his breakfast. Diane had not yet come down. He sat at the

[284

table with Michael, who had returned late from the hunt. The boy ate disgustingly of cutlets and cheese and preserves. The calendulas in the crystal swan had begun to warp and brown. Their lusty odor mingled with his food. He retreated to his office, where he might be alone with his misery.

Pencil in hand, he brushed the page of his ledger with figures. He could not escape the feeling of being scrutinized. Anne's soulful eyes had noted the scratches on his hands. The very gluttonous silence of Michael seemed pregnant with meaning. And Cyrus, who had brought him hot water for his shave, had asked, "Did Marsa Baron recovah de watch?"

"Alas no, and we searched deep into the woods!"

At ten he heard a voice singing in the rain. Well, they would have to face each other sometime. He stood up in answer to Diane's sharp rap. She entered, dripping, laughing, swathed in a rain cloak, a weather skirt and pattens. She dropped them in a heap beside the door, and came over to him radiant and unafraid.

"Heinrich!"

"Diane!"

He held her to him with a new hunger.

In her hair there were wet calendulas.

He dropped down on the chair at his desk, and she knelt beside him, her hands clasped on his knee, just as Jerusha so often knelt, to say "Our Father. . . ."

"Heinrich, I am so happy!"

"I am so happy—so miserable all in one, Liebling."

"Why are you miserable? Only last night we were born, n'est-ce pas?"

"Diane, I never knew there was love like this. . . . I always thought there must be something I . . . something I could find . . . something others had found. . . ." He stroked her hair, his fingers lingering on the wet flowers.

"I couldn't sleep . . . I tried to sleep, and you seemed to—to fill me. I wanted to go to you again. I thought I couldn't bear to be alone."

"I dreamed of you. All night I dreamed of you, Diane. Wild, tragic things. Martin Grenier. . . ."

"Non, non, non! Do not even say his name!" Her eyes darkened, and swept fearfully about the tiny office and the dusty samples of glass.

"He will be coming back," Stiegel said, his voice trembling.

"I am not afraid of him!" she cried. "Heinrich, you are not afraid of him! There is no one who can take us away from one another now."

"Diane, will you believe me . . . your love will always mean more to me than anything in life?"

"There will be tonight, Heinrich. . . . Tomorrow . . . all the days and nights until we are old, until we die. . . ."

"Oh, Diane, if we could only forget everything but ourselves!"

"But we *can*, mon cher." She turned pale, sickened by the intimation.

"You are so trusting, my darling—like a little child."

"You would not have me wed Martin Grenier!" she cried. "You do not know him, Heinrich! He would kill you!"

"Diane . . . we cannot keep on. . . ."

"You are cozening me!" hysterically.

"Nay, Diane. I would not make light of our love."

"You are a coward!"

"To give up the very core of life? . . . Oh Liebling, you do me ill——"

"You do not love Elizabeth! You cannot love her!"

She came close, stood before him anguished. "I do not believe you can cast me aside!"

He gripped her shoulders. "Don't talk to me like this . . . I love you! Can't you see it? . . . I love you so much

I can't let you live in shame. You are too beautiful, Diane, too proud. . . ."

"I don't care if they laugh! I don't care what they think! Only so you will come to me. . . ."

"Supposing there should be a . . . a child."

"I want a child, Heinrich," she said eagerly. "He will be like you when you were a little boy. And when you are away I will hold him in my arms—and so I will always have you with me, mon cher."

"Diane," he whispered, kissing her, "how can I make you see the things I see? . . . the ugliness of them. The ugliness that can come to us out of love that is so beautiful now. . . ."

"But I love you! I will not let you go!" she cried stubbornly, the angry tears gathering in her eyes.

"I'm going to Manheim tomorrow. . . . I've got to get away from you," he said quickly. "I try to think what we must do, Liebling—and I can't think—not when I can reach out and touch you with my hands!"

"Why must you think?" she retorted scornfully. "Thinking is cold! I will make you love me so you cannot think!"

The very ardor of her voice cut into Stiegel's wound like salt.

"Diane, we're not made alike. . . . You're wild and free. Like the wind. . . . I'm just human."

"If you go away I will know you do not love me," she cried. "Oh, Heinrich . . . my heart is breaking. . . ."

"But I do love you! If I go away it is for you, Diane."

"You are afraid for yourself! Afraid someone will know!"

"You don't know what laws are. Conventions. . . . You live in a world of your own. . . . You do only the things which you want to do."

"But there is only one thing in the world, Heinrich! And a liaison in the flesh or in the heart, 'tis all of a piece." Her voice was low, painfully tragic.

Stiegel, in great agitation, paced the floor. The thought of Diane subservient to Elizabeth forever was unbearable. This morning he had thought of nothing but Diane, her great black eyes soft with requited love, her hair tumbled, her finery tattered, her suppleness a palpitating thing in the spasm of lanternlight. He was so stirred and ached so with desire for her that he had braced his head on trembling hands, his ledger lying neglected before him, his pulse racing with the sound of her step and her voice.

If he stayed at Elizabeth Furnace one more day they must both let reason fly to the winds and snatch at madness. It would be better to go away, where he could not see her. Better to run away from her, as he had done before, and hope and pray that reason would come back to him again and show him what course they should take.

A scraping on the doorstep alarmed them.

After fumbling with the latch, Cyrus shuffled into the little room, a compilation of oilskin and bundles. He had been to Brickerville for a new lot of mail from Philadelphia. Letters and packages dripped from him along with rain. He deposited the whole at the foot of Stiegel.

"Yessuh, Marsa Baron, de coachman he say he nevah gwine delivah no mo' billets nigh to Judgment. De sottin' Indians 'tacked him and dramm'd de barrel o' rum to a shell, Marsa. Dey poke thumbs into de sugah, and dip de mouths in consarnless, and he yell at them, 'two cents 'thout sugah, three cents sugah in't,' Marsa Baron. . . ." Cyrus' eyes gleamed with pleasurable horror. "Dey done thought to scalp dat coachman, an' he faint with fright. When he done wake up he go to feel fo' de blood on his head—and de Indian done scalped his wig!" He slapped his knee at the dénouement of his tale.

Stiegel had opened a billet in Elizabeth's writing. Diane's finger was following a raindrop down the pane.

Cyrus was conscious of dramatic failure. "Marsa Baron,

de coachman say de tanner in Lancaster say de new saddle most ready fo' Marsa Michael."

"Thank you, Cyrus."

Cyrus gathered his cloak about him, and prepared for immersion again.

He halted beside Diane. She seemed in need of attention.

"I was pow'ful grieved 'bout yo' watch," he sympathized.

"Aye. 'Twas great good fortune to find it."

"Yo'—yo' done found it?" asked Cyrus, confused.

"Aye, under a violet leaf. 'Tis safe in my what-not."

Stiegel, chagrined, pursued his letter with diligence. He heard the door close.

So she had never lost the watch! It had all been premeditated—the bed of moss to lie upon, the portentous silence of the woods—perhaps the very scratch on her hand was cold calculation. The consummation of their love seemed suddenly contemptible. The words of Elizabeth's letter blurred before his eyes, unread, like the Latin chant of a priest. The sound of the rain pounded into his head.

No sooner had Cyrus left than the door opened again. Stiegel felt the cold dash of air, felt the shower of mist on his face. It was George Ege, just returned from Lancaster.

"Sir . . ." he greeted them, "Diane!"

He kissed Diane's hand, which dropped listless to her side, then picked it up and kissed it again, as if piqued by her nonchalance.

She suddenly took notice of him. "Come, George, I shall whip you a syllabub in trade for news." She slipped on her pattens and ventured into the soft mud, followed by her gallant.

That afternoon, George Ege came to Stiegel's office.

"Sir, I came to tell you I do not want to go away to college!"

"Afraid you will drain it of learning, no doubt." The caustic reply escaped Stiegel's lips like quicksilver. George's obvious infatuation for Diane nettled him. The boy hung about her like a leech. "College will be good for you. Discipline."

"Sir, I am twenty," reproved George, adjusting his ruffles.

"You fancy the life of a gentleman."

"Nay, you do me injustice, uncle. I would like to enter business."

"The colonies are breathless, off balance. 'Tis a poor time to throw your pence in the pot."

"I could manage Charming Forge," George suggested boldly, his fingers twisting the paper-weight on the desk.

"What does your mother say?"

"Feminine judgment is not always expedient, sir."

"Quite true. You feel you are sufficient apt in the iron business?"

"You recollect I have been reared at Elizabeth Furnace."

"Then why do you not stay here and help me?"

For a moment George did not reply, and Stiegel answered his own question abruptly. "You are in love with Diane."

George turned on him. "Yes—and I can't stand seeing her marry that damned little flea!"

Stiegel smiled in spite of himself. He felt a surging pity for the boy. He would have liked to pat him on the back and kick him from the office all in one gesture. He wondered if George would ever know what it meant to be miserable over love. Well, it would be better for everybody to get him out of the way.

"I shall give you a try at it, George," he said, holding out his hand to him. "You are right sharp. I was but little more than twenty myself and knew nought of the work. I'll give you a letter to Nassel and we'll go over matters in detail when I come home. I've a lot to do today. I'm . . . I'm going to Manheim for a while."

Stiegel left Elizabeth Furnace early the next morning. He had chosen to go in the coach, so that he might sink back into a corner and think. Fields of ripe wheat meandered past him, and luxuriant patches of beans and summer squash, asparagus gone to seed, adolescent corn. But Stiegel saw nothing. The fertility might have been a desert of cactus. His pulse quickened with the sensuous recollection of Diane's kisses, and he wondered if he would be able to face Elizabeth squarely. It was only natural that he should think of her with compunction. The prospect of the long years he must live out with her was agony. Divorce never entered his head. The few scandalous separations he had heard of branded people as queer, if not actually lettered in witchcraft.

Elizabeth didn't love him, he mused bitterly. What would she care if Diane were his mistress, so long as luxury poured in upon her?

He could imagine Elizabeth flaunting the truth before his friends, mocking Diane, not sparing Barbara or Jerusha in her spite. She would bring up Jacob to loathe his father. His one son, who should be closer to him than anyone else in the world. And it was inconceivable that Elizabeth would not divine the truth.

Also, it was natural that he should think of himself. He had lied to Diane about that. He would be the subject of cheap talk all over the countryside. The name that he had so carefully built up over the last fifteen years would be muddied with bar-room laughter. And something transcendent and precious about the love he now bore for Diane must surely vanish in the degradation and disdain which they would have to suffer together.

As the coach bumped along, he wondered just what would become of him and Diane if they should deny their love. Would she run away again? Would he ever find contentment in his work? Or in the joy of creation? How could he ever create anything again, even a little piece of glass, in the colorless and barren life that would be stretching out before him?

Stiegel's stay in Manheim lasted a month. People came to dinner from Brickerville and stayed the night. They would have made a pilgrimage to Boston to see the painted scenes of falconry on the walls. And more meticulous city folk from Lancaster came to convince themselves that no house aside from George the Third's had closets with mirrored doors. They had heard, too, of the cavernous cellar, with wine from Lisbon and the Canaries, and rum from Jamaica. The stable nearly always boarded a visiting horse or two, and the table boasted regalement of rich broths, smuggled sugar and delicacies for epicurean taste. The profusion of sumptuous upholsteries, velvets, and heavy silver plate was soon exaggerated beyond all proportion. Stiegel found himself referred to everywhere now, as the Baron.

The Glass House was rising fast, and would be ready for business in October.

He saw little of Elizabeth. She was overwhelmed with responsibility. Anna Ege had been major-domo from the moment she entered the Stiegel household, and now Elizabeth found that when a guest arrived she sometimes entirely forgot to set out the whiskey in its green glass decanter or to have the sheets washed out which he had used on his journey. During the day Stiegel saw to the completion of the Glass House, and the King of Prussia Tavern. Often he tramped about the countryside, stopping in at the farmhouses, sharing a bowl of sour milk and cinnamon with his neighbor. There was something more of humbleness in his manner, something less of German invulnerability. This was how poor people lived, who were able to live with a loved one. This was all Diane asked of life, and this must be denied her.

If only he could make her understand! Make her know that there were others in the world besides the two of them. He almost envied her the looseness of her unmorality. It would be so easy to think only of the satiation of their love. She would never understand that the motive for coming away was not selfish. Why did she feel that he thought only of money, of the glory of being rich?

One night he said to Elizabeth, "I had word from Dickinson today that our house in Philadelphia will be ready for Christmas."

"Oh, then we can spend the holidays there!" cried Elizabeth. "Think, Heinrich, 'twill be my first visit home since our marriage!"

"I may not be able to get there till February or March. The new Glass House will keep me here at Manheim. But . . . you will not mind?"

"Luddy, no, Heinrich. Why, there will be all the new furniture to buy! And Anna and the boys will come with me. They've been bestarved for a sight of home for years."

How casual she was, he thought. What a comfortable, self-satisfied matron! If he had been killed on the way to Manheim she would have gone into deep mourning, draping herself, and the picture of him over the mantel. She would have married again within a twelvemonth. He thought suddenly, guiltily, that this was exactly what he had done when Elizabeth Huber died. His poor little pink Elizabeth! Thank God he had never belied her with more than a kiss. She had loved him, at any rate.

They would all go to Philadelphia and stay there as long as he would let them. They would get rooted there in society. The houses at Elizabeth Furnace and Manheim would be solitary. Elizabeth preferred new furniture to her husband. Well, why shouldn't he and Diane have one another? Was there anyone who cared? For a month he had threshed out temptation in deep meditation, with cold reasoning, trying to eject from his memory the night in the wood. For a month he had been practical. And now all at once he knew that he was going back to Diane. He had spent the days in trying to forget her; in the nights she came to him unafraid of his weaker, subconscious self. Sometimes as he fell asleep beside Elizabeth he dreamed of Diane; then, in the stupefaction of the dawn, his gaze hovered on Elizabeth's nightcap stirring on the pillow, and the first opening of her eyes. It was Elizabeth who seemed the adulteress, whose physical presence seemed to outrage the phantom of Diane.

Now, he thought, he would no longer make any attempt to understand the girl. She was an incorrigible law, like the wind or the undertow. She was an exotic force which had swept him along in its path, making the rest of life prosaic and dull. She was beauty—the beauty and liberty of spirit he had craved since he was a little boy, and he would no longer live without her. He needed her!

"I'm going back to the Furnace tomorrow," he said to Elizabeth, and he was so filled with excitement at his decision that she could not help but note the burning in his eyes.

"Think you Diane would like to be married in Manheim?" she asked irrelevantly, as if she sensed that Stiegel were thinking of Diane.

"That's a long way off," he answered abruptly. And yet, in spite of the few weeks until Grenier's coming, Stiegel heard horse's hoofs while he ate and while he slept, dreading the dark little foreigner and his inexorable pride.

"But a month is not long when there is a wedding to be thought of," replied Elizabeth. "You had best let me know at once by the post so I can come back to the Furnace or get the house in readiness here."

Stiegel returned to Elizabeth Furnace in a queer state of mind. He was going to be another person. He was going to lead a new life. Now he was no longer going to be denied the happiness that was a man's right. For years he had been dutiful to his wife, and tolerant. For years he had been striving to live. Now he would begin to live. For some reason he felt sheepish about facing the household, about meeting the sharpness of Anna Ege's eyes. Wouldn't they all see the minute he came that he had nothing but Diane in his mind and in his heart?

He rode the horse into the stable, gave her a pat of appreciation after the long ride, and loosened the girth himself, for he had observed a sore on the mare's belly. He gave her a handful of oats out of his hand, and then turned her over to the red-nosed coachman and the stable boy. A group of servants hung about the stable door, watching him silently, gathered there for their twilight gossip. He greeted them with affability and asked them how their work had been going, but they seemed to be short in their replies.

It seemed as if he himself were purposely procrastinating. His eyes swiftly sought Diane in the garden or at the well, but the grounds seemed deserted except for the little group of men at the stable. Diane would not be expecting him. When she heard his voice she would run to him. He would not be able to take her in his arms. They would have to be guarded. All the rest of their lives. . . .

He shifted his traveling cloak over to Cyrus, who trotted before him with a lantern, curiously silent too.

"I wish I could have the locusts choked, Cyrus."

"Yassah, Marsa Baron."

"In some countries people eat the locusts. They relish them as you do corn cakes."

"Yassah, Marsa Baron."

His answer was a distinct shock to Stiegel. The loquacious Cyrus seemed cowed. He ordinarily would have replied,

"Gemini, Marsa Baron, by all de angels got wings in God's heben, you cozenin' me; dey ain't nobody could swallow a singin' spirit."

The stable boy too had winked slyly at the horse.

"Cyrus, Michael hasn't fell sick with the Wanderlust, has he? Or that Chepa Rose been shilly-shallying at the Inn?"

"Yassah, yassah—uh, no, no, no suh."

"Tell Anne to hustle a bit of cold veal or neck of mutton under the oak here. And a tankard of ale. My throat's thick with dust, and my eyes feel scorched. . . . Gott, but it's hot! The sort of night that does not move forward, but hangs still and withers the mind." He was talking now to himself. "Scarce a bit of heaven between the stars. They look as if they were a-swoon for air, too."

The air was redolent with garden perfume. It closed about him in a saturating sweetness, like the flowers at a funeral, and suffocated his nerves. As he got to the steps, fanning himself with a futile handkerchief, his foot collided with a solid object. He knelt quickly to examine it, and found it was Michael. Alarmed, at presentiment of disaster, he dragged the boy into the light of the star lantern of the hall. Could he be dead? He lifted the handsome head with trembling hands. Michael's eyes opened slowly, and then he sat up with great exertion, digging his fists into them with slow perseverance.

"What's the matter?" cried Stiegel, and then with sharp relief he saw that the lad had waited up for him and, falling asleep on the doorstep, had tumbled off.

Michael sat quiet for a moment, looked about him, looked at the chandelier, at Stiegel, and shook off the last remnant of stupor.

"They've gone," he announced succinctly.

"Who is gone, gone where?"

"George—Diane—the horses."

"You're dreaming." He shook the boy. Mysteriously the hall had filled with people—Cyrus, Anne, the Italian gardener.

Michael pulled himself up to his full height. "I tell you they've run off. 'Twas only last night."

The audience kept a respectful distance.

Diane and George eloped! He was too stunned, too humiliated to grasp the meaning of the truth. He reiterated their names, and they seemed all confused with the locusts and the dryness of his throat.

He outrageously wanted to pursue them, though by now they would no doubt be married, and the chances of finding them were few.

George—fumbling with the flowers of her hair! It was insufferable!

24

STIEGEL FLED to the Glass House early in the morning after a sleepless night. He had not seen Anna Ege; he could not bring himself to face her. His thoughts were not yet co-ordinated. His dreams had been wild, bizarre.

He flung open the door of the place; it smelled strongly of dye and stale summer air. Sinking onto a marver he clasped his head in his hands with infinite agony. He was alarmed at his own derangement, his insatiable thirst for revenge. He thought callously of their sin, of sin breeding its compensation—a delirious turn of fate!

Diane married to George Ege! She had been inexplicably hurt by his going away. Had thought that he was anxious to forget her. That was it. She had been too proud to face him again if he did not love her. It was because she loved him too much that she had gone off with George. But why hadn't she waited to marry Martin Grenier? Surely she had cared more for Grenier than for this gangling schoolboy. Yet surely she had never loved anyone but himself. . . . What would Stiegel say to the distraught man when he returned? Why had God made her so alluring, so baffling?

Why could it not have been different? Why could not their love have been normal, open? Why could she not have reared his children, a quiet, peaceful figure beside him at the hearth, instead of a vagrant of the woods? He battled these questions with distraction, and finding the problems unfathomable, walked slowly back to the house.

Anna Ege waited for him in the parlor, her keys jingling at her waist. When Diane and George had been missing for some hours, she had searched the house, and finding a note to Stiegel in George's handwriting had opened it without qualm. Now she held the note in her hand, waiting to thrust it at Stiegel the moment he entered the door.

"So!" she riled, "thy little hoyden from the woods has ruined us after all!"

"Anna, please! I'm crushed. . . ."

"Crushed! What do thee think *I* feel?"

"He's been in love with her for years." Stiegel sank onto the sofa; he had forgotten about breakfast.

"In love with her! She seduced him!" Mrs. Ege humped her shoulders.

"Nay, Anna, she's treated him like a child. . . . I cannot think why she married him."

Mrs. Ege swelled at these words like a bean in water.

"George, a child! A man six feet tall! With the manners of a gentleman. Dost think Diane such a scatterbrain she would not regard him something more than a glass-blower?"

She tossed the letter in his lap, and he saw that it had been crumpled and straightened out again.

It stated simply:

"Sir: When you read this letter Diane and I will be married and on our way to Charming Forge. I have your letter to Nassel with me, which says I am to be installed as manager. Diane and I wish to offer apology for any lack of konsiderashun we may have shewed in our Elopment and send our respekts to you and my Aunt Elizabeth and our affecshun to our mother. Your Ob'dn't nefew,

George Ege."

Stiegel crushed the letter, as had Anna Ege before him, and tossed it into the fireplace.

"How can we save him!" she cried. "How can we save him from that strumpet!"

"She is your daughter! You can at least speak of her with respect," retorted Stiegel.

"She *is* a strumpet! Everyone at Elizabeth Furnace knows what went on between her and Martin Grenier while thee were in Europe!"

Stiegel flushed at the thought of Grenier possessing her. It made no difference to him what she had been, what she was. He loved her and he would always love her. And between him and Diane there was something spiritual that no other man could ever share with her—that no other woman, would ever share with him.

"If I'd only not brought him here to live in the wilds," groaned Anna Ege, rubbing the shoulder which tortured her with this fresh emotion.

Stiegel went up to Diane's room, where the eyes of all the servants had curiously peered ahead of him. She had evidently left after cool deliberation, for her room was neat as her flower bed. He recalled painfully the time when she had been "stole by the Indians," and the floor was impudent with ribbons and bright shoes and mitts, the sort of confusion he expected to see now and did not find. The only evidence that Diane was gone was that the water had turned slimy in a glass bowl of nasturtiums.

On her lowboy lay an amazing array of jewelry, all things which Stiegel had given her on Christmas or holidays or had purchased impetuously from O'Harpigan. Set apart on a silk handkerchief were the bracelets with the

yellow diamonds, and the gold watch. The insolence of
Diane was preposterous. He pocketed the things, his fingers
burning as if he had touched her wrists. And with anger
there returned a certain salvation. He ordered the new
Negro slave girl to pack Diane's clothes in boxes. He would
see that her things reached her with insulting speed. And
he covered the harp himself and had it removed to the barn.

Stiegel spent a desultory day; he patted the horses, like
a child groping for sympathy; he pulled a weed or two
from Diane's nasturtium bed; he flung himself under the
elms and watched the clouds take shape; he sat in mourning with Anna Ege; and he prayed, falteringly, for some
sort of peace which did not come. If only he were a little
boy again, and could cry into his mother's lap!

News of the elopement had naturally spread. Stiegel felt
sensitive before his men, and unduly conspicuous. Instead
of realizing that the runaway marriage would absolve him
from any scandal or suspicion, he thought that his misery
must be written indelibly in his eyes.

He determined that he must pick up the broken frag-
ments of his life and try to piece them together. He must
make glass his ambition. He must get the blue bowl from
Diane and work on it with Martin Grenier and his other
men until they found the formula.

Going back to Manheim the end of September he found
that the new Glass House, on which he had spent close to
sixteen hundred pounds, was finished. The old glass-blowers were beginning to arrive, and also families with whom
Stiegel had negotiated in Europe—Venetians, Germans,
English. The men, delighted with the working conditions,
fell to blowing with a zest, the majority of the output at
first still being bottles and window glass, as at Elizabeth
Furnace.

Little houses sprang up, snug and small, and a few shops
on the far side of the green, not far from his own home.

There was soon a smithy, a stable, an apothecary.

Elizabeth and Anna Ege were preparing for their trip to Philadelphia. Mrs. Ege had found a school for Michael which she thought would curb any early symptoms of profligacy such as George had shown. That her peregrine son was not suited to life among the Seventh-Day Dunkers at the Moravian School did not occur to her. Michael took one frightened glance at the brethren in the long white gowns of the Capuchins, at the luxuriant beards, and at the jejune choir with its renowned falsetto chant. His heart sank in despair, and Chepa Rose beckoned to him, doubly alluring now.

It had been a perfect summer for Michael. He did not need people. He had been thoroughly content with the expanse of woodland about Elizabeth Furnace, with spasmodic fishing, with the tramping of new trails. And there had been Diane. She seemed to understand his vagaries from Conestoga wagons to voluptuous meals. He floundered now without her understanding.

Stiegel had sent for the girls to return to Manheim. He found Jerusha's companionship a comfort. She had developed into enough of a woman to anticipate his wishes, chattering brightly and filling the vacuum which came sometimes in the lonely evenings. He had not felt in the mood of company; he had neglected his farms and woods because he did not like the volubility of the farm women. His chief amusement was to run a fox into a hole or up a tree. As October approached and he knew Martin Grenier must soon come along, he became restless, irritable.

The day Grenier came back Stiegel turned on the girls with such temper that Elizabeth was astounded. Jerusha had been taunting Barbara about her Lancaster love, and the joke had deteriorated into a mental slap-back.

"Barbara," he stormed, "take these unseemly tears to your room—and Jerusha, tonight before you eat you shall recite the forty-first chapter of Job to me, starting verse twelve, 'I will not keep silence concerning his limbs.' "

"Heinrich," Elizabeth reproved him, wiping egg off of Jacob's mouth. "They are only little girls, and you expect them to be women."

"They are old enough to simper about love! They should be old enough to hold their tongues."

"I think they're . . . funny!" exclaimed Elizabeth, laughing, and she threw her head back so that Stiegel could see the wide space where her teeth had been drawn.

"They're my daughters, and I'll raise them as I see fit!" he sputtered, unable to contain the antipathy he felt for her.

"Heinrich!" cried Elizabeth, shocked, as he went off to prepare the chapel for service, and she wondered what had come over him of late. The opening of the new Glass House was an ordeal, she knew, but anyone who pretended to be godly enough to preach could be civil to his wife, at least.

"Old bear!" she murmured, dipping bread in her tea, and Jacob muttered after her, "Old bear."

That morning Stiegel had an unusually large congregation. People had drifted in from a radius of ten miles to hear his sermon. The glass-blowers sat before him, ruddy-cheeked, with renewed vigor in their eyes. Benjamin Misky's shirt was not sweat-drenched.

The village square was restless with horses, munching at oats, and the little chapel was atwitter with people who had come to worship God through the Baron's guidance. Fresh pure air drifted in to them from across the Pennsylvania mountains. They breathed it gratefully. They were grateful people, living close to God and to the land.

In competition with the organ was a flock of geese, roaming clamorously about the village. They wallowed in the puddles, pecked at the grass in the green, and looked clumsy and futile with their shingle yokes. The organ trembled to a close, and Stiegel walked into the pulpit. He had chosen as a text the fifth verse of the fifth chapter of Ecclesiastes, "Better is it that thou shouldst not vow, than that thou shouldst vow and not pay."

He had no sooner repeated the words, above the hubbub of the geese, than his eyes fell upon Martin Grenier in the doorway. He was handsome in the new vesture of a bridegroom, a rich wine, gold-braided velvet; his hair was dully immaculate with fresh powder. His eyes met Stiegel's quizzically. His mouth was austere, inflexible.

Stiegel's thoughts swept over the heads of these people. "He knows," said Stiegel to himself, his words reverberating in an empty chasm. "He knows. . . ."

He felt suddenly accountable to Grenier for his tragedy, felt suddenly pitiful and stupidly repentant and base. He realized he had not spoken for a full minute. The eyes of the congregation followed his own. There was a murmur of anticipation, as some of the group recognized Grenier.

Stiegel gave only a brief, confused outline of his sermon and stumbled across the hall to his bedchamber. It was inevitable that Grenier should be alone with him in a moment.

They bolted the door, and faced each other silently, while the shuffling of feet in the hallway bespoke the untimely end of the service.

"The damned cur," exploded Martin Grenier, his voice filled with anguish, "Where have they gone?"

"I don't know," returned Stiegel, groping for a lie. All the things he had planned to say to Martin suddenly escaped him. "They've gone to New York—taken a boat for France."

"I'll find them if I have to hunt to the ends of the earth!"

"Martin," cried Stiegel, shocked at the rancor of his voice, "if she loved you no more than that you are well rid of her!"

There was a deep silence.

"She's not worthy of revenge. . . ." Stiegel was battling for Diane, for her safety.

"Worthy! Mon Dieu, what do I care for her worth? I loved her. Don't you know what that means? . . . If I find her I'll kill her!"

He sank onto a chair, covering his face with trembling hands.

"For God's sake, Grenier," cried Stiegel, wondering what he could do or say to lessen Martin's suffering. "Don't rave like a madman. Think of the others who loved her, too. . . ."

"Think! All I have done is think! Think of her eyes, her lips. . . . She belonged to me. . . ."

Martin sprang up. He came only to Stiegel's shoulder, a little man, dignified enough in his wine velvet and powdered hair when he was calm. Now he was like some released jumping-jack, his whole body afire.

"I suppose she belonged to them all, eh? To Misky and Ege and . . . and you! I suppose you know too where the forget-me-nots grow!" Martin snatched up a box from the table and jammed it down with a bang.

"Himmel, don't shout!" cried Stiegel, doubling his fists, infuriated with the truth. "Think what you're saying. . . ."

"You love her too!" Martin burst out. "Mon Dieu, that is very funny. She makes an ass of us all. But you are married. . . . She makes the biggest ass of ——"

"If you say another word I'll smash you down," cried Stiegel.

He turned to the window, struggling to control the hands that wanted to tear Martin Grenier apart, and leaned trembling against the sash. He saw the people scattering below on the grass like ants, the black spots swimming in his eyes against the bright green of the sunlit square.

"I've had them as fine before!" snorted Martin Grenier.

"I'll have them as fine again! Thinks she can have the whole Glass House laughing at me—la chienne!"

Stiegel turned, ready to knock Martin down. Then he saw the passion through the mask of crazed words. Martin had pride—pride like Diane's. He began to pity him so much that his own pain and humiliation were entirely forgotten.

"You must laugh back at her," Stiegel cried, praying fervently that he might turn Martin into any path but that of violent revenge. "A woman of no morals. . . ."

"But I want her!" groaned Martin, unnerved again.

"She thinks you will come running after her," Stiegel exclaimed with cunning. "She will be waiting. She will be furious when she finds you have forgot her, that you are still here, making glass."

"The bowl—she took the bowl!" proclaimed Martin.

"No, I have the bowl," Stiegel lied quickly. "I will give you five hundred pounds if you stay and find the formula."

"Five hundred pounds!" repeated Grenier. He stood dazed before Stiegel a moment, and then tossed back his head and laughed long and crazily.

"Five hundred pounds! . . . A *thousand* pounds!"

Stiegel felt the sweat trickling down his face.

"I can't spare a thousand pounds. . . ."

Martin's white teeth flashed with satisfaction. He would make the gay Baron pay for the moments he had had with Diane! He folded his arms and awaited Stiegel's verdict with impudence. He could go far with a thousand pounds!

"I'll give it . . ." Stiegel stammered. If he could keep Martin here working on the bowl which he would get from Diane, that in itself would be worth a thousand pounds. Anything to be assured of her safety. "I'll give it . . . if you vow——"

"Vow!" shouted Grenier, laughing again. "What is a vow!"

"Later—October, November—when the business is running smooth ——"

He would have to see Diane now, would have to get the bowl from her without Martin's knowing.

"You know where she is!" Grenier accused him, shrewdly.

"I'll find her. . . ."

Martin grinned at Stiegel. He had the pretty Baron in a hole!

"Aye, we'll all find her again, la chienne! But the married ass—he is the most *beaut'*ful ass of all, n'est-ce pas?"

"Get out of here, God damn you!" Stiegel cried, and lurched toward the door, which slammed in his face.

His sensations were so muddled that he threw himself panting onto the bed and stared into the blank whiteness of the ceiling without a palpable thought. The organ squeaked its last vague philosophizing. October, and the room was chilly. But the sweat poured relentlessly down from his forehead.

Feeling was coming back a little, feeling other than this overwhelming heat of anger and weakness from fear. Feeling and chagrin, and a sense of frustration and victory all in one. He had been terrified of this little madman, and the whole thing had turned out to be an act of clowning!

La chienne! Bitch! But Martin Grenier still loved her with the whole passion of a lifetime. Loved her with such fire and intensity that he would die before he ever let anyone know it.

25

EORGE and Diane lived in one of the tenant houses
built close to the road above Charming Forge. The first
winter months had been bleak for Diane, though her
hands were busy from morning till night in her own house,
or helping Mrs. Nassel, the wife of the superintendent. She
spent the day washing the sweat from linen shirts, weaving
linen for new shirts, baking bread, making beds. Mrs.
Nassel had been in the harness a long time and did not
seem to mind. Her only child, Christian, was old enough to
be working with the men.

Charming Forge was originally called Der Tulpehocken
Eisenhammer. It was nestled in the curve of the Tulpehocken, where there was sufficient water power to drive
the machinery and maintain a blast in the furnace.

Near the Forge the road from Wolmansdorf climbed the
hill, paused on the summit for a moment for a breath of
wind, shivered, and hustled down into privacy again. Over
the broad, placid stream was a covered bridge. On the
other side was the tumult of the forge, with its four fires,
the rolling mill, the grist and sawmills, and the low red
brick tenant houses.

Diane was so miserable that she lived in enforced gayety.

[3 0 8]

Diane, truly happy, was a tranquil person. She scarcely dared give herself time for meditation now; the very image of Stiegel in her mind was so painful that she burst into some old French song to annihilate it.

And now she no longer had her harp. She hummed the Irish tunes of O'Harpigan as she polished her pewter, wondering if Barbara might be sitting now at the instrument, her delicate fingers picking a love song with the nicety of the first Elizabeth.

She pitied George when he was gone, and loathed him when he was near her. He was so deplorably in love with her that he still kissed the hem of her gown, moping in the chimney corner if she sang to some bleary-eyed forger who smoked and tippled.

When she told him that they were to have a child in the summer he was besieged with fear. Supposing she should die?

"I shall live as long as a myth," she had replied bitterly.

She would neglect him then for the infant!

"You rave like a child, George."

Any reference to his youth worked like a charm. He was beset with jealousy of her years. He felt vaguely that she was possessed of knowledge and wisdom which all his Latin drilling and sophistry had not earned him. He strove constantly to impress her with data and theories she did not know, unaware that this very effort was in itself a confession of immaturity. He had a feeling of never quite possessing her; of wanting to apologize for his ardor, as if she had been a bright poppy which would crumble at his touch.

Sometimes he heard laughter in Nassel's house as he scraped the snow from his boots on the porch, and when he entered, the laughter died down, and Mrs. Nassel, her hands holding down her corpulent hips, would shake the ribbons on her cap and eye him like an interested parrot.

They had been laughing at him. He knew it! He glowered
at them, tossed an imaginary something into the fire.

"Can you keep a secret, Mr. Ege?"

"Certainly."

"Chris has put white pepper in Schmick's wash gourd."

"We thought you were Schmick," snickered one of the
potters.

He laughed sheepishly with them. Each time it was the
same.

Diane laughed at him along with the rest. She endured
him only because she saw no other way out of this exigency.
If it had not been for the coming of the child she would have
been distraught. She thought of the child constantly, wondering if the vague stirring she already felt could mean that
Stiegel's son was growing strong. He would love her, love
her with so much passion that there would be nothing else
in the world for him. They would be close. He would be
the image of Heinrich.

As her foot sped back and forth on the spinning wheel
she felt impatient with the long months she must wait to
see her son. There he lay within her womb, a part of her—
and she must wait an eternity to touch his hands, to have
his eyes look up into hers, to feel his hungry mouth at
her breast. She thought of Jacob; Elizabeth could never
have felt this joy at his coming. Elizabeth could never have
known this longing.

Stiegel's desertion of her cut into her thoughts sharply.
He would be glad that she was gone. He had not even cared
enough to come to her, to find out why she had left so
suddenly. She would never tell him the child was his. She
would never let him know that she had willingly borne his
child. Or she would tell them all—would laugh at everyone
when the child was borne—George, Elizabeth, Stiegel, the
whole pack of fools—and would go off to Acadia, leaving
them all floundering behind her, smoldering in jealousy

and infamy and failure. She would go back to Martin Grenier perhaps—who would not care whose child she had borne. She would do something dramatic, something to give her a sense of revenge. But if she could only see Heinrich again—see him for one little minute . . . touch his hand. . . .

Stiegel did not go to the Forge at once because he did not want to seem anxious about following Diane. He had pledged the family to secrecy as to the whereabouts of the Eges. He told Elizabeth and Anna that George might not be safe if Martin Grenier knew where to find him. In a few months the man's fanaticism would be worn down by work.

"I think you had better send him away," Elizabeth said uneasily. "He's not—not safe around Barbara and Jerusha."

Stiegel smiled ironically. "I've made him manager of the Glass House expressly to keep him here!"

By the middle of November the new line of glassware had begun to be shelved. The Glass House had leaped to an institution. There were a dozen crucibles, and men working constantly on new ones, for the life of a clay pot was seldom over seven months. Two hundred hands labored on tableware; there were blowers, enamelers, cutters, flowerers. One worker turned out nothing but tiny glass toys— candy canes and animals—and jewelry of all descriptions.

Stiegel threw himself into the new venture with vehemence, determined that he must forget Diane enough to bring himself peace. He could never expect much happiness again. Now there were only two things left to him, the two things Diane had taunted him about time after time— money and fame. At least they would be something to work for, something to distract him. His glassware must be resonant, whole-toned and pure as a long-drawn note from his violin.

He was innately an artist, selecting neat and beautiful

patterns with discrimination. He dreamed them, saw them
in flowers, groped for colors in a pool or in a sunset. The
amethyst was the tincture of the first spring violets; the
amber, of honey, liquid in the sun. The blues—a delight
to him—were copied from all the blues of Nature. His
glassware was light of weight, thin of texture—probably
the first in America which contained lead.

The workmen he had engaged from Europe proved to be
artists too. Germans, English, Italians—their personalities
varied, but they all possessed a fine feeling for form, weaving into their work the spirit of their mother country.

The Rago brothers, Venetians, had brought with them
their own little pattern-molds and tools, and were soon producing the Venetian Diamond and Daisy-in-the-Square
bottles. The British blowers contributed the technique of
the English wineglass, and the art of making the opaque
glass of the Bristol factory. The enamelers, Swiss, came
with their native love of fine detail.

There were Venetian swans gliding atop a diamond-
diapered sugar bowl; Swiss castles enameled upon a Rhine-
wine glass; English tumblers with air-twist stems of Spanish
accent; but none of them incongruous. The domed sweetmeat jars and the footed vessels for brown sugar, lopsided
though they were, maintained a graceful outline. The
metal-mixers and color-compounders took care that Stiegel
should never find a faded blue, a murky amethyst, a dull
amber. He was a most severe judge. Walking through the
factory, he glanced at his sweetmeat jars with practiced
eye, flipping those into discard which did not meet with
his aesthetic standards. Martin Grenier, too, in the arrogant
knowledge of his supremacy, would permit nothing inferior
to be shelved.

Sometimes, loitering among the workmen, in the white
heat, Stiegel would call a halt to the work, beckoning them
out to the fresh air; there they flopped down on the crisp

fallen leaves while he extemporized on the quality of their work. He talked to them humanly, intimately, passing a snuff jar about. He loved his men, and felt imbued with the sense of camaraderie. They shared his turkeys, his beer, his glory. Their children were taught by his schoolmaster, and played about in his sight. The very chapel in his mansion belonged to them. They were at liberty at any time to leave their work and to worship there alone, unquestioned, trudging through his home as if they lived there.

The household and the entire village responded to his generosity. When the cream-colored coach returned from a journey, preceded by outriders in livery (for he would not be robbed again), the glass-blowers scattered. They seized their instruments and mounted to the platform on the roof of his house, and their pulsating German waltzes welcomed him home.

As soon as Elizabeth and Anna went to Philadelphia he would make a trip to Charming Forge, Stiegel decided. He dreaded his first meeting with Diane. It could never be anything but artificial. He would try to get the bowl from her, and she would resent that and accuse him again of building his life on love of gold. They would both be wretched looking into one another's eyes and Diane would lie to him glibly.

The preparations Elizabeth made seemed interminable. If she did not hurry she would be caught in the snows, he warned her. It was a perilous journey for two women and a child to make alone. He would send them in the coach with outriders.

Elizabeth was as excited as if she were about to be married. She washed and mended, and dropped numerous petticoats of handsome quilting into Wilhelmina's lap to be altered, for the winter had done disastrous things to her circumference.

Wilhelmina was the buxom new German indenture.

Elizabeth's conversation was incoherent. "Wilhelmina, a finger's width wider. . . . The cambric aprons are for mornings. . . . Barbara, Heinrich does not like his cherry pudding sour, you know. . . . Two ladles of —— Oh, a rent in my best mittens! Give them to Anne, Jerusha! . . . 'Twould be folly to carry pomade. . . ."

Jacob talked Indian until his mother was frantic with nervous apprehension. He felt defrauded that at the ripe age of five he had seen nothing but friendly Indians in the town of Lancaster, or "walk-abouts" in Brickerville. He borrowed his father's gun and ambitiously shot at an apple on the cocky brown head of the co-operative Jerusha—to miss it in favor of a bedroom window. He sneaked stealthily into Barbara's bedroom one night while she was kneeling at her bedside in prayer, and began to scalp the young lady. Barbara, who was timid and lacked Jerusha's spirit of adventure, screamed healthily and indulged in hysteria for an hour, while Jerusha rescued the clipped locks and said she would have them made into a bracelet. Elizabeth saw nothing in Jacob's escapades but genius for learning to protect his mother on a perilous journey, and defended him with every inch of her embonpoint. For days Barbara peered cautiously about the doorway of her room before emerging into the wilderness of the hall, ate sparingly at meals when Jacob was near, lost her pinkness at a wanton gesture of his hand, and was eventually administered calomel for her liver.

Stiegel watched the equipage start off with a great sigh of relief. He wondered when Elizabeth would come back to Manheim. She would be infatuated with Philadelphia; he had given her carte blanche to furnish the house there as she pleased. What else could he do for her? On the surface of his masculine conscience he believed that a continual buying orgy would compensate for the love of which he deprived her.

He went off to Charming Forge with a cold sort of fear. The journey was going to mean heartache for both himself and Diane. And yet he sought out the heartache and felt that it was going to bring him some little iota of comfort.

The road which led to Wolmansdorf meandered some six or eight miles through the most picturesque farmland. It was expansive but snug, one view secluded from another with huge trees, a hillock, or a bend in the road. Cows nibbled in the swampy lowland. One seemed never to meet a neighbor, though the houses along the way were tenanted. There lay over the verdure a lazy enchantment so that the locusts must always buzz in summer and the snow sparkle languidly in winter.

Stiegel had come alone on horseback. Now, as he crossed the covered bridge in an early afternoon snowfall he had a desire to turn about and gallop back the entire way to Manheim. He would have to ask for George first, of course. Or should he look up Nassel, as he had always done in the past? Supposing he should meet Diane here, in the road, now? Supposing she should be in Wolmansdorf? That somehow he would not get to see her at all? He would have to be civil to George! Appearances! Appearances!

The smoke rose from the forges; there was a stir of men, as the horse clattered over the loose boards of the bridge. He was surrounded by filthy workmen. The superintendent, Christian Nassel, senior, grinned at him and stammered a welcome.

"Where is Mr. Ege?" demanded Stiegel. George's eyes would look into his own with insolent authority, and they would say, "Who is master here now? Try to budge me from Charming Forge and the whole world will laugh at your adultery."

"Gone to Reading to wait upon a customer," supplied Nassel, rubbing his thigh bashfully in the radiant presence of the Baron.

Stiegel felt a great sense of relief. Then the thing he did not wish to say slipped from his lips. ". . . And . . . Mrs. Ege?"

He was confronted by Mrs. Nassel, who came hurriedly out of her house, a shawl thrown over her head. She curtsied deeply and settled into a stance like a ship after a gentle roll. Her face dimpled expectantly. She would make Wiener Schnitzel for the Baron's dinner.

Stiegel's eyes repeated the question.

"Oh, Madame Ege. . . . I looked in upon her a few moments back. She is home, spinning."

"I'll meet you in the office, Nassel," Stiegel said, his heart pounding. "After I have paid my respects to Madame Ege."

He tossed the reins of his horse to the superintendent, and walked over to the house toward which Mrs. Nassel had nodded.

Diane, hearing a footstep on the porch, was disgruntled. She had not thought that George would be home so soon. He was forever interrupting her dreams of the child.

"Entrez!" she called briskly, wondering why he knocked, and as she saw Stiegel in the doorway she gave a little cry and felt too weak to stand.

He observed the modesty of the room in a flash—the sanded floor, the rough furniture, the pewter and thick plates. His eyes rested on Diane. The firelight seemed to envelop her, flashing fire into her hair and casting shadows over her. She had changed somehow. Her face and her breasts had grown full, and there was a strained, peaked look about her eyes. But in spite of the hard glint of her lips, there was a softness about her he had never felt before.

He lifted the hand that trembled on the wheel, and kissed it. He wanted to fall down on his knees beside her. He wanted to cry, to bury his face in her lap and lie sobbing before the fire, as if Diane had been his mother back in Cologne.

But her eyes flared with sharp resentment at his touch. He was like flint and steel, he thought quickly, and she, like tinder. He was forever inflaming her. He had rehearsed all the way from Manheim what he would say to her if she were with George—with others—alone. Now none of the prosaic phrases came to him.

"The family is well?" asked Diane, fumbling with the flax, which had become twisted.

"Diane, why did you go off with George?"

She laughed scornfully. "You must be very curious, M'sieu, that you come in such haste to find out!"

"Diane . . . I know what you have been thinking of me. . . . It's not true. I went through Hell all the time I was in Manheim. I came back to you . . . I came back to you not caring about anything else in the world—and you were gone!"

She caught her breath in a quick little gasp and looked at him.

"Mon Dieu . . ." she breathed. "Mon Dieu. . . ."

"You believe me, don't you?" he pleaded huskily.

Her heart raced dizzily. "But you did not come here for me. Heinrich . . . if you mean that, you would have come for me. . . ."

For a moment she was filled with temptation to blurt out her secret, to go to him and cry out that she was bearing his son! She got up from the spinning wheel, and her legs felt like lead.

"Heinrich, you have come to take me away now!" she whispered, her breath coming so fast that it seemed to choke her.

"Oh Liebling, you still live in another world. . . ."

"And you are still afraid to live!" she cried out.

Was he afraid to live? Was it fear that held him back from these leaps that she was so willing to take? Was he being weak and fearful—Heinrich Stiegel who had always seemed so full-blooded and strong? Who had always thought he could never get enough of beauty and richness from life? Again and again their love seemed to go through crises of which he did not know how to be master.

There was only one solution for them. They must never see one another. They must remain far enough apart that time and distance would finally cement the breach; far enough apart that they could never open the wound by a touch of the hand or a caress of the eyes. They must never see one another again. Never. Or they would both go quite mad trying to avoid a world that was real and vengeful.

He got up and went to the window. Nassel was leading a team of mules up the road with a load of grain. How unctuously contented the men looked as they whistled about their work, across the way. Damn them! Afraid to live? He had a crazy notion that he must bar the door, bar out George and the rest of the world and crush her to him with such fierceness that she would cry out. He dared not look about and meet her eyes. . . .

He went out into the chilly twilight, wondering where his legs were taking him, and found himself plodding up the hill to the little stone office of one room. It was across the creek and faced the imposing site where George Ege eventually built his mansion.

Nassel, who was accountant at the Forge, went over the books with Stiegel. They sat close together on high stools at the desk, over a dirty candle. The books were spread out before them, and Nassel's filthy hands, washed thrice for this very occasion, rambled over the pages.

"Lisbon Salt, 13 pence. Green wafers, six shillings two-pence. . . ."

The entries in their pale lavender ink and Nassel's labored script were a blur.

Diane would keep on loathing him, loathing him as she had done when she ran off with George.

"One cask ale, 15 shillings."

She would never believe that he loved her as much as any man could love any woman. It was because they would never use the same measure for love.

He cut off Nassel's accounts with a gesture of confidence, and returned with him to his house.

The men ate at a long board in the kitchen. As a rule, George and Diane ate along with them. Tonight, however, Mrs. Nassel insisted that she set three places in the dining-room. It was cool and colorless as a vault, with dull pouty-looking blue china in the corner cupboard. The walls had grayed with time and the rough pine woodwork needed paint. Stiegel shuddered at the dreariness of eating there with George and Diane, but the more he insisted on joining the men, the more Mrs. Nassel insisted on secluding them. That *indeed* it was a pleasure rather than trouble to serve them.

Diane and George came in together. She wore the gown which she had worn several months ago in the woods. The lace had been carefully mended, and a wreath of flowers sewed over the triangular rent. It gave a look of shabby elegance, like some resurrection from an attic trunk, and Stiegel flushed scarlet as he saw the cruelty and satisfaction in her eyes.

George's face was ruddy with embarrassment, and he fumbled with the buttons of his waistcoat. There was a sharp silence, and Stiegel wondered what pose George would adopt. He was intensely relieved when George bowed.

"This is an honor, sir!"

"You are enjoying your work?" asked Stiegel, at once humiliated by the stupidity of his words.

"Very much, uncle. I trust you have found the Forge run to your approval?"

"In these times no loss is profit," offered Stiegel tone-lessly, and he waited at the door of the dining-room for

Diane to sweep in ahead of him.

George was more relieved than Stiegel that this first meeting had begun so peaceably. He helped himself generously to Mrs. Nassel's broad noodles.

"How are my mother and Aunt Elizabeth?" he asked.

"They are at the new house in Philadelphia. With Jacob. Elizabeth has just had five more teeth drawn, to her great discomfort."

"Voilà," said Diane, with mirthful sarcasm.

"And my mother?" asked George, ignoring her.

"She is not reconciled to your marriage, of course."

"She is a dragon," exclaimed Diane. "She will lap up Michael in her burning throat and swallow him, and he will writhe in her belly and not escape, eh?"

"Diane!" George protested hotly.

Stiegel watched Diane from the corner of his eye. He need not have been afraid of her. When she could caricature her enemies she was in full command of her emotion. She was showing him now that she could enjoy life very well without him!

"And Martin Grenier—why hasn't Martin come to kill me, Heinrich?"

George looked up, his expression tense.

"Because he does not know where you are!" Stiegel answered.

"What did he say? What did he do?" George asked quickly.

"What he said is better not repeated," said Stiegel. "He is manager of the new Glass House."

"He's not—not violent about it then? . . . About Diane and me?"

Stiegel smiled nicely. "He was most annoyed that Diane had taken the bowl with her," he lied. "I don't think he'd try to make trouble if he had it."

"The bowl was mine!" cried Diane, with a frown.

"Give it back," urged George. "I don't want that savage tracking us down!"

"I think you had best return it to him," Stiegel cautioned her.

"So that you may copy it, Heinrich?"

"I will buy it from you," he added, ignoring her taunt.

"But I like it!"

"I will give you . . . a hundred pounds for it!" he bargained.

"Fooh! That would not pay for the sentiment!"

"A hundred pounds! Diane, don't be a fool," cried George excitedly.

"Two hundred pounds. Will that buy sentiment and all?" asked Stiegel, angrily.

"Five hundred pounds!" proclaimed Diane. "No less. . . . George—if you do not stop gawking at me, I shall not sell the bowl at all!"

"I can't pay five hundred pounds!" groaned Stiegel. "My books are filling with credit, but no money comes in, and ——"

"Your ring—I shall take your diamond ring instead," Diane said calmly.

They sat facing each other, like two elements at war. He felt he must strangle her, and she thought she must die of the dreadful pain of her failure to win him. They were close enough that the magnetism of one was upon the other again, and held them both motionless, paralyzed.

"Diane," cried George, breaking the spell. "Give the bowl to my uncle as a loan."

Stiegel took off the diamond ring which he wore and slipped it across the tablecloth to Diane. Lightly she picked it up, and put it on her thumb, watching the flash of it with a sort of primitive pleasure. She had passed the little crisis safely, victoriously, and was serene again. Her eyes hardened.

"Glass, she is your grande passion of a lifetime, n'est-ce pas?"

"That's all I have left!" he said briefly.

"But . . . your violin!"

The violin! He had no incentive to play it any more. He had scarcely thought of it for months, and only then with a curious self-reproach that he hastily dismissed from his mind. He would not admit that he had been untrue to himself. Every youth must have an emotional outlet—women, gambling, poetry. He had chosen well. For years he had slaved toward perfection in his music. At one time he had only laid it aside for other pleasure jealously, grudgingly. But now he was a man. He had a man's aspirations and music had been an interlude. He sighed. Music had been his first love, inimitable. She had stolen from him a certain melody of living, a certain breathlessness of beauty.

Diane was looking at him intently, her black eyes flashing enmity.

"The violin was a toy," he said deliberately, as he took some of the pickled samphire Mrs. Nassel was urging on him, "a sedative for youth."

"I used to wish I could play like you." George lifted his wineglass and tossed down the last swallow. "Once or twice I ——"

"Today I have a man's work to do," Stiegel interrupted him. "I have to cope with other men, with law, with the colonies. Now with my glassware I am racing with all of Europe!"

"The German. . . . In his mind he is always surrounded by an army," said Diane.

He was not certain what she meant, but he bitterly resented her allusions to his music. He noticed that she had not touched her food.

"Some day when I have more time I'll go back to my music," he went on. "My first little tender mistress. . . ."

"And she'll be old and crude from neglect," returned Diane, maliciously. "You'll embrace her and find she is nothing but a bony hag, M'sieu."

"Diane, you're relentless."

"Non, non, non. I have the glass ball in my hands. I can read your future!"

He saw that she was really agitated.

"You will be burned for witchery," he said, chagrined.

"Il n'y a pas de quoi. . . . I only want you to *live*, Heinrich. . . . To live always—in everything you do. . . ."

They had quite forgotten their food and George.

26

*T*HE FOLLOWING February Stiegel sat in his office at Manheim one morning as Cyrus brought in a sack of mail. It was a one-room cottage a minute's saunter off to the right of the mansion.

Stiegel had brought the bowl back with him from Charming Forge, elated at the prospect of giving it into Martin Grenier's hands (for he had perfect confidence that Martin could copy it), and yet fearful that Martin would demand the whereabouts of Diane. Martin had asked no questions. No doubt he knew that Diane lived at Charming Forge. The glass-blowers and servants talked, and the men at the Furnace must know that George had been made manager of the other iron works. Stiegel sighed with relief. Perhaps he had been too terrified of the little Frenchman, who was probably combustible but harmless.

Martin had been working on the bowl now for several months. For a thousand pounds any man could surely evolve any formula, thought Stiegel. What a fool he had been to offer such a sum in a reckless moment! Martin should have been willing to do his experiments free, on Stiegel's time. When he asked Martin how he was progressing, he shrugged his shoulders expressively and said nothing, working with a glumness that Stiegel distrusted. Tactfully enough, he pretended that Diane had only lent him the bowl.

He picked up a letter from Elizabeth, a healthy miscellany of facts:

"We partook of dinner at four with Mistress Mary White, Mr. Morris' betrothed. She is uncomon plesant and easy to look upon. Mr. Morris seems much enamured of her of which I do not blame him a partickle. We formed a Party at the Southwark Theater to view Hallam's American Company who played the Provoked Husband it being a large Sucess. Mr. Lewis Hallam drew markt aplawse. Anna pled a Headake as you know it is Still esteem'd wicked by the Quakers and when I return'd I must needs tell her the whole story of the play late into the nite and what every person of fashun wore. Hair is Dres't higher and higher with perls and flowers and I would fancy some small white Glass Doves for my Hair when I return."

Elizabeth was happy, thought Stiegel, absently strumming on the desk with his fingers. Never a word about the Daughters of Liberty or the fate of those who were buying stamped paper and getting tarred and feathered for it. Aigrets in her hair! That's what life meant to Elizabeth.

He began to scribble down in his ledger what he would be worth in ten years. It was stupendous the way his glass had been selling. He had agencies in a dozen Pennsylvania towns. He was going to be rich, very rich. And when Grenier once got the formula the colonies would see something in blue glass that they had never dreamed of before.

He kept his ledgers more like a diary, jotting down estimates of the future and some of his daily deliberations.

He wondered what Elizabeth had done with the Philadelphia house. He smiled to himself. It would be a place fit for Madame Du Barry. Perhaps he'd better go and draw in the reins. Besides, Philadelphia could stand another agency for his glassware.

Elizabeth made the house festive for his coming. It was profuse with flowers, with preserved fruits of its own orchard and the dainties of the best shops in town. There was flesh, fish and fowl in the larder, hothouse strawberries and peaches and grapes on silver plate. There was even coffee on the small parlor table after dinner, and Elizabeth waiting there to cook it, a little self-assured in her new knowledge of Philadelphia. The Wilton rugs were spotless. The elaborate French furniture of her own choice was of the most elegant. She had collected enough bills to jolt even the prodigal Stiegel.

Jacob, in a fresh apron, was made to rehearse a little welcome speech of Madame Ege's inspiration. Elizabeth was effervescent.

"Oh, Heinrich, you should see the China tea plates of daffodil pattern I have bought for Barbara's chest," she chattered, "and the Ghentish sheeting Holland for Jerusha, too."

He listened to her babbling with disdain. Nothing about Elizabeth nor the house seemed warm or familiar.

"And I've engaged Copley to paint Jacob for the mantel in the hall. It irks him though to sit still for so long," she said, stroking the hair of Jacob, who stood beside her, appraising his father.

"If he were mine," added Anna Ege, jingling the household keys, "I'd send him to the Market Square for discipline. The Babes in the Woods would make him comfited with his lot."

Jacob squirmed at the mention of the stocks.

"You are too hard on Jacob," defended Elizabeth, patting his hand. "The child looks pindling."

"That's his undue appetite for mushmelons!" returned Anna Ege.

Stiegel saw little of the Stedmans, though they dined together the first week of his arrival at the Indian King Tavern on High Street.

Stiegel waited for them in the taproom, watching the innkeeper mix sugar and dried pumpkin into the flip he was making. America herself was like the flip, thought Stiegel musingly, and England was the loggerhead which inflamed it to a froth. He listened to snatches of excited political talk, and was stirred into a feeling of deep rebellion by pamphlets which were tossed into the inn by excited, dirty boys. Stiegel himself was in a predicament. The Stamp Act had given him his chance to make a great deal of money. The non-importation agreements among the merchants had helped to spread his glassware throughout the colonies. Now there were rumors of repeal of the Stamp Act. What would happen to his new business if England should repeal the Stamp Act, and imports should come flooding in again? Was he being a hypocrite? Actually, at heart, he wanted to see the colonies independent. But now he was making their misfortune his success. A parasite. The thought disturbed him deeply.

Then Alexander and Charles Stedman entered the barroom, shaking the snow from their greatcoats and slinging their muffs near the fire to thaw out. With the first flip they were at swords' points again.

"Things have come to a pretty pass when the courts are closed," Charles stormed. "Closing the courts so no stamp case may be tried. 'Tis an admission itself that stamps are legal! Andrew Hamilton and John Dickinson told me ——"

"Fooh!" cried Stiegel. "Lawyers! 'Tis only mortal they all squeal!"

"You're making a neat little profit on the Stamp Act. You needn't begrudge it!" Alexander thrust at Stiegel.

"I paid hundreds of pounds for stamped paper for my bills of merchandise," defended Stiegel. "And I'll be in good fortune if I get through without a tarring and feathering for it!"

"You don't begrudge those few dollars to the Mother Country when you turn about and make money through her loss in import?"

Stiegel did not answer directly. "You still condemn my idea of glassmaking?"

Charles Stedman leaned across the table excitedly. "Aye, you are not finished, Stiegel. You have let the iron business run itself, and we sit here in Philadelphia and suffer from it, and ——"

"Elizabeth Furnace is still making money, more money than any other Furnace within ——"

"Granted. But Elizabeth Furnace would make more money were you to expend a little effort on it! I know," Alexander Stedman went on, his gray face looking tired, "I know you think us a pair of sour Tories. But we are pressed for money."

"Why you cling to England when she bleeds you in taxes I can't see! We're treated ——"

"That's patriotism," said Alexander Stedman quietly, the two words clear above a drunken brawl that had begun in the chimney corner.

For a moment the din stopped any possibility of talk. A young tanner with his wig awry, the pigtail in his mouth like a dagger, pummeled his companion with tawny fists, and soon partisans of both sides were throwing pamphlets and muffs and flip.

"Tar him! Feather him!" came the excited cries. "Down with the Stamp Act! Down with Parliament! Down with King George!"

The shrieks rose and mingled until the whole room was abroil, and pieces of torn clothing began to fly as the young tanner was stripped, a boot darting perilously close to Stiegel's head. Then in among the commotion there was the whisk of two red jackets, and the fight scrambled out onto the street, leaving an upheaval of overturned chairs and spilled ale and sundry hats. A wheelwright who had been treated to the butt of the "lobster's" gun reeled about near the door, and the innkeeper, puffing and heaving, gave him a decisive clap on the head with a pewter pitcher, took him by the seat of the pants, and dealt him a kick that almost sent the two of them spilling onto the street.

The three men watched the little scene without much emotion. They had seen too many similar squabbles. Stiegel clapped his hands on his arms, to warm himself, for the door had been standing open and the cold air rushing in as the warriors rushed out.

Charles Stedman played with a few grains of snuff. "Down with the Stamp Act?" he repeated sarcastically. "And what happens to you, Stiegel, if the Stamp Act is repealed?"

"My glass is so superior to what is imported the colonies will never go back to foreign ware," cried Stiegel. "Stamp Act or no Stamp Act, my fortune is assured."

He swept down the remainder of his flip with a grand flourish as if he were expunging the aggregate arguments of the Tory party.

"I take off my hat to you," Alexander Stedman said coolly, as he got up from his chair. "I'm forced to mortgage my interests both at Manheim and at Elizabeth Furnace."

"You're ——" Stiegel got up too, a little dizzy with the news and the flip and the hubbub of the coffee house.

"To Isaac Cox—for three thousand pounds."

"But . . . but you have other properties you could mortgage instead!" cried Stiegel. "Why, we've been partners for years. . . . A stranger ——"

"I am mortgaging these interests first, because I do not have confidence in you, Stiegel."

Stiegel flushed angrily, and jammed down on the table

the fist that he longed to smash into Alexander Stedman's
weathering gray face. He would show up this damn cold-
blooded Tory, by God!

He hurried home to Mulberry Street, embittered with
the news, twice colliding with people on the wrong side of
the street. The Stedmans were finished with him, were
they? He would return thrust for thrust from now on. After
the years he had spent slaving at tulip patterns and ten-
plate stoves so that they could sit in Philadelphia and
pocket their remuneration without a drop of sweat! The
snow was coming down now in a melting sleet.

Repeal. Well, what might it mean to him? Wasn't he well
enough established now that the colonies would never give
up his glass for imports? What was all this squealing in
Philadelphia about hard times?

But Parliament repealed the Stamp Act in March, and
some weeks later the news came by ship. Stiegel had taken
Jacob down to the wharf to greet the ship of Captain Wise
who was a personal friend. The wharf was filled with
sailors, fish nets, "weak women," barrels, merchants, over
which a general odor of stinking dead fish prevailed. As the
brig swayed into shouting distance, people along the shore
threw up their hats and hallooed their greeting. Jacob blew
up a bag and popped it, and an urchin with a black eye
almost leap-frogged over a barrel, missed, and splashed into
the water with great ado along with the molasses. One of
the Jezebels screamed, attracting attention to herself instead, and some sailors began to shove everyone aside for
the gangplank they dragged out on the dock.

Jacob danced up and down with joy. He had become
definitely tired of Philadelphia. He had been "coated" with
gay celebration, and was intolerably spoiled. His trading
with other young men of the neighborhood had proved so
lucrative as to be uninteresting. His mother would not
allow him to wallow his toes in the mud, and he was denied

discourse with the scavengers who collected that mud in tempting little carts. He had been punished by his father for drawing pictures on the cellar doors of the front sidewalks, and for going to the wharves alone. He had no one to play horseshoe and knife with but the servants. And a few days ago when he had only sneaked into the bar-room of Clarke's Inn with a coadjutant, lapping up the drink which had been left in glasses, his Aunt Anna had cried that it was a matter for the courts, his mother had gotten hysterics, and Wilhelmina, who was supposed to watch him, had been thrashed.

Since then, one of the family had had him constantly at hand. Stiegel found himself impatient with Jacob, as he was now impatient of life and everyone about him. The tricks that the boy played seemed half-witted, and Elizabeth's constant defense of the child irritated him. They began to quarrel often over Jacob. Why, at the boy's age he had been playing the violin.

He gripped Jacob's hand tightly and they waved their hats and cried out as the ship came close. The boat was alive with burly seamen and flying ropes and flags and masts, and some of the sailors were cupping their hands and trying to shout above the bells which were ringing. All at once their words seemed to leap over the water to the throng on shore, and the cry of "Stamp Act Repealed" spread like a flame. There were screams, hats tossed in the air, tumbles into the water, and people dancing one another about in a jig. Stiegel felt a sudden sinking of his spirits. He pulled Jacob with him back to the carriage. He had no desire to talk to Captain Wise. The Act repealed! He was a traitor to feel like this. A good American would be wild with joy.

The King's birth-night would be celebrated everywhere and England would be toasted again as if she were Utopia. Punch would be made common at all the coffee houses— and the colonies would buy foreign glass once more.

He must get back to Manheim and see how Martin Grenier was coming along with his experiments. Now more than ever the perfection of his glass would count. How could the colonies want to substitute anything else for it? What would Diane say if he should fail? He could not allow himself to become a failure in her eyes. Even if he should never see her again. All the force of his thwarted love seemed now to flow into his glassware.

"By the beginning of the week I must go back and close up the Glass House for the summer," he told himself wretchedly. "Gott, why can't they work in the heat? Why can't the thing go on and on? Why can't that damned little Frenchman figure out the formula?"

But Stiegel left for Manheim the following day, after a fight with Elizabeth over Jacob.

That evening, shortly after dark, the fire alarm had sounded. Jacob, unnoticed by the family, raced to the front door and tossed out the household buckets and bags and baskets into the street for the next stranger to carry along to the fire. He slipped on a few clothes and followed the excited thread of people on to Winn Street, where he worked with the water-slingers, passing buckets down the line to the engine. For two hours the family searched for Jacob, and finally Cyrus found him, a little scorched and a good deal saturated.

It was the Hand-in-Hand Fire Company which had been called out and not the Heart-in-Hand, to which the Stiegels belonged, and the next day, when no one had returned the Stiegel buckets, Jacob's disgrace was complete.

Stiegel had whipped Jacob with his cane before Elizabeth's very eyes, and when Elizabeth refused to speak to him in the morning, Stiegel ordered Cyrus to pack his clothes.

Before he left for his journey, he stopped before Elizabeth, who was making a ball for Jacob out of ravelings of a woolen sock. "Are you going to say good-bye to me?" he asked, wearily.

She turned her swollen eyes up to him. "You will kill Jacob if you ever flog him like that again!"

"How does one punish a child that is filled with the devil?" he asked.

"'Tis enough punishment for a child of his spirit to—to have to keep to his room!"

Stiegel smiled grimly. "The last time I made him keep to his room he spent the time shooting grape seeds at the eyes of my portrait."

"He must do *something!*" cried Elizabeth, her tears beginning all over again.

"But must you feed him hothouse grapes for punishment?"

"He's just a—a baby!"

"Soon you will not be able to handle him at all," threatened Stiegel. "What he needs is Germany—the Gymnasium."

"God forbid that he will ever be as hard as you!" cried Elizabeth.

"Hard?" thought Stiegel. "Am I hard? Of course I'm hard. . . . I've been cruel to everyone I ever loved. I never wanted to be. . . . It's something there that I fight. What's happened to me? I have even been hard with myself. I've denied myself the only thing in the world that would keep me from being hard."

"Elizabeth," he said shortly, "I shall send the coach back for you and the family the end of May."

27

THE FIRST THING that Stiegel did when he arrived in Manheim was to hunt out Martin Grenier, who happened to be at the stable feeding sugar to his horse. Stiegel had thought of nothing but the bowl on his journey home. It seemed the one tangible thing to which he could pin his hopes.

He greeted Martin and the stable boys with enthusiasm. He was glad to be in Manheim again. But as he looked into Martin's face he felt a sickening shock. His one eye was covered over with a gray film. Cataract!

He turned to Martin's horse, patting him and passing some light remark about the sheen of his coat.

"Well, I have made for you another bowl!" Martin said with his old air of jauntiness. "I'll wager you cannot tell which is the old one and which ——"

"You've got it then!" cried Stiegel, shaking him ecstatically by the shoulders. "You've got it! Why did you not send a messenger to me at once? Gott! At last. . . . Show me. . . . Where is ——"

"And I have taken my one thousand pounds," added Martin brazenly, "and marked it in the books: 'Bowl.'"

[334

"But you had no right ——"

"You left the business in my care. 'Twas a debt!"

"A debt for me to pay, not for you!" Stiegel stopped, a sudden cold feeling of uncertainty taking hold of him. There was something about Martin's mood he had better not trample on.

"What was it I couldn't find?" Stiegel went on, excitedly.

"Not enough of sodium carbonate."

"Gott! It's too good to be true!" ejaculated Stiegel.

They went over to the Glass House together, Stiegel looking eagerly about him at the beloved gardens and lawn which had become so civilized since the winter months.

Martin took two bowls out of the cupboard, and held them before the fire which still burned in the clay pot. The bowls were exactly alike, and Stiegel turned feverishly from one to the other, unable to tell them apart. Both were nicked in the same place, both had the pontil mark so weirdly like Stiegel's own. He shook his head in speechless admiration of Martin's skill.

"I have made the other bowl so that Madame Ege will have the pleasure of a pair!" Grenier said, sarcastically. "Next time you see her, present the bowl to her with my compliments!"

"You will not try to see her then," Stiegel said, with great relief.

Martin shrugged his shoulders noncommittally.

"Martin, this has been a hard year for you," Stiegel said, a little awkwardly, putting his hand on his arm. "And—you've been a gentleman."

"To keep her safe for you?" spurted out Martin, tossing Stiegel's hand from his sleeve, and laughing crudely.

Stiegel turned on his heel sharply and left the Glass House, his gentle mood quickly destroyed. Martin was demented. . . . He was demented himself. . . . Diane had done this to both of them.

The next day, unable to face Martin calmly, he decided that he would say nothing more to him of the bowl or the formula until the festivities of closing the Glass House were over. He would throw himself into the celebrations with his men.

The glass-blowers and their families had stayed in Manheim for May Day. According to custom, all the young people hiked into the country, breathing in the new spring romance, gathering violets and jacks-in-the-pulpit and delicate spring beauties. In front of the Stiegel mansion there was dancing on the green, and a Maypole wound with the finest of imported ribbons which the girls received as bows. The orchestra was hilarious, and beer flowed freely at Stiegel's expense. Glass-blowers fell in love with other glass-blowers' daughters, in this ecstatic profusion of flowers and bright petticoats and tiny feet making merry. Babies tumbled out of their mothers' laps, and crawled into the scuffle, dragging long embroidered dresses behind them, like caterpillars. The visiting horses basked in the fattest of Lancaster County oats, and the people from about the countryside sat at little tables and drank beer as if they were back at some Hofbrau in the Vaterland. Stiegel wandered among them, joking and welcoming them to his hospitality. He teased the pretty girls, and sometimes, with a burst of mischief, scattered a handful of coins among the small boys. This year, because of Martin's news, his bounty knew no limit. It was a May Day to be mingled with legend down through the years.

That evening after the village had quieted down, he sank into his favorite chair and looked about him. He was very tired with the activities of the day; very tired of smiling and being gracious. The house seemed restful and luxuriant, like a mecca after the desert. The richness of it all was almost caressing, enervating. Cyrus came pussy-footing about him, mumbling "Marsa Baron" profusely

with every little importunity. There was nothing about him
that Cyrus did not know, thought Stiegel. Gretchen, Elizabeth, Diane, Elizabeth. He had lived with Stiegel through
all his loves—lived with him and understood without a
word.

He sent Cyrus for Martin, and told him to have Martin
bring the formula. There would be time now to sit down
and discuss it.

In a short time Cyrus was back again, his long face longer
with worried lines.

"Marsa Baron, dat Monseer Greneay done gone las'
night."

Stiegel jumped up. "Gone where?"

"Gone 'way." Cyrus picked sympathetically on the braid
of his coat.

Stiegel brushed past him, snatching a lantern and cross-
ing the green with long strides. Down beyond the road,
the cottages of the glass-blowers stretched off in a neat
little row. Of course—he hadn't seen Martin all day—had
never missed him in the commotion of May Day. If Martin
had gone off with the thousand pounds, had cheated him
of the formula, he would follow him with blood-hounds
until the man was chewed alive! Martin's cottage was dark,
and the door stood open, one of the new gray kittens from
the barn mewing on the doorstep. The place was empty of
Martin's belongings except for a torn shirt yellowed with
sweat, a half-spilled pack of snuff and some shaving water
with its drying suds and whiskers on the side of a basin.

Stiegel rushed over to the Glass House. Martin *must*
have left the formula, he thought desperately. Martin was
not a thief. . . . But the Glass House was neat, its tools
polished and put away for the summer, its floor immaculate, its fire blackened at last. The May air had penetrated
the place, and it was cool now as a mausoleum. Stiegel
opened the cupboard doors behind Martin's desk with

trembling hands. The two bowls sat there on the shelf—but there was no letter, no formula. He pawed through the papers on the desk, in the drawers, hopelessly, knowing well that Martin never meant him to know how the bowl was made.

For several days he searched endlessly, savagely for any notes, any hint of the formula. He grilled the glass-workers who had not already left for the New England farms. He advertised for Martin in the newspapers. He sent riders out to track him down. A thousand pounds? It was a stupendous sum. He had been quite crazy to promise him that. To have nothing for it—nothing but a pair of bowls for Diane! At night he could get no sleep, and, dressed in his cap and banyan, stalked up and down on the green. Manheim! His own village. People called him Baron. They thought he had everything in life he wanted. He had nothing he wanted. Martin had been jealous of him, jealous of his love for Diane—the deranged fool. As if Martin realized that Stiegel had possessed something of the spirit of Diane that he had never known himself.

Why hadn't he taken the bowl, the old bowl, if it was so valuable, Stiegel wondered dejectedly? Honor among thieves? Another show of insolence, because Diane had made so light of his gift? The thought haunted Stiegel, and it maddened him too because he could not tell which of the two bowls was antique. He compared them in all the various lights of day; and he held them before different flames of candles and lanterns, hoping to discern a shade of difference. Sometimes, closing his eyes, he let his fingers drift sensitively over the surface; the little beads of enamel must be sharper, or the feeling of engraving rougher on the new bowl.

Then one morning as he shaved, the truth flashed suddenly into his mind. Martin had made one bowl. He could have made the other! Preposterous! . . . He dropped his razor and ran to the bowls again, which sat on the mantel of his fireplace, turning them over for the thousandth time to look at their pontil marks. So like his own. . . . Martin had made them. Had made them both. The thought stunned him for a moment, and then the whole deception became clear. Martin had been laughing at him, laughing at him and Diane in the security of his genius. Martin would laugh for the rest of his life, Martin with his thousand pounds! Stiegel tried feverishly to remember what he had said to Martin, that day he returned. That he would give him the money for the formula? Or that he would give him a thousand pounds to duplicate the bowl? Whatever his offer had been, it was now chaos. Stiegel picked up the bowls again in two angry fists, and sent them crashing to the brick of the hearth, grinding pieces of glass into the floor with his heel. He was angrier than he had ever been in his life.

"Cyrus!" he shouted. "Come—sweep the glass away—out of my sight. Hurry, you . . . you . . ." He had been going to say "you damned ape," but his lips stopped in time, and he trembled so that he had to lean against the mantel for support. His head swirled dizzily. He could see Martin standing there in the stable before him, the smirk on his face, the contempt in his eyes. His eyes. One pupil covered with gray. Cataract. Martin would soon be blind. Martin would need the thousand pounds.

On the day in the end of May when the baby was born, George had accompanied several workers to a bowling match in Wolmansdorf. He had left Diane reluctantly, although she said the child would not be born for another two months.

As he rode home, among some half dozen workers, the thought of himself and Diane rankled. He could not understand Diane. She had always given him a feeling of insecurity and excitement, and he wanted so desperately to be sure of her! Even as she waved good-bye today, her eyes had had a hard glitter in them, like the first stinging flakes of a blizzard.

He had supposed young Christian Nassel was going to the bowling match too. Why hadn't the boy ridden along in the mild May sunshine to the village? Had he purred all day at Diane's feet, holding her yarn, listening to her tales of the Indians?

The men had become silent on the last lap of their ride. George, who rode ahead, swung a lantern. The air had tightened with sundown, and crept under his cape, pinching him with its chill. He longed for the hearth, and the comforting heat of the chimney place.

Diane would be asleep, her head nestled in the curve of her arm. He would not dare to touch her. He flushed at the memory of the night he had kissed her passionately as she slept—how she had started up like a wild thing, her eyes jubilant, piercing him for a moment, then slowly going dull.

"I was dreaming! . . ." hoarsely.

"Diane—I love you so madly. . . ."

"I was dreaming of the woods, forget-me-nots, the stream. . . ." She shrank from him. "Don't you dare touch me!"

He had fallen silent then, chagrined, blaming himself as usual because he was young.

How strange Diane was, how elusive. What a miracle that she had ever married him! How could he expect from her more than the meager crumbs she tossed him? George was not stupid enough to believe that she had run away with him because she loved him. Diane would never love any one man, he felt. She had only married him because his mother and aunt had made her life unbearable, because she could no longer endure their cruelty. That was the reason she had promised to marry Martin Grenier, she told him. But she was afraid of Martin, who had forced her into the betrothal.

George wondered if it was the same wild impulse in Diane which had made her marry him that now made him suffer because he had won her. He was so jealous of her, so inordinately jealous! And for months he had been sick at the thought of a child coming which she would love.

One of the men was telling a bar-room story now, but he was not in the mood for it, and spurred his horse over the bridge to escape their laughter.

There was an uncertain light behind Diane's window curtain, as if a candle burned on the sill. He tethered the horse quickly outside the house, meaning to stable him later, and ran up the steps into the kitchen, leaving his companions to find their way in the dark.

There was no one there but Christian, in his night shirt and cap, nodding over the settee, half a meat pie at his side. Why was Christian here, George wondered angrily, about to shake him when he heard voices upstairs. Was something wrong with Diane? Then he heard the wail of an infant. He stopped in confusion and began to bite at his nails. Diane had borne the child. Diane would be dead! He felt faint as he leaned against the wall of the narrow stairs in the blackness. He would fling the child from the window. The cry grew louder, obstreperous. He stumbled forward, bursting drunkenly into the tiny bedroom. Mrs. Nassel held a bundle lightly on the curve of her stomach, and swayed gently, like the branch of a tree.

The faded bed curtain had been pulled aside, and Diane lay motionless under a gaudy quilt. Her eyes were peaceful. They rested on his tall, dishevelled figure with a new serenity.

"We will call him Georges," she said.

Mrs. Nassel began to say something. She was proud of the child, for she had been the midwife. George paid no attention. His wig in his hand, his lips trembling like those of a child, he knelt at the side of the bed.

"Diane—you won't die. . . ." he pleaded, spreading his cold hands over her warm ones.

"I am immortal," she whispered, her eyes filled with the cry of her child.

Mrs. Nassel was piqued by George's neglect of the baby. "I'faith, Mr. Ege, you have not yet set eyes on your son. Hear how he screams for you!" She rolled the bundle off the billow of her stomach, held it under George's stupefied gaze, and added a little wickedly, so that she might not be considered *too* much of a dupe, "Ant he a strong one for seven months?"

"Is he?" cried George, looking at the infant. "He seems so spindling and—red!"

"Red? Nay, you should have seen my Christian—like a ball of fireworks. Why *this* one is only properly pink!"

Mrs. Nassel was not fooled about the child's prematurity; she had helped in too many childbirths. The tiny finger nails were pink perfection. The ruddy bow legs kicked as robustly as had her Christian's. But there was nothing to be gained by not accepting Diane's statement that the baby had come too soon—for her husband was George's subordinate.

"He is the very image of you!" flattered Mrs. Nassel.

"Is he?" Her words spun round in his head like strong rum. The child had come too soon, but Diane was not going to die. . . . He laughed hysterically. How they would have jibed him at the meeting-house in Brickerville! Now there were no years between himself and Diane. He was a father. She was a mother. He sank down beside her again, and smoothed her hair with his trembling hand.

"How guileless he is!" thought Diane wearily. For weeks

the anticipation of his wrath had exhausted her. For months she had visualized this very scene—the birth of Heinrich's child. She had supposed George would stamp about, his face scarlet with humiliation and shame. She had supposed he might use force to make her admit the truth. She had determined that she would never tell him. She would lie to him, would tell him it was a seven months' baby, his own.

"Mon Dieu, how could a man be so stupid," her mind ran on quickly, and she closed her eyes so that she need not taint her happiness with the sight of him. Despite his gullibility, she had a sudden desire to flee with her child. She felt George touching her long straight black hair which spread stiffly on the pillow, and shuddered at the thought of his thick, trembling lips and his large-knuckled, nail-bitten hands.

"Snuff the candle. I can sleep," she said, and she drew the little bundle close which Mrs. Nassel had laid beside her on the bed. Holding her lips against the long black silk of the infant's hair, she pressed the tiny body to her breast. Tonight Heinrich would come to them in her dreams.

It was not until July that Stiegel received the news of the birth of Diane's son. He had been out on horseback in the fields after an early evening dinner, to see how the corn was coming along. When he returned, the family was gathered in the garden at the rear of the house, each absorbed in his own work. Madame Ege's needle stitched at new shirts for Jacob, and Jerusha's sampler was growing another flower. Elizabeth snipped dead roses from a bush, and Jacob lay in the middle of the circle, one leg hanging in the air over his knee, trying to whistle with grass in his lips.

Stiegel dropped down in Elizabeth's chair just as the

coachman appeared through the bushes with the latest mail. Barbara dropped her knitting, clasped a Lancaster letter to her bosom, and ran toward the house.

Stiegel flipped through the mail briskly, paused at a letter from Charming Forge, and tore it open first. He had had several business communications from George since his visit to the Forge. But it was always with great trepidation that he broke George's seal. He had an evil presentiment that this would bear news of Martin Grenier.

Stiegel read aloud: "Sir: This billet is not of a bizness nature, but to Inform you of the Birth of our Son, Georges."

He looked up. His tongue clove to the roof of his mouth. Mrs. Ege and Elizabeth were aghast.

Finally Mrs. Ege spoke in a voice like distant thunder. " 'Tis a jest!"

There was a momentary pause, and Stiegel leaped to his feet, crumpling the letter tersely in both hands. He stared at the women, and they stared back at him, so marked was his agitation. He wanted more than anything in the world to utter a few words of casual explanation, but his mind was a void.

Elizabeth's fingers, hidden in the apron on her lap, went tap, tap. "November . . . aye, November, December . . . five, six, seven. . . . Jerusha, go indoors. . . . No matter if your wool has rolled away!"

The young girl jumped up obediently. Her cheeks were flushed rosy with the thought of the new baby. She could break the news to Barbara!

"I told thee she seduced him!" proclaimed Mrs. Ege fiercely. The disgrace had absolved George in her mind.

"Finish the letter. There must be something of a mishap to Diane," urged Elizabeth, maliciously. "Seven m ——"

"Last night," offered Jacob, excitedly swinging his toe, "the hound bitch brought six puppies, a dog and five bitches. I helped them get born. They were slimy. The bitch ate ——"

"Jacob!" exploded Anna Ege.

The adults gazed at him in horror. Stiegel pointed to the gate in the hedge, wordless, and Jacob, accustomed to being excluded from adult conversation, rose, yawned, and shuffled over the grass.

"Thou should never have left thy home unprotected against the wiles of a foundling," Mrs. Ege hurled at her sister.

"But you were there."

"I was abed with my bosom pains!"

"And Heinrich was there. . . ."

"All men are purblind!"

"I came to you—in Manheim," said Stiegel, and he felt as if he had pronounced a death sentence on an innocent man.

He was trying to visualize Diane with her child in her arms. He remembered her rocking Barbara, patting her with an air of abstraction as she sang French lullabies. He saw her swinging the fat Jacob on the moss, at his importunity rather than at her indulgence. He heard her cry, "Do you think I am content to bundle Elizabeth? To shush the babies in their cradles? I hate them all—the puling lot!"

There was nothing of the mother in Diane, everything of the paramour.

He was convinced that the child was his own. He wanted the child to be his. Oh, why hadn't Diane told him that she was going to bear a child? Why hadn't she been honest? She had not wanted his pity. That was it. She had wanted his love free from duty. She had been too proud to ask for anything more. The desire to see her was overwhelming, and to see the child which had been born of their love.

He was suddenly conscious that Elizabeth and Anna were still bickering over the news. The denunciation of these godly women was nauseating. What did they know of life, of temptation? He must be alone, to think out the possible consequences of this message. He dropped the letter to the grass unfinished, and Anna Ege snatched it up to glean further details.

"What have I ever done to deserve this?" she sniffled, holding the letter at arm's length, in a brave attempt to read on.

"Anna, do you think they would taint their Bible with this entry?" asked Elizabeth.

"If she thought it would devil me!"

Anna Ege wiped her eyes, and, as she saw Stiegel walking slowly to the house, she added with malice, "Heinrich is exceeding upset."

"Aye, 'twas great folly to uproot her from the woods!" returned Elizabeth with innocent enjoyment. "As if a fish could amend its mode of living out of water! It's the lack of gratefulness which cuts him. After sheltering the girl all these years he'd expect something better than . . . than. . . ."

Elizabeth now assiduously trimmed her phrases to a society matron's store of platitudes. She could not finish the sentence. Besides, she was not quite sure that George had not had a pleasurable share in the transgression.

"The thing I don't understand," she murmured half to herself, picking up some of the dead roses which had slipped from her gathered apron, "is that Diane never seemed that much enamoured of George. . . . I've often wondered if she married him to spite us. Anna—*Anna!* You're a *grandmother!*"

28

$\mathcal{S}$TIEGEL MADE a trip at once to Charming Forge. The heat of the whole summer had seemed to accumulate in this one week, the country drying up like an old man in senility. The horses spat out puffs of foam like whipped cream, and the silver on their harness reflected the white sun in a flame.

Stiegel was miserable with his thoughts of Diane. He had lived a year without her. For months he had suffered from tortured pride. Now he understood that her heart-ache had been far greater than his own. He had meant in his heart what he told her that rainy morning in the office. He had wanted her happiness above all.

He had just had her harp and the portraits of that long ago winter moved from Elizabeth Furnace to Manheim. And yet now he could not remember Diane except one feature at a time. It was maddening that he could only re-call her hands—the course of each line, the shape of each nail. Or the flower in her hair, the worship in her eyes, the white scar quivering on her forehead when she angered.

347]

He uncrossed the leg which had gone to sleep, crossed the other one over it. A few miles more and he would be at Charming Forge. He began suddenly to be uncomfortable. It was always simple to build up an immunity to Diane's passion when he did not see her. Supposing she should want him to go off with her and the child? To start life somewhere all over again? To forego his comforts and the coaches and the adulation? To have only what the poorest farmer had—peace of mind? His heart bolted with excitement at the thought of having Diane for himself.

Now the pastures began to twist and hide themselves under great trees, mingling with quixotic brooks. The goldenrod was dull mustard under the trees, flagrant ochre in the broad sun. Stiegel's eyes were filled with a grisly coating of dust; the dust covered everything as if there had been a downpour from the sky. The broad leaves of the roadside were heavy with it, motionless, as if they could not breathe. It hung lazily in the air, with the hot odors of grain and cattle.

When he tapped the quilted crimson beside him, a breath of dust leaped up and sank wearily, like a drifting feather. He gave a dry cough; he was terribly nervous, stifled more with bottled emotion than with the torpid noon. Would the child look like him?

His outriders would be at Charming Forge by now. Diane's heart would be leaping with exultation. She would be tremulously donning fresh ribbons, and dressing the child in its finest tucked gown.

At length he saw the river, broad and placid, and languid with mud. They were over the bridge. The coachman stifled a sneeze with a "ts." Stiegel stepped down, looking about him for George. He had a sudden feeling that he would like to choke George, with his great lumbering height and his pale eyes.

The men began to gather about him, a little shy, and

Stiegel followed Nassel toward his house, trailed by the group of obsequious forgers and farm hands. The Nassel house was a long red brick building of two stories, next to the house which the Eges occupied, and directly across from the barnyard. As the men approached, Mrs. Nassel waddled out, her hair straggling, her hands stained blue with the berries she was preserving. The lawn seemed to become dotted with curious chickens which strolled casually among the patch of flowers at the side of the house. The poor few blooms languished for water. Under the kitchen window of the Eges' house was a tidier garden, marguerites against the wall, and nasturtiums which had not become dry and black with aphis.

"Mr. Ege'll be here direct," panted Mrs. Nassel. "We've been ringing the bell for him."

"Good," said Stiegel briefly.

He stopped for a moment, and plucked a deep wine-colored nasturtium which had flourished cynically among all these gay yellow blossoms.

" 'Tis Madame Ege's garden," commented Mrs. Nassel.

"I know," said Stiegel, and his heart ached strangely as if it had been imprisoned for a year in a pillory. He tossed the flower away, and followed her.

The grass, yellowed from the blistering sun, had not been trimmed lately. There was a dull matted streak where the men had cut short from the road to the kitchen door. The house itself, thought Stiegel, seemed small and shrivelled with the heat. At night it must teem like a nest of worms, overcrowded with restless, sweating men. About the doorway tumbled their boots, stout sticks they had cut from limbs, tools, pots of plants, firewood, a stray hat, a scattered handful of chicken-feed, and a dog's pan half filled with food. Infant's clothing was strung from tree to post. Stiegel noticed every detail of the sickening panorama. Diane living here in the grime! It was hurt pride as

much as pity that filled him with mortification. He reached
the kitchen door and turned suddenly upon the men behind him. They were meekly aloof.

"A gourd of water, Mrs. Nassel, for my face, if you would
be so kind," he said.

"Aye, and a flip of something better for your throat,
Baron," she laughed. Now that her services were in demand she was more at her ease.

He splashed his face with water from the spring, and
drank some beer. There was still no sign of Diane. In the
chimney corner stood a cradle and on a chair beside it was
a half-knitted mitten.

"Where is—Diane?" Stiegel blurted out, at last.

"She had but started to pick peas when your trumpeters
rode in, sir. She said she would come direct her vessel is
filled."

Stiegel felt familiar anger rising in his cheeks.

"Where is the—the child?" he asked, his voice sounding
strangely hollow.

"In the field too, slung like a papoose!" Mrs. Nassel's
eyes grew large with protest. "Ach, Baron, I've warned her
that many times he'll burn to a crisp like the peas in the
sun. Baron, you can't fancy how she laughs wild-like! One
day she will bring him in an' mark you, Baron, he will be
a . . . a cinder!"

He bolted into the garden, across the road, filled with
consternation. He could not stand the tension any longer.
Beyond the large barn lay the truck garden, hidden from
view. He tried not to run. He could not see her yet. . . .
Would to God he had never found her in the forest. . . .

Diane bent over the pea plants in the glaring sun. He
heard her singing. Singing! . . . He threaded his way
down the filament of path between the beans, tried to call,
could not, stumbled on till he was a pebble's throw from
her. Her half husky voice chanted an old French folk song:

"*Sur le pont d'Avignon*
Tout le monde y passe.
Les messieurs font comm'ci,
Les dames font comm'ça."

He was in agony. He could neither speak nor move, as if he had been in a dream and was glued to the ground, unable to reach out to safety.

She wore a plain gown of orange calico, the sleeves unruffled above her elbow. Her bare feet were thick with clay-colored dust; her black hair smooth and glistening. He saw that her skin was brown and satiny as a new mushroom.

On her back, fastened in a bag made of an old quilt, was the baby. His head was covered with an impromptu bonnet made of a handkerchief, two corners knotted together on each side and tucked under his ears. He was like a weird creation out of a dream, a ridiculous looking little thing scarcely old enough to smile. His bare chest emerged from the quilting, and Stiegel saw that he clutched at a large pea pod. He must be naked!

Stiegel's lips tightened. His child, a worm in a cocoon! Diane suffering this degradation. Bare feet—naked child. He still could not speak.

When she saw him, her song trailed off into silence:

"*Les dames font* ——"

They were gazing at one another, the heat trembling about them. Stiegel felt as if he had been strapped to a stake. A milky cabbage butterfly with tired, fringed wings fluttered between them, and poised for a second on the pod in Diane's hand.

"Les dames font comm'ça," she mocked, making a deep curtsy, and trying to hide the tumult in her voice. The lucid brown eyes of the child peered at him over her shoulder.

"Mais oui, et les messieurs font——"

"Diane," he cried, gripping her shoulders. "Don't act! Diane, why didn't you come to me? Why didn't you tell me?"

She slipped away from his touch.

Dark eyes! The child had dark eyes like Diane, and straight wisps of dusky hair; shiny olive skin like an autumn leaf; a ruddy, tremulous little mouth just large enough to slip a pea pod in.

"Come, Heinrich," ordered Diane, her voice faltering. "We will sit 'neath the tree and talk."

She led the way to a great bending oak at the Tulpehocken River and unfastened the apparatus under her arms, so that the child slipped from its cocoon with a wriggle and a protracted coo. She laid him gently on the mutilated quilt, and pulled from his mouth the pod which shot back as lithely as a ball on a rubber string.

Leaning back on her elbows, she laughed gayly into Stiegel's anguished eyes. It had to be either laughter or tears—and tears, tears told too much. Laughter was a familiar fortress.

"Heinrich . . ." she murmured. "You are très élégant. Your glory travels e'en to me here . . . in the pea patch."

"Diane, I can't bear to see you in these straits; your child —my child—like a savage."

"Your child!" she gasped. "You would like to claim him!"

"God, Diane, I am not a fool!"

He had flung himself down beside her on the tall, dry grass, his hand covering hers. She closed her eyes. The old surging pain returned, the pain of his nearness. He wanted to acknowledge the child openly! He was no longer afraid! She would tell him the truth. He would go off somewhere with her, Acadia—France! She opened her eyes and found his lips close to her own. She drew him to her, trembling with his kiss, and felt his breath hot against her breast.

"Diane . . . Diane . . . to think I could not even be with you when you bore him. . . . That we have never been able to face the world in our love. What can I do for you? What can I do for him? I can't bear to find you here, so poor, Liebling . . . so alone! I am going to slave to give you luxury, Diane . . . to give you the things I give Elizabeth and Jacob. . . . How can I do it so George will never know? So you will be happy? So the boy will be happy? Diane . . . I love you. . . . I am so proud you have borne me a child!" he whispered.

The pain she felt was acute, physical. For the last time Stiegel had sanctimoniously cast her from his life. He loved her. But he did not love her enough. This then was the end.

She drew her hand from his, and fanned a crazed horse-fly from the baby's face.

"George Ege," she said deliberately with burning lips, "is the father of my child."

"You're lying," said Stiegel violently. "It couldn't be true."

"Why could it not, M'sieu?"

Why could it not, indeed? He had no proof that it was not a seven-months' child or that she had not been promiscuous that lonely summer at Manheim, as Martin had said. No proof but the beauty and passion of one night. He rested his head in his hands, and stared at an ant staggering along with a crumb twice its size.

"Heinrich," she said with apparent calm, picking the baby up slowly and hugging him fervently to her breast. "See how he coaxes for his supper." She put every effort into being casual; it was only a few minutes more until she would be alone—just a few minutes now. . . .

Stiegel watched the baby nudging her breast with his chin. He felt a sweep of loneliness. The child did not belong to him. The child excluded him finally, definitely from her life.

Her eyes were reflecting the buoyancy of the infant. The four little dimples of his fist closed about her forefinger tenaciously. In her adoration of him she obviously had no room for Stiegel. She spoke without lifting her smile from the tiny nude figure.

"If you would help, Heinrich—be so kind as to carry the kettle of peas."

As Diane drew the baby from her breast he sent up a fountain of golden yellow water which stained Stiegel's immaculate shirt ruffle with a shower of spots. She held the infant away from her, laughing, while the tears streamed from her eyes.

29

HE WHOLE ATMOSPHERE of the Brickerville house that summer was strained, and sometimes Stiegel wondered if it was only in his fevered imagination that no one's happiness seemed to be dependent upon him. Elizabeth, who until recently had defended the girls against his rigid discipline, took quite the opposite stand and seemed to feel that he favored them instead of Jacob.

"The girls ask to go to Lancaster for a month with new clothes and all sorts of liberties, and you give them everything they want. But now when Jacob gets into the bees you thresh him for it!"

"Jacob has been told to keep away from the bees. I am trying to teach him obedience."

"'Tis bad enough that his poor little body is covered with stings."

"Elizabeth, you do not seem to remember that I am still master of my home!" he said with European finality. He began to wonder if he had really shown favoritism.

Elizabeth could not understand that Stiegel did not worship Jacob as she herself did. Her sterility after his birth had always been a thorn in her contentment. It seemed as if she must forever endure the veiled reflections of other matrons who sat at tea with her and felt stirring within their wombs the twelfth and thirteenth offspring. Elizabeth Huber would have given Stiegel a flourishing family had she lived; she had died in the sacrifice of child-birth. Stiegel's growing fondness for Jerusha seemed to infer that he sorrowed for the wife who had so faithfully consecrated her body to posterity. The more Stiegel relished the wit of Jerusha, who was dark and gay and vividly like Diane, the more Elizabeth harbored a feeling of jealousy of them.

Stiegel no longer confided in her. She knew as much about his affairs as she knew about the passion for Diane that burned in his heart. They were seldom alone, and then there were prosaic details of the servant, house and guest problems to be discussed. Before his friends, he treated her with gallantry, but certainly he was no longer the gay lover of their early marriage. Elizabeth began to accept his indifference as a matter of fact, and supposed that other women knew their husbands no better than she did, and that the sexual ardor of all men wore low after a few years of intimacy.

She supposed she was happy. It took all her time to fulfill her duties, to keep her homes elegant and immaculate, her servants subjugated, and her own person in the magnificence she craved. If managing several mansions was not as simple as bragging about them in the parlor of a friend, she said nothing of it, for she knew that Stiegel would give her no sympathy. He felt that his possession now of innumerable Negroes and indentured servants must relieve her of all responsibility.

The only time she had sighed wearily with the burden of the households, Stiegel replied cynically, "Would you like to move into one of the glass-blower's cottages, my dear?"

He scorned her greed for luxury, and yet he would have had the wife of the great Baron no less splendid.

In spite of his unhappiness, Stiegel had a sense of rejuvenation the following winter. He was going to venture everything on the glass business. The Stedmans did not believe in him. Diane scorned his success and did not believe in him. There seemed only one thing to do to convince them and to forget his own misery—amass money in the face of their doubt. It amused Stiegel to see Elizabeth living more royally than royalty, and Anna Ege becoming gouty with gravies too rich for the sanction of her Quaker blood.

Stiegel was restless, nervous, stimulated by the uncertainty of colonial trade. Rumors of the Townshend Act in the spring greatly excited him. When ships brought news of the actuality of the bill, he was secretly hilarious. It was great good fortune that glass should be taxed along with tea, pasteboard, painters' colors and paper hangings.

Glass and paperware were designated as especially deserving domestic encouragement. If he should build up his glass business still more extensively, he could save the colonies an annual glass taxation of thirty thousand pounds. The stage seemed set for greater expansion.

When he went to Lancaster these days his mother eyed him askance, but she continued to send the great man on errands for a bit of spice or a pair of mended shoes, rewarding him when he returned with sauerbraten or potato pancakes.

"I am going to build a new Glass House," he told her and Anthony one night.

"Ja? But you have a new Glass House."

"Ach, Mutter, it's not new any more. And I must have a bigger Glass House."

"Ja?"

"I'm going to turn glass out as fast as rabbits. . . . People aren't going to buy foreign glass now the Townshend Act's been passed. It'll cost too much."

Anthony's feet shuffled on the fire-dogs. "But the merchants' shelves are full of foreign glass now! And it's superior, you know that!"

"Ach, but exorbitant, Anthony. And the merchants are banding together again to shut out British ware."

"Maybe the Townshend Act will be repealed, and then where will you be?"

"Ja," said Frau Stiegel anxiously, sewing on a button which had just come off of Heinrich's coat.

"I must work fast, flood the country with my glass," answered Stiegel with assurance. He knew the danger of repeal. But there was an oasis here, he thought, between the Townshend Act and its possible revoke.

"That old Glass House—you will not use it any more, nicht?" asked the frugal old lady, snipping off her thread with a vim.

"Just for the overflow."

"That new Glass House, you have started to make it?"

"Thomas Lincoln's done the design. And the bricks are ordered."

"In Cologne I could never make you wear the old pants, Heinrich, if they were mended even such a little bit. I used to have to cut them down so small for Anthony, when they were new yet."

Anthony laughed.

The spring found the village of Manheim as industrious as an ant hill. The glass-workers were all busy on the new building. The dense woods resounded with the clang of hammers. Mysterious strangers came to the King of Prussia Tavern to confer with the Baron. The glass business had not even been self-supporting of late, but Stiegel's method was always to cover failure with speculation, and now before him, a mass of bricks and oozing cement, unwashed dome and windows, rose the means of perfecting his beloved glass.

"You are a financial genius, Stiegel," wrote Dickinson admiringly in his regular correspondence, "or mayhap you have kissed the Blarney Stone."

As the building of the new Glass House progressed, he advertised extensively in all the newspapers. He fully believed that such an enormous undertaking at such a propitious time could not help but succeed. There were no loose ends. The Glass House itself, built of the finest English brick, would be vast, complete. Stiegel had spent the winter and early spring appraising his workers. He had formerly leaned toward a German personnel. Now he advertised for the most skilled workers of any nationality, interviewed them, put them through a third degree of business questions, considered, weeded out—and even dismissed one or two prize musicians.

He must have every finger in the pie, stirring a stick in the mortar as a cook would test her dough, seeing that no imperfect brick had slipped in with the cargo. He watched the men laboring blithely in the hot summer sun, forgetful of the aching eyes the winter's work had given them. He envied them their freedom of dress, the bare feet and loose pants and open shirts. It seemed very long ago that he had been a little boy in Cologne, stealing a mushy apple from his mother's Kuchen; digging his toes in the river bank after a fresh rain. How innocent of life he'd been then, when he had thought that everything must come to him with his wishing for it.

He was not happy. He seemed to be waiting for something. Sometimes in his own chapel he tried to analyze his thoughts. He was not far from forty, at the peak of health and virility. He still felt a fierce desire to meet life, to extract all joy from it. Diane had lied to him—the child must belong to him, as surely as Diane would belong to him until her dying breath.

And some day he would bring wealth to the child. And

Diane would see that he was right.

He turned to his violin seldom, always with a sense of guilt and Diane's condemnation of him in his mind. He played very badly now. It was better for one who had been an artist not to play at all rather than like this. And besides, music over-stimulated him and made him too retrospective. Some day he would have a great deal of time to give to it again. Some day when his fortune would be assured.

Yet he insisted on the weekly practicing of his men. They must drop hammer and nails and brick, no matter how eager he was to have the new Glass House finished, to struggle with the intricacies of his favorite waltzes and serenades. Their dissonance seemed to bother him little now, so long as their volume was great enough to be heard far off in the woods as he approached his home from a journey. He had mounted a cannon on the Manheim platform, and when he was expected, a sentinel watched for the first black speck of his carriage in the day, or the lantern lights at night. The signal was excitedly relayed from guard to German chambermaid, to Cyrus, to the band-leader. In the meanwhile the sentinel let fly into the heavens a salute from the cannon. The town of Manheim stirred. People hung out of windows. Sentimental young girls crushed roses into aprons that they might fling the petals into the carriage of the handsome Baron as he passed. The glass-blowers dropped their mortar and flew to their instruments. The very atmosphere became festive. Elizabeth fled from her preserving kitchen and donned a fresh cap and apron. Stiegel was ushered into his village preceded by outriders in crimson to match the upholstery of his coach. His hounds, panting from their run, dispersed to the stable where there were pans of water and bones awaiting them. Stable boys relieved the horses of their trim harnesses and helped the fatigued coachman descend from his throne.

It was a definite need, and helped to fill the vacuum of his life; it was tacit law, this circumspection.

And yet his reception was no different throughout the countryside. Wherever he stopped to exchange greetings with an innkeeper, those who had never seen him recognized the coach of the illustrious Baron. Little ragamuffins boldly wiped off the spokes of a wheel, so that they could brag they had come that close to Stiegel. Sometimes they giggled and pushed each others' dirty faces close to the window, and if he saw them he would empty the silver of his purse with a fling in the air. If a shilling dropped from the shower into the curls of a young girl, Stiegel alighted to help her rescue it, smiling into her eyes, and kissing her hand slowly, with a grave bow.

He liked to watch the crimson rise in the lovely sturdy throats of the farmers' daughters, and lost his heart to them for the moment. Years later they would say to their grandchildren with a little sigh, "Baron Stiegel—aye, he kissed my hand one day. . . . I shall never forget him. His coat was of robin's egg blue and silver lace, and his buckles of gold. Aye, he was too handsome to come to that end. . . . Now, had God but been a woman. . . ."

At the beginning of September, the air stirred with the coming of fall as subtly as a woman changes her mood. The luxuriance of the summer gardens waned. The pastel pinks and blues of rose and larkinspur were subdued and the jaunty marigolds and zinnias defied the frost.

The new Glass House opened with a vim. It produced glassware of insuperable quality, and there was the frequent rumbling of wagons as they carted hogsheads away to the agents.

The best clay obtainable was from Stourbridge, England. Stiegel had bought much of it cheaply, for ships used it as ballast. The limestone he got from his own quarry not two miles from Elizabeth Furnace. His carts threaded their way to the quarry and back, persistent tumbrils, and more than one teamster dreamed at night of "cleaning the clay."

After Christmas Elizabeth went to the house in Philadelphia. When Stiegel joined her there in the spring, Jacob had gotten the best of her nerves.

"It is time you get him a tutor," she suggested, never even hinting at the state of collapse she was in. "He is abnormal bright and it is time his mind is occupied with figures and learning."

Stiegel smiled to himself. "We will send him to the Cloisters at Ephrata."

"Oh, you know I would ne'er consent to sending him away from me," cried Elizabeth. "They would very like starve him there!"

"Michael did not seem to suf ——"

"Michael can eat anything!"

Stiegel hesitated. "I have expended everything on the Glass House this year, Elizabeth. The Cloisters will be cheaper than a ——"

"You would not save on your only son when you spend money like water on yourself!"

" 'Twill only be for this year. My agents welcome my goods with open arms, and give me credit! Whether it's iron or glass they all write back of a piece, 'We are of a sincere disposition to pay you for your goods, sir. But how can we remit what we do not have?' "

"Why can't they pay?" asked Elizabeth without any particular interest, as she toyed with a music box.

"Depression, after the war. Taxes! Every time we turn there's a new tax, a little present from Parliament. Many of the farmers have been mortgaging their homes—Wetzel just mortgaged his the other day. The Stedmans are in a terrible pinch."

"Why don't you sell Elizabeth Furnace?" she asked. She

had no feeling for the place. It was where Stiegel had lived with Elizabeth Huber, and it was shabby compared with the elegance she was accustomed to now.

"I don't want to give it away. People are selling their property at a third to a half less than its value."

"If you cannot afford a tutor for Jacob, I will sell my jewelry," offered Elizabeth stubbornly.

"Of course I can afford it!" retorted Stiegel. "It's just that now, this year. . . . It's hard to explain these things to a woman. . . ."

The tune tinkled out of the music box saucily.

"Why don't you write again to your agents?" Elizabeth asked.

"Write! It's simply a waste of sand and wafer!"

"Well, then, why don't you go to New York and get the money yourself?" Elizabeth offered her advice with a childish pout, as if this were such a simple solution.

Well, perhaps a trip to New York would be effective, thought Stiegel. He was thoroughly impatient with the long and tedious communications he'd had with his New York agents by mail.

He was naturally afraid that the Townshend Act would be repealed, as had the Stamp Act, and that foreign glass would come flooding into the country again before his own glass was securely entrenched. Through Mr. Cushing, his Boston agent, Stiegel's glass had been bringing in a good price as "imported." This was not ethical, but neither was a great deal else that was going on in the merchant's world.

"If my debtors would but pay!" groaned Stiegel, after an unsuccessful week in New York.

And yet, if they had paid, it is doubtful that he would have lived any differently than he did. He was very certain that he had been born under a lucky star. It eased his mind to saunter through a New York shop and pick up novelties for his women at home. Caps of French convent-made lace for Elizabeth (a trifle, but ten pounds); fans for the girls; a pair of gold buckles for himself (he could not resist the way the diamonds were set into the frame); a Chippendale chair for the desk; Spanish pots for the garden wall; a chime clock and new mahogany knife-box. He had not the cash, of course. Nobody had. But he purchased them all on credit with graceful aplomb.

It saddened him that Diane still seemed to haunt a shop when he fingered a pair of yellow mitts or a locket of odd design. He had not seen her for almost two years. He had supposed it would be easier for both of them if he did his business at the Forge by correspondence. Well, it had been no easier. And not a day passed but what he wondered about the boy, and how he must look now that he had grown out of babyhood.

At last he returned to Elizabeth Furnace in the summer, discouraged. He had only incurred a great expense to make the trip, and he had burned his fingers in the general brawl between the merchants and the Sons of Liberty. For the first time he felt uncomfortably trapped in the tangle of national disorder. A billet from his Lancaster agent whined about the stagnancy of business in the country, and in the same breath ordered ten gross of milk ewers in assorted colors. Zantzinger wrote too that the German Society of Pennsylvania had made eight hundred and eight pounds on their lottery. How welcome eight hundred pounds would have been in his own pocket just then. But stubbornly he turned his mind to the multitudinous orders and the thousands of pounds of credit he was accumulating.

It was just after the girls returned from their annual visit to Lancaster that an incident happened which greatly upset Stiegel. Jerusha's enthusiasm, which had soared before she left, seemed now to burst like a ripe berry. She could scarce get more than a phrase out in her excitement. She had never known there could be such quilting bees,

such beaux, such assemblies. There buzzed in her head a
hundred new stitches straight from Paris. A dozen new
dance steps twinkled in her toes, even as she ate her dinner. In her Bible there were pressed flowers from the
butcher, the baker, the candlestick-maker.

But Barbara was languid and timorous. She sniffed at
roses wistfully until they grew limp. Her eyes drooped in
conversation; her cheeks paled at mention of Lancaster,
music or the moon (for Mr. Perkins of Lancaster had
kissed her seven times). She laced herself more tightly
each day so that her waist was ethereal. And in lieu of
food, she inhaled spirits of camphor, which enabled her
to endure the coarseness of Michael's appetite. When Stiegel expostulated, Barbara grew moody. There was no one
here, she said, to appreciate her tastes, her sensibility. If
they *would* gorge, might she be excused from witnessing
the gluttony? It made her faint.

Jerusha was envious of Barbara, and began secretly to
emulate her. Barbara had already had a love affair. Supposing no one should ever ask *her* to marry? Could she help it
that she was a tomboy and only Michael would take her
seriously? Jerusha, like a gay peony, drove her delicate
sister to despair. There had never been quite so much difference in their ages before. When they were six and eight
only two years had separated them. Now that they were
ten and twelve half a world came between—the half filled
with tittering and rococo love letters and stolen kisses.

Stiegel was going through the lower hall when the girls
left for Brickerville one afternoon. He put an arm about
each of the tiny waists and escorted them to the coach.
Jerusha gave him an impetuous kiss, and Barbara, immediately compromised, lifted her ivory forehead for a trib-
ute. He waved to them as they drove off and felt a little
lonely. He always meant to spend more time with them,
to get to know them.

They had been gone about half an hour when one of the young men from the Brickerville church rode in on horseback to see Stiegel. It would be to borrow money, of course, thought Stiegel, impatiently, motioning Samuel Froelich to a chair across from him in the sitting-room.

The young man was dressed in his Sunday clothes, and they seemed to fit him ill and give him an air of fidgeting.

"Well?" said Stiegel, as the boy stared at him, unable to speak.

"It's hard for me to speak out, sir," twirling his hat.

"I know," drily. Was this the apothecary's apprentice? He could not remember.

"There's no one to help . . . at a time like this," the boy gulped.

"How much do you want?" Stiegel asked.

"I . . . I never gave it so much as a thought what would go with her, sir."

"With her?"

"With Barbara. I've been looking at her from my pew now two years ——"

"Are you making a proposal of marriage?" cried Stiegel, aghast, staring so ruthlessly at the young man that he flushed to his toes.

He disposed of the boy with haste little short of effrontery. Barbara was of a marriageable age! He had scarcely given her a serious thought these twelve years, what with iron and glass and politics and Diane. He had forgotten that she must have a dower. And Jerusha. A few years and she would want to marry, too. Perhaps it would be better to put up Elizabeth Furnace for sale. If he did lose money on the place, at least it would bring him in enough to ease this temporary embarrassment.

But as the winter came on, Elizabeth Furnace was still in his possession. The money was dribbling in in ridiculous little sums, and Stiegel conceived the idea of going to the

German Society in Lancaster for help. It would be very simple to have them run a lottery for him.

The lottery frenzy had suddenly swept the colonies like a tornado. If a church wanted a new bell, if a dog-house wanted a new dog, if a lady wanted a feather for her hat, there was always the lottery, Stiegel mused.

He left for Lancaster in his sleigh, dramming as he clipped along. The roads were well-trodden. There had been no snow for almost a week. Stiegel was not pessimistic on that cold November morning. He was as snug in his bearskin as if he had been sitting by the kitchen hearth. The sleigh-bells, made of the finest silver by Paul Revere, sang joyously as a carillon. His coachman was distinctive in a close-buttoned jockey-coat with large brass buttons, a bearskin cap which rested on the bridge of his nose, fur gloves the size of cubs, and a great scarlet sash. He fitted into Stiegel's world as a lid fits on a box, yet they had never exchanged more than a score of words.

Frosted houses stood out sharply against a painfully blue sky, and there were snow-topped trees, ice stubble, gray smoke dissolving into the blue of heaven, and pudgy noses against steaming windows. A comfortable world, thought Stiegel; comfort even in the simplicity of a meadow fence! How the colonies were squealing, as if this comfortable world would not continue to go on. Lack of money was simply a deadlock of the times, he thought. The whole problem was a challenge to his strength and skill. Stiegel was not a man to be crossed. The more the newspapers had grumbled about hard times, the more hc had advertised, and produced, and sold. He would keep his notices appearing in the important papers of every town.

He reflected on his plump little mother with puzzlement as his sleigh slid up to her door on its velvet runners. She seemed to be the one person not impressed with her son's wealth and prestige. The wig-curler's boy with his great hat-box and the printer's apprentice, his blue-inked hands shivering under a leathern apron, collided.

" 'Tis the Baron," they whispered, their words smoking in the November sunshine. Their toes became ringed with cold as they loitered to watch the famous man alight, and he waved at them jovially with his muff as he clanged the knocker on his cousin's door.

When Stiegel appeared in the taproom of Postlethwaite's Tavern that evening there was a riotous cheer. He had always been very popular in the German Society, and for years his coin had jingled louder than that of the rest combined.

The room steamed with odors—wet clothing, hot and woolly before the fire, warm wine, sweetened eggs, knuckle of veal, perspiration, and the fragrance of tobacco from the long, clay pipes. There was music too. O'Harpigan was executing German waltzes as patriotically as if they had been Irish love lyrics.

It was a surprise to the Assembly when Stiegel suggested that they run a lottery for him, and offered a hundred pounds if they would designate a man to do it successfully. There was a general laugh. Stiegel, who had been drinking, felt a little contrary, and was irritated that they should find his need of ready cash amusing.

"Is not the new Glass House so big that a boy can't throw a stone over the dome?" cried the tailor of the town, swinging a slopping mug.

"Aye, and that a six-horse team can't turn about in it?" chided another.

There was a guffaw. Stiegel blazed. "Aye, but it took money to build! Don't you understand ——" he began to blurt out, but the subject had turned to the election of officers for the coming year. They thought that the mere mention of money by a lord like Stiegel was just a pretty gesture to make them feel equal. He was at once furious and flattered. He pulled Anthony aside.

"You must see that they vote for this lottery," he told him. "They don't know the meaning of big business today . . . what it means to want money, the fools."

"Aye," Anthony answered, ambiguously.

"How is the baby?" asked Stiegel. (Anthony had lost his wife just a few weeks before.)

"Good," succinctly. Anthony was thinking of Diane. He invariably associated her with Stiegel.

O'Harpigan, in the hubbub of balloting had deserted his post, and now pushed in between the brothers in the manner of a court jester. He was wearing a thick violet suit which was not flattering to his red face, and his hands were sparkling with rings which he had not been able to sell in these hard times.

"So my student angel has a cherub!" he blubbered.

Stiegel resented his levity. "Diane has a son," he responded with dignity.

"Post-haste from heaven, so oi was told," O'Harpigan said archly, his ringed fingers dancing to an imaginary tune.

Anthony's face filled with disdain. He was slow to be gripped by an emotion, and once gripped, he was slow to shake himself loose. He had done some thinking over his books at night, grieved at the gossip about Diane which had dripped from one teacup to another. Diane had always spurned George. She had told Anthony one time that George was a pygmy-minded antelope. Diane, whose eyes had grown great and soft at Stiegel's footstep. . . .

Anthony looked across at his brother and wondered again, with a slow creeping of bitterness. . . .

"A rare beauty," persisted O'Harpigan. "Eyes like a faun, soul like the woodland—pox me, how her heart trembled on the strings! I drink to Diane . . . to Diane—Had the lady a surname?"

"Drat your insolence!" roared Stiegel, clenching his fist.

A great wateriness dimmed O'Harpigan's tiny blue eyes. "I' faith, Baron, oi would the child were mine. . . ."

Stiegel gave him a jab which sent him sprawling to the floor in a splash of beer. There was an uproar at once over the fight, and Stiegel pulled away from Anthony, slinging on his greatcoat and seizing a lantern.

"See that the lottery goes through," he muttered, but Anthony's eyes were hard and inattentive. So the thing had happened between Heinrich and Diane as he knew it would! The lottery be damned. Heinrich had gotten what he wanted before, let him get what he wanted without help now.

Stiegel trudged back to his mother's, no one recognizing him in the street, for the hour was late. He was aflame with anger, riled at the sordidness of the inn. Somehow it helped that deep ache for Diane to be able to smash the insolent red face of O'Harpigan. Why wasn't there something equally simple to do about himself and Diane? What was really the truth about the two of them? Was this the only conclusion? Did lives end this way, frustrated and empty, preoccupied with baubles and ostentation?

Frau Stiegel sat knitting before a purring fire, her corns elevated to a stool. They were bound with ivy leaves which she had soaked day and night in vinegar.

"In Germany, Heinrich," she lamented, "I had not such pains from corns. I think I will not like America."

He smiled morosely, took off his shoes and stretched his feet in the ashes on the hearth.

"In Deutschland, Mutter," he pondered, "scheint die Sonne immer."

The next day Stiegel heard with exasperation that Anthony had left the meeting early and that the matter of the lottery had not been brought up again.

30

I T WAS THE following May that Barbara's knight came riding. He was Mr. Ashton of *the* Ashtons of Virginia. His father and his grandfather and *his* father had been gentlemen with small feet and soft white hands. They had all at one time or another played roulette with some King Louis or another and it had given them a social distinction not to be ignored.

Mr. Ashton was passing through Manheim in a curricle, and Barbara, like a shy pink and white arbutus in fresh bloom, was coming out of the woods. At the moment of their meeting she had been trying to rhyme "dove" and "rove," for summer was almost at hand, and the sly growth of the earth stirred in her a renovated passion for the Lancaster love.

Now she smiled exquisitely upon the newcomer. He was what was known in that day as a Macaroni, a rare and exotic human plant that had just blossomed in Italy. If other young men wore china buttons painted blue, the Macaroni wore buttons garnished with the portraits of court beauties. If other young men wore feathers in their caps, the Macaroni wore a quill studded with rhinestones. Mr. Ashton wore his natural hair powdered and puffed at

371]

the sides, and tied at the neck with a black ribbon delicately embroidered in silver. His stock was a pale pink, blending with a suit of orchid satin, and the coat was cut away daringly just below the waist, disclosing a waistcoat of rampant yellow roses. The buttonholes were languid eyes, with silk fringe an inch long, under which hid flirtatious amethyst buttons carved in the shape of animals. From one tasseled coat pocket dangled a handkerchief of silver lace to match the silver etched buckles on his pink kid shoes. He alighted as airily as a leaf from his curricle, bowed with professional grace, and leaned a bit coquettishly on his ivory carved cane with its lapis handle. He was dazzling, rococo, superb.

If he had said, "Madame, je suis Louis," Barbara would have dropped her daffodil and kissed his hand, unsurprised.

But as he only said, "Mistress, could you direct me to hospitality?" Barbara sighed and stared, and almost forgot to answer.

He was the sort of person one did not direct to The King of Prussia Tavern. He stopped with the Stiegels themselves, and the visit expanded from one night to a month, during which time the Stiegels were introduced to more varieties of buttons than they had known existed. Stiegel, whose sumptuous dress was famed throughout Pennsylvania, began to feel dowdy.

It did not take long to see that Mr. Ashton had at last succumbed to love. The wedding was set for the end of the summer, and the household settled back with relief when he left to make preparations at home for his bride.

Elizabeth was already making elaborate plans for the wedding. It was an expense which Stiegel had not counted on, and he made up his mind that at last he must mortgage his properties. It would never do to stint on his daughter's wedding, and to deprive her of a dowry appropriate to her station.

He made the trip to Philadelphia with a heavy heart; he

had been advertising Elizabeth Furnace and Charming Forge for sale for some months, and no one seemed remotely interested in the property. It was John Dickinson, his lawyer, who introduced him to Daniel Bennezet.

Bennezet was a squat, middle-aged man of few words. Stiegel disliked him instinctively. It was not that Bennezet was colorless, or a little slovenly. It was simply that Bennezet had been able to put up eight thousand pounds on a blanket mortgage covering Elizabeth Furnace, Charming Forge, and all the Manheim holdings.

They had been waiting for forty minutes for Molly M'Call, who owned half the mortgage, to come to sign the papers. She was a widowed niece of Daniel Bennezet who had lately come to live with him. Bennezet had been her guardian since she was orphaned, and was now the executor of her husband's estate.

Stiegel poked about Dickinson's office, restless. He already had a feeling of bondage, no matter how he tried to argue himself out of it. And the more he looked at Bennezet, the more he thought him a little rat of a man. The name Molly M'Call was familiar, and he was haunted by the feeling that he had met her at some social function. He struggled with memory, but it was not until he heard her footstep on the threshold and faced her that their first meeting flashed back to him.

"You are very beautiful. Who are you?" he remembered asking at a reception at the Whites'.

And she had answered with wicked ambiguity, "Only another woman who is in love with you, Baron!"

He was surprised that he did not think her as beautiful as he had that first night. Perhaps the drabness of the office detracted from her looks, and yet the contrast should have made her the lovelier, he thought quickly.

She was only a young woman in the early twenties, and almost as tall as himself. The high pitch of her voice and the

trilling laugh were incongruous with her size; handsome
she was, rather than beautiful, disdainfully erect in spite of
her tallness. She was dark-skinned, with small, lively hazel
eyes, an aquiline nose, and a short upper lip. Stiegel wondered as he bent low in a bow if she and Bennezet had
some remote Jewish blood.

Molly M'Call was elegant today in an olive green taffeta
outfit, and after the business had been transacted, he took
her in his coach to the silversmith where she had an appointment.

"Madame Stiegel and I will be looking forward to the
honor of a visit from you," he reminded her, as she stood
beside him on the walk.

"We are going to be *very* well acquaint, I hope," she
answered with deliberate sparkle.

"Most of Philadelphia comes to spend Christmas with
us."

"As if I had not heard of your gayety!"

"You and your uncle will want to see the properties," he
added, with a tinge of bitterness.

"Nothing will keep me away—snow, Indians, nor love!"
Her voice trailed into its high laugh, and Stiegel felt unaccountably irritated.

She thought he was far more delightful than she had remembered. Young men were very stupid and egotistic; old
men, like her own poor dead husband, were doddering and
squeamish; but the middle-aged man, with a few wrinkles
about the corner of his eyes, the world in the palm of his
hand, his passion just enough under control to be interesting. . . .

What fine teeth he had! If he would only let himself smile
a little oftener. What a satisfaction there was in making
people smile a little against their will. . . . At Christmas
she would flirt with him quite madly. It would do neither
of them any harm.

Stiegel returned to Manheim in better spirits. It was characteristic of his sanguine temperament that he annexed the eight thousand pounds as if they had been a gift. The lottery would have been a little beneath his dignity after all, a public admission that he was financially pressed.

He spared no expense now on Barbara's wedding. One hundred and fifty people dined, tea'd and supped with the Stiegels on the wedding day. Punch flowed like a swollen river for two days more. For the farmers and laymen who did not attend the festivities, cake and punch and meats were sent out into the neighborhood. And Barbara's dowry was two thousand pounds.

Two weeks after the wedding the journey to Virginia was begun. The weary little face of Barbara was framed in a virginal calash of white silk. Ropes and wires barred the progress of the newly-wed coach in the road of the woods, until the groom generously paid the toll in wine. The last handkerchief was waved. Jerusha, on the lawn, burst into violent sobs, and running past the sympathetic arm of her father, fled to her room and buried her face in the discarded gown which Barbara had just slipped off.

Marriage terrified her. Mr. Ashton would be permitted to see Barbara without her stays. She herself would never marry. Never, *never!* Barbara had left them all forever for this delicate-fingered, fragrant smelling Christmas tree. How different he was from the insolent brown-limbed miller who had held her tight last fall, and kissed her. Her blood had run fast and had seemed to be one with the sound of the stream in her ears. But marriage meant that a man might see you without your stays—and there was no one who should ever see her in her shift—no, not even the brown-muscled miller. She shivered at the audacity of her thoughts, and crept downstairs to press the last rose Barbara had worn.

When the guests arrived for the Christmas holidays,

Elizabeth was wearing one of her imported gowns, the brocade of which had been on display at The Green Stays in Front Street, Philadelphia. Jerusha, who loved to be gaudy with baubles, appeared in a new set of garnets, a Christmas present from her father. The food was as sumptuous as holidays past when purses had not been tied in a knot. There were imported grapes, dripping sawdust, and odd homely little nuts with foreign names and a puzzling flavor; the decorations were more sensational than ever before, and everyone felt that the rumor of Stiegel's difficulty must be fallacious.

On the morning after the guests' arrival, Stiegel and Molly and Bennezet met in the office of the Glass House to discuss the mortgage. Stiegel saw to it that there was a bottle of Bennezet's favorite wine at his elbow. Then he showed him the ledger with its amazing number of new orders.

"Look," he bragged, "it goes as far as Boston and Baltimore, my glass!"

"The pocket scent-bottles have took Philadelphia by storm," yawned Molly. She hated business, especially when it encroached on her sleep in the morning.

For half an hour they looked over accounts, and Stiegel triumphantly showed them his newest samples. There were tall twisted and enameled cruets; inkstands, doorknobs, incense burners and bottle stoppers of millefiori; colored flint glasses with the most delicate etching.

"This is the best year the business has had," said Stiegel. "It's brought me an income of five thousand pounds."

"Is it true that Isaac Cox foreclosed on the Stedmans' Manheim interests?" asked Bennezet suddenly.

"Yes," returned Stiegel, flustered, because he knew what would follow.

"And that you purchased the land from Cox yourself?"

"Yes, but it's mortgaged, of course." Damn Bennezet and

his drilling! What business of his was it as long as Stiegel continued payment of the mortgage interest? It had always been Stiegel's ambition to get all of Manheim into his own hands. Manheim was the child of his own begetting. It was Manheim he loved more deeply than Charming Forge or Elizabeth Furnace. It was on Manheim he would concentrate in the future, and the little village would grow as his glass became internationally famous.

"Then I am not in favor of releasing Manheim and the glass works from the blanket mortgage, as you mentioned in your letter."

"Luddy, Uncle Daniel," exclaimed Molly, who was dusting off samples of glass now with her handkerchief. "How you bicker! The Baron pays us good interest."

"I'm going to advertise my other properties for sale again," promised Stiegel.

"Aye, we'd all like a little more cash these days," returned Bennezet. "Except Molly. She rolls in it."

She laughed her high little trill and squeezed Uncle Daniel's hand.

"I think Uncle Daniel and I will release Manheim," she added, winking broadly at Stiegel. "But before I consent I should like to ride over the tract with you, Baron. I'll change to my riding habit. Now, now, Danny darling, the sun's barely up and the bottle's half drammed!"

Before Molly and Bennezet left for home, dozens of bottles were empty, and Uncle Daniel had hazily consented to a separate mortgage on Stiegel's Manheim property and glass works.

Stiegel saw at once that the women were a little in doubt about Molly M'Call, and grinned to himself at their struggle between virtuous suspicion and etiquette. Molly was very wealthy, and was on the edge of the best Philadelphia society. But the things she said!

At first the whole situation amused Stiegel. But as the

days wore on, he saw that Molly was being ever so grace-
fully snubbed, and that Elizabeth herself was making only
a weak effort to be affable.

" 'Twas a very poor idea, mixing business with pleasure,"
upbraided Elizabeth. "Why, do you know what Susan
White told me? She was at a house party outside of Philadelphia with Molly only last month. And Molly stripped
down to her shift in front of the other women!"

"And they saw to their amazement that she was no different from themselves."

"Heinrich . . . what other woman you know has so little
sensibility? Would be so brazen?"

Stiegel considered interestedly.

"Diane," he mused to himself, "would never give her
body a thought."

As Molly was being subtly excluded by the women,
Stiegel felt he should pay increasing attention to her and
he constantly had the desire to prove to her that his wealth
was really unlimited, that the mortgage was a measure of
caution rather than necessity.

The night before the guests were to leave for home, Molly
was playing softly at the harpsichord while the others
hovered around an exciting game of chess between Tom
Willing and Robert Morris. Stiegel leaned against the
harpsichord, swirling the warm brandy slowly in its glass.

"Molly, have I ever told you you're beautiful?" he asked
warmly, his eyes resting on the milkiness of her shoulders
and the daring lowness of her bodice.

"Once is not enough . . ." she hummed, fitting the words
into the tune she was playing.

"You *are* beautiful, Molly."

"That is not enough, either."

Stiegel smiled down at her. "You're a little disgruntled
tonight, Mistress M'Call."

"I have not slept well at the inn," she pouted. " 'Twas

only last night I dreamed you——"

"You dreamed of me!"

"You *are* shrewd, Baron! Aye, I dreamed of you." Her laugh rippled high and soft, just for his ears. "That you had built me a tower, and imprisoned me there!"

"I shall build you a tower, Molly," he proclaimed chivalrously. "High enough for your laugh!"

"And imprison me there?" she asked roguishly.

"To the tower!" evaded Stiegel, holding his brandy high, and then holding it to her lips for a sip.

"Elizabeth," said Stiegel that night, as they undressed before the fireplace of their room. "Have you noted that Madame Weiser seemed piqued because she is lodged at the Tavern? How would you fancy a tower back on the hill, where our guests would have greater privacy?"

"Madame Weiser is very beautiful," Elizabeth remarked irrelevantly, pulling out her bosom bottle.

"But she does not have eyes like violets!" returned Stiegel gallantly.

Elizabeth looked up; Stiegel was pulling his shirt over his head. He was changing lately, she thought. He was half glib, not nearly so solemn as he had been for years. Yet she felt as if she had understood his glumness better than his flippancy.

"Well, you would like to be mistress of still more, wouldn't you?" he asked contemptuously. "A tower here—and a tower at Elizabeth Furnace, too, of course!"

Now that Stiegel had formed a definite desire for the towers, they were erected in a twinkling. The castle at Thurm Berg, near Manheim, was built out of great husky beams from an adjacent barn. It was painted red, and the lower floor was a banquet hall, large enough for an affair of state. Its cannon announced to the community that Stiegel had retreated there with two or three carriages full of guests, a retinue of musicians in purple and gold, wagon loads of food and delicacies, hounds, horses, servants, portmantuas of clothes never worn before—with Elizabeth, and Molly M'Call. The more he entertained, and the more lavish he became, the oftener he forgot Diane.

At Elizabeth Furnace the tower somewhat resembled the body of a windmill. It was fifty feet square at the base, seventy-five feet high, and had a platform on top where another cannon was erected to announce the return to his old home. It was in the banquet hall on the lower floor of the tower here that the workmen at the Furnace held their rehearsals for his coming.

There were now two orchestras, and the charcoal burners, iron founders, and teamsters practiced in keen competition with their unseen rivals.

It amused Stiegel to say to the ambitious musicians at the Furnace, with their sweat-grimed faces, "You shame the glass-blowers; 'tis only the gavotte they play better than you!" And to the Manheim band-leader, who could swing the violin bow as well as the baton, "Karl, you should hear the drubbing they give the gavotte at the Furnace! Ach, Himmel, if they could play the gavotte so well as you—but if you could play the serenade so well as they!"

Then Stiegel would charm them with a personal question, "How does the little John do at the fife?"

"Ach, Baron, he prays for you by the evening, he is so grateful you give him money to learn!"

Stiegel not only squandered money, but kindness, defiant in the face of the unhappiness which gripped him.

He would call to a teamster whose wagon was loaded with hogsheads of glass bound for Reading, "Can the little Amanda write yet?"

"Aye, Baron, she writes her name pretty; would that I could scratch more than my mark on a paper."

"You mean that, Gratinger?"

"I' faith I do, Baron."

"Then Jacob's tutor shall teach you by night, if you can hold your weary head up over a candle!"

Jacob had had his tutor. And in spite of the fact that money only trickled in, money kept rushing out. It was not until the coming of Chepa Rose the following summer that Stiegel became truly alarmed about the condition of the colonies and the effect this might have on his own business.

Chepa Rose dragged the trunk on his back as if it had been an albatross. He knew every miner, woodcutter, charcoal burner and teamster who lived at Elizabeth Furnace. He had a delightful way of stopping them at their work and laying before their eyes new bits of ribbons, for there were few who did not buy some such finery for their loves. On this particular trip he had a shabby variety of second-hand wigs, or "caxons," as the slang expression was. New York had followed London's custom of a wig grab-bag, into which one could dive for the small sum of sixpence. Chepa had cleaned out the lot, and had spent the winter renovating his ware, brushing, delousing, powdering, and be-ribboning them, so that he could sell them in the summer for some fifteen shillings apiece.

Stiegel, who had been in consultation with the miller, came out to greet his guest. He had always been helpless against the invasion of Chepa Rose. Chepa held a glass of wine up patronizingly to Stiegel, for Michael had already showered him with refreshments.

"How-do, bon jour," he smirked. "The Diane . . . how?"

"Gut," replied Stiegel, reverting to his native German in an effort to be syncopated too. He did not bother to explain to Chepa Rose that he had not seen Diane for four years— that he might never see her again.

Chepa shrugged his shoulders. He never stayed so long since Diane had left.

"What's to do?" asked Stiegel.

"The merchant roar. The Townshend Act, he—pht!"

He shrugged his shoulders again, and waved a very dirty hand.

"The Townshend Act—not repealed!" exclaimed Stiegel.

Chepa shook his head vociferously, alarmed lest he would have to repeat some of those staggering words.

"No on tea . . ." he offered.

"There is still a tax on tea?"

"Oui. . . ."

"Who told you this?"

"Philadelphy . . . all wild."

Stiegel left him to his trade. It was quite enough news for one day. He felt more downcast than he had felt through the entire depression. This was another victory for the colonies, but not for himself. Glass would again be imported; there was no doubt that the merchants would now go back on their non-importation agreement. Had his own glassware good enough reputation to compete now with a new influx of foreign ware? Was not his own lead-flint glass as lovely as anything from Bohemia, or Germany, or Holland, or England? He sent communications immediately to his many agents. The new prices must be cut in competition the minute the merchants began to import glass again.

In July it was known that the very thing he anticipated had happened, and he braced himself for a struggle.

His lawyer, Dickinson, wrote earnestly advising him to sell his works. "Sell now," he pleaded. "There is trouble ahead." Ordinarily Stiegel had great respect for the quiet little man, who had shown much foresight. But now he smiled at Dickinson's caution, and answered:

"Mr. Bartram, the well-known glass wholesaler of Philadelphia, says the glass is equal to any he saw from Great Britain, and agreed with me for a large quantity with a resolution to stop his importation and take all from me."

Then to assuage Dickinson and to show deference for

his counsel, he added, "Conserning the works, they are too high and nobody at present will give near the price for them; if you can sell them I have no objection."

He was convinced that his own glass was as fine as any imported ware he had ever seen. It was already popular throughout the colony, known widely for its thin, brittle beauty. Now he would flood the market with a rainbow of colors, and sell so cheaply that no one would consider buying foreign glass. For a year or so more he would probably suffer until the market was so well established that he could raise his prices again. He would send out a greater volume of enameled ware, and tumblers with their popular cockatoo pattern. He would spur on John and William Rago to new feats in their millefiori work.

31

STIEGEL HAD reached the point where he could not bear silence, and began to instigate one house party after the other. People were charmed to be the guest of the Baron. There were few those days who were not pulling the purse-strings tight, and all of them gossiped about Stiegel's bottomless coffer. But they accepted his hospitality with the same eager breath.

Entertainment had never been more lavish. The name of Baron Heinrich Stiegel was magic. Money evaporated. The towers were often filled to capacity, and the noisier his guests were, the deeper was Stiegel's oblivion. His life seemed to hang in suspense. He laughed at Elizabeth when she claimed that he was too effusive with the wives of his friends, or drank too much. What difference should it make to her if he left his puddings untouched?

As Christmas drew near, Stiegel and Elizabeth sat talking one evening about the guests who were coming and where they should lodge them.

"I think we shall give Madame Weiser the tower room at Thurm Berg," pondered Elizabeth, jotting down a note of this after her name on the list.

"No, that's the room Molly M'Call likes."

Elizabeth looked up astounded.

"You promised me you would not invite them!"

Stiegel shrugged. "Molly invited herself."

"Then you shall simply have to tell them we do not have the room. I'll not go through another holiday with her!" stormed Elizabeth.

"Elizabeth, Molly and Daniel Bennezet are at present our bread and butter."

"Bread and butter! Because you borrow a little money from the old miser?"

"I had great difficulty paying my mortgage interest," Stiegel said, with tightening lips. "In fact, the interest on Manheim has not been paid."

"What do you mean?" asked Elizabeth, bewildered and angry. She felt certain that Stiegel was hiding some ulterior motive behind the guise of business.

"I mean that it will pay you to be pleasant to Molly, my dear."

"You are infatuated with Molly! Everybody knows it who's seen you together!"

Stiegel laughed. "She has too much dark hair on her arms."

The argument ended in bitterness. Elizabeth was not at all convinced that Stiegel was infatuated with Molly, but she was unable to fathom the growing estrangement between herself and her husband.

One evening at Christmas time when some of his guests were going off after dinner for a sleigh-ride, Stiegel retreated to his chapel, laid his dip on the pew beside him, and paused to take a peaceful breath. He dropped his head on his arms, and wondered what was going to happen to him. He had given himself every chance to get over his love for Diane. The hilarity was an excruciating bore, and yet he continued to surround himself with it, afraid of being alone with his thoughts. Beautiful women stimulated him, and their flattery soothed his wound. After he could no longer bear the grandeur, the solemnity of the view at Thurm Berg, he closed himself up in its banquet hall, where the smell of tallow and perfumes and fruit dulled his senses and made life bearable.

He remembered one time in Cologne, when he had over-eaten on his aunt's Schaumtorte, the feeling of disgust he had had for days afterwards, a feeling of the dawn being olive green instead of rose gray. He had dined too voluptu-ously lately on flounced petticoats, and he felt a sudden distaste for women.

The fiddlers would be ready to start ahead on horseback. He could hear the twit of the violins and the excited voices of the party, and imagined Cyrus tucking the bear robe about Mrs. Willing's comely ankles, and Dickinson feeling for the violin bottle of spirits in his greatcoat pocket.

What a comfortable place the chapel was, with its cold and mingled smell of pines and candle tallow. In the past year he had turned more toward the church than ever before. He thought of the thousands of times he had read to the family from the Bible. Jerusha, her lovely dimpled hands folded on her apron, like some ripe cherry about to be plucked by a bird (in reality a little girl in love thinking of Michael who had gone off to Harvard); Jacob, ever more interested in the construction of things other than the Bible, running his finger down the joints of chairs or under a button of upholstery; the two women, models of attention, Madame Ege with her eyebrow lifted in concentration.

It was a little disturbing to know that he was held up to small boys of the community as a criterion in all things, as the man God smiled upon, and through whom God smiled on lesser beings. A man who had begun to carouse in the tower at night, and to deliver sermons to his men the fol-lowing day. Sometimes Stiegel wondered himself that he was so obviously inconsistent. Perhaps one experience was a reaction from the other, he mused, still vaguely conscious of the violins tuning up.

A feathery touch on his shoulder brought him to his feet. Standing back of him was Molly M'Call. He was annoyed. She had been clinging to him ever since she arrived. He knew that she was superficially in love with him, and that the affair might go as far as he liked. Molly was an adventuress. But he was not in the least in love with Molly. He watched her short upper lip curve into half a smile, giving her an air of childishness. She was young and handsome in a virile way; and she looked like some deep Reynolds portrait, her wine-colored suit and ermine muff standing out against the shadows.

"Molly—my heart is in my mouth!"

"You are wont to have better control over your heart than that, Heinrich. . . ." She drew the name out, softly, caressingly.

"They have sounded the horn. They will be leaving."

"You are not going, Heinrich?"

"No . . . for once I want to be alone."

She knelt beside him on the pew, picked up his dip and held it close to his face. "It is exquisite in the moonlight," she said softly.

"Molly, have you never wanted to be alone?" he returned, immediately vexed at his own abruptness.

"Not when you were so close. . . ." She caressed his hand lightly with the ermine of her muff.

He laughed at her and she was provoked to sudden wrath.

"Come, Molly," he said. "Don't be angry. I simply felt tonight that I would like to close my eyes, and see things in the dark."

"It is damp with cold in here," she replied pettishly. "And church in the dark frights me!"

"Hurry, Molly, there's the last horn, and you're going to miss ——"

"I'm not going without you. I don't want you to be here alone."

"If I close my eyes I'm not alone. . . . Close your eyes and I'll show you. Can't you see the bustle of Palestine and the bright clothes? There's Joseph's coat of many colors and ——"

"Heinrich, you've gone daft!" she cried, her voice shrilly mounting.

She dug her hands into her muff. There was a tight feeling in her throat. She had supposed his preaching was a sanctimonious gesture for his workmen.

Then the solution of his behaviour came to her triumphantly.

"You're not happy!"

He rested his head on his arms again, staring down on the floor.

"You are not happy with Elizabeth."

He was silent.

"Are you?" with grim determination.

"No. . . ."

"Is it because you are in love with someone else?"

"Hopelessly in love. . . ."

Molly's heart gave a sharp turnover.

"Love is only hopeless when it is not given back, Heinrich. . . ."

He looked up at her. Her beaked nose was making a curious shadow on the wall. God, he had not meant to let himself in for this. . . .

"Come, Molly," he said, taking her hand. "You're right—'tis very cold in here. Cyrus will mix up a flip and we'll dram together before the fire."

"We have scarce been alone since I came. You have been neglecting me, Heinrich!"

Stiegel found himself embarrassed for an answer, and instead held her fingers flatteringly to his lips. Her hand was covered with rings of all varieties.

"You and the others!" she went on relentlessly. "Even my charming hostess. Perhaps she is a whit jealous. . . ."

"You must not feel neglected, Molly," Stiegel replied ingratiatingly. "These others have known one another for years, and it's only natural they have confidences. As for Elizabeth and myself, our family is grown so enormous and we have so many to consider of a sudden ——"

Molly's hand slipped over his shoulder, and she stood close to him; he put his arm about her automatically, and she deliberately pressed her lips to his. Stiegel relaxed a little. Her kiss was soft and sensuous, as before.

"How badly you lie!" she laughed.

The holly on her muff pricked the back of his neck.

"I am going to give a ball for you, the last night you are here," Stiegel promised. "I'm going to give the sort of ball that will go down in history. . . ."

"But—the money?" asked Molly, warily.

"Yesterday I went over the books with your uncle," tartly. "I think he is convinced I have creditors enough to ——"

Molly put her fingers on his lips.

"The party. . . ." she reminded him.

They sat before the fire of the back parlor, alone, Cyrus waiting on them, his face long and perplexed.

"And what else would you fancy?" urged Stiegel.

"A muff of red roses," Molly went on challengingly. "A new loving cup of red glass, with rubies set in ——"

Stiegel winced, sensing the danger in the game he was playing. If he could convince Bennezet through Molly that there was no cause for worry, that the interest would be assured for the following year, no price was too great. Molly would leave with her head in the clouds, trampling the other women under foot. He laughed a little to himself to think of the scandal Molly's ball would create. As for

Molly, he would simply have to see that she did not find him alone again.

Stiegel's first letters from Barbara after her marriage had been full of superlatives. Her new home was more spectacular than her husband. She was surrounded by Negroes and tobacco. But of late, she had been indisposed. Her food had not agreed.

Elizabeth nodded her head wisely over the last letter, and hid it from Jerusha. With due feminine curiosity and piqued pride Jerusha ferreted it out of the escritoire one night when the family was asleep. Her pretty dimpled hands trembled as she read it. With a feeling of frustration she put it back in the pigeonhole, passing over the kisses to "sweet mama and papa and my dear little sister Rushy!" What was there about the letter that would contaminate her? She knew all the secrets that Barbara did. And they didn't suspect it, of course, but she knew that babies came by letting your husband kiss you when you had nothing on but your shift! She felt angry and vindictive and would have liked to elope with Michael at once.

But the house parties furnished continual excitement. Besides, a young enameler had fallen in love with her, and it was fun arranging a rendezvous with him among the banks of snow and ice-laden trees. Young Willing had practically worn out his fawn-colored silk knees begging her to marry him, too. And she had thought she would never have any lovers!

Elizabeth began to hint that she had better accept one of them. "Had I married before I was two and twenty I might have had a large family," Elizabeth told her with regret, whereupon Jerusha promptly answered, "What is the use of a lot of babies?"

"God meant woman to bear a man children. It is her lot in the world."

"I know, mama, of course—but they all die anyhow!"

Jerusha was not so much interested in her lovers as in her Valentines, that coming February. She had laid them on the pie-crust table before her and was reading over their poetry with avidity. One suitor had called her his sweet Calliope; another, his starfaced Myra. There were amazing intricacies of lace and hearts and cramped writing; one bore the stains of violet scent under its joined hands, another the trace of tears. In the center of one, in a painted basket, were the dried petals of a rose.

There was one Valentine which had puzzled her more than any other; it had come late in the afternoon, and she found it on her bed. The lace was real, a thin French film, and had been sewed onto a background of gay flowered velvet which looked as if it might have been snipped from a waistcoat. The stitches were uneven and awkward. Fastened to the back was a small slip of paper, which bore in elegant, slim German script:

> *"From an unknown lover who lives to touch*
> *The hand of a maiden he loves too much!"*

Jerusha fondled the limp thing with a distressing curiosity. She had not shown it to anyone; she was afraid some one would laugh at its crudity, and yet anyone who could afford a Valentine of such rich material could surely afford a more conventional paper offering. She cornered Cyrus for the second time.

"Cyrus, *don't* you know how this Valentine came upon my bed?"

"I do sweah by all de hearts ob all de lovahs, Miss Jerusha, 'tis something unnatural how dat befell you." His fingers crept to the pocket where some shillings jingled knowingly.

"Valentines can't *walk*, Cyrus."

"I' faith, Miss Jerusha, dey ain't nothing love can't do."

"Came down the chimney, I warrant."

"Now you done guess it, Miss Jerusha!"

Jerusha sighed. She had tried to extort secrets from Cyrus before. He was always conscientiously adamant. But she knew that some day the truth would pop out in an unguarded moment. Poor Cyrus. He was like a fermenting bottle of vinegar which could keep the cork in just so long!

"Cyrus, is it true that the first person you see on Valentine's Day will be your real love?"

"Why you done think Mr. Willing set reading in the hall near your room since morning candle-light?"

Jerusha flushed. "But Cyrus, he *wasn't* the first one I saw. The sun waked me and I went to the window. . . ." She looked about her cautiously. "And in the road was a traveler, with black hair and merry eyes. His chaise had broke down, and he bowed to me—*me*, standing there in my nightshift! I hurry dressed, and went to the window again, and he had got help by that time from the coach house and was about to go. A guest at The King of Prussia, no doubt. He made bold to bow to me *again*, and he was that close that I marked a dimple in one cheek. Cyrus, a man is nothing better than a brute who would bow to a lady in her nightshift!"

Cyrus chuckled. "I cal'late he don' see so good, Miss Jerusha."

It was not more than ten minutes later that Jerusha decided to go to bed, and gathering up her bounty, encountered her father in the hall. He had been called from a whist game by a stranger who waited upon him.

Jerusha recognized the young man at once.

He kissed her hand on introduction and began to pick up some wayward Valentines. She had grabbed the soft velvet concoction herself and tucked it protectively in her bosom, shielding it. But had he seen it? She glanced at him slyly, and he was smiling at her, while he said to her father, "I am William Old, sir, son of James Old. 'Twas my grandfather, the first iron-master, who named Elizabeth Township where you conduct your furnace."

"Aye," answered Stiegel cordially. "I remember him well. He named the land for Queen Bess, of England. He said he approved the manner in which she wore her ruff! Come, remove your greatcoat and join our party."

"I sorely regret I must move on, Baron. I must be back in Pottstown two days hence."

"Nonsense. We will lodge you for the night."

"Thank you, sir, but . . . er . . . my wardrobe has suffered injuries on the journey." He drew his greatcoat closed. "I merely came to exchange regards."

"No guest has ever left my door without at least a sip of brandy to take away with him," urged Stiegel.

Jerusha felt obsessed with the desire of seeing the young man's provocative smile once more. "*Do* stay," she coaxed, "and I'll make you a flip!"

"I shall have business here again almost immediate," he refused, and as if he had not already kissed Jerusha's hand in the last five minutes, his lips lingered on it again, and his eyes said peremptorily, "Wait until I return!"

Stiegel went back to his cards, and Jerusha chucked her Valentines into a box. She had miraculously outgrown them. She lay in bed watching the fitful fire on the hearth, and she said, over and over, "William Old, William Old. Mrs. William Old. . . . William, it is exceeding wet today. You had best wear your splatterdashes."

Not long afterwards, Stiegel was getting ready to go with Elizabeth to a dinner in Brickerville. Cyrus, who was shaving him, had been restfully quiet for a change (though Stiegel never liked his silences, which were portentous).

"Oh Marsa Baron, now I done sliced yo' all up! Gemini, Marsa Baron, I'se pow'ful sorry!"

"Donner und Blitzen!" cried Stiegel, mopping his bleeding jaw with a towel, "can't you watch what you're doing?"

Cyrus stood crestfallen, his fingers gingerly holding the razor as if it had been a poison arrow.

"Now finish me, you clout,—and don't even the job with a gash on the other jowl."

Cyrus worked woefully, and Stiegel, watching the ugly puckered face in the mirror, repented.

"Don't mind me, Cyrus. I'm all undone these days."

"I know. I know, Marsa Baron. Dat Judgment Day come round too soon."

"What do you mean, Cyrus?"

"It don' b'long in dis worl', Marsa Baron. Dat Christopher Koocher, he jus' a tool ob de debbil."

Cyrus had just come from an errand to Christopher Koocher, the miller with whom Stiegel had dealt for years. He had not payed Koocher for months, but it wasn't that he had shown prejudice.

"What's Christopher Koocher done?" he asked sharply.

"Dat Judgment, fo' five pounds 'n' eight shillings he gwine bring. I tol' him you don' have no button on yo' breeches flap cos' less'n twenty pounds. Fooh!"

"Cyrus," cried Stiegel, sitting up and narrowly escaping the razor again, "you mean Koocher's entering a judgment against me?"

"Yassah, yassah," moaned Cyrus, dropping the blade and playing nervously with his long black fingers. "I spose' you knew 'bout dat Judgment Day, Marsa Baron."

Stiegel leaped out of the chair and paced up and down the room, his face sticky with soap. He was infuriated. The sum was a trifle, of course, but the action was a direct insult to him. If Stiegel must wait payment from his debtors, so must smaller men; it was a condition of the times and everyone was suffering equally.

But the thought agitated him that if Christopher Koocher had lost his patience, so might bigger creditors.

"The fool," he thought, "to degrade me like this. . . . The best year the glass business has ever had! I can't fill the orders fast enough. And new agents in Philadelphia. . . . Damn the remittances! Why don't they come through? Perhaps I've been an ass to spend the mortgage money so freely. . . . People don't understand!"

"Marsa Baron," suggested Cyrus throatily, "*I* got five pounds n' eighteen shillings I done save up from brushin' folks off 'fore they leave. . . ."

When Jerusha became engaged to William Old, Stiegel felt overwhelmed by a mixture of emotions.

"I can scarce wait till fall!" she announced, and Elizabeth blushed at this unladylike zest.

The words hurt Stiegel tremendously. He had come to lean upon Jerusha more than he realized. Her buoyancy had been a proxy for Diane. Now for the first time he felt the hurt of a parent who is discarded for a stranger. Barbara's marriage had not affected him like this. She had been a little too much like the poor weak mother he never was able to love. But Jerusha he really loved deeply.

Elizabeth, who was making plans for Jerusha's wedding, came to Stiegel with suggestions for economizing. She told herself that it was not jealousy of Jerusha but a thriftiness suitable to the times.

"She will have everything as fine as Barbara!" insisted Stiegel.

"I heard you tell Mr. Dickinson that it would have suited your purse better at the moment could she have fancied young Willing!"

Stiegel flushed scarlet. He *had* told Dickinson that. Being human he could not help but think of the loan he might have maneuvered from Willing and Morris, instead of the antagonism he seemed to have incurred. The Old family had made a fortune in iron, as he had himself, but

naturally pride prevented his approaching them. He wondered if he would ever scrape together two thousand
pounds from his customers for Jerusha's dowry. He had
already approached several of his friends about a loan,
and been frigidly refused.

He thought of Molly guiltily. She was a possibility. But
he could not bear to be further indebted to her. She had
written him several times since Christmas, urging him to
come to Philadelphia. She must see him on business, she
said. Stiegel had answered the letters with difficulty. It
was hard to maintain the subtle undertone that Molly expected. He could not afford to be brisk with her. If she
had foolishly fallen in love with him, the fault was half his
own. He wrote that he could not open up the Philadelphia
house this season—and there were more reasons than one.
She must try to understand his dilemma. He wondered if
she would infer that he thought it dangerous being near
her.

God help me, thought Stiegel, if Molly ever finds out
how repulsive I think she is! How I hate all the jewels that
clutter up her fingers, and the oil of her skin. If I could only
tell her outright that I don't want her. And now she will
be hanging onto me for another year. I'll never be able to
meet my mortgage payments in the fall, if I give Jerusha
her dowry . . . I've got to find a way. . . . Why did
Jerusha have to marry now? Why couldn't she have waited?

There were many merchants in Philadelphia who no
longer extended credit to Stiegel. It maddened him to have
to order Jerusha's trousseau piecemeal, ignominiously, from
shops he had so recently considered beneath his patronage.
In his prayers he called these insults lack of Christian faith
in one another.

As the weeks wore on, other creditors began to molest
him, and he was not one to bear insults generously. There
was no reason in his mind why various merchants should

not tide him over this period of strain. His books showed
a vast profit, and he told this to their lawyers.

At last Dickinson suggested a lottery. Stiegel rejected the
idea in a temper. Although in the back of his mind he had
not entirely given up the idea of a lottery, he did not want
to admit the unsoundness of his circumstances before Jerusha's wedding. But the more he weighed the scheme, the
more sanguine he became. It was just the boost he needed
to put him on terra firma.

He knew Anna Ege did not approve of lotteries, and
would never sanction one in the family.

"It is not in keeping with thy dignity, Heinrich," she
said. "But of course, I shouldn't expect thee to put any
value upon *my* advice."

It was obvious that he didn't, for a week later he wrote
to Dickinson telling him that he had decided on a lottery
after all, and enclosed an ad to be inserted in the Pennsylvania Journal:

"The Proprietor of the American Flint Glass Manufactory at Manheim in Lancaster County, with the advice of
many gentlemen in this city and his friends, has offered a
'scheme of lottery' to the patronage of the public to enable
him to carry on a Manufactory of public advantage, and
to raise a sum of money for that and other beneficent pur-
poses in the scheme mentioned.

"This Lottery is calculated as much to the advantage of
the Adventurers as any that hath yet appeared. The encouragement he has already met with in the sale of a large
number of tickets, though but just published, persuades
himself the first class will be ready for drawing at the short
time appointed; therefore those Gentlemen who incline to
become Adventurers, are desired to be speedy in applying
for Tickets which by enquiring of the following Gentlemen, they may be informed where tickets may be had."
There then followed a list of sixteen agents.

The family seemed restless, all of them, and Stiegel wondered if the malaise were of his own begetting. Mrs. Ege was solemn over the lottery, and tractable as an eagle. Elizabeth had not been very well lately, and complained of the added work of getting Jerusha ready for marriage.

One day Elizabeth came home petulant from Lancaster. She had been shopping there for Jerusha, and had decided to get herself a new spring outfit in spite of Stiegel's sarcastic remark that she had wardrobe enough for the queen.

"Have you heard ——" a green bonnet said to the mantua-maker as Elizabeth entered. The words petered into a "Good-day."

When Elizabeth selected her taffeta, the milliner said adroitly, " 'Tis only for cash now, Mistress Stiegel. The times, you know," with a sly wink at the green bonnet. Elizabeth, humiliated, decided to look about before choosing. It irked her that all shops seemed to have gone on a cash basis. As she had no cash, she came home in a fury.

"Things have come to a pretty pass when I cannot buy a few yards of taffeta," she exploded, as soon as she arrived home.

"After the lottery ——" began Stiegel.

"Lottery! Fooh!" cried Elizabeth, angry tears surging down her face. "You are filled with promises! A new horse for Jacob—after the lottery! A new jupon for Anna—after the lottery! I have not only had to sacrifice things myself— but see my very own sister suffer. See her sew folds in her gown where the material is rotting through! And why? All because you must give Jerusha the same dowry Barbara had!"

"I can't favor Barbara," retorted Stiegel, and he thought how satisfying it would be to slap Elizabeth across the face.

"But *then* you could *afford* a handsome dowry. Now you are throwing us all into poverty because of it."

"God, how ungrateful you are!" snapped Stiegel. "You whine because you must forego a new dress for the first time since your marriage. . . . At least you can do *this* for Jerusha!"

She knew he referred to the time Jerusha had had the pox.

"How do you know you will make any money on the lottery?" Elizabeth tossed her bonnet contemptuously on the bed.

"I've *got* to make money on the lottery!" was Stiegel's answer, as he walked out of the room.

32

*T*HE COMING of spring seemed ugly. The grounds were soggy. There was a prolonged period of rain, and the usual splendor of tulips and daffodils made a desolate showing. The gardeners hung about the stable, smoking. Jacob became unruly, and Elizabeth was often close to tears. Her eyes were the color of dried violets now, thought Stiegel.

Stiegel, who seldom knew what it meant to be ill, contracted a case of influenza which kept him in bed a fortnight. He was bled every other day, and his attack left him with a hacking cough. If he were in the office, he wanted to be in the house, and if he were in the house the family irritated him and he thought longingly of the solitude of the office. Though its shelves were filled with broken glass and the miniature samples of salesmen, he was comforted by paper and figures before him, and felt that he could work out some salvation for himself.

Only Jerusha seemed very gay, very joyfully in love with life.

One night she paused, laying her sewing on her lap, and said abruptly, "Oh papa, do you think Grossmama will really come to the wedding? You know she does not like the snow in America!"

"I think she will come, if the snow is dissolved."

"I shall want Diane too," sighed Jerusha, satiate with anticipation. "George and Diane, and the little Georges. Is he beautiful like Diane, do you think, papa?"

"I—I scarce remember. But I do not think it advisable to invite them."

"Papa, it is strange Diane still has no children but the little Georges, isn't it?"

"Aye."

"And he most six. Do you think she is afraid to bear more, papa?"

"Diane does not even fear God," Stiegel replied. He knew instinctively that she would never bear a child to a man that she did not love.

"She was so . . . so different," mused Jerusha, in a soft- ened voice. "She will like my Jamie, and he will fall in love with her like all the others."

"Jerusha," Stiegel went on, his voice faltering, "I forbid you to invite her. . . ."

It was not Anna Ege's raised eyebrow that subdued him. He was accustomed to the dark, cloudy glare of her dis- approval. But he felt that somehow he could not face Diane just now. She would sense his affairs with her pene- trating black eyes, and she would make cryptic allusions to his music. It would be too hard to explain to her that this humility was temporary—that there *must* soon come a turn for prosperity. His blood began to run fast again with the thought of her.

"But I *want* Diane! I love her despite all of you, and if her baby *did* come too soon it was George's baby too!"

"Jerusha," commanded Madame Ege, like Hendrick Hudson rolling tenpins, "get thee from the room. George, indeed!"

The little bride gathered up her hemming and flounced from the room, and Stiegel, to hide his emotion, picked up an almanac and pretended to read.

"You see, Heinrich?" expostulated Elizabeth, proving nothing at all.

"When *I* was a girl," stormed Madame Ege, "a female who mentioned a baby before her marriage was threshed and given rations of bread and water for a week! Hey day, what is the world coming to?"

"She means no harm," said Stiegel, wearily. He knew these two women were bitter because Jerusha had jilted their darling Michael. He took a pinch of snuff as he walked from the room, and the subject was seemingly closed.

But Jerusha was one of the variety of hardy plants which thrive in adversity. The very fact that her family did not want Diane and that there was no good reason for their behavior, was a torch of inspiration. She had never so much as written a note to Diane, but she had always remembered her as a glamorous creature who seemed half-mythical, and her only definite sensation about her was that when she had left, the house seemed like the dark after a candle is blown out.

"Mais oui, il y a des fées," Diane had insisted and as Diane knew everything about the woods and claimed she had been born in a hollow tree, Jerusha still thought at times that she could see the fairy ring.

That night as Jerusha dipped a rag in snuff to clean her teeth, her letter to Diane had progressed as far as "Mistress George Ege: My dear. . . ."

"I wonder," she thought, "if I dare call her Nan?"

The lottery so far had not been a success. Tickets were one pound, ten shillings, and pound notes were no longer paving the streets. The first drawing made no money, for prizes were large and tempting, but Stiegel felt there must be large prizes to lure people into the second and third classes. However, when the second class was begun, immediately after the first drawings, the stream of adventurers flowed even less freely. If only he had not promised himself that he would give Jerusha the two thousand pounds.

Desperate, he tried again to sell his interest in Charming Forge through advertisements in the Pennsylvania Gazette. Bennezet had consented to release this also from the blanket mortgage if Stiegel would apply the proceeds against the principal. It was a dreadful blow for Stiegel when he had news through Dickinson that George Ege had bought the property for a thousand pounds. He would rather have sold it to anybody in the world but George Ege, and selling it for a thousand pounds in its present state of prosperity was like making George a gift. But perhaps it was better this way, he told himself after the first sweep of humiliation. After the lottery he would buy it back. And in the meantime Jerusha would have her dowry. He would only be able to send Bennezet six hundred pounds toward the mortgage, but after the lottery he would pay him the other four hundred pounds as he had promised.

"After the lottery!" He was always repeating the phrase. Thank God he had not allowed Jerusha to invite George and Diane to the wedding. He would never have been able to endure their triumph.

It was hard to keep Diane out of his mind. He felt in some unaccountable way that she had caused this catastrophe. He wondered if she would be gloating over his failure, because it meant neglect of her. She would be ruthless and vindictive, never understanding that it had cost him all the happiness he'd ever known to give her up.

He pictured her by day, working under the shadow of the house wall, in her yellow garden. Did she still go barefoot, like a pagan? Were her brown cheeks mellow again, like the last glow of a sunset? He closed his eyes, miserable, and weak still from his illness, leaned over the scrawl of calculations on the desk. He could escape with her still, could brave the woods with her into Canada. And the child. Just the three of them. She would go with him in a moment. . . . His heart beat rapidly. He was so very sick of all the pomp. He opened his eyes and watched the rain beating against the window. He was willing now to give her his failure. Mortgages, sheriff's sales! Like the boils of Job. Just a test of courage perhaps. A year hence he would laugh at it all. "After the lottery." . . . Some day he would say to Jerusha's children, "They put up a great game on me, my dears, but I always knew I would be victor in the end."

The glass factory opened as usual, his men returning from their long summer rest. It was a great burden to keep it going on its former basis. Materials were no longer sent to him on credit, and when some of the workers were told they would be paid a monthly salary now, instead of getting wages for piece work, they began to drift away. The Rago brothers, Stiegel's pride, went to Ohio, where they were offered higher pay, and soon there were only two enamelers left. It was impossible to make the beautiful glass he had turned out for years now, and he was forced to curtail manufacturing to the cheaper and more marketable grades. This hurt Stiegel as if some lovely, delicate child of his had died.

But a worse blow came when many of the Philadelphia houses wrote that they could no longer handle his output. The market was glutted with the more common ware, and unless he had his former high grade of exquisite glass for them, they would have to sever connections.

His home in Philadelphia had been closed for some time, and now, with great chagrin, he rented it—all but the ground floor, which he used as a shop for his glass. He kept the truth from Elizabeth, simply telling her that he could not afford to open the house on Mulberry Street this year.

He was suddenly bombarded with judgments and suits. A letter from Bennezet called him a liar because he had not applied the entire thousand pounds from the sale of Charming Forge toward the mortgage, and threatened to foreclose unless he remitted the other four hundred at once. Stiegel sold some of his prize hunting horses, and with his paltry income from agents was able to scrape together the balance of the amount for Bennezet. A note from Molly pleaded with him to come to Philadelphia before it was too late.

The second lottery drawings took place and prizes were duly awarded. The Stedmans and Robert Morris had spurned the idea, but other of Stiegel's close friends had been most ardent co-operators. John Dickinson himself drew out over two hundred pounds in prizes. In general however, the project was still not being well supported. People were no longer awe-inspired by Stiegel's prodigality, and they had tired a little of lotteries. The running of the lottery was a great expense, already totaling four hundred pounds, for besides lavish prizes, there were agents to be paid in many towns.

When John Dickinson wrote and said, "Shall we undertake a third class?" Stiegel wrote back angrily, "Of course we shall undertake a third class. You have benefited so well by the first and second classes, you would not wish to see the lottery come to a lingering death, would you?"

The third class was so poorly patronized that the drawings were postponed from one week to another. By early November nothing had yet been announced. Ticket-holders molested the agents. The agents molested Stiegel. But drawings must wait, he said, until more tickets were sold.

On the day before the wedding, Stiegel sat nervously at

his desk in the office, encompassed by piles of dusty ledgers. He leaned his head on tightened fists, and gazed out of the small panes that opened on the long vista into the woods. He thought desperately, "I must squeeze money somehow from my agents. This is like the feeding of the multitude with fish begot of nothing!"

He could hear the comfortable trot of horses and in a minute more the metal of harness was gleaming between tree trunks. He was curious. Perhaps this would be Anthony with his wealthy second wife! Strange, he did not want to see any of them.

As the curricle approached with its finely paired bays, he saw a little child's face half hidden in a fur robe between a man and a woman. The horses clipped past the office and slowed down, the woman tossed the robe from her relentlessly, and under the great calash bonnet was Diane!

Her coming was a shock, and he found that his processes of reasoning had completely fled. He walked up and down his office, as the dusk came on, and saw the rooms of his home light up one by one with mellow candle gleam. The little wood fire had died out and when he realized suddenly that he was shivering with cold and that the November wind was rattling the windows and stirring the papers on his desk, he put on his greatcoat. All the moments he had spent with Diane came crowding in on his fatigued mind, and he thought he had never been so weary and so God-forsaken as now. He might have sat there into the night. But soon the village began to seem a black heaven with multitudinous yellow stars, and he saw a lantern come bobbing toward the office; in the very way the lantern jogged he recognized Cyrus' amble.

"Marsa Baron, hope you finished, 'cause those gooses is ready to be broke."

Stiegel walked out beside him without answering. And

in some uncanny way Cologne came into his memory, and Minnie, with her thick, comfortable braids.

As they opened the front door he could hear sounds of merriment. The place was filled tonight with Jerusha's chosen friends, and there was Anthony with a crisp new wife, and his mother, who had been given no snow as an obstacle. He stopped short for a moment. He heard the harp strings through the din, and he was drawn into the parlor, his greatcoat half hanging from his shoulders. There was a nucleus of bridesmaids near the harpsichord —and among them, as if she had never been away, Diane sat at her harp. Many of the strings had broken from the dampness, but her fingers clung to the others nevertheless, as if content merely with the contact. A venturesome young man was amusing himself at the same moment by snatching thunder out of the bass octaves. Stiegel saw that in spite of the commotion, Diane was listening to imaginary music which she could no longer play. She had been too proud to ask him for the harp!

She seemed to know in an instant that he had entered, and their eyes met. He was surrounded with twittering young girls, with the relatives who had just come. Jerusha, like some animal escaped from a cage, flew over to him entreatingly.

"Dear papa, do please dress. It's half after five o'clock now. . . ."

Elizabeth's voice was saying in his ear, "What have you done? Sister Anna is distraught with the shock!"

As Stiegel dressed, he felt so weak that several times he leaned against his highboy, a piece of clothing hanging limply from his hand. He had seen her again! Of course he had known it couldn't be over. She was a thousand times more beautiful than she had even been with the child at her breast. Something new transfigured her beauty. Something spiritual. The boy, perhaps, living in her mind as wholly as he had lived in her body. Now he knew that her beauty had once been only the beauty of full red lips, and brown smooth skin.

For Jerusha's sake he must try to be casual. He must do nothing to spoil her happiness, to bring catastrophe to her during these days which belonged uniquely to her. . . .

He came from his room, bracing himself for the occasion, and met Diane coming up the stairs. His heart bolted miserably, and as he hugged her small brown hand to his lips, her eyes reflected his passion.

It was only when he felt a tug at the carved amethyst button of his jacket that he saw the boy half hidden behind her gold, shimmering skirt.

"Georges, this is Baron Stiegel. . . . Can you not make him a pretty bow?"

Georges greeted his new friend hastily, and scrutinized him from the largest black eyes Stiegel had ever seen. He was amazed at the boy. Strangely, he had forgotten that he would no longer be an infant. Here before him was a child of five, in a tight-fitting suit of pale striped yellow. The blouse fitted him snugly, and the pants came to his sock-tops; his sleeves were long and tight too, so that he gave the impression of a stylish little frog. A wide white collar flounced stiffly about his neck, and brought out the duskiness of his skin. The hair which had seemed so black had grown in fairly light, and had uneven bleached streaks which had never worn off from the blazing summer sun. He was a sensitive looking little person, with the features of aristocratic France. But there was something in the expression of his mouth like that of himself, thought Stiegel, with a sharp pang. He smiled at the boy warmly, and Georges hid a little behind Diane's skirts, returning the smile.

"Ah, merci, m'sieu," said Diane softly. At that moment Jerusha came up the stairs to see what could be detaining papa.

It was not until after the wedding was over that Stiegel saw Diane alone again. For two days the house rang with hilarity. Carriages came and went. In the excitement there were continuous mishaps—a fichu being torn, a white hand marred with a scratch, a dozen punch glasses broken in a dozen different ways, or a decanter of wine upset upon white velvet breeches. Elizabeth's head swam with the hubbub, and she looked haggard.

The family had not convened yet to adopt a definite attitude toward the Eges. Anna Ege had become reconciled with her son on seeing him in a fitful argument with his wife the day of the wedding. George had made himself very much at home; and as Diane blithely relieved Elizabeth of her duties as she had always done, Elizabeth was inclined to be tolerant and to forgive her.

The surprise of the festivities was over, the candles which flared up with superb white stars like fireworks in their white glass candelabra. George Ege had won the shilling in the wedding cake, and Madame Ege had bitten into the ring—which was just too ridiculous, of course. The guests had ebbed away. The house was forlorn, and disreputable looking. On the third day after the wedding Jerusha and her husband had gone to Pottstown to live. The evergreen drooped. Bric-à-brac was in the wrong place. There were a dozen unclaimed handkerchiefs about, and a woman's snuff box of handsomely painted ivory left on the mantel. The servants lagged. Anthony and his wife and the Eges had lodging at the inn and dined at the house, and Frau Stiegel stayed with her son; it was amusing how hard everyone tried to extract a smile from the old lady, and felt a stupendous sense of accomplishment at sight of it.

"Strange," remarked Diane to Christina, Anthony's new wife, "if she smiled all the time we would think her stupid. As it is, we think her charmingly reserved."

On the night before the relatives would leave, they were all gathered together in the parlor, a quiet semi-circle about a blazing fire, submitting to the anti-climax of the wedding. Everything had been said. All the news had been given about other friends and relatives. Every new gown had been shown. Anthony's heart had ached to the utmost at Diane's more mature beauty. George was anxious to return to the Forge. Madame Stiegel was not even as comfortable in this niche of America as in her own. Christina was afraid her baby would learn another word before she returned, and wondered if anyone guessed about the child just beginning to move in her womb. Little Georges Ege wanted to see his pet rabbits again. And Jacob, now eleven, in the mundane garb of a man, writhed with restlessness at adult parley, and felt a little nauseous from all the cake and wine.

In a lull of conversation, Diane said suddenly, "Play for us, Heinrich. See how we droop!"

Stiegel seemed confused by the request. "My apologies, Diane. I no longer play."

"Oh Heinrich!" she exclaimed with distress.

"I shall have my orchestra play," offered Stiegel, jumping up in relief at thought of them.

"Non, non, non, I have heard them." She rose and went over to the cabinet beside her harp, took out his instrument and handed it to him.

" 'Tis nigh two years since I have tried a note!" he said with protest.

But Diane insisted. "For little Georges!" she said.

She longed to be left alone with her harp again. She had even forgotten how to use the pedals! As Stiegel replaced a violin string and tuned, she watched him jealously. His hand shook as the bow fumbled across the "G" string, and there was something pathetic about him which held the others silent. It was as if they were going to watch the first attempt of a baby bird at flight.

Georges came over to his mother and hung over her knee. He was entranced at this box which squawked at one's bidding. He watched Stiegel intently while he struggled for a mellow note. This beautiful Baron was making a song now, and he, Georges, was quite inexplicably jubilant. His toes wriggled in his shoes, and he was humming an accompaniment in an aimless undertone. Diane's arm tightened about him. He would have been surprised to know that this waltz belonged just to her and the beautiful Baron. He looked up at his mother, and he thought her eyes seemed wavy like the river when he threw a pebble in it. But he felt too glad and curious to pay more attention to her, or to notice the embarrassment of the grown-ups at Stiegel's inaccuracy.

"I want to play, too," he cried, jumping up, and seizing the end of the bow as it descended toward him.

Diane pulled him down, not trusting herself to speak. Stiegel no longer knew the waltz. He was mutilating it. The family was buzzing at Georges' bad manners. She saw a slow horror coming into Stiegel's eyes, like that of a man coming face to face with death. And unable to bear more she clutched the boy in her arms, and ran with him to Jerusha's empty room, which was bleak and fireless.

It was the opinion of the family that she had gone off to punish him, and George sat back, chagrined and yet complacent that her action was approved. Cyrus came in with wine, and Christina was urged to play and sing. No one thought more of Stiegel's failure, no one except old Frau Stiegel, who lamented what a waste of money his lessons had been and who shook her head unbelievingly at the disgraceful attempt. America did strange things to people. Stiegel found Diane in the darkness of the room, clasp-

ing the boy to her breast. He closed the door behind him,
and felt rather than heard the stir of her taffeta as she became aware of his presence.

He struggled to control his emotion, but he thought he
had never known such emptiness. Power and ambition had
always surged along alone, and he had never had need for
understanding.

But tonight—

"Diane. . . ."

"I know—mon cher," came her words, out of the darkness.

"I'm all. . . . I don't know what's wrong. . . . I no
longer have music in me!"

"You've willed it that way."

"Diane," he whispered, and his voice was painful with
humiliation, "I beg you do not chastise him. . . ."

"Nay, I had no thought of it. I find he quietens my heart
when I hold him . . . so. . . ." She lay the child on the
bed, for he had fallen asleep in the first few moments of
complete darkness. "He is so sweet, Heinrich. He is everything I have in the world."

"Diane, if he is my son ——"

"Non, non, non," she gave a strange little laugh, her
voice hushed. "You needn't fear he will put a stain upon
your fame. You are happy now, n'est-ce pas? You have
what you want—towers, cannon, gold. . . ?"

Thank God she didn't know the worst!

"They've made life bearable," he admitted miserably,
"without you."

He could hear her breath coming quickly, as if she would
cry.

"But you must keep your music alive, Heinrich. That is
your *soul,* don't you understand, mon cher? Oh, I would
never have let this happen to you if I had been here!"

"Everything is changed. . . . I am changed. I am not

the same as the boy who came from Cologne. He was very gay. . . ."

"You are still . . . gay. . . ."

"Not from within. Music must come from within, from ——"

"It is not only the music that is gone, Heinrich. I cannot think how to tell you," desperately. "It is that you have not been able to make your life, M'sieu. You have let yourself—"

"What?" he asked, unable to endure the pause.

"Drown!"

Drown! How could she know he was drowning? For a moment he was wholly angry, though her voice was pathetic. Then a sense of shame and compunction swept over him. She was mourning him as despairingly as if he had died. Whatever loss he knew was doubly her own. The tragedy was not what he had done to himself, but what he had done to her.

"Yes," he said slowly, "I am drowning."

"Why must we both be dead?" she demanded tensely.

He put out his hand, unthinking, and it touched her cheek, and lingered on her hair. He found her in his arms, and again he could not see her, like the misty night along the creek. Centuries since he had known the touch of her lips!

"Heinrich . . ." she groaned, "'tis like slashing a wound that tries to heal!"

"I know," he whispered. "I know."

She pulled herself from his embrace and fell on her knees at the bedside where she might feel the comforting warmth of the boy.

There was the mockery of applause downstairs as Christina finished her execution. Shame swept over him again, more poignant than before, because for a brief moment he had forgotten his failure.

He opened the door almost warily, and the light from the candelabra fell across the bed. There was a warm pungence in the hall of drying evergreen, like the odor of Christmas Eve, and the chatter of his family smote him as consciousness does in the early dawn, after one has buried a beloved. He took a step toward the boy, whimsically, and lifting one of his warm heavy hands, kissed it, and fled.

33

EORGE and Diane left early the next morning for Charming Forge, and Stiegel was despondent. He had foolishly admitted that he was "drowning," and now he wanted to prove to her that he was not so utterly lost as she thought. It was ironic that Diane had no knowledge of the desperate state of his finances, though she knew of course that he had had to sell Charming Forge, and she must have heard that he was running a lottery. It was not money she had been thinking of; it was the boy who had come from Cologne. . . .

Frau Stiegel stayed on for a while, sending Anthony and Christina back home without her. Stiegel tried to keep his plight from his mother, wondering if she had heard rumors of his trouble. He seemed to feel that because no one spoke to him about it, no one was conscious of impending disaster.

Frau Stiegel went into the kitchen, and said it was time to start on Christmas cakes.

"You won't be able to make fruit cake," Elizabeth told her mother-in-law frozenly. "We have no citron this year. We can't afford it!"

415]

Frau Stiegel shrugged and her expression did not change. "Then we use something else so good as citron," she said. The way she pronounced good "gut" irritated Elizabeth.

"What can thee get that will take the place of citron?" inquired Anna Ege with sarcastic niceness.

"The way I fix it, you will never know if it is citron or it is not citron," noncommittally.

Stiegel hardly listened to the conversations that went on around him. He seemed to have forgotten Elizabeth. Sometimes he was startled when she spoke. For months he had not gone to bed till late in the night, and she had pretended to be asleep. She dreaded him more as each day came, and yet his strange, convincing faith in himself blinded her to the real catastrophe which encroached upon them.

For the sake of the assaulting creditors, Stiegel pretended to lease the works and the manufactory. Messrs. Smith and Simmund, he chose to call the pair of dummies. For a month or two he distracted the fire of the enemy by supposedly running the business for these two nondescript partners.

He labored over figures at his desk till his eyes blurred and ached with the fretful candlelight, and his brain became so fogged that at length he found himself sitting stupidly gazing at the shelves of cracked glass, saying "two thousand pounds, two thousand pounds," and meaning nothing by it but desperation.

One mild day an incident happened which changed Stiegel even in his own eyes. Martin Betz, a teamster, had been working for him for seven years. Betz, though a little dull, was reliable and honest. He had been sent to Lancaster to make an important delivery of glass, and the agent there had promised cash payment on this particular lot.

When Martin Betz returned it was discovered that he had delivered the wrong load of glass. Stiegel was as infuriated as a small boy deprived of a caraway. He had expected a pocket full of cash and here was nothing but Betz, sheepish, futilely apologetic, one hand rubbing his whiskers the wrong way.

Stiegel had always been too humane to whip his servants commonly as did other employers. But now . . . if Betz had not rubbed his whiskers and shuffled his feet in the November mud all might have been different. In the very midst of a group, Stiegel seized the wagon whip and brandished it in the air. Its lash had a thirsty sound, and the tip lapped a handful of dried oak leaves from a bough, sprinkling them onto Betz. To Stiegel it seemed that Betz typified the sordid failure of the past few years, and he suddenly loathed him with such intensity that he could have ground him into the mud.

"Damn you," he cried. "What filled your jingle brains that you did this thing?"

Betz was silent. He had a look of growing horror. He had never seen his master. . . . The whip curled about him, and agonized, he writhed from its grip. Again and again it struck, ate into his skin. The men watched tight-lipped. This was Stiegel's privilege, the privilege of a master.

At last, exhausted from his feat, Stiegel threw the whip from him and ran toward the house. His brain was boiling with words, strange disconnected words, and they reiterated themselves like pelting rain on a cold glass pane. He brushed past Elizabeth, and rushed into the chapel. The sounds of Manheim were faint, velvet-padded, but the sounds of his head were blatant. A paroxysm of coughing racked him. After a long time he began to hear the things outside of himself: screeching brakes of a wagon, the beating of a rug. He looked at his hands, curiously. They felt swollen. The lace of his cuffs dangled in ribbands. One foot felt damp, and he saw that his ankle had been submerged in mud.

Under the stained glass window Cyrus was whistling as he carried in firewood. It was a clear, sweet whistle, like the carefree tune of a mendicant, and there was something about it which soothed Stiegel's ache and shame. He crept out into the hall, where the sunlight was streaming in, and, meeting Wilhelmina, gave her his order. Half an hour later, Stiegel heard the band blaring into music from the roof. Crouched into a pew of the chapel he listened to it until he felt soothed into apathy.

Music could heal. He felt his insanity slowly ebbing, leaving him weak and humble.

The following day Martin Betz drove a wagon to Charming Forge. Every muscle of his body ached with the lurch of the horses, over the hardening mud. He cursed Stiegel with the sort of hatred that comes suddenly and lasts long. Behind him was a huge box strapped to the wagon rails with heavy rope, and in it was the harp for Diane.

For weeks Stiegel had delivered dutiful sermons, chilled a little with the cold that had penetrated the church during the snowstorms and still clung in its stillness. Now his mind began to wander so that he found himself gazing panic-stricken at the faces, as if he might find a clue there to what he had been saying. Their polite and impassioned eyes told him that the Stiegel before them had neither the same soul within nor the same romance without as the Divinity who had held them spellbound under Herr Huber's old oak tree. With every word he was conscious of reflected failure in their eyes. They were thinking of Martin Betz. That was it! They were thinking of Martin Betz.

When he wrote his sermons, thoughts ran vaguely through his head and escaped before he could catch them. He grew terrified. What if he were losing his mind? He tried to tell himself that they would endure him for friendship's sake; that they must know the strain he was laboring under, and would live through it with him.

But one Sunday noon, unable to touch the rouladen his mother had so carefully prepared for him, he left the table and went back to the chapel to be alone in his misery. Frau Stiegel followed him, and said practically, "Come, Heinrich, and eat your rouladen while it is warm yet."

"I can't preach. The words—they don't *come!*" he cried out.

"For teaching others, you must learn," said Frau Stiegel.

"Learn! God, is there a man living who has suffered as I have?"

"To suffer is not enough, Heinrich. You must yet learn from your suffering, nicht?"

"I have learned enough," dejectedly. "I have learned that my life has been a failure!"

She squatted down beside him and turned to him curiously. "You have had what you want, and you say yet you failed?"

"But I haven't had what I want," he cried passionately. "All my life I have wanted beauty. Always it has escaped me—my glass, my music, my love!"

"Escaped," she repeated thoughtfully. "Nein, not escaped, Heinrich. For finding beauty for ourselves is given youth, nicht? Not old age. In old age we find not beauty for ourselves except we give it to others."

"But I am not old!" he defied her fiercely.

"You are not young."

What did she know of him, he thought, harshly dissecting his life in a sentence! What did she know of him and his thoughts and his longings and his love? What did she mean by giving beauty to others? Wasn't that what he'd tried urgently to do in his sermons? He was so filled with agitation and regrets that it would seem impossible not to impart his emotion to these people who sat staring at him from the pews. Yet he could make none of it coherent. Had it welled up in him too suddenly? Did it lack the pigeon-holing into morals and precepts? Had he still so much to learn? Weren't they all hungry for beauty, these poor working-people? he thought miserably. The way their eyes searched his own, begging him to give them what he did not have.

His mother had tiptoed away, her shoes squeaking.

Not long afterward, Reverend Muhlenberg came to see Stiegel. For some time he had been pastor at a small church in Lancaster, and now he and his Lutheran flock would like to combine with the congregation in Manheim. That would mean, of course, that Stiegel would no longer be needed to preach in the chapel. There was scarcely room, Reverend Muhlenberg said, for the throng who now came to hear Stiegel's sermons. Manheim had grown. The people wanted a church of their own. (Not a man who belied their faith in him, thought Stiegel, bitterly.) Would Stiegel be bountiful as usual, and give them a lot on which to build a church?

Stiegel was disconcerted and hurt, for now he knew that these people had outgrown him. But why shouldn't they have what they wanted? They had been loyal to him down through the years. "I will give them the lot," he determined, "so that they can have what they really want. . . ."

The value of the property was not large, but Stiegel felt that his hands were tied. A few years ago he could have given it away with a gesture, never missing it. Today, if he wished to give it away, it would mean great sacrifice. His letters from Bennezet had been urgent and cool. Bennezet needed money also, and could no longer play the Good Samaritan. If interest payments were not prompt, he would have to foreclose.

However, with great temerity, Stiegel decided to write

to Bennezet and beg him for the sake of the church to release lot 220. How could he get together the twenty-five
pounds that it was worth? He had ten pounds hidden away
which had come into the glass business in the last few
weeks. Then he remembered that Bennezet had been fascinated by some carved Indian figures which were worth
five pounds. Elizabeth's jewelry, too. If she would give him
a piece of her jewelry!

He did not like to ask her for it. He began to wonder if
he was a little afraid of Elizabeth, and laughing away the
idea, went to her doubtfully. She had never quite forgiven
him for sending away Jacob's tutor and installing Jacob in
the Cloisters.

"Elizabeth, I would like to borrow your little gold watch
with the doves etched on it," he began bluntly.

"Borrow it? For what?"

"To give to Bennezet . . . till after the lottery!"

"I don't understand."

"I want to give a lot to the Lutheran Congre ——"

"How can you give away what you do not own!" she
taunted.

"I'm buying it back. Don't you see?"

She looked at him in amazement.

"You are giving away a lot when Anna and I are walking
about in last year's clothes?"

"Elizabeth, try to understand. . . . I can't preach to
them any more. They—they don't want me!"

"Why must you give strangers what they want when
your own wife can't have what she wants?"

"Oh, Elizabeth," he said pitifully. "I've got to give them
something for . . . for what I've taken away. . . ."

"My gold watch with the doves on it was the first present you ever gave me. Heinrich, are you going horn mad?"

"I don't know. Perhaps I am. . . . The little French
clock. . . . I paid fifty pounds for it in Paris."

"It doesn't run!" scornfully.

"No matter. . . ."

Stiegel collected the things and sent them at once to Bennezet with a pleading letter. In ten days his messenger returned.

Bennezet said, "I am releasing Lot 220 as you request, and will accept your unusual payment of it. However, it greaves me to add that unless your mortgage interest is paid by the end of the month, as I notified you, it will behoove me to foreclose."

But the lottery will bring in the money by then, thought Stiegel feverishly.

The following day he made his gift to the church, Reverend Muhlenberg fawning upon him as if the creditors were not waiting outside the door. Well, he had done it. He would no longer have to pray at a sickbed, a feeling of guilt in his heart. And he would no longer have to stand before them, their eyes accusing him of whipping Martin Betz.

"You will require a nominal cash consideration?" asked the pert little lawyer briskly.

"Five shillings," said Stiegel, and he thought . . . "thousands of pounds, thousands of pounds. . . ."

"And the balance of the payment?" proceeded the lawyer, his quill poised for action.

Stiegel looked out at the first flakes of the coming storm, and felt terribly alone. No one understood him, he thought, how jealous he was of his men wanting to leave him. No one knew the emptiness in his heart, the same emptiness he had felt when Jerusha was married. What would the men think of his gift? That he was still playing the role of a feudal lord? That he couldn't bother with them any longer? If he could only tell them somehow that he was leaving them because he loved them. . . .

"The balance of the payment?" repeated the lawyer, with a note of impatience.

"One red rose in June—forever . . ." Stiegel said slowly.

One day Stiegel was suddenly confronted in his office by Daniel Schman from Lancaster, who was in charge of the lottery. He was a tremendous red man, with a booming voice, and Stiegel felt that most of his vulgarity was an affectation.

"Stiegel," roared Schman, without circumlocution, "I have come to close up the affair of the lottery."

"But the third drawings ——" exclaimed Stiegel, shocked.

"I can't proceed with the third drawings. Enough tickets have not been sold!" Belching, he emptied his heavy leather purse of eighty-three pounds, three shillings and tenpence, bellowing out the amount of money as he shoved it across the desk to Stiegel.

Stiegel scattered it with an angry, childish gesture.

"Eighty-three pounds!" he snapped, with the utmost scorn and rage.

Daniel Schman sucked his lunch loudly from his teeth, and spat out a piece of gristle. Then he yanked an itemized account from his heaving vest pocket.

"It cost me close to 650 pounds for operation and prizes!"

Stiegel waved it away, the angry tears leaping into his eyes. The lottery had been his only staff. Now he would have to crawl to his friends, crippled, and supplicate for mercy.

He dismissed Daniel Schman curtly and sat staring after his big bulk. The paltry earnings of the lottery were scattered over the desk and dribbling onto the floor.

In a few weeks the settlement of the lottery brought up new disputes. In Heidelberg alone there were suits amounting to four or five hundred pounds, Stiegel learned. There had been deficiencies there due to diverted funds, and prize money had been withheld from winners. Everywhere, people clamored to retrieve ticket money for the third drawing. It was like being plagued with locusts.

"Let them give me time and I will repay every dollar," Stiegel wrote to Dickinson despairingly. "Can it be that my former friends in Lancaster County will drive me to ruin when I have increased the wealth of the county by at least one hundred and fifty thousand pounds?"

The very crash of his last hope seemed to give Stiegel renewed energy. It seemed as if he were being released now that all uncertainty was gone. Something must be done quickly.

He wrote at once to his more intimate friends and business associates of Philadelphia, begging them for a loan. He sent sheets and sheets of figures to John Dickinson, who had never deserted him, giving him a complete statement of his financial condition and begging him pitifully to hold the family together.

"At last," he said, "I am closing down my beloved Glass House!"

Dickinson only replied that Stiegel had better come to Philadelphia. Of course! If he once got to Philadelphia there were any number of old friends there who would help him. Morris would certainly come to Stiegel's rescue. Tom Willing too, when he knew the seriousness of Stiegel's plight. Even Molly M'Call. She had been warning him that her uncle was not so patient as herself. Molly would be his mistress in a moment. He laughed ironically. Would pay him to be his mistress! The thought was so ugly, so obviously a last shameless resort that he shoved it from him. But he was a drowning man. Each new idea was a spar to cling to. Philadelphia was large. The very magnitude of the place would give him comfort, would offer innumerable possibilities of salvation.

Stiegel ordered his coach and horses. The town came forth snuggled in greatcoats to see him leave. The coachman sat stoically upon his box as if he did not smell a mouse. Stiegel waved his muff gaily at his people and the fires in the Glass House lagged while the chapped fingers of the workmen played to him from the cupola. The keeper of Stiegel's inn slapped his hands under his leathern apron and mumbled something to Thomas Lincoln about "Pride goeth before a fall."

Stiegel's smile was forced. He was obsessed with the idea of getting away. The people were stamping their feet on the frozen ground, chafing their hands, blowing on their wrists; some of the younger ones danced hilariously to the music, and as the cannon boomed, a cheer went up, and the horses lurched, and the smiling faces moved by his coach window like portraits in a gallery. The music lasted till he could no longer hear it but in his mind, and the bleak November morning seemed more bleak because a moment of festivity had brightened it.

He took his hand from his muff for a moment to touch a gray streak in the crimson upholstery of the seat. It was the horsehair scratching through. Dingy, he thought, and the people too; they were haggard through their smiles.

34

STIEGEL STOPPED in Philadelphia at his favorite inn, the London Coffee House. He thought the barmaids not so pretty as they had been when he first came to America. He remembered the chambermaid who had come for the candle stubs, and who had sat in rhapsody at his playing, but he put the memory out of his mind quickly. He wondered just what course he should take. First he had better wait upon Dickinson in the morning.

There was an hour before the shops would close, and he wandered out; it was growing dark and an old man who looked like a sea captain was lighting the street lamp. The effect of the city upon Stiegel was magic and stimulating. His step was lighter, and he found that for a moment he could banish the cares which had so weighed on his mind for months. He did not want to be recognized, however. He was not in the mood for trivialities, toasts to beautiful belles, or slogans for rebellion. It was peaceful being independent and alone at last, though life stirred about him with encouraging briskness. In a tailor-shop window was a new gray velvet cloth so thick and rich in the light of a lantern that it almost seemed to purr.

[426

He was very soon in Front Street near the Bank Meeting House. John Gualdo lived there, a music dealer whose shop had always drawn Stiegel with its beautiful musical instruments. He saw, to his disappointment, that the shop was closed. Nevertheless he clapped the knocker, and when he had done it wondered why. He could scarce afford these days to buy food, much less say violins and flutes. He was about to turn away, humiliated, when the door burst open and a young apprentice with a quill in one hand peered out into the dark.

"Mr. Gualdo still keeps shop here?" asked Stiegel.

"Aye, sir. But he be out at tea. Won't you step in from the cold, sir?"

Stiegel complied. He seemed to be living on impulse. The boy held up a dip and a cry of recognition came from his lips. "Baron Stiegel!" He repressed a desire to add, "Aye, the master will be that sad to miss you. I'm a-wearied o' hearin' about that hundred pounds you owes him."

"Himmel! 'Tis Pat," returned Stiegel. "Still copying music, my young friend?"

"Aye, and my eighth note shall be a whole note if I hold it too long," bandied the boy. "But come warm your feet, sir, at the fender, and I may put on another peel full o' coal now there's a customer."

Stiegel followed the youth into the upstairs living quarters, where he had been laboring in a sitting-room at a large table. It was filled with sheets of paper. Pat's job was copying music by hand for those who ordered it, for the book which contained the printed music was Mr. Gualdo's and not for sale.

"Enough notes in that bar to be a flight of birds, Pat," commented Stiegel, looking over his shoulder.

" 'Tis music for Mistress Ewing's harp, sir, that's why. Trills, frills."

Stiegel thought suddenly of Charming Forge—of Diane.

She would be playing in the twilight with the boy starry-eyed beside her. Good God! He had not sent her a sheet of her music. . . . He stared into the shadows of the room.

"Pat, Mistress Ewing must wait," commanded Stiegel in his old voice. "I want a score or so of sheets sent immediate to Madame George Ege, of Charming Forge!"

The boy curled his feet under the chair. "A shilling six-pence a sheet, sir!"

"No mind the cost!" Stiegel thought for the fraction of a moment the lad's quill halted in its work. "Tell your master as soon as business rights itself. . . ."

Pat looked up at him. His left cheek was smudged with ink, and altogether his appearance was not prepossessing. Stiegel felt vaguely annoyed. He fumbled in his pocket, gave the boy two shillings for himself, and said, "I must go on."

He was glad to be alone again in the darkness of the walk. The street seemed more dismal now; in those few brief moments the roar had come back into his head. The walks were more or less deserted. The shutters of the houses were closed, and all along one could see nothing but cracks of light. Now and then a chair would go by with its driver so submerged in a robe that the horse seemed to be running away. Passing two Negroes on the corner of High Street, Stiegel felt their luminous eyes riveted to his gold buckles. He hurried on, tense with the biting wind which had come on with the evening, and thought he had never been more lonely.

The following day seemed a mockery. Wherever he waited upon a gentleman, he was not to be found at home. Tom Willing had made a business trip to New York on the last coach, and Robert Morris was that very morning confined to his bed with creeping pains. It seemed to Stiegel as if Philadelphia, the city of brotherly love, had closed its doors on him. John Dickinson was closeted with three Congressmen on the most secretive business. Stiegel made an appointment by note to confer with him that evening at his home. The fact that he had not been invited to dine with the Dickinsons hurt him more than his aggregate losses.

He had hoped to borrow money from one of these men before he went to see Bennezet, but now he felt that he could no longer stand the suspense of postponement. If he could not cockily lay down the borrowed interest money he must begin by making a plea to Daniel Bennezet to have mercy a little longer.

Stiegel had sent a note to Molly M'Call at noon asking her if she would meet him in her uncle's office at four. He would send his coach for her. He had thought it would be much easier seeing her first under the chaperonage of her uncle.

As Stiegel entered the dingy office, Molly seized his hands, and eyed him very much like a coy parrot.

"As handsome as ever! All but a wrinkle or two on the brow!" she exclaimed.

He resented her obvious infatuation, and wondered if her uncle had noted it. There was something encouraging about her breeziness, however, and Stiegel's spirits began to revive.

Daniel Bennezet had ordered tea, and a tin tray with some very thick cups stood on the desk, with a little ewer of milk and a few sugar loafs.

Molly picked up one of the toasted buns, assuring herself of its coldness, and dropped it. Then she peeked into the pot of tea, sniffed it, and settled back to look at Stiegel.

For an hour the men heatedly discussed the mortgage. When they had finished Daniel Bennezet shoved the untouched tea things a little roughly near the corner of the desk, and pounding a bell, nodded to a gangling office boy to remove them. Five o'clock and the dusk had come on, and Daniel Bennezet had not changed his mind.

"I am still of a mind to foreclose," he concluded relentlessly. "You have made no sacrifice to pay your interest!
You give balls that are exorbitant; you buy new horses for
your coach; new buckles for your shoes ——"

Stiegel flushed haughtily. The ball which had been given
to impress Bennezet! Horses, buckles—trifles!

"I'll get the interest money for you if I must risk my life
to do it!" he retorted.

Molly stirred. "*I* do not want to foreclose yet," she murmured.

The men looked at her a little astounded, for until now
she had expressed no opinion. A little morose, toying with
her gloves, she had been watching Stiegel and they had all
but forgotten her.

"In these things, Molly, you must trust me," retaliated
her uncle, vexed, shuffling some papers about in front of
him.

"Half the mortgage is mine," she reminded him, jauntily,
"and I like the way Heinrich wears his gold buckles, Uncle
Daniel."

There was a moment of embarrassing silence.

In the last few months, after so long a separation, her
interest in Stiegel had lagged a little. But now that she saw
him again, her pulse quickened at the memory of his touch.
She might soon get tired of Oliver Stein's wealth and his
funny little hop; but to drive about in the streets of Philadelphia in Heinrich Stiegel's carriage, to laugh at the gossip
which would reach her, to have secret visits from Stiegel
on his trips to Philadelphia—that would be a thousand times
more amusing than a dozen Oliver Steins! She smoothed
the mustard velvet of her coat, and gathered together her
gloves and perfume bottle and muff.

"This is too dull!" she expostulated, anxious to be with
Stiegel alone. "And the fire's gone out! Come, Heinrich, take

me to the tailor where I must fit a riding skirt."

She tucked her hand possessively through Stiegel's with a glance of defiance at her uncle.

Daniel Bennezet rose stiffly. "I will see you on the morrow then, Stiegel?"

"Aye, after I contract a loan with Dickinson," Stiegel growled at him.

When he and Molly were alone in the coach he felt self-conscious. She was as big as Stiegel, and her easy manner of proprietorship riled him. He had again the old feeling of antagonism. She was dressed luxuriously as always but without taste. Her gloves were tinged slightly with a green that did not match the mustard, and the sallowness of her skin was only emphasized by her costume. The short upper lip which he had thought so intriguingly childish when he first met her, seemed pouty now and inconsistent with her massive frame. She should have had a full wide mouth, he thought, and large strong teeth instead of small white irregular ones.

Stiegel frowned out upon the houses of the shopping street, as they lighted up.

"It is not so serious!" cooed Molly, sitting close to him. "Uncle Daniel is a little pressed for money now. But I can manage him!"

He exerted himself to smile, remembering that much might depend on Molly's attitude toward him.

"I am poor company at this time," he apologized.

Her funny little laugh trilled up and ended in mid-air.

"No, Heinrich, just a little pensive, mayhap, with so many troubles in your heart! Come and unburden them tonight. I shall expect you for dinner at seven."

"I'm . . . I'm engaged. John Dickinson ——"

"Of course. How stupid of me." Her emerald earrings in the shape of a lyre jingled energetically. "But after you leave John. Then you will come to me."

"Molly, that will be late. . . ." Stiegel faltered at the implication of her words.

"Certainly," she said warily, "we must plan our campaign when Uncle Daniel is snoring."

"He will be home. . . .?"

"I shall make his flip myself when nine o'clock comes. It will be strong."

"I still have not recovered from my jour ——"

"You are afraid of me, Heinrich," she laughed, exultantly.

"I'm not afraid of you!" he said with emphasis.

"Then I shall be waiting for you to come. Here—here to the left!" she called to the footman, rapping on the window pane.

Stiegel wanted to remonstrate, but she had jumped out ahead of him and said, "Don't wait. I'll be a considerable time."

He drove on, hating the strong perfume which filled the coach. It reminded him of the incense which had been burning in Molly's house the few times he had been there, and the heavy tortuous Chinese furniture with its strangling serpents.

Going back to the inn, he laid out his most elegant clothing, his last square-cut coat with its stiff buckram expression, and the gold and diamond buckles he had bought in New York. The feeling that Molly already lay in his arms disturbed him. He could not seem to get her out of his mind, nor the sensuous perfume lingering on the coat sleeve which had been close to her.

He was very tired and hungry. He wondered aimlessly if he would ever enjoy food again. The room at the inn was cold, for the fire he had left blazing there was long since burned out. He washed absent-mindedly, shivering as he splashed water from the basin onto his face and neck. Strange how he could not stop shivering, as if the coldness he felt came from within instead of without. Hunting in his portmantua for his spirits bottle, he took a generous dram, and wrapped himself in his flannel robe. It would do him good to lie still for a few moments before he should dress for dinner. How old he felt! How old the entire world seemed tonight. He was grateful for the hot narrow path the brandy had made to his stomach, and the gradual diffusion of warmth through his body. Diane's rancor would soon be eased when the music arrived, he thought. How did they live now, at Charming Forge? He had purposely avoided any intimate business talk with George.

He rolled over, still shivering, listening to the noise of the street subdued through the closed windows and drawn curtains. The candle was burning evenly, and the room was gray and impersonal. He felt for a moment as if he were in a cell, except for the English prints of hunting scenes. What would failure actually mean? For months he had shoved that question from him, deliberately filling his life with commotion so that he would not have to answer it. He knew now that he was not afraid of failure because it would mean a cottage instead of a mansion. What he dreaded most was Diane's mocking recognition of his covetous pride—her knowledge that the property and position for which he had tossed aside their love, were now unavailing. Diane's voice, a palpitating thing in the darkness, came to him again—and the smell of evergreens. "If I had been here this thing would not have happened to you!" Drowning!

Was it possible that he had *already* failed? Yes, in her eyes he had failed. The news of his bankruptcy would be the merest anti-climax.

"But I won't fail!" he told himself again with the sharpness of agony that this vision brought. No matter how he dismissed the idea, it seemed to surge back again like the recurring waves of a tide, edging in a little closer each time.

"I don't *have* to fail. There's always Molly." How strange it would be to humor her. To save his family and himself by yielding to her whim. People would know. Philadelphia, Manheim, Elizabeth would know. Elizabeth would not care too much. Elizabeth would close her eyes, he felt, and thank God that she had not had to relinquish her brocade. Some day Molly would tire of him. He would not make a good lover. He had no desire for Molly, no more desire for her than for any other woman who could give him a moment's sympathy and understanding in these troubled hours. For a while Molly might make him forget his shame, of course. She would tide him over, and he would regain his fortune and she would go on to fresh conquests.

But he would never look into Diane's eyes again. He would never raise his face to meet hers.

God! What was this thing he was considering? This filthy intrigue that was going to keep him riding desolately in his coach? That was going to keep Elizabeth fat and flouncing in finery? That was going to keep Jacob from ever using his hands? What was he coming to? He, the paramour, waiting for the favors of a woman!

Unable to bear the detours of his imagination longer, he tossed off his clothes, and began to dress for the evening. He must keep moving. He would have liked to kill the colorless little fool of a Bennezet for bringing him to a crisis like this.

He put on the fresh linen he had laid out, and the pale and dark blue suit and crimson hose which were new. His own darkening blond hair was unpowdered, and in spite of his despondency, he looked upon himself with a certain feeling of satisfaction. He was so weary of the feeling of suppression, the feeling that Bennezet held him in chains! So anxious to forget sordid failure. And he must show John Dickinson. . . .

He took another long drink of the brandy. Then he looked

at his reflection for the last time and knew in his heart that it was only his indomitable pride that had arrayed him so meticulously.

Drowning . . . drowning. . . . Oh, if only he could reach out and beg Diane to save him—to pull him somehow from the tide which was sweeping him out. What could she do to save him? Nothing. . . . How flighty he was getting. . . . The brandy perhaps.

Stepping out into the blustery night he looked for his coachman. The damned chump was late. He fumbled for a pinch of snuff, saw a whiff of it disappear like a swarm of gnats in the wind, and waited deliciously for the first sneeze. The wind was penetrating, and he sauntered to the corner to keep warm. Two men were huddled there against the wall of the inn. He thought of giving them a few pence. As he reached for his purse he was seized with a series of tardy sneezes, and at the same moment felt a hand upon his shoulder.

"Baron Stiegel?"

"Aye!" haughtily.

"I take you prisoner," said the one man, while the other whistled for the Black Maria which waited around the corner.

"Stop," cried Stiegel, lurching from his grasp. "I am a free citizen. What does this mean!"

"It means, sir," bowed the man, with unctuous tones, "that I have here an affidavit made by John Gualdo that you are one hundred pounds in his debt, and have been so brazen as to contract further debt without effort to pay. This little paper which I hold in my hand. . . ." He brandished a parchment coquettishly at the prisoner.

Stiegel stared at them vacantly. His mind refused to move. Then he felt a hand about each wrist pulling him to the curb. He braced himself against a hitching post and struggled.

"Don't touch me!" he commanded, "I am able to walk alone!"

He stepped into the coach proudly ahead of them. It smelled rankly of the stable.

"To the sponging house, Rob," caroled the man with the unctuous voice.

Debtor's prison! Stiegel cringed. All his heart and his hope and his emotion stuck in his throat. He must get John Dickinson at once! John Gualdo—and he had given him hundreds of pounds of business! Diane's music; it would never get to her. . . . Inconceivable—arrested for a few sheets of notes.

Following the summary arrest was the conventional hearing and judgment without appeal. His threats and his pleas meant nothing. He must accept this fate for the moment. When the court allowed him three pence a day from John Gualdo to clothe and feed himself he laughed out sarcastically. He wrote a hasty note to John Dickinson to come at once, and sent it out with Trollope, the errand boy of the prison. The procedure might take hours, and Molly would be waiting. He laughed. He had not wanted to go to see Molly M'Call. Gaol was a safer place. . . .

The Debtor's Wing of the Old Stone Prison was in High Street, adjoining the Workhouse for Criminals on Third Street. Stiegel was escorted ceremoniously to a room which looked down at the market, pillory, stocks and whipping-posts. He realized in the semi-darkness that he was not alone in his misery. There were half a dozen wretches who looked as if they had been there for months. They blended into the shadows, stirring a little like worms, thought Stiegel, shrinking from them. The wind rattled the window panes and leaked in briskly at the cracks. Huddled in the chimney corner were two middle-aged, filthy men, one shivering in a torn shirt and breeches and the other naked except for a loin cloth and tattered shoes. There was only a faint spark of fire in the ashes, and yet they clung to it.

Under a blanket on the floor someone was snoring, and at intervals a gayly painted woman glanced at him and tittered. She was sitting on a high box, her toes crossed and swaying as if to some tune she hummed, and her soiled quilted petticoat was smoothed out before her. The only respectable looking person was a well-dressed Quaker standing before a desk improvised from a board fastened on nails in the wall. Stiegel's eyes clung to him for a moment, hopefully, but the man was busy writing and did not turn around.

Not knowing what to do with himself, Stiegel faltered to the window, and tripped over what he thought was a heap of bedding. He halted, panic-stricken, for the thing rolled over and groaned.

The woman slid off her box and strutted over to his side, leaning so close to his ear that he could smell the gin on her breath.

" 'Tain't only the starved 'un, m'lord. He don't know nothing, n'more; till Yuletide he'll be in a box."

Stiegel's toe burned curiously where it had thumped the rags, and he covered his eyes with his hand. He could not get his breath in this place, this cage where animals lay rotting and the stench of human sweat hung in the air.

The noise of the room seemed negligible compared with the noise in his head, and his blood pounded through him with violent jabs. Why didn't Dickinson come? Why didn't the boy return?

The woman's hand was coaxing on his arm, and he flung it away from him, furious. There was no place to sit, and he remained at the window, staring out into the darkness.

Trollope did not return with an answer for several hours. Stiegel tore the letter from his hand:

"My dear Stiegel, It greaves me sorely to hear of your arrest, and I shall attempt to intervene for you as soon as possible. Unfortunately, you cannot be released at once.

Imprisonment may be several days; it may even mean several months, but I hope you will be of strong heart. . . ."

Days, months! But he couldn't bear to lie here longer in this nest of crawling worms! Dickinson *must* come with the hundred pounds—*must* release him now! Didn't he know, didn't he realize what it meant? That it meant not only the hundred pounds but everything he owned? That when his creditors heard of John Gualdo's action they would sweep down on him like so many cannibals?

He jotted down pleading notes of explanation to Robert Morris and the Stedmans, and sent Trollope out again, unmindful of the late hour. And again he feverishly waited for help. There was no answer at all from the Stedmans, and at last a short note came from Mrs. Morris. Her husband was ill and sleeping after much pain, and according to the doctor's order, could not be disturbed. Mary Morris, who had led the dancing with Stiegel in Thurm Berg. . . . Mary Morris, who had asked him to be god-father of her child.

What had happened to his friends? Why were they deserting him? Men and women he had known since he first came from Cologne? Men he had worked with and loved; women who had shared his friendship and hospitality year after year? Had some scandal been started and passed from tongue to tongue?

The lights of the street blurred, and the room swayed. Sinking down onto the hearth, Stiegel lay there quiet, so stupefied with his catastrophe that he did not think to send Trollope for a blanket or bedding.

The Quaker had stretched out under the desk, and was sleeping, and the woman, Maria, removed a few petticoats and a pair of stays, and nestled close to the lump under the blanket which had been snoring. For a while the snoring ceased, and there were vague whisperings and more titterings. The blanket pulled and jerked and rose and fell, and

Stiegel thought he would scream with the foulness which seemed to envelop him.

The wind began to howl through the windows and as often as Stiegel dozed off into troubled unconsciousness he felt the shaking limbs of Hogan warming themselves against his body. The contact horrified him like the stiffness of a corpse. Finally, shivering with cold himself, he pulled off his coat and tossed it to the poor creature in his loin cloth.

"Here!" he cried under his breath. "For God's sake— wear it!"

The man let out a queer noise that was neither a whimper nor a word, and, staggering to his feet, he thrust his bony arms into the sleeves, looking ridiculous, with no breeches, and the skirt of the coat standing out like the tarlatan of a ballet dancer.

But he continued to chatter, and his companion sniffled every few seconds, rubbing his snotty nose on the satin sleeve which lay close to him.

The noise of the night quieted down, and now that the low medley of sounds in town was muffled like the far-off roar of a tide, Stiegel seemed to realize what had happened. The thing had happened which he had been dreading through sleepless nights and tortured days. It had happened unless tomorrow he would call to Molly for help. There would be no loan from Dickinson now. There would be no help from anyone else. There was only one alternative to absolute failure. To sell himself to Molly M'Call. He repeated the words harshly in his mind. He would sell her his self-respect, his honor, his very manhood. He would become a toy. He closed his eyes, and visualized Molly, vindictive because he had not come. Strange, how he had supposed the first moment of meeting her that she was beautiful, with her curved nose, her air of hauteur, and her small bowed lips. Skin so dark that it had an olive cast— and long strong arms and hands—with too much dark hair.

Jeweled, perfumed to suffocation. Her body muscular, faintly oily. Dominating, not yielding. Some day when she was old, Molly would be like a hawk.

His passion was roused, in spite of himself. But along with it came a swift revulsion of the woman. What would this thing do to him? It would save his fortune, but what would it do to himself, Henry William Stiegel? Would he become like a hawk too, ever so gradually? Unable to escape her ravenous appetite? Were these hallucinations? If he were poor—he would still be free. . . .

What did he care after all if the pomp continued! It was only a façade to hide the bleakness of life. Drowning, Diane had said. Since he had known Diane he had never wanted any other woman but her. Never wanted anyone with more than his flesh. So different if he had been in love with Molly M'Call. . . . And he might tell Diane that he had loved her. . . . How his mind was rambling—without any sense to it. The boy would despise him some day. . . . He could never do this thing and face Diane and the child. They would know instinctively what had happened. Already he had taken everything precious away from her. Almost everything. . . .

Stiegel shoved the chattering Hogan away from him roughly.

"God, can't you stop shaking!" he cried, swallowed at once again by his revery. "Drowning . . . but not gone," he pleaded with himself. "Poor. . . . They will take everything. How strange. . . ."

He did not know that he was crying until he felt the warm tears on his hand. He brushed them away shamedly, looking hastily about him. The room was almost in total darkness now. No one stirred, but the pile of rags trembled now and then as it emitted a weak groan. In a box at Yuletide. . . .

The bedfellow of Maria Penrod snored evenly in a minor key. He had loathed the prostitute. But he was no better than she. . . .

Inchoate prayers formed in the weary emptiness that was his mind. He was alone with God. Why shouldn't he weep?

35

*T*HE DAYS dragged on, interminable. Stiegel had long ago sickened of the stories of the prisoners. Maria Penrod had been a "bloomin' belle" and later a "woman of fortun', " according to her own vernacular. Her advances nauseated him. Poor Hogan of the loin cloth had in vain been trying to sell himself into bondage to someone who would pay off his puny debt and take him into his establishment to work off the amount.

Stiegel threw the remainder of his penny's worth of tripe into the fireplace, where two new beggars pounced upon it and scratched at each other like dogs with a bone.

He had learned to sit on a box, head against the wall, arms folded, eyes closed, utterly heedless of the snivelings and wrangling which went on about him. There had been much to think about. He had just sent out notes to all his creditors which said:

"Sir: "December fifteenth, 1772."

Please to take notice. That I have appealed to the Honorable House of Assembly for a Law to relieve my person from Imprisonment. If you have any objection please

to attend Thursday next at Three o'clock in the afternoon
at the Gaol in this city, before the committee of Grievances.

Your humble servant,

Henry W. Stiegel."

The faithful and busy Trollope delivered these messages,
and when once they left the prison Stiegel felt that now
there was hope of being freed. It hurt him incredibly to
think about the landslide of his fortunes. Sometimes in a
wild moment of remorse he blamed himself for not having
sent for Molly. He had heard nothing from her in the two
weeks that passed. He had been duly informed that Bennezet would foreclose the mortgage. There had been no
word from Elizabeth although he had written her of his
plight. He could see her eyes dim with tears, a patch of
violets in the rain!

Dickinson had communicated with him by letter. As
Stiegel's lawyer he was doing all within his power to effect
his release, he said. The lack of faith of these old-time
friends was something that Stiegel could not fathom. Of
all the wounds he had had, this desertion cut him most
deeply.

And Diane—what would she say? Some day she would
know. He wondered if she would ever find out it was because of her he had been imprisoned. Of all the people in
the world, it was Diane who knew him best, understood
his needs, cherished him. Understanding was instinct with
a woman who really loved a man, he thought. Loved him
without shame or without reservation.

Sometimes he longed for her so much that his pent-up
feeling became a definite ache which seemed to leave his
throat dry and his heart beating hard. Diane, so wildly
beautiful, so totally his in spirit—so impalpable. If only he
could talk to someone—anyone—about these things.

There was a scuffling outside the room, and then Trollope

banged on the door with one husky boot. Maria Penrod admitted him. He had an armful of dishes which he unclothed and sampled with a hungry finger.

"Baron Stiegel!" he announced with a flourish. "From Grandmother Whitsun."

Grandmother Whitsun, who had once lived next door to Elizabeth Hölz, and who must be eighty? Stiegel was deeply touched. Kindness always seemed to come in this world from the sources least expected, he thought.

The prisoners drew around the steaming food like tenacious flies. There was a beef pie, and a mound of plum pudding with pungent sauce. Trollope himself remained. They scarcely waited for a nod from Stiegel before they dug into the dishes with dirty fingers, and Maria Penrod stabbed a piece of crust with a hairpin and shoved it into her mouth so voraciously that she spread the rouge from her lips onto her chin. Stiegel left them to their orgy, nauseated at the sight.

He gazed out of the window. The people were crowding about the market stalls. It was cruel to have to look down on food that one could not eat. In this fortnight he had grown thin. He knew what it meant to be hungry. It seemed as if the second day of the week would never come, when he got his few pence from Gualdo. He picked up a mug of stale beer which he had been sipping slowly, and which he had sent Trollope for in the early morning. (The sheriff ran a bar in the gaol contrary to the law.)

He watched the women fluttering about the stalls, baskets on their arms. There were turkeys hanging by their feet, geese, and great bunches of holly. On Christmas his mother would cover her face with her apron, as she had done when his father died. Jerusha would hear the carols and would burst into sobs.

He would not turn about, for he could still hear the smacking of lips as the pie was consumed. Oh well, if it warmed their poor ribs! His heart bolted as he saw the sheriff and several assistants approach the whipping post in front of the market. A group of curious pedestrians immediately thronged about him. A genteel shopkeeper who had made too free with the names of others to support his sinking credit was strapped to the post and lashed with a leather whip which curled over his naked blue body like a serpent. In addition, his face was pelted with eggs by the standersby. The sheriff moved on to the stock, where a youth, screaming in horrible anticipation of further punishment, tossed his head hysterically. But the sheriff had an appreciative audience today. With a graceful gesture he took from his pocket a pair of delicate, sharp scissors; the head of the youth was held firm by two aides-de-camp, and the sheriff clipped the boy's ears, adroitly, holding up the red shavings to the populace which shouted with approval. Stiegel's clenched fist crashed against the window pane. He could see the head of the boy fall backward in a swoon. The frozen walk was stained with blood as the sheriff dropped his tidbits on it, and kicked them to one side; he wiped off his hands on his handkerchief, and strode away, leaving his victims to their conscience.

Each person who came along was entitled to toss one stone at the heads of these miserable creatures. For a moment Stiegel watched them. Then his hands leaped to his head and his fingers clove to his ears; his whole body throbbed. The prisoners above him in the garret never ceased their shuffling, nor the woman in the next room, her wailing. He thought feverishly of the servants he had whipped—of Martin Betz whom he had scourged in a tantrum. Was this going to go on forever, this nightmare? Was there to be no end?

On Saturday, December the twenty-fourth, the Speaker of the House presented to the Governor five bills. One was for the release of Henry William Stiegel. It stated that the prisoner was willing to assign over all his effects for the use of his creditors and the payment of his debts. He was to be allowed an exemption of "wearing apparel and bedding for himself and his family not exceeding ten pounds in value in the whole." The bill was amended by Governor John Penn, accepted by the Assembly and returned to the Governor for his signature. His Honor enacted it into a law, and signed a warrant for affixing the Great Seal of the Province to it. The Assembly would refer it to the King in Council the following July. But the Assembly had taken to doing as it pleased and asking the king's consent later. So on Christmas Eve, Stiegel was freed.

It was only as he stood on the frozen walk outside of the gaol that he felt himself truly a prisoner. He thought he would never be rid of Maria Penrod, and that he would see her rouged cheeks in the bloom of every whore on the street. He knew that the faces of his wretched fellow-prisoners were crowded before the window pane to watch him walk out of their lives. He did not turn or look up. The frost of the December night smote him through his greatcoat. His suit coat still clung to the loins of Hogan, its jauntiness gone now, and its braid already unrecognizable with the gray of ashes from the hearth and the drooling of tobacco.

Shivering with the excitement of being released, Stiegel turned toward the Dickinson house. John would lend him a suit. He would have the chance to defend himself in the eyes of Philadelphia, to explain. Ah, there was no height he could not attain now he was free again. He would regain his fortune in a few years. And he would soon have men believing in him once more as he believed in himself.

His hands and face stung with the biting wind,—and his breath was lost at times with the sweep which came from the north, so that he choked and turned his back to the gale. His feet were so numb that he could scarcely feel their

contact with the walk. Frequently he slipped on the frozen
bricks. The twilight had deepened, and festive candles
shone from the windows. He longed for warmth. He
thought that he would never again know the joy of hot grog
slipping down his throat, or the tingling of his feet as they
thawed before a fire. As he came at last to the Dickinson
house, glowing with light, he could hear the violins; on
Christmas Eve the Dickinsons were "at home." Memories
of Manheim and the brilliant house-parties of the last few
years paraded before him. Elizabeth—how she had relished
them. And now she would be sitting before the fire, a damp
ball of handkerchief in her hand. . . .

He banged the knocker and a colored servant admitted
him. The sensation of warmth was as poignant as the sting
of a sweetmeat before a meal. The great hemlock tree in the
hall revolved in a German musical base. It played Tannen-
baum confidently. There were scores of pastel tapers,
lighted angels and gingerbread men of Susan Dickinson's
making. Droll, carved people dangled from the boughs, and
beneath the tree lay an amazing countryside, with miniature churches and fences, a pond of real water, and wee
stiff people and animals which seemed in a hurry and never
arrived.

In the parlor, a rainbow of pretty women was languishing
about the harpsichord, singing to the accompaniment of
Mary Morris. A group of flushed and persistent men in the
dining-room haggled over the threatening war. Spurts of
conversation came out to him.

"No tax at all means war then?"

" 'Twill ne'er get to the point of no tax."

"The King says there must always be one tax to keep up
the right."

"Whose right?"

"We are abused! Let us all fight for freedom. . . ."

"Treason ——"

"*Complete freedom!*"

A roar went up. Hot speech and hot blood throbbed quickly. The sideboard table exchanged full flagons for empty.

Stiegel felt thrillingly outside of himself for the first time in weeks. He waited for Dickinson in the back parlor.

On and on went the haranguing, and the virtuous sweet singing of the women. In Stiegel's brain there were two currents. One drifted along smoothly: the men's voices, the carols, the bayberry candles, the fragrance of warm, sweet fruit, and wine. Another beat at him powerfully, hopefully. It was his own life coming back.

The room looked unusually luxurious to him, with its ornaments from the continent, and yet there was nothing here which he had not seen many times. He looked at the bric-à-brac now with an avid appreciation, and picked up an amethyst bowl which he had sent Susan Dickinson one Christmas when she couldn't come to Manheim. He fingered it tenderly. He loved it. He loved the beauty of life, the glamorous colors and the feel of rich velvets and the satiety born of exquisite silver turned gold in the candlelight. His throat ached. God . . . it had been hell in gaol! He had tried to close his sensitive eyes to the squalor. But it had given him constant anguish. And now his own life would be niggardly. Ten pounds of worldly goods!

His hands crept over his eyes, and he thought, "Oh God, give me courage and strength to face them. . . . I can build again. What I can do once I can do again. . . ."

"Stiegel," said Dickinson abruptly, in satiny black velvet.

"God bless you," cried Stiegel, jumping up, and seizing his friend's hand. "You've been a God-send, John. On Christmas Day I should have died in gaol."

"We're all . . . very happy . . . for your release . . ." Dickinson said slowly, avoiding Stiegel's eyes, and affected

by his friend's dinginess in spite of himself. "You are planning to spend the holiday with Jerusha in Pottstown?"

The remark was like a dash of cold water.

Stiegel gazed at Dickinson in unbelief. Dickinson was
staring down at his gold buckles. Stiegel was suddenly conscious of his fringed cuffs, of the runners in his soiled crimson hose.

"You no doubt wish to borrow presentable clothing,
Heinrich. And a horse perhaps," Dickinson relented. "We
will not call it a loan. I'll be glad to give you the clothing—
for the sake of old times. The horse you may return at your
leisure."

Stiegel looked at him bitterly. Dickinson was washing his
hands of their friendship casually and coolly as if it were
not Christmas—as if these two had not been bosom friends.
. . . And the others, too. Fawning guests, earning their
board with magpie chatter, clinging like seagulls till the
ship went down.

The shrill mercurial laugh of Molly M'Call climbed above
the high notes of the harpsichord. Stiegel felt sickened. If
he had willed things differently they would have accepted
him here tonight with Molly M'Call. He turned from Dickinson sharply and faced the fire. He would not swallow this
condescension.

Dickinson pitied him, and for a moment was tempted to
reconciliation.

"Heinrich, you surely have no desire to see your former
friends?" he asked.

"I can't understand . . ." returned Stiegel brokenly.
"What's happened. . . ."

"They have burned their fingers. 'Tis a long time before
they'll be rid of the scars!"

"Burned their fingers?" stupidly.

"The lottery. . . ."

"They can't believe the lottery was not fair!" Stiegel gasped in amazement. "It failed . . . but God knows I have done no wrong!"

"I do not attempt to judge." Dickinson straightened himself, as if this task took more boldness than he cared to admit.

"But you, John, surely *you*. . . . You must have told them. . . ."

The two men stared into one another's eyes.

"You believe it too. . . ." Stiegel said, tonelessly.

"I'll have a suit laid out on my bed, and you'll find a horse saddled for you. My respects to . . . Elizabeth."

Stiegel was blinded with chagrin. So they thought him a thief! Dickinson had slipped away to his guests. They were greeting him with a tippling enthusiasm, voices dropped guardedly low as they discussed the curious fate of Stiegel. There was an appalling silence—then Molly's laugh trilling above the murmur. Molly, boasting no doubt that Stiegel had made advances! He could imagine her framing the words in a witticism that would preclude any doubt.

All of them—men and women who had generously eaten of his hothouse grapes and drunk of his exclusive Madeira! And had not even given him friendship in return! They were the thieves, Stiegel cried out to himself.

He thought he must dash out into the blustering night and drive the mad sorrow from him by rushing through the wind. But he was still a prisoner. He had nowhere to go. He was banned. He would have to accept this bitter charity from Dickinson. And he would start off to Pottstown while other men were dining and drinking to good will toward men. He was indebted to Dickinson for his freedom, and now he hated the man as keenly as he had loved and respected him for years.

He dressed hurriedly in the purple suit and fresh linen that had been laid out for him, asked the Negro servant for hot water, and shaved. He felt his self-esteem creeping back. The suit was handsome, made by Stiegel's own tailor. He stood in the doorway of the bedroom when he had finished dressing. Dickinson was through with him. This gift was like the last delectable dinner served to a man doomed to the guillotine. Charity!

"I shall pay for the suit," thought Stiegel desperately, "if I must nurse the pox-stricken to do it!"

Dickinson's eyes had avoided him, had lingered on his shabbiness—and his antithetic gold buckles. Stiegel looked down at them, and one of the diamonds seemed to expand with a sudden ray of candlelight. He knelt and touched it, hesitating only for a second before ripping it fiercely from his shoe, and tossing it contemptuously onto the lowboy.

He had not accepted charity from Dickinson after all.

36

F STIEGEL ever needed courage he needed it as he approached the town he had founded. It was not that he had lost faith in himself, but that those who had built up the glory of his past had lost faith in him.

He dreaded Elizabeth. She was a coward. To Diane he would have said, "Ten pounds of bedding and clothing . . ." and she would have answered, "Ah, but that is too vast a wealth for the woods, M'sieu. . . ."

It was late when he reached Manheim. The mare Dickinson had lent him dragged along pitifully, and fell often on the slippery, frozen roads.

The house was dark. He stabled his horse and went into the house, sleeping in Jerusha's old room so as not to disturb Elizabeth. In the morning he was downstairs before dawn. After a long time he heard the stirring of the household, and Elizabeth's step in the kitchen. He leaned like a criminal against the dining-room fireplace, and waited. Finally she came into the room with a tray of breakfast dishes.

He was shocked with her appearance, for she had lost a great deal of weight, and her face under its fresh muslin cap was pale and peaked. He started toward her with a new humility, and she gave a sharp cry and dropped the tray of Wedgwood, which smashed into bits.

"Elizabeth—forgive me!"

He took her into his arms. He was a little boy again, needing sympathy. She was heavy in his embrace, and he felt her breast heaving with sobs.

"Jacob," she cried. "What of Jacob? You have ruined his life!"

The words trembled on her lips as if they had been there for weeks, awaiting his homecoming.

His arms dropped.

She stood there shaking, her face hidden by her apron.

"God knew best that I conceived but one child . . ." she sobbed. "And then to have you . . . you drag him . . . into poverty!"

"I shall make a fortune again, Elizabeth, I swear it!" he answered tensely. "I shall find a way. . . ."

He was afraid she would be seized with a paroxysm of self-pity if he talked to her any longer. He walked into the parlor and stood numbly beside his desk. The closed shutters barred the early morning light. The room seemed gaunt, critical. He picked up the sandbox which he had brought from London. The touch of its soft leather was like the grip of an old friend, but it no longer belonged to him. Even the cold ashes on the hearth were no longer his. . . . He looked about him unspeakably frightened as one feels cold and frightened at the thought of death.

For several days he secluded himself in his office, and sat there before his desk, bemuddled by figures. He would regain his fortune. Of course he would regain his fortune! He would give poor Jacob his due, would prove that Henry William Stiegel was invincible. But in spite of his bravado, he refused to enter the gaunt Glass House, the mausoleum of his hopes, with its cold pots of fire-clay and its idle tools.

If only Elizabeth would cease her whimpering! Anna

Ege who had come from Elizabeth Furnace to spend the holidays with her, dolefully helped her to pack away her treasures and to select the few pieces of clothing she was allowed to keep. Michael and Jacob had both gone back to school after Christmas, their tuition having been paid up to the following summer.

Then one evening Stiegel ventured into the kitchen with Elizabeth and Anna Ege. They sat before the fire in black dresses and warm knitted shawls, for the house was damp. The shutters had been closed to bar curious eyes. Two smart youths of the village had frightened Elizabeth to hysterics one night by peering in at her. After that there was only one fire kept burning, and that was in the kitchen fireplace.

The black alpaca of Elizabeth's skirt was shiny with fallen tears. Stiegel thought of the night he had forgotten to take her to the Assembly many years ago—how she must have cried. He approached her indifferently.

"I have had word from the sheriff today. We are to vacate the house tomorrow."

"Into the . . . highway!" offered Mrs. Ege.

Elizabeth covered her face with her hands.

"Come," said Stiegel more gently. "At least we shall have a roof above us. They have consented to give us Cyrus' cabin for the moment."

"Cyrus' cabin!" exclaimed Madame Ege and Elizabeth in joint horror.

"Oh, my poor Jacob," Elizabeth added, the tears flowing freely again.

"God," thought Stiegel, tossing a few more sticks of wood on the fire, "are tears infinite?"

The minutes seemed to drag. He himself had selected one change of clothing, an olive green suit. Ten pounds of clothing! He owned not even a pair of breeches under ten pounds. His bedding to be included in that paltry sum too.

And his coverlets all satin from Europe! He laughed grimly. How did they think he had lived? It did not occur to him that he might take some of the servants' more common bedding as his quota. He sat on a kitchen stool before the fire, his head in his hands.

Anne's burnished copper pans and pewter plates twinkled industriously on their hooks and shelves. The ceiling was strung festively with drying herbs, and a large kettle of Schnitz was on the mantel. The room was no different than it had ever been. There were the same familiar nicks in the fireside bench, on which Jacob had experimented with his first knife, and the same scratches on the chair rungs, for the kitchen had always been haunted by some hungry villager or other. But it seemed very barren and desolate tonight. Anne, the cook, like a sick dog, hung apart in her corner, and there was no cheering smell of mince meat and roasting fowl.

Elizabeth's sobs continued tirelessly. At length she broke the silence. "I w-w-wager they shall e'en take m-my p-p-plumpers!" These were little ivory balls to fill out the cheeks of those whose teeth were extracted.

Stiegel rose, and laughed so long that Elizabeth pulled over closer to her sister. Bolting out of the kitchen, a dip in his hand, he stood shivering in the front hall, trying to sort his emotions.

"God," he cried aloud, "thousands of acres of land gone— my beautiful glass—my coach, my horses—and she whines of her plumpers!"

The hall was silent again, and he looked about him, as if he half expected to see this man who had groaned his losses. The shadow of Diane's portrait moved with the flickering candlelight, and the girl was so alive in her yellow gown that he could hear her low coaxing response.

"They cannot take your music, M'sieu."

He stared at the portrait stupidly. "My Stradivarius—they

will take my Stradivarius! Diane, they will take you! They
will toast you in some tavern with their drunken glasses!"
She did not seem to mind. She had managed his own
tippling friends, she smiled.

He loitered in anguish about the parlor, holding the
candle close to beloved objects. The stool Jerusha had
made, verdant with rose leaves and blooms; the wax flowers
under glass which Elizabeth Huber had fashioned with her
own wax-like fingers; the hunters on the wall, galloping to
the hunt; the desk where he had written his scores. Scores!
Had he really written music? Had it really ever sung
through his body? Surely that Heinrich Stiegel who had
been jubilant in his creation was not this Heinrich Stiegel
with the shaking candle!

He touched the cabinet wherein lay his violin and his
fingers lingered on the lock. A waltz drifted into his melancholy. Diane's waltz. He saw her playing it on the harp, her
dark head cocked with assurance and animation. Young
Baron Stiegel was watching her. What a queer light the
young man had in his eyes, thought Stiegel. He was surely
in love with the girl. Yet never so much in love with her as
with himself, with the luxury about him. The years of extravagance and ambition and satisfaction shimmered by
and he tried in vain to feel that he had been a part of them
and to place himself in the picture. But they passed him in a
tantalizing panorama.

His fingers trailed over the top of the cabinet caressingly,
and left three parallel lines in the thick dust.

"I am not the same," he whispered. "I am an old man.
And I cannot even afford plumpers for my wife."

By the end of March Stiegel was established at Elizabeth
Furnace as caretaker. Bennezet had generously told him
that he might use the food which was stored away in the
cellar: big cheeses, honey which Michael had gathered

from hollow tree trunks, crocks of preserves which Frau Habicht had made before she died.

Stiegel had regained his poise, but it was difficult and painful living ignominiously in the house which had once teemed with servants' activity and the hilarity of youth and guests. He trudged back and forth from the old homestead to the furnace much as he had twenty-five years ago, always vaguely thrilled with the burst of the fire and the molten iron, and the snow ruddy as a winter sunset.

Anna Ege had returned to the Furnace with a passionate desire to pack her clothes and get away from the morbidity. She was planning to go to Philadelphia for an unlimited length of time. Michael ought not to see this degeneration, she had said.

Elizabeth was no longer interested in the house or how it looked. She and Stiegel had not exchanged kindly words since his return from gaol. They seemed to irritate one another with every word or action, and he had come to hate the definite bulge in her cheeks which meant that she had salvaged her plumpers from the estate.

Late one afternoon Stiegel dropped into a chair before the kitchen fire, lighting his pipe. Elizabeth and Madame Ege were taking tea with Mrs. Klingerman who had been asking them occasionally out of pity.

His whole body ached with the strain of simulation. The new manager of the Furnace was overbearing, and it was hard for Stiegel to realize that the business did not belong to him; it piqued his pride when the men still called him Baron, and offended him when they didn't. In the presence of his old workmen he held his head high, but at night, alone, he drooped.

He hoped fervently that Herr Huber would never hear that Elizabeth Furnace had passed into strange hands. The old man had been hurt enough! Some day Stiegel would buy it back. Some day after he had regained the Glass

House which David Rittenhouse of Philadelphia was now taking over. He *must* regain what he had lost! If the colonies should go to war with England, perhaps then. . . . He began to figure again. Pounds, thousands of pounds! He was so absorbed with his dreaming that he gave no second thought to the sound of a carriage before the house. A moment later the kitchen door opened slowly, and Diane stood before him, her great dark eyes filled with unhappiness.

"Heinrich!"

"Diane!"

The words were frantic, both of them; in another second she noted the solitude of the kitchen and crushed his hand to her lips.

His heart beat terrifically. "What brings you here?" he asked, half in a whisper.

"I had to come to you when I heard. . . . You must know that!"

"I am poor. . . ."

"I know. . . . 'Tis why I came."

"I can't take help from you!" painfully.

"Ah, beloved, think you I would offer feathers to a peacock?"

She kissed his hand again tenderly as if to assuage the insult, and sank down on a stool beside the chair where he had been sitting.

"Heinrich, where is she? And Madame Ege? The old dragon!"

"Taking tea with ——"

"Dieu merci! Then you are alone. . . . How I hate them, Heinrich! How I hate all the world but you and Georges!"

Stiegel made no answer. She seemed to him an utter stranger. The absurdity of her appearance stung him worse than her words. Her powdered hair rose to a steep climax and was topped with a basket of flowers and an enormous calash bonnet. Even, fat white curls fluttered out and clung to her brown velvet bodice. Little silk nasturtiums nodded from her head. She was no longer the old Diane, and he sickened as he would have done at news of a death. It was absurd to think that this woman in her ermine had actually lolled on the banks of a brook, fishing with the dandy who was now her husband; that she had rocked children to sleep with deep mellow lullabies and had knelt among the flowers, trimming them tenderly. She had been a wild young creature fit for dreams, and now even his dreams must be denied him.

"Mon cher, do not look at me so! What have I done?"

"You are very splendid!" he mocked.

She wanted to remind him of his own ostentation, but she had already hurt him too much.

"Ah Heinrich!" and she shrugged her shoulders. "I have nought to think of but feathers and turnips in my hair. You would not deny me these?"

"Nay, they become you," caustically.

"M'sieu . . ." softly. "Do you remember—you must be gay, you said—without me?"

Stiegel understood. "Yes," he returned slowly. "I remember. I'm sorry, Diane."

"They are very foolish—feathers and turnips. But George fancies them. It seems so small a thing to do for him, being a lady."

The intensity of her words began to melt him.

"George is insane with love of me. He is building me a mansion on the hill at Charming Forge. I don't want it! . . . I don't want any of the things he gives me!" Stiegel winced. George was building a mansion for Stiegel's son!

"But Heinrich, I must give him something in return besides hatred, n'est-ce pas?" She spoke with such fervor that Stiegel looked down at her in amazement.

"Then why did you marry him, Diane?" A thousand

times he had answered the question to himself. But he must hear from her own lips that Georges was his child. As always, it was fatal to watch her lips as she spoke. He was scarcely thinking of the answer.

"Oh, you fool," she cried, the angry tears springing to her eyes. "What does it matter! For years I have borne his foppery till I am quite mad. If 'twere not for Georges I should be eating acorns in the woods."

Their voices had dwindled again to a whisper.

"Georges . . . loves him so much?" Stiegel flushed hotly.

"Apes him as George Ege once aped you, M'sieu."

"Diane, why must you always come back to torture me?" Stiegel asked huskily.

"Heinrich, I love you so that my heart breaks, mon cher." She clung to him, her cheek pressed to his.

"You see, it is always the same. . . . We belong together, no matter what years come between," she whispered. "And now at last you have nothing left—and we must go away, you, and Georges and I. . . ."

"George Ege is in love with you ——" grimly.

"He will have his Forge and his buckles of gold!" she cried.

"Elizabeth ——"

"She will have her memories. For fifteen years she has had you to husband—and we have had one another but an hour! Heinrich—you do love me still! Say it!"

He turned away from her feverish eyes. One cannot stem the tide nor turn the sun from its course forever, he thought rashly.

"Say it!" she demanded. "I hear their footsteps and their voices. Heinrich, you must say that you love me or I shall not bear this stupid life any longer!"

"I love you, Diane . . . I love you. . . ."

"And you will take me away, Heinrich. . . ."

"You are young and passionate and without reason. . . . I am getting old. I have failed everyone, everything. . . . Elizabeth and Jacob—they need me."

But he knew as he spoke the words that no one needed him, neither Elizabeth and Jacob, nor Diane and Georges. And the loneliness of the thought was unbearable.

Diane was stirring a pot of soup with trembling hand, glad of a pose to hide her desperation from the two women at their moment of entering.

Startled by her elaborate attire, they greeted her coolly.

" 'Tis a great honor, a visit from Madame Ege," sneered Elizabeth.

Diane made them a curtsey. "I have just delivered a packet to Brickerville for George. I passed too close not to give you the season's greetings."

"My son is well?" inquired her mother-in-law.

"Aye. He sends his respects."

"Diane will stay the night, Elizabeth," said Stiegel, trying to make his voice calm.

Elizabeth stiffened.

"But the bedding. . . ."

Diane laughed gayly. She laughed so gayly that there was the sound of far-off tears in her words. "The first night I slept under this roof I slept on the floor!"

All during the meager supper of soup in the kitchen they talked of the coming war, of Charming Forge, of things outside of their hearts. Madame Ege and Elizabeth were glum. Diane and Stiegel kept up the conversation nervously. Once or twice their eyes met in painful confusion.

Diane, who had been through the rest of the house, felt half choked. The rooms were gray with dust and neglect. Shutters closed out the light. She longed to throw open the rooms to air. Supposing the house were no longer theirs. Supposing there would be an auction soon when all the beloved things would be snatched from the place. Why could not these two healthy women give Stiegel one last bright moment? Give him his soup in Dresden china? Give him his meals in a dining-room bright with sun or candlelit silver?

"This is all I have to offer. We have nothing but soup," complained Elizabeth, tears welling in her eyes. She rose from the table and began to stack the dishes.

"At least you could serve it on lace and mahogany!" Diane could not help but answer.

"Think you I would lay finger on another man's goods?"

"You could scarce harm what you have loved and tended all these years!"

"Never did I think to come to this!" began Elizabeth, and Anna Ege handed her an encouraging handkerchief and patted her shoulder.

"Come to what?" demanded Diane. She refused to meet Stiegel's eyes.

"Come to destitution. Do you not know we have l-lost everything in the w-world?"

"Everything in the world!" laughed Diane scornfully. "So you have lost Heinrich's love! 'Twill be great find for another!"

"Diane!" cried Stiegel.

Elizabeth burst into angry sobs. "Hold your tongue! 'Tis very well for you to m-mock my poverty—you w-with everything in the world yourself."

Diane stood with her back to the wall, her head lifted proudly. "Is it so hard then to use your hands for the man you love?"

"It's his own f-fault I'm l-lowered ——"

"Or *do* you love him!" cried Diane, feverishly.

"Diane!" threatened Stiegel.

"Oh, I've watched! The velvets and the coaches were the things she's loved. Not you, Heinrich. . . ."

"Stop!" exploded Anna Ege, but her voice was swept

away in the greater outburst of Diane.

"She's cheated you—cheated you of love! Oh let me rave! For an eternity my tongue's been clove to the roof of my mouth, since you first found me in the snow. All through the years of misery I never told them what I thought, slaving for them and their babies till I prayed God to strike them dead!"

She turned again to Elizabeth, who was white with rage.

"And now *you*—you whine because you must work for him *with your hands!*"

She snatched her wraps from the settle, rushing toward the door.

"You can't go off in the night!" cried Stiegel, pulling her back by the arm.

"And why not!" she retorted fiercely, lurching away from him. A second later the door slammed in his face.

Anna Ege was helping the collapsed Elizabeth from the room. Stiegel dropped onto the stool before the fire, holding his throbbing head in his hands.

Deranged. God, were they not all deranged? Sometimes lately he truly doubted himself as he rehearsed bitterly the misfortunes he had to bear, and he had a peculiar sense at these times of being outside himself, of seeing his mind objectively.

Diane. . . . He loved her, of course. He had spent his whole life wanting her. How could he turn away now from the one happiness that life had left to offer him?

Finally he trudged upstairs and stood inside the doorway of the bedroom, his eyes riveted on the colorful patch quilt which shook with Elizabeth's body. He put his dip on the table and began to undress slowly, not noticing the chill of the room.

Once more he lay beside his wife, and his blood ran wild with the thought of Diane. Months it had been since he had taken Elizabeth into his arms with something of the passion of youth. Now the thought of her flabbiness repelled him. She was a pitiful thing. Perhaps Diane was right. Perhaps Elizabeth had never even known love. His hand crept to her shoulder. Her night shift was damp and the sobs still shook her plump body like recurrent pain.

"I'm sorry," he murmured, with contrition in his voice and the ache of truth in his heart. But she made no answer, and he did not speak to her again. Yes, she was pitiful. Anyone who had never known his overwhelming sort of love was pitiful. Now she no longer had her brocade; he could not bring further shame to her.

The following day Elizabeth's face was distorted and swollen from tears. She laid Stiegel's boiled salt mackerel on the kitchen table before him without a word. He adopted her mood, though he felt nervously talkative. Diane's fury seemed an hallucination now in the cheery presence of the early morning fire and the little Betty lamp which sat at his elbow. Stiegel left the tempting fireside and tramped through the snow to the fire of the furnace. In a kettle there had bubbled corn meal for a noon pudding.

In the middle of the morning, when the snow had become a sticky softness, a carriage rolled up the road through the woods and stopped before the brown stone steps of the house. It was a fine coach, painted modestly in brown and deep tan, with brass lanterns which gleamed in the sun, and two bay horses. Stiegel hurried from the supply store where he had been buying snuff, his curiosity leaping ahead of him.

The footman stiffly descended and flung open a shining brown door. But no one got out. Stiegel hastened up to the coach and peered into its empty, practical depths as he addressed the man.

"Have we the honor of a visitor?"

"Madame Edmund's coach for Madame Ege," announced the footman without opening his mouth.

Stiegel felt a bit bewildered. Her sister-in-law's coach, arrived from Philadelphia to take Anna Ege out of his life. Well, he was not sorry. She had been a tyrant in his home. And he owed her nothing. He had educated her boys and given her enough wool to knit a thousand Quaker socks. She had ridden on the crest with them. What need now of her exploring the depths?

He walked thoughtfully through the kitchen and servants' quarters, for the front door was kept barred like the lonely front door of any farmhouse. His eyes were still dazzled by the sun. He found the women standing in the dark, cold hall in an entanglement of hair trunks and carpet bags. He did not notice that Elizabeth was wearing her black bonnet with the faded pink roses, and shabby old mantilla. She was sobbing again in Anna Ege's arms.

He stood there for a moment, uncertain what to say; this would be the first time in their married life that he and Elizabeth would be alone. It was a tragedy for her to have her sister leave. Another sorrow he had heaped upon her. He touched her shoulder sympathetically.

"God willing, we shall have a home for Anna again," he said simply.

She shrank from him, unbolted the door, and clung to Anna as the older woman majestically went down the steps and was ushered into the coach. The footman was brushing past him to collect the baggage in the hall. He ran down the stairs, stupefied, threw open the carriage door, and cried, "Elizabeth, where are you going?"

"Thou art a fool to ask," retorted Madame Ege, unburdening herself of a long pent-up speech. "She goes back to friends and civilization . . . and *morality.*"

Words died on his lips; the sting of her inference was too plain. He gripped the hand of his wife as she huddled into the corner, a handkerchief over her face.

"Elizabeth," he cried at last, pathetically. "Do not go! I

vow you shall be happy again. I shall slave for you and Jacob . . . *Jacob.* . . ."

The coach was shaking with the new weight of the baggage, for the horses were pawing the snow. The footman was looking past him at duty, the doorknob in his fur-mittened hand.

"Diane . . ." sobbed Elizabeth.

Stiegel had been delicately shoved to the side. The door of the coach clicked. The horses slipped for a moment before the carriage wheels turned in the snow. Stiegel was stumbling alongside the window, crying something, but his voice faded away, and the carriage lurched into the woods like a brown beetle.

He slumped down onto the top step next to the hitching post, sitting in the slush. Elizabeth was gone . . . had left him. . . .

Now that she was gone he saw her smiling at him from her fresh violet eyes, her cheeks blooming with young blushes, her arm tenderly about Barbara, a radiant new mother with Jacob hugged to her breast. . . .

Elizabeth would never come back to him. And now even her tears were preferable to the emptiness of one's self . . . to the maddening tick of the clock . . . to the vastness of a vacant bed. . . .

37

TWO WEEKS LATER the starched crocheted doilies of his mother covered everything, and the flowers from the funeral of Anthony's Maria Glessner lay as the pièce de résistance under glass on the parlor table. In the very height of a snowstorm Frau Stiegel had come to Heinrich at Elizabeth Furnace, bringing with her a motley collection of furniture she had acquired during the years of grace, and the five hundred pounds she had hidden against a snowy day. She had challenged the roads with a vim miraculous in an old lady of seventy years, unable to do more than sputter at mention of Elizabeth's desertion.

Frau Stiegel took possession of Heinrich as absolutely as if he were only ten, putting her own furniture just where she wanted it and hanging her sparkling pots and pans about the fireplace. At first Stiegel thought he could not bear the irony of his life, the plainness of the few rooms which they occupied. But the first nut torte completely changed his outlook. After all, he must stop being a sentimentalist. He must make a real effort to forget the delicate Dresden which had hung in the cupboards and the beautiful little works of art which had stood so proudly on the tables. It was a great comfort to know that Diane and

George had bought Cyrus and Anne and his Stradivarius at the auction sale. Stiegel had not been able to witness it. He had driven aimlessly through an April mist to escape the torture, stopping at taverns to dry himself and heal his aching throat with syllabubs.

It seemed strange to have no domestic ties. Elizabeth did not write to him, and he told people who inquired for her that she had gone to Philadelphia to visit relatives. When school was over, Jacob went to his mother.

The spring which followed seemed just an interlude in Stiegel's life. The duties of caretaker were not laborious. The house and grounds and furnace—the whole estate was in excellent condition. He had taken a personal pride in the immaculacy of each stone, and though these houses and gardens no longer belonged to him, they would always be his in his heart. Not a day passed but what he tended the yellow garden with his own hands. It was the first time since he had dug for night-walkers in Cologne that his hands were brown with earth. It was a silent communication with Diane. She seemed close to him when he smelled the queer spicy odor of calendulas.

In June the roses bloomed luxuriantly and he thought with longing of the gardens of Manheim, of the little chapel, of the men who were flocking now to their own church—a log cabin on the land he had given them. One red rose in June forever. . . .

One night he dreamed that he had demanded the payment of the Rose. It was late afternoon and he was fumbling about the Manheim garden. The house seemed to be deserted, except for Diane. He heard her singing. He followed her from one room to another—and yet he was not in the house, but fumbling about the garden. The day was humid, and Manheim lay in a quiet apathy. The shadow of the sundial began to grow long, and the garden wall shaded the stone bench on which he sat, waiting. . . .

"After the lottery," he was saying to a frog which stared up at him from the gravel. "After the lottery. . . ."

Time was standing still. The shadows on the sundial were restive. He wanted Time to leap ahead months, years, centuries. He began to tear the petals from a rose in his hand, and as he dropped each petal the churchbell tolled.

It was not until the congregation had almost reached the mansion that Stiegel was conscious of their singing. It was a picturesque procession, gay with color; the soft satin of the women's gowns held the luster of the setting sun. They came in single file, first the musicians, then the children, and the women, and the men.

> *"Sur le pont d'Avignon,*
> *Tout le monde y passe.*
> *Les messieurs font comm'ci,*
> *Les dames font comm'ça,"* they sang.

And then their clothes began to turn into the brilliant robes of Egypt. And there were donkeys and palms. . . .

Reverend Muhlenberg, who rode on a mule, was saying, "Dear Brethren, we are gathered here together . . . to make payment of three thousand pounds to our beloved Baron . . . three thousand pounds. . . ."

The smiles of the children were red roses opening their buds. They grew in the garden, the children . . . swaying slightly with the turbulence of his heart. . . .

Then the smallest one came forward, prodded on by a feminine hand in a pink lace mitt, and handed him the loveliest rose of all the gardens of Manheim, and the child said, "This is for you, God."

The Rose began to laugh, and turned into Bennezet, but a shower of red roses filled the air with a chorus of hallelujahs. One nestled on his green brocade shoulder; others hid his gold and diamond buckles from view. They clung to the hedge, and bloomed from the larkinspur, mingled with the faded lilacs. They lay like the Red Sea all about him. . . . Like blood.

"My hand. It's wet," said Diane, and blood was diffusing from a long scratch.

"Does it pain you?" he asked tenderly, and tried to touch her but she faded away.

Three thousand pounds. He needed three thousand pounds. . . . And he had nothing but a sea of roses. . . .

As the autumn came on, Stiegel shuddered at the thought of another inactive winter, and having no resources, he was a lonely man. Music was denied him now, though once or twice to please him his band had pathetically murdered an old repertoire with home-made instruments, the others having been included in the auction. Often Stiegel sat talking with them in the supply store, which was alive at all hours, for the colonies were in utter confusion and exciting reports of war drifted in. It seemed strange to him that their voices should clamor above his, that he should have to shout his opinion above the theories of sweating men. Though he was amused with the workers at first, they soon bored him. The discussions of these men were not the debates of lawyers, governors and business magnates to whom he was accustomed.

He had never more than nervously perused an Almanac or the Gentleman's Magazine. Fiction had always seemed to him an elementary thing for young ladies like Barbara. The Bible which he read daily, was no more diversion than duty.

He and his mother were forced to live very simply. Though Frau Stiegel knew how to make a shilling stretch to a pound on the table, still salmon was not turtle. Stiegel became thin, and his pale blue eyes had a new searching look, like the desperate eyes of a woman hunting her lost child.

The thought continually galled him that no one needed him, and he did not know how to go about filling this emptiness. When Jerusha's first child was born, the news did not reach him for weeks.

"His name is James. For his grandfather," Jerusha wrote.

Stiegel felt a pang of jealousy. He was the grandfather too.

Now that the close relationship with his children was over it was a shock to realize that he had only been a monitor in their lives. Jacob would always spurn him as a debilitated money-bag; Barbara, still surrounded and pampered by luxury, would remember him as a social failure. She had never even answered his letter telling her of the catastrophe. Jerusha, with a tender and sympathetic husband, could never miss an understanding with her father that she hadn't known. All the glitter, all the munificence had made them selfish, impregnable. They had read their Bibles absently, said their prayers indifferently, thinking the while of rose satin, or "The Spanish Friar" which they had seen played at the inn. Now they needed him neither to share their joys nor their sorrows. Was there no one in the world who needed him?

Was that indeed what made life so barren? Not this new poverty, simply the insignificance of the years he had lived in the past?

He had not seen Diane for months. She was beautiful. She would always be beautiful. Some women were like that—or was it just one woman who would always be beautiful to one man? He tried to recall the mid-summer night when she had belonged to him, but he could remember little of their love but the friction which had always poisoned it. He thought of the intervals of her life which had been hidden to him, and how jealous he had always been because of them.

Daily he hoped and feared that she would come again

and force him away against his better judgment, so that at last he might know what it was like to live with a woman he loved. As often as he dreamed of her he dreamed of the boy, too, and what it would have meant to him if this bright black-eyed boy had been his son instead of George Ege's. Then it would be his duty to take the boy and Diane away. Georges was still young. Stiegel might yet mean something to him. Somewhere the three of them could be sitting before their own hearth fire together. Drugged with stolen happiness. But the boy would know that he had run away from failure. The boy would loathe him. Still, there would be Diane. . . . This inhuman loneliness was more than he could bear any longer!

"Once I only longed for the touch of her hand, for the madness of holding her to me," he thought. "Now I long for her to sit on a stool at my feet. Strange how passion ebbs a little with age. Strange and . . . restful. . . ."

Shortly before Christmas he trudged home in the trampled snow of the Horse Shoe Pike after giving a violin lesson to the son of a farmer. The boy was a dullard, and each visit Stiegel made he vowed would be the last. But the two shillings were more than welcome. He could stop at Mrs. Kreider's in Brickerville and get some currants for his mother.

In two days he and his mother would be having dinner with the Kreiders in their dingy back parlor. He would try to be grateful to the Kreiders, try to forget what Christmas had once been like—spicy odors for weeks before, secrets and surprises, minuets, sleighing parties, radiant red glass candelabra with cathedral tapers, plum puddings gloriously afire, Diane playing on the harp, her eyes soft with happiness. God, life was endless.

He noticed that the sharp wintry air made him short of breath. These long tramps into the country were strenuous.

Several sleighs and cutters passed him, gayly indifferent.
He looked after them longingly. He seemed surrounded by
glazed snow, and bare silhouettes of trees. Diane had loved
their labyrinth of branches in winter, snug against the distant yellowed sky. Gypsy lace, she had called them.

When he reached home, his mother was sitting before an
ambitious little fire, her hands folded idly in her lap, her
Bible on the table beside her. He kissed her forehead, and
stood thawing moodily on the hearth. Soon she brought in
a kettle of boiling water and a pot, with a dish full of coffee
beans, which she would grind and infuse herself.

"I shall make the coffee, kleine Mutter," he told her. He
was glad lately to occupy his hands.

After a moment she said, "George Ege left a billet."

He stopped grinding the coffee.

"He was here, *himself*? . . . Alone?"

"Nein, Diane and the boy."

His heart catapulted. He had missed her!

His mother was looking at him curiously, like the canary,
which said nothing, but had a sharp eye. He pulled his
wits together. "Give it me," he demanded.

The message, written on some of his own birch bark
was:

"Sir:

Diane finds herself happy in restoring to you an old
friend long in her possession in memory of early kindness
shewn her by her foster father. We regret not being able
to bide your return.

Your humble serv't,

George Ege."

"Has Diane left a packet?"

"Ja, on the mantel."

He unwrapped the big bundle curiously, then wildly, as
he half-guessed its content. A violin! No—not just a violin

—his *own* violin! He gazed raptly at the mahogany red of the instrument, touched the "G" string reverently with his finger, gripped the bow in his shaking hand.

It was La Finesse, the violin tenderly made and named by Antonio Stradivari, the violin his uncle had bought for him in Cremona in 1735, the violin he had played to the chambermaid with the scented apple. Played with infinite daring and genius.

His mother was swimming in a blur of tears. He hurried from the parlor to the cold, bleak dusk of his bedroom, to be alone.

Tucked under the strings was a little Christmas greeting from Georges, a few labored words surrounded by hand painted pine trees. For some unexplainable reason Stiegel did not show the card to his mother.

After Christmas he began to give violin lessons to several other boys. He worked daily on his music, sometimes for hours at a stretch. The old ambition which had first come across the water with him began to stir again. He would be able to play the violin now as he had never been able to play it in all his years of success. He would write music again, and put into his score the emotion which was so new and so poignant.

He played always for Diane and the boy. Sometimes she seemed to be sitting on the worn red sofa, her yellow taffeta spread out before her. Again, he saw her at the window, twiddling a nasturtium, gazing quietly out into the blue mist of the mountains, but always listening. He strove to show her that he still felt the power of his old ambition.

But his fingers no longer ran up and down the scale with unconscious ease. Now that he had the desire again to create, his fingers were no longer glib enough to obey him. Sometimes a horrible thought came to him in the very midst of his playing.

"You will embrace her and find she is a bony hag,

M'sieu," Diane had said to him in their bitter quarrel at Charming Forge.

Several years later the war commenced in earnest. Robert Coleman leased Elizabeth Furnace for a period of seven years and engaged Stiegel to superintend the work. The British had begun their campaign on the middle states, hoping to cut off Massachusetts and Virginia, the two ringleaders of the colonies. Elizabeth Furnace would be needed for ammunition, Coleman thought. He had guessed correctly. The demands on the Furnace were so great that the fires never stopped blazing. Orders flooded in from Continental Congress—small shot, cannons, cannon balls.

For months Stiegel almost forgot his debasement. From gray dawn until dark he was in constant demand. At night he was so exhausted that he fell heavily into sleep. He had lurid nightmares of the war, of the fireworks of battle. He was happy in a negative way. Here was something which diverted his mind from himself. He would no longer bemoan the loss of his Glass House, which he realized now he would never regain. Here was something constructive he could do for the colonies, since he was not able to make blue glass bowls for them or take a gun over his shoulder.

George Ege too, he heard, had devoted his business to the cause. He could fancy Diane, her eyes gleaming with the fun of the excitement, watching the output of Charming Forge and coaxing George into daring exploits. He had not seen her for a year, since the time the whole family had stopped in to call on their way from Lancaster. He had tried to accustom himself to the thought that now she was definitely out of his life. She had seemed happy.

It was late in 1777 that Washington sent a force of Hessian prisoners to Stiegel at Elizabeth Furnace. The best output of the Furnace was too meager for the needs of the army, and Washington ordered a tunnel to be dug there to double the capacity of the works. The prisoners had been dumped ceremoniously in Hessian Camp on the mountain back of Reading. Captain Crook, the patriot in charge, watched the Stiegels with surly suspicion, for Stiegel was kind to the men.

Stiegel sat with them at night, smoking his pipe and reminiscing. They brought news of Germany. They were young blood, adventurers, fighting because fighting was romance. Old songs came back to his lips, and there sprang into his memory old Hofbraus, mountain walks, peasant dances, handfuls of wilted flowers, and the University, where he had looked through the spyglass of knowledge.

Frau Stiegel spent her last pence making coffee kuchen. She sprinkled the top far too generously with cinnamon sugar and slits of almond, and passed out her chef-d'oeuvre to her favorites. And they were all her favorites, though she never smiled at one of them. In her heart she wanted these Hessian boys to go home jubilant—and in his heart Stiegel would have liked to keep them here safely until their British allies were defeated.

38

ONE NIGHT the following April, Stiegel, dreaming into the fire, felt that his mother was gazing at him, or rather, through him, as if she were seeing other days.

She seldom talked, ministering to his comforts in silence. He was still her little boy in Cologne, and he must be well fed and patched. If she understood his vagaries, his longing and melancholy, she showed no sign of it. She continued to mumble about Elizabeth, but otherwise it was as if she had been swept back to Germany on a magic carpet, or as if they had never left and Frau Stiegel knew nothing of this enigmatical America.

"Morris has bought my home in Manheim as a retreat for his family." The thought of Morris in his old home stung unbelievably.

"Ja?"

"He is a hero. 'Twas he who begged from door to door and raised money for Washington. They say the city is very gay now General Howe has occupied it."

"Ja?"

"Washington has camped his men at Valley Forge. 'Tis heart-rending, the reports of disease and death and bleeding feet. And in Philadelphia," Stiegel went on bitterly, "the British give a Meschianza, balls and gayety such as have never been seen! They rack the homes and the wine cellars like vermin—even Franklin's. The damn red-coated monarchs tar and feather the Quakers and flip the wigs from their heads with the insolence of a monkey. And I hear that Major André and his officers think of nought but fishing parties and horse races and regattas."

"Ja?"

"But Washington is no man's fool. Rumor says he gathers regiments from all parts, and Baron Steuben is teaching them the maneuvers of Frederick the Great!"

Frau Stiegel sighed. She looked pinched, and now Stiegel saw her knitting less often. But to show that she would never succumb, she sat beside the fire, her work clutched tightly in her hands. Why, she must be almost seventy-five.

"Mutter," reproached Stiegel, "you care not a fig for the war!"

"Ja!" she exclaimed, obscurely.

"You still do not like America!"

She was silent.

"You came to America just for me. And look what I've brought you to. Rags and starvation. . . ."

He wondered now how he could have kept body and soul together without his mother, his little solemn mother whose very silence gave him strength. She had been bedridden twice this winter with severe colds, and had been blooded both times. Her cheeks were no longer like rosy, dried apples.

He sighed deeply. It was when he looked at her that he really mourned his riches. He wanted her to luxuriate in feather beds with French comforts of satin. He wanted to give her wine from Madeira, and huge succulent grapes, and breast of guinea hen.

There seemed to be no words, no action with which he

could show her the contrition in his heart; he fumbled hopelessly for expression.

Then as if she could read his mind, she rose from her chair with a little grunt, handed him the stockings which she had been warming on the fire screen, and patted his shoulder. "I think I am going to like America!" she conceded for the first time in her life.

For a long time they sat in silence, and Frau Stiegel's head began to sink on her wrinkled neck, and roll around a little as she snored.

Then Stiegel took a lantern and went out into the rain. From his own house he could hear the uproar of the Hessians at their evening games. He walked over to the temporary dormitory which they had built near Martin Grenier's old cottage along the creek, and there a blazing fire was going. Some lolled on the floor playing at dice. One buzzed on a comb covered with paper. Another tapped on the white pine table with a pilfered pair of Frau Stiegel's knitting needles. Quite independent of the orchestra, three of them with locked arms were singing in close harmony. There was almost a revolting odor of sweat, and cheap tobacco, and mud.

Stiegel laughed at one of the boys who was attempting to scrawl a letter home to his mother in spite of the clamor. He lay on his cot, a finger in one ear, a pillow stuffed up against the other, frowning.

Stiegel began a game of chess with their lieutenant.

An hour later, in the midst of a loud guffaw, a volley of sweet cold air blew in, and before them stood Frau Stiegel, her gauze cap covered with an old red capuchin, and her pattens leaving little fat soles on the clean scrubbed floor.

"Was ist los, kleine Mutter?" queried the comb-player.

She paid no attention to him but beckoned to Stiegel who followed her out hastily.

"Jakob!" whispered his mother in his ear, and then trotted ahead of him with her lantern, refusing more information.

Stiegel's brain was a jumble of fears and emotions. Something wrong, undoubtedly, and with Jacob!

The boy was standing boldly before the kitchen fire in his bare feet, and before him hung two huge filthy woolen socks, and a pair of boots shining with neat's-foot oil. He faced his father briskly.

"I am a Loyalist," he greeted him curtly, and offered his hand, as if his father were at liberty to take it or leave it, now that he knew the worst.

Stiegel clutched it without thought. He was overcome at the size of Jacob. Almost seventeen, he was a tall, slender youth who had grown unaccountably like his mother; handsome, too. Stiegel glanced quickly about at the windows. The shutters had been closed and the dips snuffed.

"Jacob. . . ."

Stiegel sat down on the settle, and Jacob flopped down beside him, his long gangling legs sprawled out. His grandmother, who had already found him a pair of Stiegel's woolen stockings, began to beat up an omelette of duck eggs.

Jacob continued to rub his hands which were cracked and chapped. The fire stung them unmercifully. He had an air of slight pique as he continued to look about the shorn kitchen. It was no longer redolent, epicurean. It was a living-quarter for paupers, where soggy, steaming socks were hung to dry. By rights it should be teeming with preparations for roast goose and snapper soup and soufflés, for him, its heir. His mother had impressed him strongly with his injury, and he now gave Stiegel no more deference by word or action than what etiquette required.

"Jacob, what's to do?" asked his father tautly. "You—a loyalist."

He half whispered the word, and looked about him.

"I am not frighted; you need not hush so!" haughtily.

"There is a captain here to oversee the Hessians. 'Twould please him if he could take you prisoner."

"Some great clout from a farm. . . ."

"Jacob, you know not what you do—abetting the English."

"Ho, don't I though? What I do is to raise a company of Tories in Lancaster County." He leaned over to take a glass of wine from the table. "To George the Third!"

The wine slipped smoothly down his throat, and he tapped the glass on the gleaming knob of an andiron, looking gratified as it tinkled into bits about the hearth. He had learned tricks in Philadelphia.

Stiegel felt more and more as if he were oppressed by a bad dream. This his son . . . a company of Tories!

"I had no money today," continued Jacob, amused. "I pledged my gold watch to a bumpkin of a farmer for a bullock."

"Ach, Himmel," groaned Stiegel. " 'Tis an outrage to raise a son to treason."

"You are the traitor, sir," replied Jacob glibly.

He was beginning to enjoy himself now. The omelette was puffing up to combustion before his very eyes; and he had shocked his people as thoroughly as he had anticipated.

"Have you no thought of your mother?" demanded Stiegel.

"She is an ardent Tory, too. The Stedmans, Mr. Dickinson. . . ."

"But she worships you; 'twould kill her should you come to harm."

"I am not an infant to be coddled!" Jacob hesitated as he drew on his father's socks, and announced petulantly, with six-year-old emphasis, "I wish people would leave me alone!"

Stiegel smiled at the futility of trying to curb the youth. If Jacob had nothing else he had spirit. Thank God for that! He had not grown fast to Elizabeth's apron strings.

"Your mother, how is she?"

"Pukish! She has great pain in the belly."

"And Michael?"

"We fight. At times I think he talks Patriotism just to incense me."

"Jacob," and Stiegel touched his cold hands. He was filled suddenly with a tenderness for his son, with apprehension for his safety. "Jacob, each day I shall pray to God to guard you, to. . . ."

A curt knock on the door filled the room with silence. Jacob, transfixed for a moment before his father, shot like a rabbit down the cellar stairs. Stiegel slung the boots and bearskin cap after him, and opened the door himself. Before him stood Captain Crook, who strode in uninvited, and looked curiously about.

"You are in excellent time to join us in an omelette, Captain."

"Aye, news reached me that you had left post-haste for sustenance."

Stiegel looked him squarely in the eye. He loathed him. "Take seat, Captain."

"I should rather fancy looking about. They tell me 'twas spectacular here in its day!"

Stiegel picked up the Betty lamp, his hand shaking. Captain Crook snatched it from him rudely, without explanation. A quick glance passed between Stiegel and his mother, who was casually sprinkling a little pepper on the omelette.

As Captain Crook reached the doorway there was a sudden rumbling noise from the cellar, as if a barrel had been upset and started to roll. Then a heavy thud.

Stiegel's heart went still, and Captain Crook turned on

his heel. They glared at one another in a swift second of comprehension. As the Captain bolted for the cellar door Stiegel ran over and threw his whole weight against him. They began to fight, their fists swinging out at one another fiercely.

They were swearing in spasms like two spitting cats, and Frau Stiegel watched them now in breathless horror.

"Damn you. . . . I'll get you. . . . Open that door. . . ."

Stiegel's nose was bleeding and the blood spread garishly over his face and into his eyes. Even a few seconds might save Jacob, he thought distractedly. The boy knew all the doors. . . . He *must* know the danger, must be trying to escape! . . . Stiegel smashed into the Captain with his last ounce of strength. But Captain Crook had found the latch. The door flew open behind Stiegel with a bang, and slipping, he felt himself swallowed suddenly by the black opening of the cellar. Crashing down the stairs, he had a last vision of Captain Crook looming above him, framed against the dim light of the kitchen.

There was a moment of terrific pain in his ribs as he lunged against the corner of the bottom step, a burning agony throughout his body, and then relief.

Several hours later when he became conscious, his mother was sitting beside his bed, and one of the Hessians was nodding in a chair, his arm braced on the washstand.

Stiegel looked about him, vague. He breathed softly, so that he should not be cut in two with pain. Then he remembered, and tried to frame the question with his lips.

His mother shook her head violently. "Safe . . . gone," she whispered.

Stiegel closed his eyes. He could imagine Captain Crook searching the cellar, blood oozing from the cut on his chin; pausing silent in the attic, where he could hear the treading through the cold damp rooms of the house which branches of the oak scratching against the window pane;

had so long been unused; returning to the kitchen, standing there puzzled in the comforting warmth. Finding no trace of Jacob.

Stiegel smiled grimly. He was thinking with strange emotion of the tall, impertinent boy with the huge bare feet and big raw hands. He had done something for Jacob which had not cost money. . . .

39

IN THE FALL of 1780 Diane and Georges came home one afternoon from nutting; it was dusk, and George Ege was perusing the papers.

Georges dumped his bag of nuts unceremoniously on the parlor floor, and went off whistling to get a piece of bread and honey. Diane dropped down before the fire, leaned against a chair, and propped her feet on the sack.

Her face was flushed and her eyes sparkled, and George was painfully conscious again that the two of them had been in perfect harmony and never missed him. They laughed together, fought, worked and played together. Georges was fourteen, but Diane still romped about the gardens with him as she had once run through the woods with Michael and himself. Sometimes he felt ashamed of her unrestraint. Always he felt envious that Georges was having his turn and that he himself was now a sedate man of business. Diane spent her anger or her gayety upon him, but never any of the beautiful intimacy which she shared with her son.

George never ceased to be jealous of Diane. He worshipped her frantically, and he still had a childish horror that she might disappear into the woods, that she was not quite human. Not once in all these years had he felt that she was securely his.

He dropped his Gazette and watched her as she unfastened the gay handkerchief which had bound up her hair like a West Indian. An old woman past forty, yet handsome and spirited and somehow utterly unchanged. Perhaps because she had only borne him one child. He had always regretted that there were no more children, after the first fear of losing her in childbirth had worn away.

Diane looked up with an untimely question, almost as if she divined his yearning for her and wished to divert him.

"What did Michael say in his billet?"

"I think he would quit Boiling Springs; orders have fallen off there as they have everywhere else, now the seat of the war has changed to the south."

"Guerre à mort," Diane murmured with regret in her voice. "But it has been diversion!"

George found her incorrigible about the war, and he did not like the way Georges' eyes brightened at her radicalism. General Sullivan, who at last punished the Indians for their attacks, was just another brigand. Had not the French and Indians owned this country in the beginning, she challenged? It would be exciting now having a war with France and becoming totally French!

During the war Michael had been prosperously manufacturing cannons at a furnace about five miles from Boiling Springs, building there a spacious stone mansion for his mother. She was aptly termed a thorn in the side of the British. Although they lived but an hour on horseback from the English barracks, she had encouraged Michael to cast cannons at night for the Valley Forge troops. They had had to take the utmost precautions. The life suited militant Anna Ege to perfection. She was a grand old war horse, and hostilities superbly brought out powers which had lain dormant while she merely superintended households. When she heard that Jacob was a Tory and abetting the English, she turned both him and Elizabeth out of her life without the slightest compunction, and a few years later died without a word of regret.

Diane smiled wistfully. She knew Michael had not found this adventure as serene as those of his dreams. Wealth had accumulated too quickly for him to know what to do with it, now he was alone. There was something pathetic about Michael shackled by convention.

"Still restless, my poor Michael," Diane mused. "I think he was truly enamoured of Rushy, and wishes she and her four sons were his 'stead of William Old's."

George nibbled at his nails. "Like you, still mourning that damned French glass-blower who fell at the Battle of Brandywine."

"P'r'aps, mon cher," agreed Diane, just to be perverse. "Martin Grenier was a most *beaut'*ful lover!"

George crumpled his newspaper, and Diane laughed.

"What are you laughing about?" he asked hotly.

"Michael. . . . 'Twas only a month back Chepa Rose asked news of him, and I said Michael was a rich gentleman with a big house. Chepa Rose looked as if I had said Michael was dead. '*Jhentil*mon!' he said. 'Ah, trop fort!' . . . You know, I don't think he's ever quite forgiven me either for becoming a lady!"

Diane tied the kerchief about her waist.

"Making cannon was never quite to Michael's taste," spluttered George. " 'Twas my mother who wanted to make cannon."

"I think he always envied you the wagon loads of flour and grain and straw you sent to the army from your Berks County Farms, and your placid gifts of money."

"What mean you, placid? Did I not give over every inch of my iron establishments for General Washington's consumption, the same as Michael?" He began to bite at a hangnail, and she watched him scornfully.

"Aye, and made a great deal of money—without so much as a drop of sweat!"

"Must a man sweat to be patriot?" he demanded hotly.

"Non, non, non, not a gentleman," she returned with quick sarcasm, and began to look over the nuts she had collected. "But what will Michael do if he quits Boiling Springs?"

"He asks me to make him a partner here," tartly.

"You owe it him; he has been a good brother."

"I don't relish family ties in business. You know what happened when my uncle kept books for me at the Reading Furnace. He could never keep his own books straight. I do not wonder he made a tangle of mine!"

Diane looked at him solemnly, and it was a moment before she could speak. "Heinrich was born to be an artist—and he is so alone, George!"

" 'Tis his own ado!"

"While Frau Stiegel lived, there was someone to care for him. Her death must have been a heavy blow."

"Anthony's been a good enough brother, giving him Thurm Berg to live in."

"It must be a hollow place to live in," she said, shuddering. "George, I scarce think he is well!"

"Ill of wherriting."

"I can't bear to think of him in that draughty little schoolhouse in Schaefferstown," she said feverishly. "George—we shall take him here!"

"Preposterous!"

"But he raised us both!" she pleaded tactfully. "And now he is alone 'tis only our duty to help him."

"If he'd treated my Aunt Elizabeth fair he'd have a wife today to look after him."

"Fair!" Diane slung a wormy nut viciously into the fire. "She wanted everything!"

"I don't know why you always hated her."

Diane was silent. She had always been very careful not to give George any inkling of her feeling for Stiegel. There was Georges to think of now.

"And there at the end there was even talk of another woman," George went on.

"What . . . other woman?" asked Diane, her heart lurching.

"The one who had the mortgage—Molly M'Call."

"It wasn't true."

"How do you know?"

"There's never been any . . . other woman."

"Well, Michael told me once that's why Aunt Elizabeth left him."

"She left him because she didn't love him," cried Diane. "It's the only reason any woman leaves any man."

George laughed cynically. "I suppose you'll be happy to hear she's dying."

"Dying . . . who told you?" asked Diane tensely, getting up and staring at George queerly. Was it really over, she thought? . . . Had the time come for her at last?

"Michael heard from Madame Edmund. She said Aunt Elizabeth is very weak, and her belly big as if she were with child."

Diane continued to stare at George, visualizing Elizabeth grotesque in her pain. She was not sorry for her. She had been Heinrich's wife. . . . How much longer would she live? How Elizabeth would cry out and agonize. How terrified she would be to give up life, thought Diane scornfully.

"I hope she is soon out of her pain," she said coldly, to hide the turmoil of excitement within her.

It had been a particularly trying day. Stiegel had come to school to find a drift of snow broken through one of the

windows which was stuffed with oiled newspapers. It had
entirely blanketed the horde of vegetables and grain which
dribbled in from parents as payment of his labors. They
were so frozen together that they looked like a massive
compote glacé, and now he would be unable to sell them
to passers-by and make a few shillings.

The supply of wood too, was ominously low today, and
Hansel Grau had the grit to appear again without his share.
Stiegel barred him from the fire, according to custom. If
his parents did not care how he shivered, then he must not
share the warmth which did not belong to him. But at noon
Stiegel could no longer bear to see the boy shaking under
his mammoth leather apron, or to hear the deep rumbling
cough which half choked him, and he ordered him near
the fire once more. He did not like to relent. It was weak.
And yet the boy looked ill. He set him making ink from
soot and vinegar so that Hansel would not feel himself
absolved.

The schoolhouse was a mean affair, scarcely as comfortable as the neighboring stables. The land had been
bought from the village after a successful lottery, and the
log cabin built in a few days. The schoolroom itself was a
cyclone of draughts in winter, and a rendezvous for butterflies and wasps in summer. It was entered through a
little shed where were accumulated coats, dinner pails,
hats, kites in season, marbles always, and stray hornbooks
which had lost their owners.

Stiegel's desk was in the middle of the room, close beside the fireplace. The older boys sat at wall boards hung
on pegs shoved into apertures. The younger scholars shuffled before the wood-fire, their brains dulled with the buzzing of lessons, and their six-year-old capacity for wakefulness strained to the limit with the dim light. It seemed
anything but a place of learning, thought Stiegel—this mixture of odorous human growth and spilled ink.

He had rather surprised himself with an aptitude for teaching. But his work not only filled the hours of the day. It brought along with it duties which kept him busy long into the evening. He was expected to sweep the church floor and ring the bell on Sundays, providing water for baptisms and bread and wine for communion. Even delivering invitations to a funeral came into the field of pedagogy. If the Germans in the community had had their way, schoolmasters would have done everything but teach, for the early German settlers were a stubborn lot and argued that too much education made the boys dissatisfied with farm work, leading them to doubt religion itself.

Shortly before school was out, one of the scholars came up to him with a pen to be mended. He was a boy who loved to be slyly bad. Now he dug his boot into the ground floor, pretended that he tripped, and sent a cloud of dust into Stiegel's face. There was an uproar of approval from his cohorts as their master choked and sputtered. The day had been a dull round of addition and division, and here was diversion at last.

Stiegel sent them home early, his eyes burning with the onslaught. He sat at his table, his head in his hands, and flinched from the clatter of desk boards yanked from their pegs to be converted into toboggans.

He was utterly miserable. He could scarcely see through the stinging veil of dust, and his side hurt him with the old pain he'd had since his accident. It shot through the middle of his body and stabbed his back with relentless precision. He was dreadfully tired of having pain, not patient with it as he had been at first. His hands were stiff with cold, and the room smelled faintly like new steaming dung.

The shouts of the boys filled him with slow anger. They seemed to revive all the turmoil and misery of the last half dozen years, all the groping for happiness, all the shame of unfulfillment.

His mother had died over a year ago of pneumonia, and something of his courage had died with her. She had been contented there at the Furnace, with the young Hessian boys to pamper, and again at the Brickerville parsonage, where he had preached for so short a time. Strange, about his silent little mother; she had known how to be happy wherever fate put her. Perhaps happiness lay in little things, Stiegel thought suddenly. In the carving of a whistle for a child, in the gathering of moss from a tree. It must have been the endless little things she did for his comfort which made her happy—the shirts she patched with her failing eyes, the German kuchen she baked to tempt him, the few flowers she kept on the table. Yellow flowers. Almost as if she had known of his love for Diane and the romance of the yellow garden. . . .

He was startled at the touch of a hand on his shoulder. It would be little Punkie Zimmerman, always sympathetic.

He looked up and saw Diane. She held out her rose kid gloved hand to him, and he hugged it to his lips without speaking. He had a strange feeling that if he talked she would vanish.

She sat down on a log bench near him and it was a moment before she spoke. She began with little circumvention. Stiegel lived in her mind and she was never conscious of months or years that might intervene between their meetings.

"I have had the news of Elizabeth," she said briefly.

"Aye, Elizabeth is dead. . . ."

"So it is true. Elizabeth Huber, Elizabeth Hölz."

"Think of it, Diane. I had not even the money to bury my wife."

"Non?" Without interest.

There was a tense pause.

"Poor Elizabeth. I gave her nothing of myself. . . ."

"Heinrich, you did not love them. . . . Say it to me—

'twill not hurt them now." She leaned close to him.

"Nay—I did not love them, Diane."

"Ever since you found me in the woods I have loved you, Heinrich. And I have always known that no one else could make you happy. You are free. . . . You will not turn me away now. They've had their chance to make you happy. Now so shall I!"

Her eyes were pleading.

"How faithfully you have loved me, Diane."

"I have never really belonged to anyone but you, M'sieu."

"I had forgotten how beautiful you are. . . ."

"I have never wanted to be beautiful, except for you. Heinrich, we will go away! You want me still. I can see it in your eyes!"

"George Ege wants you too!"

"I have told you before that I loathe him. I can't bear my life with him any longer!"

"If you belonged to me I would kill any man who touched your hand."

"I do not belong to him!"

"A weak little law of your own."

"He owes to you everything he has, M'sieu. Fortune, wife, son! Why cannot you take back what you want?"

"What do you mean he owes me his wife and his son?" Stiegel asked slowly.

Diane shrugged, refusing to answer, and played with the turnip on his desk which held a stub of a candle.

"I don't understand you. I have never understood you. . . . I think you must be a mystery even unto God, Diane."

"Non, non, non, I am so simple, Heinrich. All I want is to live!"

"You think to live is but to have what you want!" he reproved her gently.

"Happiness is not much to ask. I don't love gold or the stupid feathers in my hair."

Stiegel touched her hand.

"I have been the same to you as to the rest. I have always taken from you, Diane . . . and given nothing."

"Non, non, non, that is not true, Heinrich. For years you let me stay near you—let me live under the same roof with you. . . . 'Twas something just to be able to say 'bon jour' to you, M'sieu."

Her words affected him keenly and for a moment he could not answer.

"I've been so weak, Liebling. I've always wanted you to keep on loving me. Living on your emotion like a parasite—getting courage and hope from you . . . from the touch of your hand. . . ."

He had not even been honest with himself, he thought—a man who supposed he held God and the church in his heart.

"Diane," he whispered. "I have ruined your life. . . ."

"Non, non, non, my life is just going to begin!"

"If we should go away together. . . . Oh Diane—without me you still have a chance to be happy!"

"All these years I have been waiting only for this!" she said tensely. "There is no sacrifice I would not make for a day alone with you, M'sieu."

"A year or two, perhaps—and you would be hating me. You have always hated what was weak. . . . I'm a failure. Nobody needs me. I'm . . . ill. . . ."

"Non, non, non, you are not really . . . ill?" Her voice trailed into a whisper.

He made no answer.

"You could soon be well again, in France! Heinrich, we shall run away to France!"

It was a mad suggestion, and for a moment it swept his reason away. New life, new country, new soul!

"A little cottage with a thatched roof," she cried eagerly, "you and Georges and me!"

"It would be like heaven," he returned agitatedly. "I think all my life I have been searching for . . . peace."

"France will be so beautiful, M'sieu," she cried, crushing his hand to her cheek. "Oh my Heinrich—my beloved Heinrich. . . ."

"I can't tell you how I want it, Diane!"

"Ah, mon cher—at last you are not afraid!"

The triumph in her voice hurt him, and reality flooded back once more. It was no use trying to make-believe. There could never be ultimate happiness in such a fantasy. Now the fear of his illness brought all the tenderness of her love to the surface. But if she must live with that illness! That would be different. Diane, who had always scorned the weakness of pain in others—would she not be jealous when it took the place of the passion she would expect from him? And what would be the meaning of life to him with the prop of her love removed?

"Liebling, you would come to hate me. I couldn't bear it!"

"Non, non, non. Si bête!"

"I would come to hate myself. And Georges—we would break his world to bits!"

The long desperate struggle had commenced again. She pressed her hands to her forehead, getting up to tread back and forth in front of the thinning fire. Finally she turned and stood still, staring at him with a strange fanaticism in her eyes. She had built her life on the attainment of his love. She had vowed to herself that he should never know he had fathered her son until he proved that he loved her as unreservedly as she loved him. And now cold calculation was coming between them again. Damn his conscience, she thought. Must it ever stand between them? It infuriated her that she must use this last resource to gain her point.

She leaned close to him, her cheeks scarlet. "You would mind very much, M'sieu—if Georges loathed you?"

"Aye," he faltered. He was suddenly ashamed of the

fondness he harbored for the child.

"To have a son is to live again, n'est-ce pas?"

"I have scarce lived again in Jacob," bitterly.

"He was not born of love," she whispered.

The vague implication of her words stirred him.

"How many of us are born of love, Diane?"

"So few," she answered softly. "Heinrich—I would have borne your sons proudly!"

"I would have lived again in those sons, Diane. . . ."

"I shall still bear your sons," she went on breathlessly. "Heinrich—Georges is not born of duty. . . . He is born of love—moonlight—the brook. . . ."

Stiegel jumped up and faced her, trembling.

"Heinrich! He is your son!"

Quick tears crowded into his eyes.

"You see!" she went on swiftly. "We belong together . . . the three of us!"

He had her in his arms once more, and he had forgotten poverty and hunger and pain. The boy was his! To build for ——

"Diane," Stiegel said softly, trying to steady his voice. "I could never begin to tell you my happiness! 'Tis so deep and sweet . . . I can scarce. . . ."

They stood for a moment, wordless, lost in complete joy.

"It frights you . . ." she whispered.

"How can you know?"

"I feel it, too."

"Diane, I have never loved you like this before."

"The night beside the brook. . . ."

"Nay, then you were part of another world. Now you are my very . . . breath."

He looked into her eyes, kissed her solemnly, and sank down again behind his desk, his head in his hands.

"Georges—my son," he said queerly. "I must think. . . ."

Diane's heart beat so hard that she felt it must sound out

above the cries of the boys in the snow. For a very long time Stiegel did not move.

"It is all going to be different from what I thought," he said half to himself, breaking the infinite silence at last.

"Heinrich!" cried Diane.

He fingered a hornbook absently.

"You do not mean you will not go!" she cried out again, in amazement.

"If it should make him a failure. . . ."

"Non, non, non," desperately. " 'Twas why I told you. So you might see how he needs you, Heinrich!"

"What could I give to him?"

"Your love, your knowledge . . . everything! Oh mon Dieu, Heinrich, you can have no doubt!"

She began to pace the floor again and wring her hands.

"All my life I have waited and waited," she cried frantically. "All my life I have been in agony waiting for you to love me!"

"Georges loves his father," said Stiegel irrelevantly.

"The boy dotes on all that glitters!"

"Ah, my poor Diane—if I should die and leave you alone in a strange country. . . . Deserted in some Paris alley. I am poor, poor. . . ."

"I am not afraid. . . ."

"You are still young and beautiful, my Diane."

"Ah Heinrich, I would sell my soul for you."

He pressed her fingers to his lips.

"Heinrich—you see now that we belong together?"

"Aye, we belong together. . . . But we have no right to take his fate in our hands. George can give him so much more than I. . . ."

"You have tossed away all I have ever given you!" she cried, distracted.

"Diane," brokenly, "do not be cruel to me, I beg of you. I have enough to bear. . . ."

She made no answer, wrenching her hand away from his grip.

"I must try to build again—alone. . . ."

There was a formidable lull.

"Diane, beloved, try to understand. . . ."

She was motionless, her lips thin, her scar like a shimmering, living web. She had done everything that she could. And he had said that he loved her. She could not understand. She had been made so simply, with such primitive desires and instincts. She picked up her muff and the rose kid glove from the table, and she looked at him with her great dark eyes empty of expression.

"Diane, you have made me very happy. . . ."

She squared her shoulders. "You will die triumphant after all, and I . . . Mon Dieu, I will live to be a thousand cruel years!"

Her cry rang in his ears long after she was gone, but echoing in his mind was only one thought, "Georges is my son! Thank God! Georges is my son!"

40

GEORGE WAS waiting at Charming Forge, terrified for Diane's safety. Dinner had been served long since. When she arrived at last, he was uncontrollably angry.

"Did it take so long to give him money that you must return at such an hour?" he rebuked her.

"I tied my horse to a tree. I walked through the woods for hours. I was lost," she answered mechanically.

"Woods! Have you no woods to prowl through at home, but you must experiment in some strange place?"

She scarcely knew that he answered her. Anne was taking her wet clothing.

"Won't be no time 'fore your dinner's hot," Anne exclaimed.

"I don't want food."

"I'll jus' brew you a pot o' tea."

"I don't want tea!" cried Diane. "Go away, all of you! Can't you see I want to be alone!"

"Diane—I'm sorry I was so quick; I was worried," said George, utterly contrite now that he had given vent to his temper.

But Diane would have nothing to do with him, and he

499]

spent the night reproaching himself for the passion which he could never seem to control. Would he and Diane never be at peace?

That night Diane was unable to sleep, and the house once settled, she paced up and down the lower hallway, unconscious of fatigue. George had finally dozed off, chagrined and enraged that she would neither listen to his apologies or anything else he had to say.

Ever since she could remember, she had built her thought of the future on the time when she and Stiegel would belong together, and had felt confident that if she waited long enough they would find happiness at last. Now with the very weapon with which she had hoped to defeat him, she had defeated her own ends.

As she rolled the candle wax into soft balls, she tried to think calmly what would become of her. She knew that either she must never see Stiegel again, or she must accept his decision. What would happen to her if she never saw him again? What would she do with her hours, with her hands? Even in the intervals when she hadn't seen him her hands had always worked for his happiness. A few years more and her child would be gone from home. She thought of George again with a swift revulsion.

Of course it would be painful to be near Heinrich. Now that he knew Georges was his son he would have eyes for nothing but the boy. Would it not be better even now, she thought, staring into the blackness of the night, to tell George Ege the truth? To let him throw her and Georges out into the world? Then Stiegel would have to accept them. Her eyes blazed for a moment. I could *make* Heinrich take me that way, she thought. He would have to accept our love in spite of himself. With a few words to George I could end this torture.

She ran her finger tensely down the strings of the harp, and was amused at the thought of ripping open the quiet night. Heinrich had given her this harp as a symbol of his love. Heinrich, who had once loved music more than anything else in the world. He had been made for music, and now he was a failure. She felt sure that the failure was inexplicably her fault. Why hadn't she made him cling to the thing that he really loved? She had been the one woman in his life who could have resolved his inner conflict. Hadn't it been her duty to find a way to help him? Wasn't the failure her own—not his?

The humiliation of the day swept over her with increasing bitterness, and she thought that any second she must shake George Ege from his fitful sleep and sling the truth in his face.

"I can still have what I want!" she said aloud, and in the empty room her words came back to her like the roar of the sea.

But Heinrich too was to be reckoned with. She closed her eyes and recalled the joy in his face today when she had told him about Georges. After all these years of despair he could be happy. Truly happy, perhaps, for the first time in his life.

"He can still have what he wants, too," she thought painfully. "He wants someone who needs him. He wants . . . Georges."

Georges would go to him willingly, eagerly, she knew. She had talked to Georges about Heinrich since the boy was old enough to listen to her stories, and she knew he thought of Stiegel as some sort of god who had been shabbily treated on earth.

All the years of his childhood she had prepared him for the time when he would hear the truth. And all the years of his boyhood training she had taught him the things Stiegel would want him to know. His early love of music had filled her with a boundless joy. She remembered the poignant moment when he had pulled at Heinrich's bow, and wanted to play the violin, too. Then the cornstalk fiddle Cyrus made for him when he returned to Charming Forge. With what style Georges played it, little as he was! And how Cyrus danced, his old bones creaking with the unaccustomed effort. George would never forgive her, she knew, for having bought the expensive Amati violin for Georges without his knowledge. And yet she had known when he was only ten that no ordinary love of music was hidden in his stubby fingertips; not with his ardor for the sound of wind in the trees; the even clap of the horses' hoofs on a frozen road; the murmur of the brook over stones.

No teacher had ever thoroughly understood his preoccupation, his unformed dreams. They had never been able to hear the deep, soundless things that Georges heard. If Heinrich needed Georges—how much more Georges needed Heinrich, she thought, jealous and weak at the idea that they would love one another, and forget her.

Oh, if only she could learn to be patient! Some day Stiegel must turn to her in spite of himself. Some day after she had built up his pride, and he felt that he had something to offer her. Some day . . . and she would never give up. . . .

She heard heavy bare footsteps above her. George would be charging down to see why she didn't come to bed. She thought fiercely that if he spoke one word she would strike him across the mouth.

"Non, non, non, I shall keep bearing him," she cried aloud. "I shall keep bearing him so that I can give Heinrich what he wants!"

Several days later Diane brought up the subject of Georges' schooling very abruptly as the three of them sat at breakfast.

"The time has come for putting forth Georges," she said. Georges looked up, his spoon poised in the jam jar.

"His place is here with his tutor," replied George. "If he is to follow in my footsteps as he desires he may well learn both his Latin and his ironmongery at once."

"I don't like Rudolph Bechtel," said Georges.

"Then you must learn to like him."

"But he laughs at things I say!" Georges piled the raspberry preserve thickly on his bread.

"Georges has a real talent for the violin," said Diane.

"A violin—that is child's play," retorted George. "Certainly he has talent, but no son of mine shall spend his life strumming a tune!"

"I don't want to spend my life strumming a tune, father. I'm going to make money, too. But I want to keep on studying the violin always—and I know as much about it now as Rudolph, don't I, Cyrus?"

Cyrus stood grinning, a water pitcher balanced on his hip.

"He plays nigh's well as Marsa Baron!"

"Bravo, mon cher!" cried Diane, waving her napkin.

George was snorting. They had a tantalizing way of forgetting that he existed at all. He shoved his coffee cup over to Diane.

"If you know as much as Rudolph Bechtel the time has come for another master," Diane persisted. "If you wish to play better."

"Of course I do!" expostulated Georges, his mouth bulging with bread and jam. "Living jingo, I want to be so many things! Musician, and iron-master. And go to Princeton, and——"

Diane looked up as Georges' eyes dropped self-consciously from his father's gaze. "Then——?"

"Well—I thought if I make a lot of money in the iron business——"

"Oui?"

"I will build a theater for people to hear concerts."

"Then you shall go to study with Baron Stiegel," Diane said calmly.

"By God, that he won't," cried George Ege pounding his fist on the table so that his coffee slopped over. "I'll not have my son going off to some hut to live!"

"Heinrich can teach him the violin better than anyone else," replied Diane haughtily.

"Yes, father!" cried Georges, delighted. "Oh, please!"

" 'Twill give him a sense of value," pursued Diane.

"If he doesn't like Bechtel, I'll get him a new tutor from Philadelphia, and he can live here at the Forge like a gentleman!"

"Where will you find a greater gentleman than Heinrich?" Diane defended stubbornly. "Or a man with more learning and savoir-faire?"

"A man who's a total failure?" scoffed George.

" 'Tis scarce his fault the times and his friends have failed him!" she cried bitterly. "And now you would fail him too, after all you owe him!"

But she knew that he had failed himself and that she was going to make reparation because she loved him.

This was only the beginning of a week of argument. Georges, drawn into the vortex of their battle, scarcely knew how he felt about the change. Diane had always painted the most romantic picture of Stiegel and his prosperous days, and Georges felt that now he was fourteen he was entitled to leave home and see another side of the world. The prospect of studying the violin with Stiegel enthralled him. And yet, he had been very happy all his life at Charming Forge. And if his father was too busy a man to give him much time, he was certainly rich and important. The more they talked about the problem, the more elusive and arbitrary Diane became.

Finally, furious at her tyranny, George went off on a three-day hunting-trip without saying good-bye, and when he returned from this self-castigation he found that she had made the journey to Schaefferstown with Georges alone. She had taken matters into her own willful hands in this crisis. Deliberately given their son out to a broken, old man. Duty! It was amazing that she should be so suddenly obsessed with duty toward Stiegel, a mountebank long ago exposed and punished by fate.

He had been frantic until her return, for he had not even been sure of her destination or her return. But when at last she came home, braced for an explosion of the worst kind, he recalled the bitterness of their recent quarrels, and held her to him in a jealous penitence. It frightened him to think of the destruction they might be heading for, but if she was still angry with him, she seemed only weary and devoid of resistance.

The meeting with Stiegel had been an anti-climax which took all the courage she possessed. She went about her plans as if she were deaf, unheedful of Stiegel's remonstrance.

With her usual celerity, she changed the tenor of his life. He was transferred from Thurm Berg, the formidable empty tower, to Anthony's little vacant house on Market Street.

She spent the nights at the inn, and during the day she made livable the kitchen and the bedroom which they would share. She borrowed furniture from the overwhelmed Anthony, who now lived in Schaefferstown, and who would have still given his wife and his roof and his soul for Diane. She engaged a neighbor's daughter to do the cooking and tend the clothes, and deposited the stunned girl in front of the oven with explicit directions about the cherry pudding. She slashed chintz and hid the heavy four-poster bed inside it. New pots and pans hung from the chimney-place, and shelves were lined with provisions. Even Anthony's wife, Christina, entered into the spirit of the thing, and donated some preserves that had not been popular with her own family. Although she had paid little attention to Stiegel, she declared that from now on he and Georges must spend Sunday with them.

When she left, Diane shoved into Stiegel's hand a five-pound note.

"Georges will need all manner of supply," she said. "A Latin Grammar, a little rock candy, a new strap for his skate, mayhap. . . ."

She touched Georges' fingers lightly to her lips, laid her hand for a fleeting second on Stiegel's arm, and was crying "Au revoir, au revoir," as she flew out to her sleigh.

They watched her from the window.

"Isn't she beautiful?" cried Georges, waving wildly, as Diane flourished her muff.

"Aye. The most beautiful woman in the world."

"And so good!"

"She has been good to me," said Stiegel, touching the boy's shoulder.

"And my father," bragged Georges. "He is known all through the countryside. I would like to be famous too."

"Why?"

"Oh, 'twould be very exciting!"

"Excitement is a short-lived thing. One man can steal it from another. But happiness is deep. No man can take it from another because he cannot reach it."

Georges frowned.

"What is the matter?" asked Stiegel.

"Oh, nothing, sir. Only sometimes I don't understand what you say."

"Then will you make me a promise?"

"Aye," said Georges absently. Diane was tucked in now with bear-robes, and in a moment she would be gone.

"If you do not understand, promise me you will say it over and over to yourself sometimes after your Latin."

"There she goes. . . . Good-bye, *good-bye!* . . ."

They watched her, both of them, until she was out of sight.

The boy lowered his eyes, which were hazy with tears, and turned miserably away from the window.

Alone with his son, Stiegel was more serene than he had been for months. As he watched the boy's dark head tilted close to the violin, his heart raced with pride, and all the dreams and aspirations of his early youth seemed united in him. Georges was part of Stiegel. He loved music. Perhaps the great music that he himself had composed in his hopes would materialize in this boy. He taught him avidly, never weary as long as Georges would concentrate.

Georges was carefree, though sensitive, with high ideals half formulated, a lovable mixture of artist and adventurer. He preferred Stiegel's companionship to that of his schoolmates, who thought he was proud because he was the son of a rich man. The "olden days" in Germany had a peculiar fascination for him, and his eyes sparkled at description of the lavish Philadelphia assemblies, or the early skating parties on the river.

"They must all have been very rich!" he exclaimed.

Stiegel did not answer. He recalled the frown which had crept into Diane's face one time as she ejaculated, "Fi donc! The boy talks ever of money!"

One night, not long after Georges had arrived, they sat in the kitchen, which made an intimate study.

Georges nibbled at a few raisins from a cornucopia. His lessons were spread out on the white pine table before the fire. Stiegel sat on a stool near him, cleaning a rag wick.

"Spargere voces in vulgum ambiguas," murmured Georges, leaning back in his chair at a perilous angle, and seeming to enjoy the brief moment of unbalance.

"You have spoke the same phrase three times," teased

Stiegel with a smile. "Do you specially fancy it, or does it give you trouble?"

Georges' chair erected itself with a surprised jump.

"Ah," laughed Stiegel, "you do not even know what words you have spoke."

Georges laughed too, a little sheepishly. "I was . . . I was wondering if Mozart had writ his music by candle-light."

"Why, Georges?" curiously.

"I could never write music in the day, with the forge a-blazing."

"You would be a . . . an iron-master, like your father?"

"Oh yes, I shall be very rich, but then I——" Georges stopped, suddenly bashful.

"I shall not laugh at your thoughts, Georges."

The boy colored. "My father does not like . . . my maunderings."

"Your father wants you to be an iron-master?"

"Aye, or a student at law."

"And—and your mother—what does she wish you to be?"

"She says I am 'vouloir prendre la lune avec les dents!' "

"The wish of every mother for her son, Georges, nicht?"

The boy shrugged his shoulders. "I do not like laws."

The true son of Diane, thought Stiegel!

"Then do not study law. . . . What else do you think when your grammar lies open before you and you say 'spargere voces in vulgum ambiguas,' and know not that you say it?"

Georges looked for a moment at his master, and then decided to take the leap.

"I think. . . . when I see shadows dance on the wall at night ——"

"Aye?"

"I'faith, I could write music as gay as the Baron's."

Stiegel was agitated.

"My music, how came you to know of it?"

"My mother plays it on the harp. It goes '*la,* la la, *la* la la,' n'est-ce pas?"

Stiegel could not answer. He got up to stir the fire, and threw another log on it. Georges' shadows scurried about the walls and ceiling like mad. Finally Stiegel turned to his son.

"Georges," he said, "put the Latin grammar aside. Perhaps this very night we shall save your soul!"

"But I do not know my lines, sir!"

"'Tis much more important to hark to the shadows. Come, I shall teach you how to mark down what they say."

For an hour they labored over eighth notes. Even the raisins lay deserted. There were strained, excited words, pithy phrases: "More—more Aufschwung! No, a quarter note. Aye, Bestimmt. *La*-la-la . . . like water, nicht?"

The clock striking midnight startled them both. For a moment Stiegel could not think where he was. For hours he had been young again.

Georges sighed deeply and stretched, picking up the violin to play the first note of his amateur composition.

41

As the winter and spring progressed, Diane returned. But George always came with her, and their visits were brief, lacking honesty and spirit. Diane's eyes met Stiegel's furtively, as if they would ask him so much. They always began to talk as strangers, on the subject of the war, drifting off to news of the family which was now so scattered.

"Jerusha is well?"

"Aye . . . and she writes great news of Jacob. He makes his home with Barbara in Virginia, and has took a Rachel Holman to wife. There is an infant son, another Jacob!"

"Jacob, a . . . a *father!*" laughed Diane gayly, and even George smiled at the thought.

"Aye, and a farmer and High Sheriff," added Stiegel proudly.

Diane became solemn. She was jealous of Jacob. The son Elizabeth had borne. She did not want Stiegel to love him as he loved Georges.

When the Eges had gone, the routine of the day always seemed dull. But neither Stiegel nor Georges ever tired of

[510

talking of Diane. At the end of the term, the Eges came to take Georges away.

"Georges has been waiting to play for you," Stiegel said tactfully. "Georges, do the Mozart first. . . ."

The boy got out his violin, and tuned it with a well-practiced air of assurance. His sticky fingers fluttered on the strings.

There was a little ripple of gravy on his shirt-frill. But the bow swayed like wheat in the wind, with utter grace and abandon, thought Diane, her face radiating pride. George Ege sat listening stubbornly.

When the boy finished he inquired, "And what have you learned of ironmongery during all these months?"

Georges, expectant of praise, was a little crestfallen.

"Oh, I know all about that already!" he answered.

George Ege laughed. "You are grown cocky."

"Black shame, George!" cried Diane. "It was *beaut'*ful, mignon. . . . Ah, Heinrich, *you* have done *well!*"

Georges brightened.

"Come, mon cher. . . . Play some more! Your progress is magic!"

"I have a surprise," he admitted, glancing dubiously at George Ege.

He tuned once more with veteran accuracy, and launched into a bright little piece which sang of youth. He repeated the short simple bars with growing ardor, slid his bow into the air with a grand gesture, and bowed.

"Bravo!" cried Diane, moved almost to tears with the success of her child.

"*I* did it," cried Georges, "*I* did it myself. I shall do more. Lots more. Serenades and . . . and symphonies!"

The eyes of Diane and Stiegel met for a brief, painful moment.

"Diane," said George. "Are you ready to leave? I would like to get home before dark."

One night, the following fall, after school had begun, Georges lay before the fire, his Latin grammar dutifully open while Stiegel read before his whale oil lamp. Now that the boy was maturing he seemed to have drawn himself into a shell. He often sat dreaming. Perhaps he was growing too fast, thought Stiegel, or was he still watching shadows dance on the wall? When he sat idly strumming on the desk, Stiegel wondered if a new waltz was being born, for the boy's progress on the violin was amazing. But he no longer chatted with Stiegel as he had formerly, and Stiegel knew that it was of no use to urge his confidence. Georges loved him—that was obvious by the kindly little things he did for him—but he seemed troubled. Georges loved his home, and spoke of it whimsically.

Stiegel read the Bible to him always before they went to bed. But Georges seemed no more moved by the Bible than had Jacob or Barbara. He preferred the Psalms, because they were a pleasing background for reverie, and their rhythm seemed to melt into the apathy of his mind.

Stiegel knew instinctively that things could not last as they were. Georges had begun to be curious about the outside world.

Suddenly he said, "I had a billet from father today. He has been up in a balloon, sir. Fancy, up in the air, and nought to hold him there!"

"Aye, I have heard before of such daring," replied Stiegel, slightly envious in spite of himself. "But what is the use of a balloon?"

" 'Twas the very thing a scoffer said to Benjamin Franklin. What think you Mr. Franklin told him? 'What is the use of a new-born babe?' "

"An excellent rejoinder."

"I told my father once I wanted to go up in a balloon and he said, 'You are always up in the clouds,' and my mother said, 'Dieu merci.' "

Georges paused. "My father says in another year I am to go to the New Jersey College at Princeton and settle down to the business of being a man."

Stiegel's heart leaped painfully.

"You mean . . . you would no longer have time to study your violin?"

"Oh, I shall always find time for that," and he returned to his Latin again, strumming out the declension of a noun with his fingers on the floor.

Stiegel felt saddened. He wondered what it was in youth that caused self-deception. Was it the eternity of years ahead? The belief that time was illimitable? What would he not give now for time, he thought miserably. And yet, after a fashion, he was happy.

All the meaning of life had suddenly resolved itself into his love for this son, into the molding of his talents and a yearning for their fruition. At fifty-three he no longer dreamed of the time when he would reclaim his wealth. A pound was now a treasure which would buy him food, a thing to be slaved for, and not a handful of shillings to be tossed from a carriage window. Money now meant to him only bread and butter for his supper; his world was Georges, and his world had never been so great. A few years more, he and Diane had decided, would see Georges ready to go to a University in Germany. Away from the influence of George Ege, he would be able to give free vent to his genius.

"That is what he really wants," Stiegel told himself over and over. "And no matter what the cost, I shall get it for him."

That year George Ege was appointed a member of the General Assembly of Pennsylvania, and often was away from home for a long period. Diane began to come to Schaefferstown frequently, alone.

One day in the following January, when George Ege had gone to Reading, Diane planned to surprise Stiegel and Georges with a goose dinner. She arrived in Schaefferstown early in the afternoon. Besides roasting a goose, she had decided to experiment with a new fashionable root called the Irish potato, cooking it with butter, sugar and grapejuice, and disguising it with lemons, mace, cinnamon, nutmeg and pepper.

While she was waiting for them to come, Diane lay childishly curled up in the settle before the fire. She was radiantly happy. Her cotton dress was simple, and the thick leather shoes with the peaked toes made her feel that the cottage was her own and that the three of them had always lived there. She glanced occasionally at the table set before the fire, to be sure she had not forgotten the salt or the napkins.

They would be alone again—the three of them! Sitting before the fire, talking of little comfortable things—things that did not matter.

She remembered the first time she had had a meal with them alone in Schaefferstown. Georges had fiddled for her a little, his mouth pursed in concentration—a little streak of brown gravy on the frill of his shirt. She had wondered if he would learn to love Stiegel. If he would ever rouse him and bring the light to his eyes once more. Supposing Georges should inherit his father's genius?

Now two years had gone by; Georges, almost seventeen, was as tall as Stiegel. He no longer had a trickle of gravy on the frill of his shirt. Everything had happened as she planned. Stiegel was supremely happy. And in a year or two when Georges went to Germany, she and Stiegel might at last live out their lives together in poverty and peace.

She spun the goose slowly about on the spit, and took a peek at the steaming cherry pudding. Would they never come? The steady drip, drip of goose fat was counting off the seconds lost.

"C'est l'amour, c'est l'amour, qui tourne le monde ronde!" she crooned, and jumped up again to rearrange the holly which she had draped over the mantel.

Suddenly she heard a scraping of boots on the flagstones, and her heart careened. She opened the door an inch, and stood behind it, elated, her apron thrust over her head to help prolong the secret. They were on the door-step now— on the threshold.

"Bon jour, tout le monde," she cried, curtseying as the door closed.

But as Stiegel came in, Diane saw that he leaned heavily on Georges, and that his face was white. It seemed to her as she helped Georges drag him to the settle that her hands and feet had turned to water. She tried to pull open his stock, but her fingers caught in the worn threads of the linen. Tears of fright trickled down her cheeks, and choked her words.

"D'vin, bête," she cried to Georges, lapsing into French in her excitement.

"Oh, mon Dieu, qu'y a-t-il?" she pleaded, stroking his face and praying desperately for one word of response.

He clenched her hand and his nails cut into her flesh.

"Heinrich—Heinrich . . . speak to me! Ah, mon cher— mon cher. . . ."

Stiegel could die! She was overwhelmed. She had always thought of the two of them as immortal. One day they would find happiness together in vague Elysian fields. It would go on through eternity—through fleeting springs in bloom, through wars, through infinite caress. . . . But now he might die! He was not immortal, like herself. . . .

At last she revived him with smelling-salts and warm wine, but he was so drugged with the apathy which follows

severe pain that he consented to have Georges help him
to bed.

Diane watched Georges while he ate his meal alone.

It was almost midnight before she felt content to go back
to the inn. Georges had tumbled off to sleep on the settle,
and Mrs. Wagner, a neighbor who had agreed to sit up all
night with Stiegel, dozed before a slothful fire. Her knitting
lay on her lap, a mere gesture of industry. She had already
done the work of three women since four o'clock that
morning.

Diane felt exhausted. Her endurance had always been
boundless but tonight she was unbelievably frightened. She
saw that Stiegel was too sick to care whether he lived or
died. She had fought against his will to live ever since she
could remember—but it was quite different fighting against
his will to die. But he could not die! Simply exhaustion from
walking through the deep snow, the doctor had said as he
bled him. Stiegel could not die! This was a silly fancy, bred
of midnight and a darkened room.

What would life mean without Heinrich? So vast, so inconceivable was the answer that she could not call forth
one picture to her paralyzed mind. She looked over guiltily
at Georges; she worshipped her son, but he was someone
she had loved first because of Heinrich. His eyebrows were
puckered crossly as he slept, and his red sensitive mouth
drawn into a pout. His upper lip was covered with a fine,
dark down. He had grown away from her, these last two
years, she reflected with a heartache. She no longer knew
his thoughts and his dreams. Those were for Heinrich, now.

Before Diane left she stole up to Stiegel's room. Leaning
over him as he slept, she realized that he was no longer
young, and her heart cried out again in anguish for their
happiness together, and for the maddening, futile years that
had escaped them.

She kissed his lips softly. His eyes flickered open, and she saw the panic in them was equal to her own.

"Ah, mon cher, where have you been?" she whispered, holding his hand to her breast.

He wondered if she would ever know the pain of the place he had been, and he did not answer.

"Heinrich, you shall come to me to live, and I shall nurse you back to health!" she whispered, and turned away sharply so that he could not see the unaccustomed tears on her cheek.

Diane stayed on for several days until she was certain that Stiegel was recovered, but her heart lay heavy within her as Cyrus drove her back to Charming Forge in the sleigh. It was late at night when she reached home, and the sleigh-bells, like a flippant old music-box, seemed incongruous with the frozen quiet of the hour. The tinkle of a bell for each absurd twinkle of a star. . . . She would not let Heinrich die and go to "the happy hunting-ground" beyond those heartless, glittering stars. . . .

But suppose he would not come to live with them? The two thoughts battled in her weary head without solution. She lay back drunkenly against the bear robe and the stars swam in the inkiness of the heavens. At last she was tired. Very, very tired.

She had utterly forgotten about George—that he might have returned from Reading. The days had sped and she had given them no thought. George stood facing her as she entered the hall; he was wearing his greatcoat and hat, and in his hand was a lantern which teetered a little as he dropped it onto the stairs.

"Where have you been?" he snapped.

Diane held her hand over a candle. Warmth was good. She supposed she must answer him, but she was too tired for a scene. She wanted to be drunk with sleep.

"Where have you been?" George repeated, staggering over to her.

"I have been to Schaef ——"

"Damn you. You're lying to me!"

"I said I have been to ——"

"Stop! You're lying, you little hussy! You told Anne you'd be gone for two days. You've been gone five days. You have a lover!"

She began to laugh in his face, and he was so enraged that he grabbed her arm.

"Don't you lay hand on me, George Ege," she thundered, "or I shall go into the woods and not return. I shall go into the woods . . . to my lover!"

His hand dropped.

"You are bedlam-crazed," she added wearily. "And tomorrow after you have worn yourself insane over my lover I shall tell you about Heinrich's illness!"

"Why didn't you tell me he was ill! Why didn't you send word?" he groaned.

"I never thought of you—even once," she said coldly. She took a Betty lamp from the table, and began to go up the stairs.

George leaped up ahead of her, stopped her.

"Where were you, Diane!" he begged.

She thought of the fiery scenes she had had with George Ege since her marriage, of his incredible jealousy and childishness, of the magnificent egotism which had never let him suspect her love for Heinrich. How she had loved to torture him, and how she had loathed his repentance after a quarrel! She had never been fair to him, of course. She had never really tried to be fond of him. She had only tossed him morsels of affection when she was radiant with hope. Tonight George did not even seem worth the fun of melodrama. There was no use in withholding from him the news.

"Heinrich is very ill."

George faltered a moment. "What's the matter with him?"

"I don't know. When he is better I am going to bring him here."

"Never!"

She stared at him in contempt. "I am *not* going . . . to let him die!"

42

SEVERAL WEEKS LATER, Stiegel came to live with the
Eges at Charming Forge. Diane was too lonely without
Georges, she said, and Georges must continue his lessons
with Stiegel. Besides, Samuel Weiser had just dismissed
the convict who was teaching school in Wolmansdorf because he whipped the boys too cruelly, and Stiegel would
be the very one to take his place.

Stiegel was given a spacious attic bedroom which was
dormer-windowed and bright, overlooking the river and
the orchard. The mansion sat on the hillside, its back to the
fruit trees, gazing down upon the avenue of tenant houses
and barns and offices, like a feudal lord above the salt—
elevated, remote, astute. If George Ege had wanted to surpass his uncle's grandeur, he had well succeeded.

In the spring Diane cooked fat asparagus for Stiegel, and
garnished it with a savory Indian sauce of cornmeal and
peppers. Soon she produced tortes which would have made
old Frau Stiegel envious.

Each morning Cyrus wakened him with a bowl of yellow
flowers of Diane's arranging. Again, of his own accord, he
would bring some mittens that he had knitted in his spare

time, or an old bearskin muff or pair of breeches that George had discarded. It was seldom that he came up empty-handed. Sometimes he had a demijohn of wine or some candied lemon-peel that Anne had made specially for Stiegel. He loved to wait on his old master, polishing his shoes, cleaning the hearth, and shooing dust from one object to another with a turkey-wing. He knew that no matter how long he lingered, or however many duties he forgot, Diane would never reprimand him if he said he had been with Marsa Baron.

The attic room which George had so gracelessly given Stiegel became a galaxy of comforts. His lowboy held a red glass jar of rock candy, a container of snuff, and the latest almanacs and news-letters. There was a desk for his papers and books, and a cabinet filled with music. Michael and Georges lounged there often, keeping him company.

When summer began, Stiegel protested that he must leave, as Georges' studies were over. Pride would not allow him to remain unemployed under George Ege's roof, he told Diane. She laughed at him. Georges must not get lax during vacation, she argued; and who would give him lessons on the violin if Stiegel left?

Because Stiegel's love for Diane and Georges was greater than his pride, he relented, and spent several hours a day with Georges over philosophy, teaching him in German.

Sometimes they took their books and violins down into the orchard, and Diane joined them, listening in silence. Summer had coaxed the phlox into bloom. There were brilliant beds of it edged with sweet alyssum, and deep purple morning-glories rambling over everything from the ice house to the barn.

The house seemed almost a part of the outdoors. The interior was a cool green and white with unexpected splashes of color or chintz. The wide front door stood open always, and bees and butterflies and men alike were free to enter and wander through. Flowers were in profusion everywhere. Ivy twisted itself from a little table up through the posts of the stairway, and sprays of blossoms hung from the chandelier in the hall.

At first the informality of the household upset Stiegel's systematic German mind. There were no laws. Anne was allowed to smoke her pipe in the kitchen while she peeled potatoes, and her pigtails of tobacco hung from the rafters within easy reach. Georges and Michael, who was now a partner in the business, began their fencing on the little plateau to the rear of the ice house, and often one would spike his opponent into the hall of the mansion and out of it again, spearing him into a boxwood shrub at the top of the stone stairs. Kittens and dogs of all colors and varieties dozed throughout the place.

Often, Stiegel and Georges and Diane hiked into the woods, finding a stream in the shade beside which they ate the lunch Diane had brought in a pannier. Diane lay back then on the fresh summer moss, her calash hung on an infant spruce. Happiness seemed quickly to bloom within her when she could look up into the sky. She gave every insect, every tiny shoot some pompous Indian name, and her pupils laughed over them and tried to repeat the gibberish.

When they rested in the meadow, she made long clover chains for Stiegel, and crowns of dandelion for Georges. She nibbled at curious berries which would have poisoned any mortal. They stained her fingers with bright dye, and she laughed—as she sighed that she would ne'er be a lady again, alack! She brought back to the house an extravagance of wild flowers, tied with one of her sheer lace mitts, and arranged them in a wooden porringer. If the heat simmered lazily in the valley, she took off her shoes and stockings at the first little creek, and heedless of her company, gathered colored pebbles which attracted her eye. Once, as the day lay gloaming in the brook, she sang softly to them—melodious French songs and uncanny Indian chants, and Stiegel listened to her, bewitched and thrilled, fearful of seeing her mingle with the underbrush and become a myth.

These hours in the woods were mellifluent, infinite. They put a certain peace into Stiegel's soul, a composure he had prayed for in desolate moments, and never found. There was nothing that mattered when the sun beat mightily into his blood—neither poverty nor lingering pain. Even death could not be so formidable if it came softly in the August sunshine, with Diane smiling close.

He had never been afraid of death because it had always seemed so remote, and he had never considered it with any philosophy of his own. But the thing that seemed to hover about him now with every attack of illness was not what he had distantly thought of as death. It was too close, too personal, something he dreaded because he was only learning now to live. And yet infirmity was creeping on him so persistently that he could no longer do a man's work. The short walks to the village tired him, and the oppressive noon heat. He was old. But he must not worry Diane. If he could help it, she must not see that he wasn't well.

One evening Georges and Diane sat on the floor of the parlor, mending music with flour and water, an oil lamp between them. Dinner had been dull. The cutlets had been dry (Anne was growing too fat for easy locomotion, thought Diane). George had a headache and had lost his temper when Cyrus dropped a wine glass on the hearth. Now he was scribbling at his desk. He had a thousand letters to write, for he was making contacts with some new wholesale houses in Philadelphia. Michael, who was usually jovial, had gone sparking to the next little village.

After a short walk on the terrace, Stiegel joined them.

"Shall I help you now with that andante movement?" he asked Georges, watching him with affection.

"I'm going to ride over to see the clothes Mr. Williams bought in Paris. Father says they're the finest he's ever seen," Georges replied without looking up. As an afterthought he added, "Thank you the same, sir."

The eyes of Stiegel and Diane met uneasily as Georges scraped the flour off his fingers. A moment later he ambled out.

"Clothes!" cried Diane scornfully.

"He's young," Stiegel defended him.

"But *clothes!*" she repeated skeptically.

Stiegel smiled at her with lenience.

"Sometimes I can't understand Georges," she said in a low voice, glancing at the back of George Ege. "He says one minute music means everything in the world to him and the next minute he forgets all about it and counts the days until the Christmas parties."

"Genius won't be hurried."

"Do you *really* think he has genius?" she asked, as if the question were new.

"I don't know. I had genius in my fingers, too. . . . But that isn't enough."

"Oh Heinrich, I am so afraid for him," she sighed, crumpling the Turkey cotton of her dress with anxious, pasty hands.

As the mantel clock hammered out seven George rose and stretched. He had become more wiry with age; his hair, which had grown thin and grayish, was dyed a rich brown, harshening his face, and seeming to emphasize the fullness of his lips. But he dressed in the latest mode.

The fresh odor of sealing wax sweetened the air. He came over to where Diane was sitting, stooped beside her and examined a mended sheet. He was in a better mood now. He lifted her hand and kissed it, laughing at the little crumbs of paste. When Stiegel was present, she doubly resented any show of affection from George.

"I must go over an account with Nassel. I shan't be long," he said.

"How is the bad head?"

"Something better. 'Twas hunger, p'raps!" He kissed her hand again.

She leaned against the wing chair, passive, and he bent over and pressed his lips to hers.

"Good-bye," he said aloud, and then whispered in her ear, "Diane, I have never enough of you. . . ."

"Then why don't you give me what I want?" she asked cruelly.

Stiegel's eyes clove to one word of the almanac in his hand.

George pulled over a stool and sat on it, close to her. He began to twiddle a marcasite button on his waist coat.

"*Stop!*" Diane wanted to scream, but she bit her lips.

"What have I ever denied you?" he asked with real solicitude.

"A dozen times I've broached the subject of Georges' schooling, and you won't even listen," she said darkly.

"You both want him to go abroad!"

"Mais oui, he is the son of a gentleman!"

Stiegel laid aside the almanac. He did not like talking to George Ege. Beneath George's pseudo-deference his lack of respect was obvious. But this matter had been so close to his heart for months that it was difficult now to keep the concern from his voice.

"Send the boy abroad," Stiegel pleaded.

"You deemed the Princeton school good enough for me!" retorted George.

"But Georges has dreams. . . ."

"He will get nothing in Germany which he cannot have here in the colonies!"

"Why do you hate his music so much?" Stiegel cried.

"Do you think I want Georges soft-eyed with love songs

and waltzes? I want him to do a man's work in the world!"

Stiegel flinched, and Diane's eyes blazed with fury at the insult.

"Soft-eyed if he goes abroad; soft-tongued if he goes to the Princeton school," she exploded.

"Come now, Diane," George rallied, "What would you do if you were to lose him to music? Germany is another world."

"For once," she answered scornfully, "I am not thinking of myself!"

"I can't help the boy much longer," begged Stiegel, "his knowledge and his skill are beyond me. Now he needs a master! And the kind of life which will keep his mind on his work. If you could but take him to Leipzig, George. . . ."

"Georges has told me he wants to go to the New Jersey College. He's all but eighteen. He's man enough to speak for himself!"

"George," and Stiegel's words trembled with pent up emotion. "Think if he should reach forty or fifty—and then find that it is too late! If only you would give him a year or two abroad—now—while his dreams are real! If he were unhappy he need not stay. . . ."

"If he's unhappy at the Princeton school, he can change his mind."

"But then it might be too late! Even now he has lost something. . . ."

"I don't want my son to be a musician," George summed up, sharply. "What would he ever give to the world but half-starved children?"

"A man can give nothing to the world if his soul is not at peace," miserably.

Diane was white with anger. Sometimes she thought she must pound George with her two hard fists. "Can't you see how he—he *wilts!*"

" 'Tis natural he's glum! He needs companions of his own age—youth and levity!"

The words smote Stiegel as if they had been a physical blow. George might be right, he thought painfully. Perhaps this music had only been a flare after all, and the boy's ultimate happiness lay in conventional paths. Perhaps this was just selfishness, wanting Georges to know the career he himself had missed. But somehow he could not help but believe his son was destined for greater things than merely becoming rich. They had worked together on notes too many times late into the candlelight, seeing visions and hearing music that mortal ears couldn't hear. It was not so long ago that Stiegel had been a tow-headed boy of seventeen in Cologne, filled with his own dreams, hating the intrusion of the outside world. Not so long ago that now he couldn't recognize the same dreams in another when he saw them.

"I only want him to be . . . happy," Stiegel murmured, half to himself.

George Ege walked over to the desk, as if the subject were closed, and picked up a report.

"Till fall twelvemonths you will scarce know him," he said with assurance.

Diane crumpled the sheet of music that she had been mending. "If you will not let him go abroad, then neither shall I let him go off to college with a parcel of fops! He shall stay at Charming Forge and Heinrich shall tutor him!"

Stiegel went out and slowly climbed the stairs, and George slammed some books on the desk to show that no matter what Diane said he would still have his way.

The argument went on for weeks, and ended in compromise. In the early fall Stiegel agreed to stay on as Georges' tutor. But the decision had been difficult for him. It would not be easy living in the house with George Ege's hostility. And he knew that his staying would only increase the discord between Diane and George. It was strange, he thought, how he wanted Diane to have happiness and yet did not want her to be happy with George.

Diane had been adamant about his remaining.

"If you do not stay I shall leave George Ege," she told him.

"Perhaps we've been wrong, Liebling. Perhaps we're only trying to fulfill our own dreams in Georges."

"Non, non, non, Heinrich, you *know* that's not true. And now when he needs you most, you would desert him!"

It was hard to tell what the boy was feeling. He worked for hours every day on his music. Sometimes he worked on it late into the night, with zest. Most of the time he was moody. Often he deserted it for some apple-butter boiling, or for a business journey into Reading with George Ege. For days afterward he would be filled with a feverish gayety, neglecting lessons, and seizing his mother about her slim waist to skirmish her off in a waltz.

Stiegel felt that if he could be sure of Georges, he would be completely happy for the first time in his life. Every minute that he worked with his son was precious. If only the boy would talk to him as he had when he was still a child. He wondered painfully if he had ever said or done anything to rebuff him. Now the thought even came to him in his most harrowed moments that perhaps he wouldn't live to see Georges a man. It was enough of a punishment that the boy would never carry the name of Stiegel. But to die with anxiety for him in his heart. . . .

That fall and winter Diane did all she could to force Georges to some conclusion about himself. Stiegel could never be perfectly well without contentment, the doctor had said. And he could never be contented without being sure of Georges. The three of them played together often at the harp and violin, and she worked on music so difficult for her that only her invincible spirit could master it. To encourage Georges to work up programs, she arranged small musicales at the church in Wolmansdorf and at home.

George Ege disregarded her doggedness and she did not seem to care what he thought or did. She was only living with him to give her loved ones what they needed. Nor did she feel guilty in her shabby treatment of him. He had already had more than he deserved, and it did not occur to her to measure in love rather than in years.

In October she made the long journey with Georges to Philadelphia to introduce him to a famous violinist who was giving concerts there. She had taken him on the pretext of having him outfitted for the winter, and George Ege was wild-eyed when she told him nonchalantly that Georges had had an audition with Fenili.

"What did he say?" Stiegel asked eagerly. He had known all along the purpose of her trip.

"How he kissed Georges and hugged him!" laughed Diane happily, throwing aside her shawl and calash. "He thought he *must* have him in Italy to teach! Mon Dieu, he said Georges played like a seraphim, and he played not half so well as he plays at home!"

Georges flushed. Fenili's kisses had not flattered his manhood.

The evening of his return Georges went to Stiegel's room to watch him play chess with Michael. After Michael had departed with a yawn over his defeat, Georges fingered a castle silently, and Stiegel waited till the boy was ready to talk.

Finally Georges said, "Signor Fenili—is he very great?"

Stiegel paused, his stock in his hand. "Aye, Georges, very great."

"I played for him—Bach, Mozart—your waltz."

Stiegel's pulse gave a lurch.

"And he said, 'Surely, this cannot be something *I* have never heard!' I told him aye, and he said, '*You* have writ this? Ecco! I can see the very mountains and the eyes of the peasant Mädchen in love. There—that is the shuffle of their feet. Now their hearts beat to the moonlight as they dance!' "

Stiegel waited, his stock in his hand.

"I told him I had composed the 'Marche Fiévreux,' but that I could not do music so good as the valse. And he said, 'Ah, but signor, if you will but try you can!' "

Stiegel laid his hand gently on his son's shoulder.

"Are you going to try, Georges?"

"I don't . . . know."

"My score is all yellowed with age," Stiegel said slowly, "and I thought not to part with it so long as I live. But tonight I will give it to you. Do with it what you wish. . . . Make it . . . come to life, Georges!"

43

CHARMING FORGE was never quite so gay as the following winter. The house was filled to overflowing with guests who came for Christmas and stayed into the New Year. There were all manner of festivities, charades, a masquerade including half the countryside, and games and practical jokes. At night Stiegel could see the fires of the barbecue on the frozen river, and hear singing and shrieking and the music of fiddles.

When there were guests, he ate meals in his room. It was a tacit agreement between him and George Ege that he should not partake of their social life. Nor had he any desire to do so. The emptiness of their carousing struck him again and again, and he thought the house must be filled with Molly M'Calls.

Georges had moved up to share his room. The boy flew in and out like mad. He seldom seemed to have enough time to throw aside his skates and woolen scarves, and change to velvets. His books lay untouched in Stiegel's desk, and for days his music huddled in a slovenly mass where Cyrus had dumped it when he dusted.

"Marsa Baron," said Cyrus, hobbling about with his turkey wing, "Marsa Georges ac' like he done los' his brains and was scurryin' round to find 'em."

"He's young," commented Stiegel. "He needs youth and levity!"

"A'int no parties so gay as de olden days."

He set Stiegel's tray of lunch on the little piecrust table before him. "Mistress Ege make the cherry puddin' 'thout no help, Marsa Baron."

"But Mistress Ege, she has a thousand guests!" He did not trust himself to look up from the perfect brown crust of the pudding.

"She done say . . ." Cyrus glanced over his shoulder, his face puckering into myriad wrinkles. "She done say de guests can hobnob wid de debbil!"

Stiegel looked over the tray of tempting food, the pheasant with its sherry sauce and the wild honey and hot biscuit. Every day the lunch had been just as appetizing. Every day Diane had looked in on him once or twice, flopping into a big chair, and murmuring, "Mon Dieu . . . what peace!"

Occasionally, with her arm through his, she had sauntered with him on the verandah in the dark. On New Year's night she left the company to its hilarity and slipping on a fur cape, joined him in a stroll.

"I could kill her!" she exclaimed, flinging back her head to breathe in deeply the cold night air.

"Who is she, and what crime has she committed?" laughed Stiegel.

Diane walked quickly up and down the verandah, past the two great boxwoods with their mushy hoods of snow.

"Tabitha, the little green-eyed cat! And she's crushed every ounce of sense out of Georges. Why, he's only a baby!"

"He must begin sometime," laughed Stiegel, thinking of Minnie in Cologne.

"But this is no innocent flirtation. She has her eye on the wealth of the Forge—I'll bow to that!"

"Come, Diane, 'tis only normal for a boy of eighteen to be flattered with pretty words and a pretty face. Don't distract yourself further."

"But she's a widow," cried Diane. "All of twenty, with a child running about our feet. And she's up to Georges' shoulder, which makes him seem twice the man!"

Stiegel was amused at the tiger attitude of Diane toward her young, and yet her conviction disturbed him a little. Georges was a handsome boy, tall enough for twenty, and with a certain air of reserve that seemed to give him added age.

So Tabitha's child was the little man who had ridden in so gallantly on the Yule-log! The little man who sat drugged with sleep watching the grown-ups long after dark. And Tabitha ——

"There, that's Tabitha—in the deep red velvet," exclaimed Diane, stopping before the widow.

"She's pretty ——"

"She's a cat!" said Diane.

They stood silent for a moment, watching the people shift like bits of colored paper in a kaleidoscope.

"Isn't he beautiful?" she asked, warmly, as Georges picked up his violin from the harpsichord.

"Yes, he is beautiful. He is like you, Diane."

"Non, non, non. He is like you, M'sieu. So tall and . . . and proud."

After a moment, she whispered, "You are lonely, Heinrich. . . ."

"No—I am very happy."

"But I am lonely. I wake in the morning and it is another day. Another day which does not belong just to the two of us. And in my heart I am always waiting. . . ."

He gripped the small hand which lay in his own.

"Heinrich, hold me close to you. . . . Please, Heinrich. I am very lonely. . . ."

He drew her close to him and kissed her, touched with her sadness. "Don't feel alone . . ." he said. "No matter what happens . . . beloved."

And he watched at the window as she went slowly back to her guests.

All the impressions of Christmas which he would carry into the New Year were glimpses of luxury seen from the dark. It was strange that he should notice things about the house and people he had never seen before, now that he looked in from the quiet, frosty night. There was the infinite row of R's of the white painted molding, so evenly carved by hand; the long satin candles quietly tipped with flame; the cupboards—no orderly row of books or sedate gathering of plates, but a chaos of birds'-nests, music, glass flowers, and tiny china men.

Diane sat at the harp, holding the maudlin gathering hushed as she sang and played. What a lovely picture she made in the palest of yellow, a coral brooch at the top of her fichu; mirth on her lips, and loneliness in her eyes:

> "Mariann' s'en va-t-au moulin,
> Mariann' s'en va-t-au moulin,
> C'est pour y fair' moudre son grain;
> C'est pour y fair' moudre son grain;
> A cheval sur son âne,
> Ma p'tit mamzell' Marianne,
> A cheval sur son âne, Catin,
> S'en allant au moulin."

How the eyes of George Ege devoured her while she sang, and how his fingers nervously picked at the grisly-edged music!

Stiegel turned abruptly away and paced up and down on the wet flagstones, and the applause and shouts followed him.

How they all drank and lolled and screeched! Yes, Georges was a prisoner. Stiegel had seen the lace of Tabitha's fichu brush his hand as she made a pretense of looking at the musical snuff-jar. They were all prisoners in there, after some fashion or other. Prisoners to lust, or gold, or wine. Or like George Ege, prisoner of a love which would never belong to him.

No one even half free, thought Stiegel, but himself, looking in from the dark.

He was dozing off to sleep when Georges came up to bed some hours later. Georges threw off his coat, and in the reflection of one mirror, Stiegel saw Georges surveying himself in another. For a moment the boy gazed at his reflection quietly, his black eyes gleaming with excitement. Then he put his hand to his cheek, and proudly caressed his whiskers. His chest expanded slowly, his shoulders pushed back, and for the first time he seemed conscious of muscles and hands.

"Tabitha," thought Stiegel, "has awakened him."

Georges undressed slowly, munching at an apple, and Stiegel lay quiet, for he did not want to embarrass him. He felt rather shamefully that he was stealing a glimpse into Georges' soul. It seemed hardly fair to spy on his first intoxicating love. Surely each youth had a right to protect this from the eyes of cynical middle age.

Georges' hum seemed fitful, like the spurt of the candle which held him in relief for a second against the shadows. The melody was a new minuet which Stiegel did not recognize. Through half-closed eyes he watched Georges bowing low over an imaginary hand.

"Tabitha," whispered Georges throatily. "Tabitha, I love you!"

Somehow the words hurt Stiegel more than any rebuff. The tall dark youth had belonged to Diane and him—until now. After this he would always belong to some woman or other.

Georges handed his phantom about until he had hummed the minuet to a close. Then he stood solitary and dejected in the middle of the room, and glanced cautiously at Stiegel.

"If I play ever so softly . . ." he mused, and pulled out his violin from a muddle of clothes.

There seemed no music sweet enough for Tabitha tonight, and he began to improvise, beginning with an unfinished phrase of Stiegel's score. The perfume of Tabitha was in his blood. He must create something for her far more beautiful than mortal ears had ever heard! Surely she must be infatuated with him, as he was with her. . . . Why weren't there any notes to sing her fragrance, her softness, the magic of her touch? . . . Sometime she would inspire him to write whole operas, whole symphonies!

"Life is very long," he thought dreamily, his fingers hesitating, "and life is very sweet. Tonight for the first time in my life I am completely alive! No one could ever have felt quite like this before. If only I could tell Tabitha these things. . . . Yet how exquisite a pain to keep them hidden in one's heart! She let me kiss her. She let me kiss her long! She loves me. . . ."

He repeated over and over again the little melody that had come to his finger-tips, and when at last he jotted down the notes on his score the moon shone in with a long white light.

Before he stepped into the high bed beside Stiegel he held the candle still and looked down at his tutor with mingled affection and pity.

"It will break his heart when I start work here at the Forge," he thought ruefully. "And I can't bear to tell him why I'm going to stay. . . . He'd never understand that it would be torture across the ocean from Tabitha. . . . Never understand what it means to love like this. . . . He's old and broken. I'm young, thank God! And I have all of life ahead of me. . . . I'll have everything. Everything!"

Several days later George Ege sat in his office, taking care of some neglected business. A few of the guests had already departed. There was a mid-afternoon lull now in the activities, and George found it an unexpected relief to be in the quiet of the office with work spread out before him.

He was a little surprised when Georges knocked and walked in. The boy was not in the habit of seeking him out. They faced one another a little self-consciously.

"I'd like to . . . to talk to you, sir," Georges stammered.

"Of course! Sit down. . . . No trouble with your mother?"

"No . . . but . . . but there will be!"

George pushed his chair around, curious at the feverish statement.

"I . . . I don't know how to go about telling her. It's going to break her heart!"

George fingered his box of snuff. "What are you trying to tell me?"

The boy took a deep breath. "I'm going to marry Tabitha!"

"You're going to . . ." George burst out into a laugh.

"Don't laugh at me!" cried Georges, turning scarlet. "I've already spoke to her. . . . She's going to marry me as soon as I become a partner in the business."

George Ege sobered. "I'm sorry. . . . You seem so young."

"I'm eighteen."

"Almost eighteen. . . ."

"Father—I want to start in the business at once."

George did not answer. He was thinking of Diane, that Diane would not allow the boy to marry. That she would be furious, and if he took Georges into the business now, there might be the permanent breach between himself and Diane that he had dreaded for years. She would accuse him of deliberately ruining Georges' career.

"I would prefer to see you continue your schooling until you are older," he said.

Georges' eyes were stubborn. "I've got to make money. I can't marry her on a . . . a song."

There was a note of smug satisfaction in his father's answer.

"So you are giving up your music?"

"Not giving it up—no, sir. It's just that now I've got to have money. . . . I thought you'd understand," miserably.

"Georges, I do understand. I've always understood you. Always known that this passion of music would occupy your mind until something more important came along. I know what it means to love. Know all the normal things you are going through now. If you were twenty I wouldn't hesitate to say yes at once. I'd feel sure you knew what you wanted. But seventeen. . . ."

George paused, picking at the sponge on his desk. "You've never come to me in your life. The only reason you come to me now is because I can give you what you want and your mother can't. But Georges, I've always had hopes for you the same as she has. And if they were different maybe it's because I can see farther ahead. Because I can understand better what a man wants as he grows older—a home and children. They take money, Georges. Money and hard fighting with the outside world. . . ."

"Then you will start me at work?"

"This has come to you very sudden, hasn't it?"

"Aye—but that makes no ——"

"Georges, you would do well to consider before you take this step. I don't want to influence you. Wait till Tabitha is gone. I know what she does to you, now. You no doubt think I'm too old to . . . to know passion. . . . Well, I'm not. . . ." He got up and stood before Georges, his fingers crumpling the paper beneath his hand. "I love your mother more madly than the day I married her. Every time I hear her voice . . . her step. . . ."

"That's the way I feel about Tabitha, too," thought Georges, strangely stirred at his father's emotion. But his own love was too new to share with anyone else in common words.

"Don't marry her until you make sure that she loves you. . . . Don't marry her and go through the years waiting . . . and hungry. . . ."

"I know she loves me!" triumphantly.

"Tabitha's older than you. She's . . . we'll talk of it again when she's gone. . . . I want to help you, Georges. But you must decide for yourself. You're going to be giving up music as a career, something you've wanted all your life for something you can't be sure about."

"But I *am* sure, father."

"Come back to me in another month."

Georges hesitated; he had wanted to tell Tabitha tonight that as soon as she left he would be starting in work at the Forge. If only they could all see Tabitha through his own eyes!

"There will be no use—mentioning it—to anyone else then," he suggested.

He returned down-heartedly to his room to get his hiking boots.

Stiegel laid aside "Hamlet," which he had been reading, and getting down his long clay pipe from the mantel, began to smoke.

"The house is strangely quiet," he remarked.

"Aye. The ladies are packing, and the gentlemen have settled down to dramming and Congress."

"By tomorrow the company will be gone, then?" Stiegel surmised.

"Aye." Georges looked up for a moment as if he would add something, then flushing, proceeded to change his shoes.

"Are you going to brave the weather?" Stiegel asked.

"Michael and I are making a trail in the fresh snow."

"'Twill be well to get the heat of the parlor out of your brains!"

Georges did not answer. He was in no mood for banter. The hours between now and tomorrow when the last sleigh should go were dwindling too fast.

Stiegel stood at the window watching the two boys heading for the orchard. Darkness had begun already to creep out of the woodland and settle in a violet mist in the valley.

Stiegel looked over the music which Georges had hastily jotted down. He was tempted to play it, for the tune had lingered in his mind the entire day. But it seemed sacrilege to attempt it, a lovely haunting song not yet perfected or dedicated.

It was some time after Cyrus had been up to light the candles that Stiegel was taken unaware by a knock on the door. He was amazed to find Tabitha before him. The fragrance of her scent was borne in to him with a warm staleness of pine from the decorations below. Stiegel could hear the mingling of voices and laughter.

"Georges is not yet returned?" she inquired, her eyes sweeping in the details of the room, and then she went on without waiting for an answer. "I've come for his violin and music! You can't think how dull it is; Madame Curlin has told all her jokes for the millionth time. But now Thomas Waite is inspired. We are compiling an orchestra! Luddy, but 'tis cold up here."

She drew an Indian shawl about her, and her wrists in their long tight apple green sleeves jangled with a dozen hair bracelets.

"I can't give you Georges' violin. I'm sorry," said Stiegel.

"Ah, that's where you are wrong, Baron. You are Baron Stiegel, of course? I have seen Madame Ege take refuge from our noise!"

Stiegel restrained himself from giving a tart reply.

"Thomas Waite plays the violin, and Henry Jackson the mandolin. If we can find Madame Ege we will coax her to play the harp. With a paper comb 'twill be quite complete. *I* shall be the prima donna. . . . Oh, what think you of a musical glass or two, and a portmantua to drum!"

"If the glass has been too well drained, I would not advise it!"

"La, Baron, what wit!" She picked up Georges' violin, and fingered the pile of music.

"Madame, be so kind as to lay down the violin. Georges permits no one to touch it."

"What odd notes—like a flight of angels. . . . Has Georges writ this, Baron Stiegel? 'To Tabitha.' . . ."

Stiegel reached out to rescue the music from her, but she was too quick. She snatched it from the pile and hid it deftly behind the apple-green taffeta of her skirt.

"I am Tabitha, Baron," she announced. "The piece is writ to me. Who has a better right to it than I? Georges would only sing it to the midnight. And that would be great waste. We shall thump it out gayly downstairs."

He saw that she had enough punch to be refractory.

"Please, Madame Tabitha," he begged. "The boy would die of shame to have everyone see his effort!"

"I'll be able to console him!" she laughed.

"His music means more to him than anything in the world!"

"Ah, then he belies me, the rogue."

Stiegel was so furious that he could have shaken this tantalizing little woman until she was limp.

"Madame Tabitha, I beg of you! . . . Georges is a sensitive boy. He is young. He is not hardened."

Her stubborn green eyes thwarted him. "Is he so tender you must still rock his cradle, Baron?"

" 'Twould break his heart."

She smiled at him impishly, and Stiegel repeated the words to himself. " 'Twould break his heart." But would it break his heart? "It would have broken my heart once," thought Stiegel. "If his music means anything to him but play. . . ." The thought lingered in his mind as he stared at her challenging green eyes.

"I'm sorry, Madame Tabitha," he said shrewdly, "I have forgot myself. A guest of the house has free access to the house. Here, another composition of Georges', Marche Fiévreux. And . . . his score."

Stiegel handed her the music with a bow.

"I have been told the ladies could not resist you, Baron Stiegel!"

He turned abruptly and walked to the window, and in a moment he heard the door close behind her. Georges would never forgive him for this. But no matter. He hoped to God they would be murdering the piece as Georges entered the house, slicing it to bits with buzzing comb, shrill singing, and shrieking violin.

Surely Georges and Michael must return soon. He paced up and down the room, unable to keep his hands from trembling. Finally he opened the door; the din of the new orchestra pierced the house to the ceiling. In the distorted notes, Stiegel recognized Georges' song. Someone must have written impromptu words, for Tabitha's voice wailed of love and hearts, and trembled on the high notes independent of her orchestral accompaniment.

Sickened with the fanfare, he went back to his room again, to stare into the blackness of the night until Georges should come.

44

A SHORT TIME later Stiegel heard the stamping of Georges' heavy boots up the stairs, and the moment of hesitation before he entered seemed eternal. Dropping his violin on the bed, Georges stood staring at Stiegel, rage and unbelief in his eyes.

"She—she told me . . . you gave them to her!"

"Does it displeasure you so much?" answered Stiegel calmly.

"My violin—he was sawing at it. . . . He—he broke the bridge! And my score. . . ."

"Your father gave Madame Tabitha permission before me."

"But you knew how I felt—you must have known!"

"I thought you would be proud to find them playing the song; Madame Tabitha said you had writ it to her, and ——"

"I tore it to bits under her nose!"

Georges turned from Stiegel furiously, and began to pull from the drawers of the lowboy a tangle of stockings, skates and small-clothes, dumping them in a pile on the floor. He would not sleep in the same room with this Judas another night.

"They were all so very bored," said Stiegel, "and they
thought ——"

"They . . . they laughed at me!" cried Georges, sinking
down onto a chair, and letting the angry tears slip through
his fingers.

Stiegel walked up and down the room, aching to comfort
him.

"Nobody understands," sobbed Georges. "Nobody cares.
. . . I thought you knew—thought you knew what I
felt. . . ."

"Georges, I beg of you ——"

"I hate everybody in the world!"

"Perhaps it is only yourself you hate. . . ."

"Your score—'twas all spilled full of wine!"

"Georges, these are your guests!"

"Pox them for a tipsy lot of fools!"

"But they are the friends of your father," said Stiegel
tensely, "you will go to college with them, do business with
them, marry among them. And some day you will be tipsy
with them and laugh at . . . today!"

"No, no, no, never. I have told them to get out of the
house at once!"

Stiegel was stupefied. "You have told them ——"

"Aye, my father will probably horsewhip me; then I shall
run away ——"

"Georges, you must forgive them, and apologize! They
are the fortunate rich," Stiegel went on desperately. "And
you—*you* are the fortunate rich!"

What had he done? There was little triumph in seeing
Georges as disillusioned as this.

"You must forgive me, Georges—for bringing you this
heartache!"

"Why should I forgive you when you've betrayed me!
I thought you loved the things I loved, and—you knew what
I felt. . . . Why have you sat with me late in the night

over one note? And—and why did you give me your score? Why have you done these things, I say?"

"Georges, please try to under——"

"All I can understand is that you've all been deceiving me. . . . And I hate you. . . ." Georges straightened, his back against the wall. His eyes glowed with a black intensity. "And you—I hate you most of all!"

Georges gathered an armful of clothes, and dragged them out of the room, trying to wipe the tears from his face on a velvet coat which he carried.

Hours later in bed Stiegel listened to the dripping snow, and somehow it soothed him to think of it running in little rivulets out to the sea. There was something calming in the flux of Nature, he thought. Tonight a quivering pain like burning wires ran through him. He had not felt it so sharply for months, and now he caught his breath in the terrible agony.

Before he slept, he heard Georges' step on the stairs. The boy paused in the doorway, his wretched eyes finding Stiegel's.

"I shouldn't have said that. . . . I'm sorry. . . ."

"God bless you, Georges," whispered Stiegel, rejoicing.

Georges was gone. The room was lonely without the brightness of his scarlet cheeks and his anger. Georges had hated him most of all, he said. Then surely Georges had loved him most of all! Foolish that he had ever had any fears for the boy.

The next afternoon Stiegel dragged himself slowly through the oozing road to Wolmansdorf to buy a peace offering for Georges. He wondered what the boy would like best. Some day he would tell Georges why he had betrayed him. Soon winter would be over and they would be out in the orchard again. The thought of the lazy summer days to come was warming. Summer and winter, and summer once more. Georges would be going to Germany. "Diane always gets what she wants," he thought.

With the confusion in the house Stiegel had not seen Diane all day. When he left, the halls were filled with the last portmantuas, and Tabitha's child sat wearily atop some baggage. Cyrus brushed everybody and everything a dozen times over.

The last guest had scarcely departed when a special messenger arrived on horseback, with black moonstone rings and gloves, and the announcement of Anthony Stiegel's death the day before. Diane was curiously shocked. She warned the servants at once to keep the news a secret from Stiegel; first she must tell him that Anthony was ill and in danger. She looked for Stiegel with dread until Cyrus said he had gone for a walk.

Her thoughts ran fantastically. She was very tired, and she loathed the thought of death, a stuffy, unnecessary thing. Anthony had worshipped her. With a shudder, she wondered if somewhere poor Anthony still worshipped her. Anthony, queer soul, who had only half lived in the reflection of her smile. Big, ugly hands. She shivered. Death was horrible, a gruesome end to flowers and sunshine and wine —and forget-me-nots in a brook. . . .

The afternoon seemed infinite. Now that the company was gone the thought of them sickened her, for the house was disreputable with their carousing. She looked through the rooms they had occupied, untidy with spilled snuff and bits of powder and combings of hair. Tabitha's child had left a broken toy, and the counterpane of their bed was splotched with ink. How she had slaved for them, and they cared not a fig for her! Sacrebleu! but Georges had had spunk! She had been proud of his tantrum! And Heinrich would be so happy to know what his music meant to him!

It would be peaceful to sit quietly beside Heinrich, planning again for the spring. Planning walks in the woods and lessons under the trees. . . . What could she say to him now about Anthony? That he had been thrown from a horse, perhaps, and was badly hurt?

She waited with growing impatience for Stiegel to come, trying to sort out music and changing a harp string which the dampness had snapped. The house seemed stifling and she thrust open the windows, but the muggy air did not enter, hanging about the curtains like a wraith. . . . Why didn't he come? Was it possible he had come in through the kitchen as he often did, and she had missed him? She ran up to the attic, but when she reached the top of the stairs she saw that his door was open and the room was dark. It was almost dinner time, and he must soon return. . . . Anthony had been out hunting, and his horse. . . . She would go down to the kitchen and see that Anne's partridges were brown enough. Dinner would have to be perfect, to close out the thought of pale Anthony. Six o'clock. . . . With the fog and darkness she could no longer see down the road. Perhaps she had better send Georges. No, it would be wiser to go herself. She could never bear to sit quietly before the fire. She slipped on her pattens and a cape, and was drawn curiously back to look into the hall drawer where she had shoved the articles of mourning. They fascinated her.

She took the lantern from Cyrus' hand, and when she saw that he shook, she was angry. She loathed people who visibly weakened, and she marched out staunchly into the damp fog. It was like stepping off the edge of the world. She crept toward the light of Mrs. Nassel's kitchen, and saw through the window that they were sitting gossiping over beer and a mound of cheese; she wondered if Christian Nassel might know where Stiegel had gone, and knocked briefly and entered.

For a moment the firelight seemed to allay Diane's fears. "'Twas a bit sudden, Mr. Anthony's death," remarked Christian, allowing a fine froth to settle on his lip, then ruminatively licking it off in scallops. "A bad shock for Baron Stiegel!"

"But he mustn't know yet!" cautioned Diane, looking out of the window. "Don't you know where he went? I've been waiting and waiting. . . ."

A guilty look passed between the Nassels. Christian tossed down an imaginary fragment of beer, and shuffled over to the fire. Diane felt deeply irritated at the moment of silence. And the very manner in which he had shoved the cheese aside, the prominent veins of his bear-like hands. . . .

"You've seen him," exclaimed Diane, catching her breath. "You've—you've told him!"

Mrs. Nassel smoothed her apron in great agitation.

"He passed by at six o'clock. Christian . . . Christian ——" She could scarcely stand the fire of Diane's eyes. "I'faith, Mistress Ege . . . how was Christian to know 'twas secret?"

Diane slipped past her, forgetting her cape and pattens and flying through the fog as she had once fled through the wood with bow and arrow.

Cyrus was in the upper hall, on his way to the attic, a Betty lamp in his hand.

"Gon' light Marsa Baron's candle 'gainst he come soon," he said, but Diane had shoved past him to Stiegel's room, and the damp cold struck her more sharply than the fog.

"Heinrich!" she cried, trying to peer through the darkness.

As Cyrus puffed into the room the shadows began to shift gayly. Diane snatched the Betty lamp and looked about her, and a sharp little cry escaped as she saw Stiegel. He lay on the bed, huddled in his greatcoat, his arms flung from him in pain, his face livid.

"Heinrich . . ." she cried again, but he did not move or answer, and she stood looking down at him, paralyzed with fear.

Cyrus' black hand crept trembling over his master's cheek, and Diane came suddenly alive, ordering Cyrus about quickly now—water, the doctor, wine. . . .

If he should die. . . . The conception of life without him was numbing: a constant ticking of the clock, an endless dripping of rain, a slow mechanical sound which would beat in her brain through the coming of light and the interminable echo of dark.

"But I shan't let him go," she thought fiercely, "I shan't let him go. Nothing . . . nothing else matters."

She watched Stiegel for hours, her hands folded on the cover close to his face, her fingers insensible, her throat so dry and aching that she could not utter a word. She was in a world alone in the aura of candlelight with Heinrich, a world which took no cognizance of familiar voices and footsteps and Time. He belonged to her, and she would not let him go. For hours she held him to life with her indomitable will.

Toward midnight Stiegel's eyes drifted slowly open, and Diane pressed her face to his.

"I have been dreaming . . . of Anthony . . ." he whispered. "The day . . . we came to America . . . he was frighted . . . of the Indians. He hid . . . under the . . . bed. . . ."

Diane smiled wanly. "Do not talk, my Heinrich. . . ."

He heard the drizzle of fresh rain against the panes, and he thought, "It will run in little rivulets and puddles to the brook, and out into the magnificent strength of the sea. . . ."

"He used to steal . . . the raisins . . . from the kuchen. . . ."

Diane touched her fingers to his lips. "Do not talk, I beg of you, my Heinrich. . . ."

"One day she . . . whipped him. Diane . . . Anthony is grown now. Anthony loves you. . . ."

"Heinrich—now you must sleep, mon cher. Tomorrow—tomorrow we will talk of these things. I shall make you a cherry pudding for dinner! And we will sit before the fire, and talk of all the happy times we have known. The day Barbara was born—the Assembly balls—the night in the woods. . . ."

She was twisting the ring that he had given her for the bowl, and her eyes gleamed with a hard brilliance.

"And we will talk of the happy times to come, Heinrich —how proud we shall be of Georges. . . . How he is going to be great because of you. . . . Before the fire, M'sieu. I will sit on a stool at your feet, and rest my head on your knee. . . ."

Her words seem to rush into his being like a gale.

"Diane—how beautiful . . . you are. Diane, what peace to die . . . with your hand in mine. . . ."

"Non, non, non," she cried sharply, shrinking at the loudness of her own voice.

Hot hands pressed the words into his consciousness. The sea was rushing up to him now, victorious, jubilant, roaring, "Anthony . . . Georges . . . Diane." He was overpowered with happiness. "Anthony . . . Georges . . . Diane!"

He did not need the burning hands. He tried to say goodbye to them.

"Diane!" he called triumphantly, but the hands seared his flesh. He must try again. *"Diane. . . !"*

Now the burning hands were vague. Now at last he was going to be free. How beautiful was the blur of Diane, and the soft words that mingled with her image. They filled his being with quiet, like the deep sweet reverberations of a cathedral chime.

"Heinrich . . . Heinrich . . . I'll be waiting here . . . when you . . . waken. . . ."

A NOTE ON THE TYPE

The text of this book is set in Caledonia, a Linotype face designed by W. A. Dwiggins, the man responsible for so much that is good in contemporary book design and typography. Caledonia belongs to the family of printing types called "modern face" by printers—a term used to mark the change in style of type-letters that occurred about 1800. It has all the hard-working feet-on-the-ground qualities of the Scotch Modern face plus the liveliness and grace that is integral in every Dwiggins "product" whether it be a simple catalogue cover or an almost human puppet.

The book was composed, printed, and bound by H. Wolff, New York. The paper was made by S. D. Warren Company, Boston.